THE TALES SAGA
BOOK ONE

TALES OF A FELDSPAR PRINCE

D1714564

Cody Rex

ISBN: 9798832782027
Illustrations by Brittany Cecilia Co.

Dedicated to Marky "the Rock" Jaquez

2000-2021

You fought your battle

and made us all proud

Thank you

To you, the reader:

Thank you for reading this story. *My* story. I am not a writer by trade. My goal is not to make a fortune off this series, as I have a day job and a separate career path. Writing is my hobby. A fun hobby. I would love for this series to build a strong community of people who enjoy the tales of Petrus and end up making stories of their own.

I have always enjoyed tales of old and what we can learn from our past. Countless ages came before us, and countless will come after. This story (and those to come) were made to highlight many aspects of our past and how those historical events shaped the path of history. I hope that, regardless of what age you read this story, the thoughts, cultures, and ideals of our past can be relatable and spark an interest in our collective history.

If you would like to join our community in discussing the past, present, and possible futures, find me on social media. I have made accounts to help bring us together in discussions. As of writing this book, you can find me on LinkedIn, Facebook, and Instagram. Our community is the most active on Discord and links can be found on my other media pages. Anyone and everyone are welcome to become a fellow Anthoran!

Your Fellow Anthoran,
Cody Rex

CONTENTS

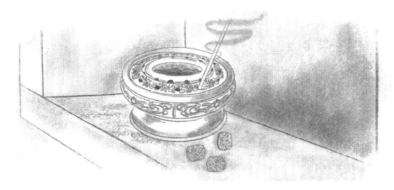

CHAPTER 1

Incense On A Warm Breeze

19th of Beryl, 453 of the Age of Discovery

*T*hunder *crashed against the cliff walls as rain clouds burdened the humid air. A woman faced outward and extended her bare arms to the sea, overlooking a bay of dark water. Her olive skin and umber hair clashed in stark contrast to her snow-white dress. Adorned across the embroidered hem of the dress were strands of gold and facets of deep red gems. As the arcs of bright light flashed across the tall granite pillars that lined the outer edge of the courtyard, wind currents swept and rippled across the marble tiling. Her smile widened at the sight. Crimson pools trickled across the tiled floor, seeping between the intricate mosaic designs, and staining the grout. Golden eyes stared directly forward as a final strike of lightning illuminated a titanic form in the distance. Large and terrifying, its shape was swaddled by the fog and clouds. It dove beneath the waves, water displacing in tidal waves towards the shores. The woman's smile faded as the waves distorted into the bay. She muttered one word before the scene darkened.*

Awoken at the end of the vision, Castor sat upright in his bed and allowed his mind to wake from the dream. Or was it a nightmare? Either way, it had taken a toll on his sleep. Dim yellow light slowly crept through the edge of the window's curtains, warming his skin. A flicker of dust floated through the rays of light and settled on the granite frame of the window. The warmth of the morning light was a stark contrast to the cold, tan plaster covering the sandstone walls of the room. The sheet of linen underneath his body cooled his skin as the cold sweat of the vision started to evaporate across the wrinkles and folds. The smell of salt lingered in the air and very faint crashes of waves could be heard in the distance.

Getting out of bed, the cypress wood boards creaked under the changes in weight. Castor stretched towards the ceiling and moved the large piece of fabric covering the windows of his bedroom. The cool tiles on the floor prickled his feet as a flow of warm air entered through the window and across the room. The light of the early morning seeped through the elaborate brass window bars and warmed the surface of his arms. He could smell the petrichor in the air, last night's rain had left its mark on the surroundings.

His sight focused on the valley below the sandstone estate walls, the view giving way to the small village of villas he lived in. A few shepherds with their flocks took advantage of the early morning light and walked the verdant hills between the winding path towards the end of the valley. The usually thin creek at the bottom was much deeper today. The flow of water had taken some bramble, mud, and floating leaves with it out into the estuary downstream. While hazy from the high humidity, the reflection of the ocean's surface in the distance shone brightly.

Castor grabbed a stick of incense and slotted it within the bronze censer that sat on his windowsill. With his hands clasped in the shape of a tent, he muttered a short prayer to Ignus, god of the sun and carrier of the sacred flame. He thanked his patron deity for the warmth of today's morning sunlight. As his short prayer finished, a spark ignited at the end of his finger. The small flame flowed as though fueled by an oil lamp. The heat it produced was enough to kindle the tip of incense to an ember. As the room filled with a gentle scent of sandalwood, Castor once again gazed out across the landscape he had seen since he was a boy.

Slowly stumbling over to his stone chest, he unclasped the lock and raised the hefty slab of sandstone. From within the chest, he took a cyan *chiton*, a short linen tunic, and his *xiphos*, a short bronze sword. A mantle of white linen was also near the chiton, so he grabbed it for the road. Castor considered the bright light coming through the window and knew the white fabric would help keep the midday sun off his body, keeping him cool. Walking out of the room, he grabbed a plain leather belt that was only adorned with a brass ring and a studded belt end. The end was encrusted with a pair of lapis lazuli cabochons. He slid a small leather pouch onto his belt and fastened it on his right side with his trusty xiphos on his left. The bronze pommel was engraved in ornate, repeating shapes and a sphere of amazonite was inlaid within the grip of a metal clawed hand. The dense stone helped balance the blade while its teal hue and speckles of white feldspar gave the weapon's design a balanced aesthetic.

He fastened the ring belt with a standard knot at the center. Puffing his chiton out above his belt, he checked to make sure he had everything he needed for the day. After grabbing a few silver drachma and one electrum stater off his counter, he tossed them into his pouch and closed and clasped the stone chest. He then headed out for breakfast.

Leaving his room, he was greeted by a familiar sight. As he stepped on the terrace overlooking the open atrium below at the center of the home, his mother and older sister walked across the open space and waved to him.

"It seems you have finally awoken after such an eventful night!" his mother Xenia announced across the atrium. Her thunderous, controlling voice did not match her slender build.

"Does that surprise you?" Aretha, his older sister, quipped back loudly. Her tone was matched with a mocking smile across her face, "It is not often he would choose to wake early after a night of drinking with his friends at the docks."

"I hardly consider myself a lush," Castor retorted, grabbing onto the sandstone banister lining the edge of the terrace, "and it is quite the journey back from the docks in a storm. Even with our gems to support us, we could not hold the rain off for the entire trip back."

"And what is all that training you do good for then?" Aretha shot back, "You cannot just rely on the energy in your gems. If you want to be a good and proper guard captain, you will have to work on your channeling far past your current limits."

Using the banister as leverage, Castor tossed his body over the edge, tumbling through the air. He was around ten feet off the ground when a burst of wind swirled around his legs. Channeling his mana, he controlled the air around him. The gust of wind pushed back onto his body, acting as an invisible spring to dampen his fall. He landed safely a handful of feet away from his mother.

"Oh, so impressive," Aretha smirked at him with a fake round of applause, "Now show me how you jump back up to that height with your gifted abilities."

Castor bowed a bow so deep he almost fell over, jesting with his older sister to prove his point. "I can if you would like me to, but I think that would just be showing off. You know what humility is, right?"

She rolled her eyes, not wanting to continue their fake argument so early in the morning.

Xenia blasted wind out of her fingers in tight tendrils. She combed through her son's thick, wavy hair to set it into a decent shape. Her fashionable earrings glowed a light scarlet as she drew mana from their stores.

"Clean yourself up, will you?" his mother doted, "Just because you have the day off does not mean you should look unkempt and wild in front of our staff and guests."

Her hair was the same mahogany brown as his, but her skin was slightly lighter. She spent most of her days within the city buildings while Castor spent most of his time outside, so his skin was as swarthy as any working Anthoran. Her nose was smaller too, as he acquired his aquiline nose from his father.

"Guests?" He looks quizzically around the atrium for anyone he would see out of the ordinary. Columns lined the inner edge of the courtyard, holding up the terrace above. Between them and the walls were many potted plants, tables, and benches. The eldest tenant of the estate sat across the atrium in a wooden chair and smiled gently at Castor with her old, squinted eyes. Lydia had lived with and served the Daimos house since Castor's grandfather ruled the region and always had a way to make the estate feel more like a home than just a house. Penelope, a teenage girl with short curly hair, was a newer tenant who sat near Lydia. Shyer than the old maid, she continued to work her loom as Castor surveyed around the yard.

"They are not here yet," Aretha said flatly, "Father has a meeting with the forgemasters of Tyressos today to increase the city's weapon stocks. I asked to participate this time since the shipments will be traveling with my supply company and we need to decide proper terms for late deliveries."

"Have you had issues with travel recently?" Castor asked, raising an eyebrow. It was his job to know about any bandits in the region.

"Yes, unfortunately. It seems to be harpy season again. They keep going for anything they can find that shines or twinkles. Even with precautions in place to make sure all crates and containers are covered with dark cloth, they still somehow know when interesting items are being shipped. I understand they are not far off from being mindless animals, but they could try and not attack every caravan I send across the mountain line." Aretha huffed.

"Well, it could be worse, it could have been goblins..." Castor realized the topic he had brought up after it was too late. The mood instantly got colder as he cut his sentence off. His sister focused her eyes off to the side and his mother frowned.

"Hey, uh... I am sorry about that..." He rubbed the back of his neck in response to the awkward mood.

"It is alright," Aretha said, "It has been almost two years since Theron passed. I know I should be over it by now."

Xenia put an arm around her daughter's shoulders as she moved closer. "And you know his death was not in vain. His horse still made it back to us with his information on that nest. If he would not have, who knows how many others would have been taken by those creatures? Dozens? Hundreds?"

"I know, I know." Aretha shyly said," but having to sell off our house and move back home to pay off his family business still feels weird to this day. I know they do not blame me, but you know commoners love to spread nasty rumors when they can. This whole ordeal has only added fuel to their fires."

"Everyone likes to blame those who they do not understand." Castor remarked, "Theron would not have cared what anyone else would say. He built that company with you, and he wanted you to run it in his absence. Just because the Daimos house rules over this land does not mean the Othanos house can waltz in and claim government overreach. They cannot claim direct control of a business they had no hand in founding."

"Very well put, my dear," Xenia said proudly. A twinkle in her eye confirmed that Castor's words struck true and reflected rightly on his wordsmithing. "Their claims of patrilineal inheritance laws would give their family a better claim in future generations, but not when they had no heir. We had combed the law books for weeks before the courts decided the outcome."

"I know, I know," Aretha forced a weak smile. "I just miss him, that is all."

Xenia grabbed the back of each of her children's heads and caressed them in opposite directions. "Come now, my darling children. We have a full day ahead of us and preparations are left to be done. Castor, go and tidy yourself. Get down to the amphitheater for your morning training sooner than later. And off we go, Arie. We still have to do something with this rat nest you call your hair."

Aretha smiled and walked towards the back of the house with her mother. Off to the side, Lydia gestured for Castor to come to visit her, and so he did. He had always taken a liking to the cute elderly woman. As he got close enough to see every wrinkle on her old face, her smile dropped into a frown. "You have not been eating enough, child. Day after day you train but look at you!" She pinched his forearm, and he instinctively jerked his arm back.

"Grab a big bowl of soup in the kitchen before you leave. I put a lot of fish in it this time, and you need your meat. I saw the way you landed earlier. That took a lot out of you, didn't it?" the smile returned to her face and her already squinting eyes became even more shut.

"You have good vision for someone with their eyes closed." Castor beamed, leaning over and lightly patting the top of her head. Her hair, pulled back in a veil from cooking earlier in the day, was gray and bluing. Her friendly attitude always made her seem a few decades younger.

"I appreciate you not worrying my mother with this. Training my body and channeling all at once can be very tiring. I know it is expected of noble families to have full control of their physical and mental prowess, but that only adds to the stress of the training. I am already learning the ways of law as I keep up with my martial and channeling training. What I need more than anything is a two-day nap. "

"I know, my dear. I know," Lydia commented. "You should have seen the training your grandfather did back during the insurrections. Bless his soul, but he was not particularly good with his channeling at the beginning. He relied heavily on his control over his blade and his command of his soldiers. He was quite skilled before adulthood, but his peers still teased him for many years after."

She shrugged, "Although, he was an amazing hoplite fighter and a sword master as well, so he never really relied on his channeling to win his battles."

She smirked and waved her hand dismissively. "It will always be a funny story to me."

"I do not plan to let that happen anymore. Which is why I have to get down to training before Nikitas decides to find out how far he can throw a noble before it becomes illegal." Castor kissed Lydia on the forehead and squeezed her hand before stepping away.

This whole time, Penelope looked on shyly a few paces away, working the loom as she had for the past hour.

"Good morning," Castor said. He always made sure not to ignore her, regardless of how timid she seemed.

"Good morning," Penelope said back.

The timidness did not falter.

Castor had not pried into her background or how she ended up getting a position within his household, but he knew his parents would have good reason to hire such a young girl. Her skill with the loom was commendable, and her cooking skills had added variety to Lydia's homely recipes, but Castor was still curious as to why she was hired instead of finding a husband and starting a family. She was cute, with pudgy cheeks and dimples. She seemed quite healthy too, as she was always running around and performing fetch quests for Lydia. Either way, simple and polite gestures were the way he could communicate without coming off as too overbearing.

He knew her situation did not concern him. His sister and mother had the most experience with running and maintaining the household. Overall, there were six tenants of the estate at peak capacity. Two stewards supported Hecantor, Castor's father, with regional affairs whilst doubling as bodyguards for the family. Maya, an archer in her late twenties, was Aretha's bodyguard at her workplace as well as supporting her at home and on travel. Lydia and Penelope bring the number up to five. The latest member of the estate was the house boy Perseus, who took care of buying from the market and tending to the garden and shrubbery.

Taking a second to appreciate the cool air flowing through the atrium, Castor walked toward the kitchen. The smell of fish and garlic permeated the flow of air coming towards him as he passed by Perseus, who was dropping off a food crate next to the kitchen. After his eyes adapted to the meager light within the cooking room, he could see the glow of the central stove's coals radiating off the mosaic tiles covering the floor.

Chopped carrots and young onions littered the countertops on the far side of the room while white clay amphorae lined the side walls. A large wood barrel of clean river water sat next to the stove and supplied the house with their non-alcoholic drinks. Small clay pots holding oils, honey, and cheaper wines sat on the wood tabletop. Copper pots and pans hung from hooks on the walls and glittered the room with small rays of light when they were hit by the sunlight coming through the windows. The central stove sat between the two main casements on the back wall with the smoke seeping up through the clerestory above its mantel.

On the wood counter next to the stove was an ordinary wooden box covered in a single teal cloth with silver embroidery. While the cloth had seen some wear over the last two decades, it was nonetheless folded up and cleaned for use as it was every morning. Lydia always made sure to keep the villa clean and tidy. Castor smiled at the thought that Lydia had prepared his bowl like she always had for his family over the last fifty years.

Lydia knew from experience that giving Castor a ceramic bowl was destined for ill fate. The difference was trivial in their form and function when using wooden items, but their quality was unimportant when their durability was in question. He laughed to himself and accepted the old maid's decision.

Removing the lid and grabbing a ladle, Castor stirred the contents of the cooking pot. Small flakes of smoked fish rose and fell in the thick white broth. Chunks of finely chopped fresh greens and potatoes stuck to the ladle as he moved the contents around. The brass ladle rubbing against the ceramic cooking pot made for a gentle grinding noise as he moved the stew in a circular motion. The smell of dill, parsley, and thyme filled the air as the hot steam aerosolized in front of him.

As he stirred, the light of the stove dimmed. Out of a basket in the corner of the room, he grabbed and tossed a few small firewood logs onto the coals to keep the meal going. He ladled some stew into his bowl and closed the lid.

"Ouch!" Castor gasped as his hand was scorched from the rim of the heated ceramic pot.

The warm liquid splashed onto the floor, prompting him to set his bowl down abruptly on the detailed cloth towel he was given. He took a rag from a counter and wiped up the mess. *Lydia knew me a little too well*, he thought to himself as he cleaned up the mess. He did need a break. After returning the dirty rag to a cleaning bin, he went to the wood counter and cut a slice of rye bread for himself. He sat it on the side of the bowl. Its spongy internals soaked up the creamy broth.

Walking out of the room, Castor took a sharp right and walked into the left corridor of the house. At the end of the hallway was the family's home shrine where many would sit in retrospect or pray for a sign to aim their lives towards. Some, like Castor, went for veneration. He had many reasons to appreciate his life and chose every day to show his thanks for what he had been given. Before eating, he went to the shrine of Ignus and cast a large piece of fatty fish from the stew into the brazier. The chunk burst into flames and disappeared within seconds, the bright yellow flames dancing across the chiseled mane of golden fur around the neck of the defied Maudian.

While the cat people of the eastern continent of Maudif were not common in these lands, their culture was still noticeable. Their god of the flames and sun was a part of the pantheon of Castor's nation, Anthora. Ig' Nataz, the Maudian form of the Anthoran Ignus, held the sacred fire and was well respected across the Maudian empire. This flame was the purest form of elemental control over heat and fire. He was said to be the first to control the elements and his flame signifies the start of an age of improvement and enlightenment all those years ago. The flame was maintained within his giant golden mane, flowing around his head like a halo made of pure sunlight. As the climates and cultures in these two lands were remarkably similar, his holy form was easily adopted into the Anthoran pantheon many centuries prior. For most Anthoran believers, his Maudian form was turned into an Anthoran with a lion's pelt worn around the neck like a scarf. As one of the less popular gods in Anthora, Castor was happy he had a seat at the Table of the Gods, the Kalotrapia, in the holy banquet halls of Elysia.

Castor took a moment to appreciate the workmanship of the statues around him. The gods of the Kalotrapia sat around the room, each one around two feet in height. They were all made of stone, carved meticulously to engrain every detail of the god's or goddess's visage. Highlights were given to the cold tone with threads of colored silk and plates of flattened brass. Ignus, made of white marble like the others, had his mane gilded in bronze. Polished to a mirror finish, the metallic glint of the wreath of flames cast small reflections across the room with the light from the early morning sun coming through the windows.

After a few words of reverence towards his patron deity, Castor felt a surge of relaxation rush back into his body. It was common to find your patron deity before turning twenty in Petrus, but Castor was a special case. His connection to Ignus showed on his sixteenth birthday. His early connection to his nana channeling had given him a head start on his path toward becoming a great leader for the region.

Castor never regretted devoting himself to one deity so early in life. It was the more honorable choice in his eyes. His sole reverence made him feel closer to the god of the sun. He even believed when he was younger that doing so fervently would allow him to become a god-kissed. A god-kissed was not a common feat to achieve but becoming one would bless him with great boons of strength and control over his channeling, or so the legend went. A god-kissed had not graced his home city of Thyma in over a hundred years. The young prince no longer kept his hopes up as his younger self would.

After he finished his morning prayers, Castor ate his meal on a wicker bench in the atrium. The wind blew through the central corridors of the house, cooling him with brisk winds on this muggy summer morning. He sipped from a pitcher of watered-down wine as he enjoyed the creamy fish soup that Lydia prepared the family a few hours prior.

Days like this were days Castor could appreciate. The wind on his face, his faith restored, and no rush to return to his normally hectic schedule. His only plan for the day was some light sparring in the morning and checking in the market for any gems he could add to his collection. He had saved up a decent number of coins from his guard position over the last month and wanted to find the proper gems to facet into his sterling silver bracelet. The torc he wore came from the Durulian mountain homes across the sea, forged within the capital of Hem Durul itself. While Castor was a proud Anthoran, he always admired the skills of the expert smiths from that short and sturdy race under the mountains. This solid silver bracelet was his favorite piece of jewelry. Castor liked the torc's exotic design but felt it needed a gem to make it stand out as useful in daily affairs.

Maybe I will stop by the watermill and practice my channeling on the way home. Castor thought to himself as he ate his brunch. A day like this would be perfect for training around water to cool off and get some extra favors owed with the local miller would not be a wasted effort. He would most likely repay the effort with a few loaves of rustic bread, and he liked the thought of that.

Castor took his bowl to the kitchen and left it in the pile of used dishware. After meandering over to the storage jars, he grabbed a few figs for the road. Figs were not natively grown on this side of the Sideros mountains but having a sister with trade connections had its benefits. After Castor was finished with his morning meal, he went to prepare himself for the day in the washroom.

His mother's plea to clean up his appearance had to be appropriately taken care of. He knew he would not hear the end of it if he showed up unkempt to practice for the day. He removed his mantle and placed it with his chiton on a wicker chair near the door. Grabbing a bone strigil off the counter, he scraped his arms and legs to remove any oils and dirt left over from his run through muddy fields between the city and his home the prior night. The humid air made his cleaning even more important. He did not want to smell terrible if they were having important guests over in the evening. He took a rough stone of pumice to his cheeks and chin which removed any stubble that grew since he had last shaved. He brushed the loose hairs off his chest and shoulders and moved over to the water basin.

Leaning over the open tub, he massaged a weak solution of vinegar and salt in his short dark curls. The acidic grit dislodged the dirt and detritus in his hair and made washing the grime out much easier. He rinsed the solution out with clean water and dried his hair with a linen towel from the towel rack. He dabbed his curly head with the tips of his fingers, careful to make sure he applied a very slight amount of olive oil to texture his hair. He rubbed his teeth with a cloth covered in charcoal powder and rinsed his mouth with a salty vinegar solution. Making sure his face and teeth were ready for a day out in the town, he headed upstairs to ensure his gems were placed properly on his windowsill.

Before he made it back to his room, he remembered to stop and wake his brother up next door. Acco was a heavy sleeper when he worked his extra-long shifts at his forge apprenticeship. He asked Castor to wake him when he had the chance. His notoriety for sleeping into the late mornings was something Castor wanted to relate to, but his guard position meant he usually kept to a strict time regiment during the week. Today was an exception, not the precedent.

While they shared the same age, Castor and Acco were not twins. Acco was not a part of the Daimos house by blood. He was the child of a business associate of Castor's father. His parents were dignitaries in the Anthoran colonies on the western continent and perished right before his first birthday. His grandfather was his sole caretaker until he passed of old age and was transferred to the Daimos clan when Hecantor offered to take care of the child at age four. Castor knew him no different than a brother, as they had grown up together and shared many fond moments and typical sibling arguments. He had no gripe for waking him up from a nice night of sleep. He owed his brother back for messing with his stash of incense in the storage room, so abruptly waking him would be his pleasure.

Castor quietly opened his room door and crept in. Considering his options, he figured the figs were the best choice to wake the slumbering giant. Hefting one in his right hand, he lobbed the small fruit at Acco's head. The lopsided fruit whiffed off to the left, bouncing against the wall and rolling onto the floor. Luckily, Castor grabbed two of them. On the second throw, the fruit landed directly on his forehead, leaving a loud thud. Instinctively Acco shot up in his bed. He looked around, still comprehending what was going on while his brain fully awoke from a deep sleep.

Acco made direct eye contact with Castor before a block of stone shot past Castor's head. Castor knew his brother's abilities all too well and saw the launched chunk of mud far before it had gotten close. He moved out of the way like he has done many times in the past. The chunk of dried mortar hurled into the mosaic behind Castor and dirtied the design as the chunk blew into a fine powder.

"You know mom hates it when you do that," Castor said flatly.

"I do not like fruit while I sleep," Acco retorted. Castor laughed under his breath at the strange response.

"You do not like eating your fruit when you are awake either," Castor shot back.

"Hmph," was Acco's response. He was not a morning person. He looked out the window. "What time is it?"

"Halfway through the morning, I presume," Castor said, going over to the other side of the room to retrieve his midday snack that was now laying across the floor.

"Ah," Acco said gently. "Thanks for waking me up."

"Mhm. Do not forget to clean this all up. Mom will have your hide if she finds mud throughout the house again." Castor pocketed the figs for later, their bruised surfaces would make peeling easier anyway.

Acco walked over the wall and waved his hand across the area he had impacted with the block of sand and clay. Small sparks danced across his fingernails as his chantless channeling removed the dirt on the wall and clumped the material into a near-perfect sphere. The levitating mass of dry dust held together tightly, no particle escaping the grasp of the mosaicist's spell. He bent over onto one knee and continued the control of the clay near where the rest of the clay had splattered onto the tiles below. The ball grew bigger and wider, its mass increasing as his hand passed over more surfaces. By the end, Acco had claimed more mass than he had originally thrown at his brother as his spell claimed the residue of muddy boots and dusty work clothes that had coated the area near the entrance of his room.

"Do you think this will suffice?" Acco asked coyly. He sat the mortar ball on his wood cabinet, and it held its shape after he released his metaphysical grip.

Castor bent onto one knee as well, wiping a finger across the side of the wooden dresser that sat on the same wall as the mural he had so meticulously cleaned.

"Probably? Maybe get a little more behind this dresser while you are at it?" Castor smiled.

"You are lucky you are the blood heir to this land," Acco's simple statement held a typical mocking threat behind it, and Castor was glad he knew his brother's humor so well. Some princes would take offense to an adopted orphan's dry humor, but Castor enjoyed his brother's sassy nature.

"I am aware. You make sure I never forget," Castor brought his attention to the mosaic on the wall in front of them. A small stack of old tiles was sitting in the corner of the room. "I always liked this one. When were you planning to expand it? It has been at least six months since I have seen any shipments of tiling come to your room."

They both looked at the other walls in the room, their plain white stucco leaving the room feeling open compared to the elaborate mosaic next to the door. Acco had prepped all the walls before starting his first project in anticipation of finishing the entire room, but his busy summer job at the foundry kept him from making much progress.

"I will get to it when I get to it," Acco muttered. He sighed loudly in exasperation. "The smelteries have been working me longer every week as the autumn rolled around and my apprenticeship at the Stelios Workshop has been more of a menial labor position than a paid apprenticeship."

"That's too bad," Castor said. "I know how much you enjoy working on these."

Acco shrugged in digression. "If you want a definitive answer, I plan to work on it this winter when the smelteries bring in their extra labor support from the fishers and farmers who need something to do in the cold months."

"That is a good point," Castor agreed. "Your apprenticeship comes first. You know you do not need the extra money from the smelteries. Father would support you financially if you let him."

"It's a matter of principle," Acco stated. "I also must consider personal experience. Becoming a trained smith is a distinguished career path, especially for someone with my lack of heritage. You know I feel welcome here. But my projects can be.... expensive."

Castor understood. The wall of mosaic tiles in this room currently would cost enough to feed a lower-class family for a year. Castor appreciated Acco's altruism, but he did not want him to feel like a second-class member of the family.

"If you ever want a better-paying position, I could always get you a spot as a Decanus," Castor offered. The soldier who led a squad of ten men within a century was in a position with higher pay than a common smeltery hand, and Castor knew Acco had the physique to lead a city guard patrol.

"Ugh," Acco scoffed, "by Brömli's beard, I have told you not to tie me in with the guard. I will not dance and charade my way through those webs of politicking I have seen you do at your meetings and public events."

Acco made a good point. Castor knew what hoops he had to jump through to keep those of high positions happy, and he knew Acco was not one to do so. The adopted son of a noble would have many more hurdles within the Anthoran hierarchies. He was well aware the long nights of paperwork and overly extravagant festival roles would not suit his burly brother.

"That is fair," Castor sympathized with his seditious views. Politics could get quite tiring after a while. "Then keep on keeping on, I guess."

Acco grunted. "I do not mind too much, to be fair. The demanding work at the smeltery keeps my muscles strong and my mind sharp. Aretha keeps the smelting lords in check... mostly."

He sighed, "We are not worked to the bone. I am only tired of working in both positions when my coworkers shirk their duties. Twelve times this month I had to claim a double shift to keep the fires lit," Acco thought to himself for a second. "Maybe I will talk to Aretha again about this."

Castor patted Acco on the shoulder. "There you go. Use your resources to your advantage. Now you are thinking like a Daimos."

Acco nodded in approval but warned, "Just make sure that father's attendants do not hear you speaking like that. They may be overly kind to you, but you know they take family lineage seriously."

"I do not care for what they think," Castor responded naturally, "They will eventually serve me, and I do not plan to allow them to treat you like some foreign cart boy. You have been my brother since I was able to walk, so my brother you will stay."

"I appreciate the sentiment," Acco grunted. He pushed the hardened sphere of clay across the top of his dresser. The chunk kept its shape even rolling it a few feet across the stained wood surface. Its shape started to falter by the end, covering the top of the wood surface with a powdery layer of dry clay.

Now that the dirt and dust were cleaned, the mosaic Acco had been designed and created was clear to see upon the southern wall. Black and white tiles created the design of intertwined bare branches across the edges of the substrate. The obsidian tiles countered the brightness of the white alabaster and gave a layer of shadow around the edges of the andamento. Small orange flowers bloomed from some of the branches, giving a small amount of vivid color to the otherwise monochrome design. In the center of the wall, the scene showed the first stag hunts of Thyma's Arietia. In the scene, three men surrounded a giant deer. Lightning crashed at the men from the top of the mosaic. Each man was wielding a long spear in their main hand and a xiphos in their off hand. The giant stag was at least twice the height of the men, its massive antlers fusing into the jagged lightning of the sky. It reared up onto its hind legs, giving off a threatening aura. Castor always liked the pieces Acco made, but this was his favorite. He had considered patroning a wall like this from his brother in the past, but he had not planned to do so until Acco had more free time and was able to finish his room.

Many of the colored stones in this design were imported from various regions around Anthora and Maudif. Castor remembered that the orange stones were blood carnelians usually found in the mountains near Hem Durul. Friends of Acco's parents were able to acquire them for him, a late birthday present for the growing colonial. Castor was happy to see his old family still affecting his life, even after the passing of his parents. Acco's family had lived within Hem Durul for at least a hundred years. They kept good relations with the Durulians in the region and had even lived within the mountain homes for a few generations. When civil wars broke out between the great clans of their nation, Acco's parents were executed for siding with the wrong side. He had no wish to visit those lands in his lifetime, especially after what the locals did to his parents. The presence of blood carnelians was a good sight to see, showing that Acco was opening to his heritage a little more. Castor thought their presence was a small piece of what could have been for the Hem Durul orphan colonist.

"Make sure you eat your fill before you leave," Castor said to his younger brother, "Lydia made our favorite soup again."

"Mm," Acco rubbed his belly, remembering the meal he always asked the old maid to make, "I hope she put a lot of smoked fish in it today. Some meat would be genuinely nice on a damp morning like this."

Castor nodded and left the room, closing the latch as he left.

Upon entering his room, the smooth scent of sandalwood immediately graced his senses. Wisps of gray smoke curled and swirled around the room, dancing in the breeze. Going back to his stone chest, he took out a smaller, ornate wooden box from the bottom underneath the rest of his clothes. Unclasping the front hook and lifting the lid, a brilliant bed of multifaceted gems and cabochons was revealed. Looking as though a rainbow had condensed itself in the bottom of the container, Castor started to ruffle through the stack of rare gems. As he touched each cut crystal in the container, he could sense the mana within it. He unclasped the two cabochons from his belt and put them away, grabbing two identically shaped rubies from the container as their replacement. Their design, while similar in shape to the cabochons from earlier, shone brighter from the way their facets were cut and spiraled out from the center of their oval geometry. They fit right into the belt end's clasps and snapped smoothly into place.

As the weather today was much nicer than the few days prior and the sun streamed in through the windows with bright intensity, Castor put all the yellow and orange gems in the container into the palm of his hand. Walking over to the censer he used earlier in the day, he laid the yellow gems around the base of its foot and made sure to line them up in the sunlight. He then grabbed a piece of charcoal from a little wooden box that was sitting next to his nightstand and lit it within the censer much like how he lit the incense when he awoke.

As soon as the charcoal had small sparks dancing across its surface, he sat the orange gems on top of the smoldering chunk. They started to glow faintly as soon as the gems contacted the open flames. The yellow gems at this point also started to shimmer from contact with the sun's intense rays. Naturally recharging a gem with mana was not a challenging task if one knew what one was doing.

Downstairs he heard a shrill yell. Running out to the balcony, he notices Lydia reaching for Penelope's hand. The thin bone needles she uses to sew and stitch outfits together slipped past the thimble and stuck her in the thumb. A small bead of blood flowed down her pointer finger and onto the hem of the outfit. Seeing the disturbance that the scene had caused and the attention it drew from the young lord, Lydia informed Castor that the situation was all right and under control. He saw her take Penelope into the washroom.

Castor went down and ducked his head near the door, making sure not to look inside in case they had undressed the blooded outfit from Penelope, and checked to make sure everyone was safe before he left. Lydia reassured him that she was all right, and Castor told her that he was departing. Across the atrium and out the front door, Castor headed off toward the port of Thyma.

CHAPTER 2

A Tilling Of Loamy Soil

19th of Beryl, 453 of the Age of Discovery

own the side of the estate's outer walls and through a few flagstone streets, Castor passed his neighbor's estates on his way out of town. While the insides of the houses were coated with plaster and murals cover the walls, the outside of the villas were bare, chiseled stone blocks, void of any detailed designs.

The houses were mostly tan and gray, which was based on the home's construction material. While the higher levels were coated with petrus-colored plaster, the first floor had bare stone exposed to the elements. The light, muted colors kept the Anthoran summer heat from penetrating the villas. Orange, yellow, and light red pigments were used to give the homes a slightly vibrant appearance. The colors were mostly located on the wood shutters which sat next to any windows that were not lined with bronze bars. The same stone was used to build each estate's border. Head height walls outlined the properties to separate the public streets from the sanctity of the private households.

Castor meandered through a stucco-covered arch at the end of one street and walked into the open, rolling fields of the southern Thymian countryside. Many minutes passed as Castor walked over the sandy trails towards town. The humidity of the prior night's storm was beaten back by today's harsh sunlight. The gravel paths started to kick up dust as he walked down the hills towards the main gate a few miles away. The morning dew was gone now, and only a few shepherds still walked the fields with their herds.

Wild and domesticated aurochs grazed the knee-high wild grasses, nibbling at any roughage the shepherds' sheep had missed in the days prior. The large beasts were enjoying the new growth after the storm, flicking their tails back and forth in amusement as well as to keep the flies off their bodies. The weeds and wild herbs had taken over the once tilled fields and became a local hotspot for any foragers in the region while they laid fallow this year.

The most popular of the wild foragers were large, red-tailed deer that fed on the fresh lavender sprouts whenever they could. They were a local delicacy amongst farmers and nobles alike. The Ephysian deer would often roam in packs of twenty to forty and migrate around the western side of Anthora depending on the season and weather. The fields were not just limited to the migratory cervids, as farm-owned aurochs also grazed the fallow fields around Thyma in peace, much to the chagrin of local poachers and their clientele.

Many locals without livestock tossed their food scraps into the fields to fatten the herds before the annual deer hunt festival started on the last day of Jasper. The Arietia, the celebration of the bringing in of the winter season, was a massive celebration in each of the smaller communities around the Thymian region. While the hunters were celebrating what they caught during the ten days of the chase, the giant feast and meat preparation that happened after was much more important. The prepared meats stocked the larders of local houses before the snow reached their lands. Castor was excited about this year's hunt.

The young prince saw a lone shepherd guiding his flocks of sheep across a nearby hill. They were the only two Anthorans on the local hills and Castor felt obliged to acknowledge him as they passed. While he was the one leading the sheep, his demeanor was sheepish towards Castor as he caught up to him on the trail.

"Good morning, sir," the balding, middle-aged man said to Castor. He politely gestured toward the well-fashioned teen while trying to keep the conversation brief. His short tunic was dyed a mellow yellow shade and was kept in good condition. Keeping one's clothes tidy and untattered was commonplace in Anthoran culture if one was going out in public where his neighbors and peers would see him. Castor noticed faded streaks of mud pressed into his left side and back. Castor assumed he must have fallen earlier in the day on the western slopes of the hills and tried to wash out the dirt at a stream before returning to his duties.

Castor dressed like a nobleman, so it was common for him to be treated as such. Not every citizen knew that he was the heir prince, but it was common courtesy to speak to nobles with a polite tone.

"A fine morning indeed," Castor responded. "Are you looking forward to the Arietia next month?"

"Yessir," the man said timidly, albeit with a smirk forming on the edges of his face. "My boys love trying spiced venison. It is their favorite meal of the year."

He was used to locals he was not acquainted with becoming shy during their first meeting, as his regal clothing and speech made him stand out compared to an average citizen. He made a personal goal to always try and crack that hardened heart when he could. The people of his lands were important to him, and he wanted them to feel comfortable around him. While folks from the denser parts of the big cities and docks had a reputation for being unruly or violent, those who lived out in the pastures and paddocks of the countryside tended to live mundane, relaxing lives. Castor sometimes envied their ability to ignore the rest of society and enjoy their simple lifestyle. If there was any group he wanted a good standing with, it was the local villagers.

Dirt scrunched under Castor's bare feet as he walked next to the shepherd down the hill. They crossed a small stone bridge, which was not more than ten feet long and five feet wide and had a small trickle flowing down the center of the otherwise dry creek bed. Summer droughts may have been prevalent in decades past, but the climate was much wetter over the last few years. The sheep, following the two men closely, were not all able to cross at the same time, as they numbered closer to fifty. As some passed across the bridge, others ran down the embankment and across the small ditch holding the flowing water. They muddied the bottoms of their fluffy coats in the process. The shepherd, although cautious at first, became more relaxed with the prince as they walked.

"And who might I be spending this nice morning walk with?" Castor asked, hoping to open an easy dialog with the shepherd.

"Glaucus, sir. My family lives in Olynthia. The fields around here were on my way back and I figured I would get the herd to good grasses after that storm."

Castor was taken aback. "Well, I am Castor. You looked like you were coming from the northwest. If you were stuck with your flock in the mountains during that storm, I am sorry for you. I hope you did not lose too many of them."

Glaucus was surprised the young lord knew about such trivial matters in herding and appreciated his concern. "It was quite alright, given the circumstances. I do not remember the last time we had a storm of that size this late in the year. Vrontir, praise be his divine justice, has not sent any tempest we could not handle in Sunstone, Fluorite, or Beryl for the second year in a row. He must be preoccupied somewhere else if we went another summer without a serious gale."

The sheep followed behind the two men a few paces back. They mewled at them, ensuring the shepherd they were following closely.

"Only one ewe was lost. She ran off into the slopes up the other side of the river. I wanted to go looking for her but..." he trailed off, clearly holding back." Either way, I will be able to return home by tomorrow's nightfall so long as the herd keeps up today."

For a long time, the trotting of soil and the occasional mewl were the only noises around them.

The shepherd's hesitation piqued Castor's interest. He seemed worried. Maybe he was not sure he could trust the young lord with his troubles, or maybe he just did not trust nobles. Either way, Castor's job was to protect the region. He wanted to get more information regardless of the man's hesitancy.

"You should know you do not have to hide anything from me," Castor said gently to the man, "It is my job to help you if something happens. If something is causing you stress, do not feel as though you would be hassling me with your troubles. I have never met a man whose issues were too much to handle."

Glaucus hesitated and rubbed his neck with a wide, fake smile on his face before looking down and giving in to his worries.

"I did not want you to think I was trying to be a bother. I was going to leave it with the guards after I stopped in town. I let them know yesterday, but they just laughed me off."

"That does not sound like the men I train with. You mentioned it here in Thyma?"

"No," the man shook his head, "I talked to the guards at the lookout tower near Tegoe. They thought I was seeing things, claiming I was drinking, and quickly shooed me off." Glaucus looked upset for the first time. "What use would I have had drinking in the mountains by myself during a thunderstorm with a bunch of sheep? They just did not want to do their actual jobs!"

Worried that he overstepped his bounds by accusing the prince's regional guard of failing in their duties, he pulled back and bowed his head in apologies for his outburst.

As they walked again in a short silence as Castor digested the information. His men were well trained and would not disregard a citizen's request so lightly. It was possible a mercenary group hired by the Traders Guild was stationed at the tower. The autumn harvest arriving soon meant the town guard had fewer hands to run the border defenses. Hired guards did not perform as well as those who willingly chose to protect their lands.

Before Castor could respond, they came upon a cluster of wattle and daub buildings. A family crest sat above the main home's lintel, one of an important lineage in Thyma. Their house had diversified into multiple professions over the generations, and they were well respected in the community.

Castor, realizing the rancher was preparing his tools to plow a fallow field near his home, waved and made idle chit-chat while they passed.

"Good to see you, Castor!" the portly man bellowed from behind his cart. "I am about to get this area prepared for winter. I appreciate your family letting us use some of their mana stores for this. I do not think I can handle this all by myself anymore. Not without my farmhands. My back just would not take it!"

The man, in his late forties, had seen a lot of wear and tear. His build was muscular and tough, but his face was wrinkled like that of an older grandparent. His hearty belly laugh reverberated across the buildings surrounding the motley crew. Castor recalled his father mentioning why the neroine was not in the storage shed when he was checking their inventory a few days prior. He now knew where it ended up.

"Having your labor leave so suddenly is quite unfortunate," Castor remarked. "I had not heard of any labor shortages. I thought you all got along fine."

"We did!" the farmer shot back, "They all just up and left after getting an opportunity to sail across the sea! I did not think sailors made any good money, but all three of them left the following morning without more than a half-hour conversation with me. If it was as profitable as they made it out to be, I should have joined them!" he chortled and scratched at his long sideburns.

Castor saw the size of the cart the man was trying to haul into the field. He was struggling to get it through the damp soil. He looked up to the sky and tried to guess the time of day by how far the sun was in the sky. He had a few hours left until the half-day rolled around. He left home earlier than he expected, and he was not too far off from town at this point. A half-hour, forty-five minutes at most. With that in mind, he shrugged and joined the man at the front of the cart.

"Would you like some help?" Castor offered to the farmer, grabbing the yoke from the other side and helping pull it out of the muddy divot, "I would expect another set of hands could make the process go faster."

The farmer was confused, then shocked. "Oh no, young master. I could not impose by taking up time in your day! Your family has already done so much for us."

"If I am honest, I could use the practice," Castor responded. "And I have a bit of time before I am due into town. I know you donate a good portion of your summer harvest to the Arietia every year. My father has mentioned your generosity before for our public events. That holiday is my and many others' favorite before the winter cold. I can at least return the favor by making this process go smoothly for you."

The man paused, then nodded towards the shepherd behind Castor. He was not sure what the shepherd was doing, walking with their prince towards town.

Glaucus noticed their stares and said, "If you do not mind me using your well water, I could use a short rest." A few sheep bleated behind him, as if in agreement.

The farmer shrugged his shoulders and smiled at the consensus. "Ya, that would be simply fine. The trough next to the well can be used for your animals. Feel free to relax while you wait for the young lord," he shook his head whilst turning towards Castor, "Your kindness really will give you wrinkles like mine. You may start to see them by the time you turn thirty if you help every farmer out standing in his field."

He smiled a large, toothy grin and slapped Castor on the back. The force knocked him forward a little and heightened his senses. It was for the best, as he was taking the morning in a too relaxed manner and needed to wake up before his intense training in a few hours.

Castor removed his outer mantle and handed it to Glaucus to hold while they worked. Slipping his right arm through his chiton and draping the extra fabric below his armpit, he manipulated the folds until it sat loosely around his shoulders and waist. He hiked up his chiton through his belt to give him more flexibility and tightened the bindings near his shoulders. Knotting his belt snug after adjusting the fabric, his outfit was far more comfortable for manual labor.

More like the size and weight of an Anthoran war chariot, the neroine was set up so that it could be moved around with one or two yokes. Since this cart was made to be pulled by humans, the two men moved into position and pulled the small wagon into the field next to the farmhouses. Out in the field, the farmer had marked up the circle where he planned to start his first crop in the spring. While some farms still used oxen and aurochs to plow their fields as beasts of burden, farming was also done by channeling the soil with mana. Farming done in this manner led to the pattern of concentric circles being created across the fields of Anthora.

Settling the cart into the center of the field, Castor and the farmer each took a side of the dappled gray tarp that covered the array of crystals below. They both brought the oiled linen taught and carefully removed it to reveal a mound of beautiful pillars, crescents, and other geometrically shaped structures. In the center of the cart sat a massive green jasper chunk, polished on its outer surface to resemble a pyramid in design. Small iridescent flecks of red impurities glittered under the surface. Its mass made up half of the surface area of the cart's bottom, with chunks and slabs of other sparkling shapes sitting around the central object. Tall towers of Tiger's Eye sat at each corner of the pyramid. Agate geodes lined the outside between each pillar with their sharp internal surfaces glistening in the sun. Every piece was connected with rods of copper and the twisting of the wires made the bottom of the cart look like reddish brown roots gnarling through the ground. The metallic webwork continued across the sides of the cart and up the corners, ending along the cart's railings. While most of the exposed copper was patinated with a dark teal, the sections along the railing were shining from the contact with Anthoran hands. The connection points on the crystals also did not have any corrosion, as though the flow of mana prevented such damage from occurring.

Castor recalled charging a few of the agate geodes from this device. When he was not training, patrolling, or relaxing, he spent a few hours at a time helping the town recharge their mana pools, these crystals included. This mana pool on wooden wheels, called a neroine in Anthora, was owned by the state and given for use to citizens who petitioned for its abilities. Storing such a vast amount of mana on a person was only possible by the most trained and wizened conjurers in the nation. Devices like these allowed less experienced people to use a lot of mana at one time without draining their energy to the point of passing out. This neroine was over two hundred pounds of low- and middle-grade gems, which has a substantial capacity for storing mana. A middle-grade channeler could channel for hours at a time.

Castor could feel the mana within the neroine as his fingers brisked over the copper edges of the railing. He looked out to where the fallow field extended fifty feet in every direction. *This should not take too long*, he thought to himself.

The farmer nodded at him and asked, "Do you know any of Gargrin's Laments?"

Gargrin, the Durulian god of mundane dirt and rock, was a well-respected god for Anthoran farmers, miners, and masons. As the patron of mining and digging, Gargrin's name was usually invoked for easy tilling or digging. His followers tell the tales of the time he was betrayed by his twin brother Hongrin and spent ten days alone at the bottom of a great ravine. Gargrin's Laments were hearty songs sung by native Durulians and Anthoran colonists who prayed to the rugged god. They always remembered to tell the tale of his strife within the ravine and his labors towards digging his way back to the surface. As the lament goes on, the power of his words becomes stronger. These short verses were the basic chants used to channel the ground.

"I do!" Castor responded, "I have read the first three, but I only have the first one memorized. Is that all right?"

The farmer nodded. "It should be. The soil is not frozen, and the rain made it all that much softer."

"Great. Would you like to get started? I will watch you once to pace your speed." Castor asked.

"I would." the farmer cleared his throat and laid a hand on the railing of the cart. Feeling the power welled up within the array, he made a connection to the flowing veins of mana. With a long, thin strand of copper tied to his belt, he took a step away. As his hand released from the edge of the cart, a small flash of lightning arced from his palm. With the extra mana, they started chanting the first verse of Gargrin's Laments.

Falling forms passed, in deep hole, he was cast
Far below ground, the deep pillars were vast
land above pit fell beyond a karst hill
From stone moonlit, he laid there like stone still

Strike the ground hard, the dig up was deeper
Underground dark, the great stone's deep keeper
From lands renown, the stark light was too dim
Followed far down, where he made this dark hymn

Dirt moved as the sun-beaten man sunk his feet into the soil. The loam parted around his sandals and gave away until his ankles were covered in damp mud. His stance was deep, his knees were bent, and his feet were splayed out like one would ride a steed. Energy flowed through him, rising and sinking as his breath went in and out.

In and out.

Palms fully open and fingers tucked, he pulled his arms close. Welling up the mana within him, the farmer focused on that which came from the cart. Like the paws of a tiger and his hands tucked up to his shoulders, he breathed a heavy breath in as he spoke the first section of the first line. As his breath expanded in his lungs and grew in his chest, he just as quickly released the air. He pushed his hands down the sides of his body and out towards the lane of land he planned to move. The entire movement continued circularly and ended where it started again. They continued to plow the field as they spoke the next verses of the lament.

Why was it I, who was cast aside
No hate or ire, nor brother defied
Friendship betrayed, a kinship was lost
Random of day, and no words accost

Tumbling down, the light grew so faint
Struck upon brow, was the stone-loved saint
Woken from pain, covered in raw ore
Vision was faint, he rest on the floor

As he spoke each line and the motion of the farmer's arms completely cycled, a burst of energy ran through the ground and split the channel. The sundered trench of open space was only a foot in width, but each pulse of the verse moved half a dozen feet of dirt out of the way and onto the tilled mounds between the furrows. The hum of energy from the neroine could be felt from a few feet away.

Castor watched the older man work and mimicked his pose on the other side of the neroine. Touching the railing, he connected himself to the vast amount of energy stored within the hundreds of pounds of stone. His hand discharged a bolt of energy just like the farmer, albeit much larger and with a loud crack. The shockwave was enough to make the farmer flinch, but he kept the pacing for the laments and did not falter in his motions.

The prince widened his stance and waited for the farmer to finish his current row before joining him in the laments. As the energy flowed from the cart to his body, he channeled the energy down through his hands and into his feet. While Castor's training focused on combat skills, his ability to control mana was far superior to the average Anthoran citizen. Channeling stone was his weakest affinity, as his focus has always been fire and wind. Even with his focus to be on the other elements, his raw capacity for his channeling and his overall training in channeling make him more than capable of plowing ruts into a loamy field. The prince had no doubt he could do this level of channeling with his mana store, without so much as needing the help of his personal jewelry and gems.

Each pulse of power rippled under the surface as he channeled his energy through the ground. The soft soil moved away from the center of the channel and, while a few pulses were unruly and not straight, Castor tuned his flow of mana to match the length and magnitude of what the farmer would output.

As each pulse went out, small chips of soil and rock launched forward and separated from the flow of the divots. As soil went left and right, any stones were tossed away from the center of the circle, building up increasingly until a pile of loose stones and dead roots were left at the end of the rows. The stones built up at the edge of the plowed circle until the field had started to develop a natural wall of dry-stacked stone around the outer edge of its circumference.

As the men toiled away, they worked through the rows in a clockwise motion. The circle went from being covered in small tufts of tough weeds and residual stocks from the prior harvest of rye to a fully tilled field of crumply loam in the freshly cut furrows. Sweat grew on their brows as the late morning sun started to beat upon their skin and clothes. Halfway through, the farmer took a short break to grab straw hats for both of them. As they finished the first circle, the men went and placed the copper strands back on the edge of the cart and removed their connections with the neroine.

"If you ever get tired of lording over these lands, you could always come work for me as a farmhand!" the farmer chuckled to Castor from across the cart. The hum of the stones dampened to silence as their connections were broken.

Castor smiled. "I appreciate the offer. I am not sure how that would go over with the city council." He wiped the sweat from his brow and used a small, clean towel the farmer threw at him from across the clearing. While he was overheated, the only dirt on his body was from his feet burrowing into the soil. One benefit of moving the soil from a distance was keeping the soil from your outfit. There simply was no dirt to dirty your clothes.

After cleaning themselves off with their towels, they moved back to the front of the cart and towed the neroine to the next clearing a hundred feet away. Each circle butted up to the next, with the next rows' centers lining up with the outer edges of the prior row. This offset allowed for little wasted space between circles with only a small triangle between each area.

Working each circle took about a quarter of an hour at the slow pace the farmer set. Having Castor there had them completing their fields in less than half the time it would have taken the farmer alone, and Castor could tell the man was struggling to keep up as they progressed. As a field this size would take a normal human half a day to plow by hand and a few hours to plow with a beast of burden, they were able to cut a good portion of the farm's work for the week down within one morning. As it was not even noon yet, he had no worries about getting to the training on time. Anthoran's days were thirty hours long, so he still had a bit before noon hit at 15 o'clock. Powering through, the two men were able to finish six fields before Castor let him know they had to get going into town.

After pulling the shade cloth back over the top of the cart, the men pulled the neroine back to the farmer's homestead, placing it within the barn to the left of the farmer's house. As they walked back, cart in hand, an older portly lady sat by the front door with a small table full of snacks next to two recliners.

"Hello, young lord!" exclaimed the older woman from a distance away as the two men returned to the homestead. She had a tray of cheese and dried meats on the table and two pitchers of wine in her hands.

As they approached, Castor saw Glaucus washing his tunic at the well. His sheep nibbled at the weeds around the edge of the barns, baaing timidly at the men's return. They hauled the cart within a wood stall inside the barn and attached it to the wall with a few strands of rope around the chassis. The farmer returned to his wife and kissed her on the cheek while Castor went over to the shepherd and let him know he would only be a few more minutes before heading out to town.

"I do not mind, my lord." the shepherd said as he nodded, "A break like this with clean water is always welcome on my travels. I would have rested here or near the front gates, and this is a more than welcome respite over the city walls."

He used a dry cloth from his belt pouch to dab at the wet spots on his tunic. The mud from earlier in the day was mostly washed out and was barely noticeable even when one was looking for the stain. Satisfied from his cleaning, he leaned against the edge of the cobblestone well and chewed at a piece of dried mutton he pulled from another of his pouches.

Castor walked up and onto the porch of the farmer's homestead and came up to where the portly woman had set up the recliners and food table. As he got closer, she smiled and gave him a bear hug, squeezing him to the point where he felt a few of his bones move in his chest. As her head was tucked under his chin due to their height difference, she pulled her head back and looked up at him.

"Look at you!" she bellowed in a deep tone to not hurt his ears at such a close distance. "My, have you grown over the last few years?"

Castor had to think hard about what her name was. It had been a few years now since he last saw her. *Varos?* He thought. Or was it *Garos?*

He remembered that she was one of his mother's old friends from many years back. The last time he saw her was at his sister's wedding, which was a few years ago at this point. Baros. He remembers seeing the embroidered letters AB on her apron.

"I appreciate your kind words, Missus Baros."

It took her a few moments to realize how Castor had referred to her. Her smile turned into a wry frown.

"There is no need for 'missus' or 'mister' around here, Castor." she said in a mockingly bitter tone. "You are the future prince of our region. I cannot have the heir prince calling me 'Missus Baros.' I would never hear the end of it from the neighbors!"

Glaucus the shepherd all but choked on his snack of dried meats. Hearing someone talk so informally and even give commands to the next lord of this region was something he would not even consider. To see an old farmer's wife make such brash statements was stunning to the man from out of town.

"I will make sure to remember that going forward." Castor chuckled.

"Avgi, dear. My name is Avgi."

He nodded, "I will make sure to remember that going forward, Avgi."

After she unclasped her arms from the young man, he and the farmer lay on the recliners and had a snack of cheese and honey. The curds, made within the last week, were savory and tart. The tanginess sat on his cheeks while the honey on top soothed the acidity. The men spoke of the coming autumn and the festival they were to prepare for. Castor learned that Avgi was the one who donated the cheeses for the festival, made from the milk of the auroch they owned that roamed the hillsides on this side of town. Castor was looking forward to the event since it would be the first year he could take part. Usually, you must wait until you turn twenty and become a full adult, but the local families usually bend the rules a little if a birthday was close to the time of the event. Since Castor's birthday was only two months after the month of Quartz at the beginning of the year, no one would complain about him joining in on the hunt this year, especially about the young man who would be ruling over these lands in a few decades to come.

They spent a half-hour talking, eating, and resting from the harsh sun. Once they finished, Castor thanked them for their hospitality and prepared for the rest of their journey into town. The farmer assured him that he was always welcome to help on the farm. And Castor chuckled. He assured the man that he would keep an ear out for more workers who would be looking for farming work. As they parted, Avgi handed Castor and Glaucus a small chunk of fresh feta cheese. The men nibbled on it as they walked down the slopes towards the port town's main gate.

Rolling hills let out into flatter lands as open pasture turned to farmed fields. Trodden gravel paths and small wooden stairs made up the road system in these rural parts. As they were not on the main state roads between towns, the state funding was extremely limited for rural infrastructure. Considering how only a dozen or so people would pass through these parts a day, it simply did not make sense to make a heavier road system in between the local farmer's plots of land.

The two continued for a bit as Castor picked away at the feta cheese in the palm of his hand. Once he was done, he wiped his hands on a patch of tall grass by the roadside. The fresh cheese helped give him a boost in energy after such hard labor.

Castor found it difficult to keep up with the lively sheepherder. For his age, the man could keep a quick stride. He wondered how the middle-aged man's feet were able to keep up with his current pacing all day. Considering his job was to walk through fields and countryside to lead his flock, this was not out of the question. It would also have helped if Castor put his sandals on for this trip. The occasional large stone caused him some pain every ten minutes or so.

Days like this made Castor nostalgic about his childhood before his appointment as a guard captain. Although young, it was common for princes of Anthora to take higher positions as training for their future careers. While not one of the most populated or one of the wealthiest regions, Thyma was still a province of over 30,000 people. He wished he had a little longer to roam the fields and enjoy his youth before his daily chores of work had taken hold of his life.

After a bit of walking, the prince spoke up about their prior conversation. "You have every right to be upset. There are issues that should be handled with more care at those towers. They are there for people like you to report anything you see on your travels. No one should have to feel as though a threat was being played off as drunk ramblings."

Glaucus looked puzzled and then remembered their prior conversation from a few hours back. The two walked a little farther in more silence. Castor felt bad for the older man's issue. He did not want to make him feel worse about it all, but it was his job to fix these issues when they arose.

"Goblins." the man said under his breath.

Castor instantly stopped walking and turned toward the man. "What did you say?" The expression on his face was clearly distressed even if he was trying to mask his full emotions from the conversation.

"I saw goblins," Glaucus said again, this time a bit louder. He did not look up from the ground near Castor's feet.

Castor spent a second trying to compose himself and calmed down to the point where he could continue the conversation without overreacting. He patted Glaucus on the shoulder and had them continue their travels once more. There was no point standing about. A tepid stream gurgled underfoot as they crossed another small stone bridge. The water's surface was foggy and muddled, the mud from the prior storm's runoff still lingering.

"I believe you. I do." Castor said in a confident voice. He did not want to alarm nor offend the man who clearly just put his trust in the young lord for bringing up such bold accusations. "But, if that is the case, then I am not surprised the mercenaries wanted nothing to do with your case." Castor thought back to the conversation this morning with his sister. Some of the men that Glaucus had talked to may have been the very men that were working for Theron two years prior and knew the dangers of the topic at hand.

"I want you to put your worries aside." Castor put his hand on the man's shoulder. "This will be something I will personally bring up with the patrol captains in town. I will spare you the trip into the barracks for an official interview. Considering the circumstances, I see no reason for you to lie. Just tell me everything you saw while we finish our walk to the front gates."

Castor peeled a fig from his pouch as Glaucus explained what he saw. The road they now traveled was one of the major roads connecting the region with other cities. As Glaucus spoke of his encounters in the mountains, the two encountered many other travelers on their way to the gates. Amongst them were merchant caravans who flew flags of countries or cities he had only seen in books and scrolls. The caravans made sure to fly their flags high above their carts, not only to advertise their business as upstanding representatives of their homelands but also as a means of deterrent towards bandits and highway robbers. Stealing from a lonely shepherd was one thing but gaining the ire of a military state was a completely different topic.

Another reason for keeping your flag on your cart was to help identify comrades from the same nation. Fellow citizens would exchange news and pass along trade tips to their own people within these foreign lands. On their way, he had seen two caravans with the same flags meet up and set up camp on the side of the road.

Around a mile out of town, a small village of tents, carts, and carriages was seen in an open field. They were huddled against the hillside on the left side of the road. This area was where traveling merchants, dignitaries, and pilgrims had set their campsites up for the nights ahead. As cities did not allow for large groups of foreign parties to set up their camps within the city walls, this area was sanctioned by the local authorities for their stays. A group of guards was assigned to help keep the peace, protect the travelers if issues arose, and gather information on who and what was coming from outside the region. The guard patrol also stationed a government official to keep track of any tariffs that would be levied, plan for meetings with any local dignitaries, and help those unaware of the city's layout on where to visit the town during their visit.

A stone tower two stories in height sat by the roadside near the campsite. The tower was surrounded by a wooden palisade and only able to be entered from a single ladder that led up to the first floor five feet off the ground. The second story had a full wood balcony that encircled the top and allowed for easy vision over the surrounding landscape. A single archer sat at the top of the tower. Castor waved at the guard and the guard nodded back. Castor and Glaucus passed the community with no issues except for Glaucus needing to call his sheep a few times more than normal. The small animals were easily distracted by the colorful tents and groups of different people.

As they got closer to town, Glaucus let Castor know he planned to skirt past the outside of the port town's walls. Bringing an entire herd of sheep into a town was not the easiest task and was only usually done during their sale.

As they got closer, the tall looming walls of Thyma started to grow on the horizon. While they had been able to see the town earlier in the morning from the hillsides, they had traveled into the valley and taken the main road to the front gates. The Mena River quietly burbled on the right side of the road. Small boats traveled down the river and out into the split bays of Thyma's port. The river passed on the western side of the town walls and created a natural moat for a third of the city's defenses. A large stone arch bridge could be seen in the distance, connecting the two sides of the valley.

Once they were near that split in the road, Castor and Glaucus said their goodbyes. Castor thanked him for his information and assured the man that the topic would be investigated. As he left, he crossed the arch bridge and took his herd across the Mena River. The sheep could be heard baaing in the distance as Castor approached the line near the gate.

In front of him was the only gatehouse on this side of the city. Three arches made up the central gate. Two smaller gates about ten feet in height flanked the central, twenty-foot main gate. The central gate was a set of bronze-clad doors with ornate carvings and details. They were currently closed and on the right side, a smaller arch was being used for the entrance to the city. As caravans were cleared to enter, the heavily reinforced door would slide open and close soon after.

Castor got into the line queuing outside the gates and saw a few of his guardsmen on duty. They were performing gate checks on all incoming and outgoing traffic to the city. The gatehouse sat back from the rest of the long stone walls, the recessed section allowing for better angles of sight on anyone near the entrance to the city. The walls were thirty feet tall and six feet wide. The gatehouse was the same rough-hewn sandstone that the rest of the city's fortifications were made from. A relief of two dolphins made up the keystone of the center gate's arch. The two heralds of the town were the pets of the city's matron goddess, Keanas. The keystone was carved from a single slab of white marble. The outlines and details of the animals were inlaid with turquoise slabs, giving the reliefs a pop of color to accentuate their fine features. On the top of the walls sat a flat roof of wood framing and slate shingles which were held up with tall circular columns. Two guards stood near the entrance by the ground and two archers stood near the pillars atop the battlements.

Castor smirked as he kept a low profile in the lengthy line. He wanted to see how his guards would act when not under the scrutiny of their leaders. Minutes passed as guests were allowed into the city. As he got close to the entrance, he noticed a caravan giving his guards a tough time at the front of the line. A palanquin sat off the ground near the guards, its raised platform carried by a dozen Maudian cat men. These Maudians looked like they were the same subrace as Ignus, the patron deity of Greater Maudians, who looked like an anthropomorphic lion.

One major difference between Ignus and these Maudians was their lack of a mane. They were built large and muscular, so Castor assumed they were all males. Female Maudians were shorter and sleeker than their male counterparts and their faces were much longer. Every Maudian that was visible in this entourage had their manes cut to a short length and only a single long dread of hair was visible on the back of their heads. A higher-ranked emissary stood proudly in front of the entourage and wore an ornate robe and headdress. Two braided dreads could be seen protruding from the edges of the head covering.

Within the Empire of Maudif, only royalty and noble families could have their full mane grown out and unbound. The length and volume of a Maudians mane could display their position in the empire's hierarchy. Based on the level of extravagance this group traveled in, Castor could assume the noble upon the dais was full-maned, one from the noble classes. The person being carried on top was not visible as the entire palanquin was covered in sheets of silk and gossamer that hung from the ciborium overhead. The palanquin had exquisitely carved murals on every side of the wood base.

The emissary talked with the guards. One of the men on the ground gestured for them to pass through the gate, but the lion man kept pointing towards the larger gate. The palanquin would easily fit through the smaller gate, but the party did not seem to budge.

"Open the main gate." the emissary growled gently to the guards standing near the door, a smile on his face and his hands wrung in front of him. Castor recognized the recruits as Alec and Icharo, two of the newer trainees who were under Castor's command during his normal shifts during the week. Since this job was good training for them, Castor stood back from the confrontation and kept an eye on what was brewing while he waited. Stuck with working the weekend shift, the boys were clearly tired of the demands of the emissary.

"As I have already informed you, we do not open the bastion for any carts or travelers small enough to fit through this gate," Icharo said. He and Alec had stood to the side, but the group of lion men did not budge.

"His majesty does not simply travel through side gates." the emissary hissed. His constant smile and squinted eyes never wavered, becoming increasingly forced as the conversation progressed. "He should be welcomed into this city like how he is welcomed into the rest of your cities. Pynos was much more... accommodating."

"This is not Pynos, and the capital has many more guardsmen to staff the gates on weekends. We cannot just be opening the bastion every time someone asks. We would not be able to lift our arms after a few hours of moving those hunks of metal."

The lion man, still smiling and hands clasped, bared his fangs for a second before composing himself. Whiskers twitched on his furry cheeks as his mouth opened and quickly closed. Alec instinctively put his hand on his sword's pommel, as the sight of a six-foot-tall cat man with bared teeth can be very intimidating for a sixteen-year-old Anthoran boy. Icharo, who was twenty-four and around the same height and not nearly as furry, did not react to the action.

A low rumble came from the palanquin and the emissary retreated. He tucked his head in between the silk sheets which separated the royal from the outside world and kept it there for a few moments before returning his head outside.

The emissary whistled. The twelve palanquin bearers, averaging a little under seven feet in height and close to three hundred pounds each, lifted the platform from the ground and moved into the city through the small gate. The emissary led the group from the front. As he passed Ichiro, the Maudian hissed, a sign of disrespect within the satrapies of Maudif. The noise was enough to startle Icharo, and he stepped back as they passed.

The line moved forward, and Castor waited his turn. He was in no rush and enjoyed seeing his underlings work. Being able to understand and balance the strengths and weaknesses of those under one's command was a trait Castor aimed for. He knew his father, although capable of his martial training and channeling of the elements, was renowned for his silver tongue and ability to work his allies together to benefit the region. While Castor was not brash nor bull-headed, he was still a nineteen-year-old boy. He was fully aware of his limitations both in his age and reputation. He strived to learn when he could.

From watching the two gate guards, it was clear that Icharo was the more experienced of the two. He was the one who initiated conversations and would lead any searches of property. Alec stood next to him, albeit a small bit behind, and did what he was told. He made for a good foot soldier, but his leadership skills were not his strong suit.

As he waited, he took the time to admire the White Tower of the East that sat upon the ridge in the mountains. Few had the privilege to see the alabaster tower up close, but all could see it from a distance. Its bright white walls stood out against the dark blue skies that lay behind it. It was but a speck on the horizon from this distance, but Castor knew of how big it truly was. Taller than the great lighthouse within the Thymian port, the

White Tower of the East was the third tallest structure in all of Anthora. It soared over five hundred feet into the air and sat upon the highest peak on this side of the Sideros mountains. At the very top of the tower held a giant crystal, or so Castor was told. No one he knew was allowed access to the top of the tower. Only the Oracle and his head priests were given that privilege. They lived in the temple complex attached to the base of the giant white monolith.

As one of the five oracles that led the nation in times of turmoil and strife, the immortal oracle of the White Tower sat in contemplation for centuries right within that very tower. He would only grace the city with two visits a year, during the summer and winter solstices. His time outside the temple's walls was spent foretelling the next year's prosperities as soon as the new year rolled around. While the event did take place on the coldest and darkest day of the year, many would gather in town for the event just to get a glimpse of the Oracle. Only once in a decade or so would the oracle personally choose to read the fortune of an individual from the crowd, and they were usually blessed with good fortune for the rest of their lives.

Following the tide of incomers, Castor looked at the tower and the glistening beacon that sat at the top for quite a while. He finally noticed how close he had gotten to the gate when Alec called the guards to attention. Bringing his focus back to attention, Castor turned to see both gate guards and archers standing at attention, saluting their captain. All four had their weapons drawn across their chests. Their other hand was tucked behind into the small of their back. Their helmets were off, held by the offhand behind them.

"At ease, friends," Castor said, smirking at the attentive guardsmen. "Let us not make a scene here."

The men sheathed their swords and donned their helmets. The archers, lighter armed and constantly holding their bows, put their hoods back up and disappeared behind the pillars they were stationed at.

"Captain, good morning!" Alec's stark black curls brushed out below the brow of his helmet. His hair was long enough to be a nuisance when wearing a helmet but not long enough to be pulled back into a braided knot. The sun on this hot and humid day was not doing him any good. He was able to stand within the shade of the tall city walls while he performed his duties.

Castor walked up and inspected his brow, putting his hand on his chin in a quizzical manner.

"Hmm...." Castor grunted with one eyebrow raised while getting quite close to the younger boy's face. Alec smiled shamefully, knowing full well what his captain was looking at.

Alec took a step back, turned around, and took off his helmet. He quickly pushed his hair back off his face and tucked as much as he could behind his ears. Hastily donning his helmet once more, he turned back to Castor and took a step forward to return to position.

"Much better." Castor smiled. "Skills are important but having the look of a warrior is half the battle when on duty."

"Yessir!" Alec said so enthusiastically that he slurred his response. Castor patted him on the shoulder and turned to Ichiro.

"Will your squad be joining me for supplementary lessons today at the amphitheater?"

"We will still be on patrol, Captain." Ichiro shook his head.

"Ah, well there's no way to get you out of your duties," Castor responded. "I am sure I will see you all during our standard meetings this coming week."

"We look forward to it, Captain."

Castor opened his belt pouch and showed it to Alec. "I am free of contraband. May I enter?"

Alec looked surprised and gestured for Castor to pass.

"Thank you," Castor said confidently. "I hope the rest of your shift goes smoother than what you put up with this morning."

"Thank you, sir," Ichiro responded with a nod. Castor passed Alec and entered through the archway.

CHAPTER 3

Dry-Shod On A Granite Road

19th of Beryl, 453 of the Age of Discovery

s soon as he passed under the central arch of the front gatehouse and entered the port town of Thyma, the smell of local foods flooded Castor's nose. A handful of food carts littered the edges of the streets and crowds of people passed through the narrow roads. In front of him was the western plaza. Many flocked to it for food and relaxation on this side of the town. As he walked towards the naturally open area, the bustle of the front gate quickly died down. Tall sandstone buildings lined the streets surrounding the plaza. Some of the walls were rough-hewn while others were plastered and painted.

Castor, now slightly hungry after having a light breakfast and knowing his training session would last far past lunch, needed to find something heavier to eat before the session he was to lead.

Fired clay bricks clad the paths of the town and kept mud from building up in the streets. Off to his right, a man selling grilled kebabs out of his cart waved to the passersby. Castor was already on his way over before the man noticed his approach.

The shop cook roasted the cut pieces of meat over an open pit of wood coals sitting within a square ceramic bowl. The wooden tips of the skewer sticks went through the meat and sat upon the lip of the ceramic bowl on each side. The height of the container held them up off the smoldering embers far enough to give the chunks of the lamb a crispy golden outer layer. The ceramic bowl sat in a divot on the top of his wooden cart. His home was stationed behind his street setup just like all the other food vendors selling to the midday crowd. The food stands allowed the shops to make some money during the morning hours while the home kitchen was dedicated to preparing the evening meal. The stand had a few chairs and small tables next to it; a few patrons sat around and chewed on the kebabs under the cloth canopy. The cart owner sprinkled a mixture of spices onto the meat as he twisted the skewers over the glowing coals.

"Hungry again today, young master?" the cart's owner asked coyly as Castor ordered four grilled lamb skewers from him. The tan, skinny man turned the skewer over to allow for even cooking on all sides of the meat.

"As always, it seems." Castor nodded. It was starting to get close to midday and Castor would not have time to grab a proper meal before heading to his training. He was a growing teenage boy. His constant training regimen meant he had to eat a lot more than the average young adult.

He paid the man with one of his silver coins, a drachma, and received two copper obols in return. Two obols for a single cooked skewer of meat were a competitive price for street vendor food. Although a whole roast was worth the same if sold in bulk or bartered between families, the convenience of street food raised the price. Castor was not in any worry about becoming destitute, so he happily paid for the convenience of grabbing a meal before he went to the training field.

Taking a short break, he sat in the plaza on a stone bench. His body was shaded from the harsh midday sun by shade cloths that lined the outer area. Tall, milled columns of pink marble lined the outside of the circular plaza, spread out every fifteen feet. An inner row of columns sat within the outer circle, shorter in stature and numbering only eight within that area. The capitals at the top of the columns were plain in design. Between the outer and inner circles was the stone-lined path that Castor took refuge in. The path below his feet was made of the same pink marble and tiled the floor within the shaded area. The stone bench Castor sat on was accented in the same plain Anthoran pattern as the columns. Around the outer columns were small shrines. A statue of a god was interred within a wooden pergola at each location. Castor found the shrine to Ignus and sat across from it.

He recalled the history of this plaza from his tutoring lessons as a teenager. This city park was dedicated to a prince from over two hundred years back when the last ruling dynasty still controlled Thyma. Polybolas Drakos of the Drakos clan was a notorious leader that had many books written in his honor. His family was knowledgeable of masonry and had connections within the region to many mines and quarries. They had the pink stone shipped in from across the seas from a satrap in Maudif. Lord Polybolas had sent himself along with a battalion of well-trained city militia across the sea to help with the overthrowing of a corrupt governor in the southern steppes of Ecardis. The new leader of that satrapy gave the ancient prince many shiploads of pink marble in return as compensation for his support. The resistance leader turned governor, Bashir Khezri, led Ecardis into an age of prosperity and many beneficial trade deals flowed from the dominant trade city to Thyma over the centuries.

As he sat, Castor watched the townsfolk go about their daily lives. He saw shop vendors opening their shops for the day, children running through the plaza to play tag, and guards making their rounds through the many areas they patrolled. He saw the children had decided to climb the statue in the center of the plaza. The pink marble fountain sprayed water in every direction within its basin. Atop the fountain was a painted marble statue of the goddess Keanas. Her net was in her left hand and her oar was in her right. They were gilded in gold and shimmered across the plaza. Keanas was the goddess of oceans and seas and made for a fitting matron of this growing port town.

While many of Anthora's oceanside towns had taken her as their matron, Thyma's historians believed that Keanas originated within the Thyma region. Legends say she had taken refuge from Vrontir, the god of thunder, storms, and clouds, within this town over a millennium ago. He had pursued Keanas for her beauty and wit but was angry when he was spurned by the ocean goddess. It was for good reason, too, as Vrontir was married to Nerea, the goddess of rivers and rainfall. This family feud had Keanas hiding from the storm god for many years. The infighting between the husband and wife can be seen to this day, as storms of thunder and lightning bring the flooding of rivers and cause havoc in the mortal world. Oceans were safe from the wrath of the sky and do not tend to rise in level when a heavy storm hits, but those who travel her waters were always wary of the damage the god of thunder could do on the high seas.

Once Castor was finished with his lunch, he walked over to the shrine of Ignus. Around five feet in height, the small wood canopy housed the statue of the lion god in his Anthoran form. Much like his Maudian counterpart, he stood upright and in a heroic posture, the sacred flame wreathed around him. As an Anthoran, he had the pelt of a lion wrapped around his neck like the mantle Castor wore that day. The sacred flame radiated across the fur of the lion and concentrated near the brooch in the center of his chest.

Below the statue sat a few offerings to the god of fire. The dried foods and assorted baubles sat next to a small ceramic cup to light incense. While Castor did not bring incense with him, he did have the wooden skewers from his lunch. He stuck the cyprus sticks into the sand inside the cup and said a prayer to his patron. A small flame ignited from the tip of his finger and lit the tips to an ember. The fragrance of cypress wood and grilled meat filled the air. After a short pause of prayer, Castor headed off down the path outside the plaza towards the Thymian barracks.

He passed through a small alley on his way through the city, saving himself time from walking down the busy corridors in a U-shaped fashion. He frequently participated in patrols around the city during his week as a guard captain. While the patrols were good physical training, he saw it as an opportunity to build connections with local citizens within the different districts of the city. He knew he had a legacy to live up to with his family and wanted to get an early start on fostering connections he could use when he became the crown prince of the region.

As he walked, an arm came around his neck and yanked him back. Castor tucked his chin and quickly drew his xiphos from his belt. He burst forth a focused gust of wind from his left hand. The funnel of air propelled him forward while tossing his assailant away.

As Castor turned, he lifted his sword and bent his knees, dropping his weight into a more comfortable stance for fighting. He was about to chant a more dangerous spell before he noticed who had grabbed him. Across the alley was his dear friend Kyros, laying in a pile of someone's dirty laundry along the back-alley wall.

"That's no way to greet a friend," Kyros grunted as he got off the ground and dusted himself off. His blonde hair was very oily from his adventures and was formed unnaturally after the strong gust of wind. His straight locks were twisted and knotted in abnormal shapes as the grime within his hair kept it in place.

"Attacking the heir prince on your first day back? That's a bold move." Castor said with a grin.

"I like to live boldly." Kyros retorted. He grinned widely as he approached the prince.

"You smell terrible." Castor squinted as he sheathed his sword. He went towards Kyros and gave his friend a strong, solid handshake. He would have given him a strong, solid hug, but the smell coming from the seasoned mercenary was not something Castor wanted to take with him to the training.

Kyros lifted his left arm and sniffed his armpit. "I can't smell a thing." He then let out a hearty laugh.

"I do not doubt that." Castor joined in and chuckled back. "What happened to arriving home at the end of the month?"

"Our trip to Bythea was quicker than we expected." Kyros stated, "Our client cut negotiations short due to the current rebellions in Maudif and did not want to stay away from home any longer than he had to."

Kyros Delkínitos, now twenty-three, had been adventuring across Anthora as an armed caravan guard for three years. Castor looked up to Kyros growing up, even though he was born to a middle-class family of merchants within the port town. His father had many dealings with the Nephus family and would let the boys play together when they visited. The mercenary wore his full set of armor and had his traveling rucksack on his back.

"Where are you off to today?" Kyros asked Castor as they walked out of the dingy alley and into the next street. "I thought you had the weekend off."

"I do," Castor responded, "I may have the days of Ignus and Pyrros to spend on myself, but I spend part of Gargrin's day teaching the newer recruits and aspiring channelers how to better hone their skills."

It was common for Castor to spend his weekends doing volunteer work. Having three full days of rest out of every ten-day week meant a decent amount of free time for the heir prince. The days of the week were named after each of the major deities in Anthora. The weekend was made up of the days of Ignus, Pyrros, and Gargrin. The workdays were days dedicated to Brömli, Vrontir, Nerea, Keanas, Beltunias, Calcothwyn, and Arimilia.

"Well, look at you! Our amazing prince is sacrificing his precious time off to help those in need. You are living up to your gracious personality." Kyros patted Castor forcefully on the back whilst donning a wide, sarcastic smile. His friend was easily over two hundred and fifty pounds of solid muscle, which made knocking around a two-hundred-pound prince easy.

"What are your plans? Care to join us in the amphitheater?" Castor asked, disregarding his friend's quip against his altruistic intentions.

"Well, as you so politely pointed out earlier, I have some washing to do. I think I will hop in the ocean down by the docks to get the smell off and then head to the bathhouse after to clean myself up." He turned and pointed to show Castor the large gash in his linothorax that had cut through most of the layers of the linen armor. "Oh, and I need to get this mended as well."

"Well, that does not bode well. Did you forget how to walk and trip down a hillside?" Castor asked coyly.

Kyros stuck his foot out in front of Castor to try and trip him, but the young prince was far more agile than the mercenary. He skipped over his foot, making sure to step down softly on his exposed toes. Kyros yelped in pain, laughing off his regrettable decision.

"No hillside did this to me, but instead a clamor of harpies!" Kyros exclaimed, "We were attacked on our way back through the mountains. There were over two dozen of them and only eight of us. My shield brother was tossed to the ground during one of their barrages and the opening got me a claw in the side. Luckily, no one was killed. We slew four of them before the rest retreated up the mountain."

"Mhm," Castor said. His disbelief was showing on his face.

"I was able to skewer one with my spear and almost took a beak to the head before my shield brother got up and pushed it out of the way," Kyros said valiantly.

"Oh!" Castor said. He nodded sarcastically, but the mercenary did not notice his tone.

Kyros continued imperiously as they walked, "I dislodged my spear from the one bird and threw it into another that was trying to get to our client."

"Fascinating," Castor said. His sarcastically distant expression took a bit for Kyros to notice, but he did eventually realize the disbelief Castor was showing.

Kyros squinted at Castor. "You are lucky we are in the town limits. I could hang you by your heels in the river, you know."

"I am already clean from the rain showers last night, but I appreciate the offer," Castor tried to say with a straight face, then cracked a large smile.

Kyros let out a deep sigh and put his hands up in exasperation. "Have it your way."

The two friends passed some shops on their way through the merchant district. A pottery shop boasting a plethora of shapes and sizes sat across the street as they left the alleyway. Next to it sat a clothing store selling many vibrant outfits personally crafted from the displayed swaths of fabric. Their colors and patterns were not only inclusive of all Anthoran styles of the time but also held a few patterns seen in faraway lands, across the sea in Maudif, or even hailing from the mighty mountain homes of the stout Durulians. Not only were fabrics made of linen and cotton, but many bolts of cloth were made of exotic materials from faraway lands. Two bolts on display were made of Durulian crystalhair, special silk from a cave mushroom that resembled beard hair only found deep within the Hem Durulian Mountains. The bolts were shown off on a podium in the front of the shop to adequately display the foreign to local passersby.

When walking past, Castor saw a sign in front of the building calling out their latest shipment of Tecuanti spider silk from the dense, infested jungles of Sangmarta. That material, while incredibly light, was even stronger than the crystalhair of Hem Durul, making it one of the rarest commodities in the known world. Getting enough silk for one bolt would take hundreds of hours in dangerous locations. It was so expensive that even Castor would not buy it in excess if he did not have a good reason to.

The mentioned bolt of silk was not on display. It was held in a secure location, so no thieves had any funny ideas. That fabric took months to get to Thyma and took a year overall to create. It was the month of Beryl now, the seventh month, but it was close to last Beryl when the silk was first gathered. The ten months of the year, Quartz, Jade, Calcite, Emerald, Sunstone, Fluorite, Beryl, Jasper, Azurite, and Moonstone, each had their own weather and temperatures. As the winter would be much cooler, it was far easier to gather the spider silk when the spiders were less active.

As they walked by, the shop clerks smiled and waved. This mercantile street was often patrolled by the city guard since the stored wealth made it a prime target for any high-end thefts. Castor smiled and waved back as the men walked down the tiled path.

"I was not joking before, by the way." Kyros said as they walked, "We were attacked by harpies."

Castor smiled. "I believe you, friend. I was just giving you a hard time, that is all. You used to be quite an exaggerator back when we were younger."

"I grew out of that once my adventures became tales that needed no exaggerations," Kyros replied with a smirk and a raised eyebrow.

"It's a good thing you were attacked while traveling and not when you were camping for the night," Castor commented. "Having armor and a proper formation surely helped against their numbers."

Kyros nodded. "That is true. Our client was safe within our shield wall, so he had no issues with the trip either. The only unfortunate parts were that Jason lost an eye and we had to reroute back to town away from the maintained roads. It was higher in the mountains, and we had no running water to use for the last few days. We survived from what we had stored in waterskins to drink and no excess to bathe."

"Ah, which explains the smell," Castor remarked.

"Yes, that explains the smell." Kyros agreed.

The two men made their way past an artisanal street of shops within the merchant's district and passed Kyros' family estate. The storefront was open by the street, and their family home sat behind. Large tapestries and vibrant carpets hung from floor to rafter outside the storefront.

"I am going to stop home before heading for the river." Kyros said, "I should let my parents know I am back in town. I will be around for at least a few weeks so if I cannot stop by for your lessons today, I will catch up with you this coming week during your evening patrols."

"That sounds like a good plan," Castor said. He offered out his hand. "Stay out of trouble while you are home."

"You know me, I am as innocent as a priestess of Nerea!" Kyros chuckled. They shook hands and Castor started heading down the road towards the entertainment district. Before he got too far away, Kyros called out and caught up.

"I almost forgot, I grabbed you something!" Kyros said between breaths, panting from the sprint over. "I grabbed these for your helmet since I know you still like to use that older design."

Kyros took off his traveling backpack and reached into the side of his bag. He tenderly pulled out four vivid orange feathers from the opened pouch. They were all about a foot long and a couple of inches wide. The central quills of the bright fluff were pitch black and led up to a black diamond at the part between the quill and the main section of the feather. Their design was surprisingly beautiful for a batch of feathers, but the way the black quills blended into the bright orange plumage gave them a majestic composition.

"Since I was the one who finished off half of the four beasts, the client allowed me to take first pick at the bodies. Luckily, none of us aimed for the head so I was able to salvage their crest feathers. Not like I was going to claim their rancid meat anyway." He handed the feathers to Castor, who held them gently.

"These are for you." He extended his hand with a bright smile. Castor was very appreciative to have such a good friend.

"These are amazing, thank you," Castor said kindly as he tucked the feathers into his pouch, making sure not to tighten the drawstring to the point of crushing them. The tops of the feathers stuck out of the pouch by at least six inches, which gave a nice accent to his teal chiton. The pouch was not big enough for all four without the risk of crushing the contents.

He took two and, crossing them a few inches up from the quills, tucked them into the bronze brooch that held his mantle together. The feathers draped over his left shoulder and added a flare to his outfit that was far more fashionable than what he would normally choose for himself.

"Make sure you make time for me while you are in town, I will prepare an ample amount of wine to celebrate your victory," Castor said confidently, showing off his new accessories.

"Of course, of course, my lord." Kyros bowed a deep bow mockingly at Castor, who in turn smacked him on the side of the head. They both laughed and parted ways properly this time.

Off through the city streets did Castor walk. Many shops lined the fronts of houses as personal businesses were what drove the middle class within Anthora. While other nations were known for their slave-driven economies and theories of quantity over quality, Anthora had taken the opposite approach over the centuries. Crafters like these had honed their skills in their trades. Their work ethic was not for the meek and humble but those aspiring for fruitful and satisfying lives. That is not to say that their work is easy. It was far from it. Anthorans in the artisanal crafting industry saw their work not as a chore but as a way of life. Their pantheon had a matron deity just for these people. Calcothwyn, the Elvari goddess of fine crafting and art, was a deity most welcome in households across Anthora. While The Elvari had little presence in these arid lands, their culture and dedication to their crafts were accepted with open arms.

Down the stone street of the upper district, known as the street of Calcoth, sat many more shops like what Castor and Kyros saw earlier. Two channels were worn down the center of the stone street where the heavy carts of goods would come through every day to restock the storefronts. As the morning was just ending, the shops were slowly opening for the afternoon shopping wave that came during the lunch rush. Light *tings* of

[62]

hammers on metal could be heard down the corridor. The sound of a silversmith or goldsmith starting his work for the day was a welcome sound to hear.

Noisy and frequently filled with foul smells, the industrial region of town housed a good portion of jobs for the lower classes. As Castor walked, he noticed the difference in architecture and road structures between where he came from and where the district split towards the docks. Rather than well-maintained buildings of quarried stone and tiled walls, the buildings in this area were mostly of timber and daub. The edges of walls and roof framing openly showed the wooden structure beneath and cracking at the edges from a lack of maintenance was visible. Warehouses of bulk goods sat in large pots or wooden crates within some of the open bays along the street. Smaller apartments were stacked on top of some warehouses and workshops, their bare wooden balconies overlapping the street and making the road feel cramped. Glances of local workers and beggars made Castor feel uneasy in the open as they eyed his colorful clothing. Their jealous stares stabbed daggers into him.

While the supplies in the warehouses were left out in the open, they were not left completely unguarded. All warehouses had staff walking in and out of their open timber frames. Dockworkers focused on the tasks they were given for the day as they paced between locations. A tall man, dressed in a single plain white chiton with stains in the edges, rolled a wooden barrel down the cobble streets as Castor walked by. His frame was gaunt, but his ability to move a full barrel of goods across long distances from warehouse to warehouse seems to be something he had done many times before.

As Castor passed one building, he looked in and saw large piles of salt open to the humid air. Next to the salt were containers of local fish that sat out in the sun. The fish were all small and not large enough to be eaten on a plate. Castor watched for a moment as two of the men started shoveling layers of salt and fish into barrels. The process of salting the fish and allowing them to ferment in the barrels created a local delicacy. This condiment, known as garum to the Anthorans, was an ingredient held in high regard around the world. Many cities would import this fishy fermentation and use it in Anthoran cuisine. Their high salt content kept the mixture well preserved over time and the fermentation allowed for a deep, albeit pungent, aroma.

As he walked, the prince saw a small boy and a dog run by him. As the dog passed him from the front, he could sense a light padding upon his waistline. Catching the boy's hand in his pouch, Castor gripped tightly and yanked the boy forward as he turned around.

"I'm sorry, I'm sorry!" the young boy said over and over as Castor dropped to one knee to match his height. The child, obviously ashamed of his actions, looked down at the ground, knowing that thieves were not treated well when caught. Castor assumed the boy was between the age of seven and ten.

Castor tilted his head and stared at the child, but the boy refused to look up from the floor. The dog behind him growled and snarled, and Castor looked directly at the hound. Loyal to his small master, the dog did not back away, but it did stop growling and waited for the situation to unfold. While loyal, it knew better than to attack someone with a grip on his owner.

"What is your name?" Castor asked gently.

The boy kept his glare at the dirty cobbles beneath and did not answer. His bare, muddy feet fidgeted near where his vision was fixed.

"I asked you for your name," Castor said flatly. He did not tighten his grip on the child's wrist, but he did turn his hand to try and get the boy to look up. He made sure not to cause him any unneeded pain.

"I'm sorry." the boy responded. His downward stare did not waver.

"That's not a name, that's a statement," Castor said back. He noticed bruises and cuts along the boy's small, frail arms. He knew many of these children, whether abandoned or neglected, were out on the streets alone. These orphans had no choice but to fend for themselves. Castor had seen many of his kind during his time as a guard but never had he run into one who had tried stealing from him or his comrades.

"If I was planning to hurt you, wouldn't I have done so already?" Castor tried to reason with the boy.

The boy started to quietly cry, small tears rolling down his face. He did not make any noise. Castor could assume the boy had been in situations where loudly crying had gotten him unwanted attention and learned to hide his fear and sadness behind a facade of quiet acceptance.

"You have a strong will, I commend you for that," Castor said aloud. The boy, noticing he had started crying, quickly wiped away his tears with the hand that was not in Castor's grasp and hardened his facial features.

Castor let his grip on the boy loosen a little, but not enough that he could pull away. These types of situations needed to be handled carefully if he wanted to get the results he was looking for. Allowing crime to fester at such an early age would only add to the city's problems but becoming overbearing towards a starving child would only leave a sour opinion on the young thief.

"Can you tell me your name now?" Castor asked for the third time. This time the boy glanced up towards him for a moment before turning his gaze downwards.

"Atticus." the child said in a stern but defeated tone. He was past the stage of being startled by his failed theft. His embarrassment made him sound irritated.

"Atticus. That is a nice name." Castor doted on the boy to try and weaken his guard. "Why were you trying to steal from me?"

"Let go!" Atticus yelled. He tried to pull away, but Castor's firm grip from years of martial training was like a vice on leather. No quarter was given; Castor's hand barely moved as the boy tugged as hard as he could. Finding no way to escape the prince's grasp, the boy's shoulders shrugged down in a sign of surrender. The mutt behind Castor growled deeply, but Castor paid no mind.

"I'm hungry." the boy said at last.

"Where are your parents? Shouldn't they feed you rather than a stranger's purse?" Castor questioned further.

"They left me," Atticus said. His somber expression finally showed through. As tough as a street urchin could be, the boy was only a toddler in mind and spirit. His composition was clearly on the brink of falling through.

Castor put his left hand up towards where he gripped the child on his arm. The boy seemed used to harsher treatments. He looked away and braced his stance as if to expect a lot of pain as payment for his nefarious actions. Castor was no abuser of children, but the boy did not know that. Instead of a beating, Castor held the boy's hand gently. His hold was much weaker, but also less imposing.

"Well, that was not nice of them, huh? Atticus, I am deeply sorry that all happened to you." Castor stated in a firm yet kind tone, "And I do not think a child like you should be starving in the streets. But stealing from others will only get you in trouble. If one of the angrier adults would have caught you instead..."

Castor trailed off, remembering the bruises and cuts he had already seen on the bare arms of the child. The boy knew what happened when an angrier adult caught him, it would seem. But the boy was hungry enough to try this again after all that. Castor assumed his situation was as dire as Atticus let on.

"We have orphanages in this city. They may not be like having a real family, but you would have a place to stay and food to fill your belly."

"No!" the boy yelled. He did not recoil from Castor, who now only held the boy by the hand like a caring older sibling or parent. "I am not going back there! They beat me and stole my food! None of them cared!"

This topic seemed to upset the boy. His small frame was almost vibrating from the stress of the conversation. Children were not good at hiding their emotions.

"Who did? The Priestesses?" Castor knew a good portion of the Priestesses of Pyrros. Pyrros was the god of home, hearth, and family. His priestesses cared deeply for the children they protected. Abandoned children were left at the orphanages of Pyrros and in turn, became priests and priestesses of Pyrros when they grew up. The priestesses knew of what Atticus went through because they were like him. Castor could never expect a priestess of Pyrros to abuse a child.

Atticus shook his head. "No, the other kids. The older ones. They always took my bread and would throw me on the ground if I refused." the boy started to cry, subconsciously taking comfort from Castor's hand. "They teased me for being small and never let me play with them." Castor saw nothing more than a beaten and battered child in front of him.

Castor pulled the boy in and gave him a gentle hug. He caressed the back of his head as he patted the boy on the back with the other hand. He teared up a bit, knowing that the boy had gone through so many hardships at such an early age. No child should be abandoned. Being constantly put down by others was not a situation a child should have experienced.

"It's ok, It is ok." Castor cooed to the boy from up close. At this point, the dog behind him walked forward and laid down by Atticus' feet. His droopy, nappy hair flopped around as he lay upon the stained stone path.

Noticing his interaction had gained the attention of dockworkers and passersby alike, Castor grabbed the boy by the shoulders and continued their conversation.

"Would you like some lunch?" Castor asked.

The boy's eyes lit up for a moment before he quickly hid his excitement.

"Yes...please," he said.

Castor took his hand once again and the duo walked down the cobble path out of the industrial district and towards the barracks. The dog followed close behind.

As Castor and Atticus made their way past the wooden warehouses near the shoreline, Castor's gaze fixated on the entertainment district in front of them. The central hub of Thyma was sprawled out in front of him, sitting just off the coast and in between the growing hills of the northern district and the main street of the city's merchant district. As the location where all foreign trade passed through and public events were held, this area held most of the city's public civil buildings.

Before reaching the Thyma amphitheater, which was nestled into the stone cliffs on the far side of the entertainment district, the two reached the open-air market. This sprawling canopy of merchant stalls kept the city's international trade alive. The market had the hustle and bustle of midday traffic starting to kick off in the narrow walkways between the many vendors. The stalls held an assortment of tables, stands, and chests full of trinkets and baubles from across the lands of Petrus. Old rugs, reinforced cloths, and matted pelts covered the floors of the shops. Barely any direct light made its way through the array of sunshades held up by tall, wood posts.

As they walked through the tents, they were bombarded by the sights and smells of trade goods, foods, and clothing from faraway lands. While most of the inhabitants were humans from other Anthoran cities, people of all races sat and paced the stalls. A Durulian merchant, wearing fine crimson robes, stood stoutly within the closest booth. His wares in front of him were all types of hand-forged jewelry. The well-crafted rings were made from precious metals and adjourned with well-cut gems. He knew his way with his trade, as he was wearing a good portion of the items on display. His hands had at least one ring on every other finger and each ring was designed uniquely. A gilded leather girdle kept his highly ornate robes in proper order and around his neck sat a collar of ornate bronze reliefs. His long gray beard was expertly braided into three long cords, their ends tipped with large bronze orbs. The orbs that held the ends of his hair in place were inscribed with runes of the Durulian language and inlaid with silver. While Castor could not read Dwoma, the ancient language of the Hem Durul people, he did know that they were highly reverent of their beards. The writing upon the beard beads were names of their deceased ancestors, carved as offerings to their memory. These beads could also be inscribed with short prayers to the most famous Durulian gods, Gargrin and Brömli.

The Durulian, noticing the way Castor was eying up his beard and outfit, greeted him in the common Durulian greeting of a tap on the forehead with his middle three fingers. Castor, aware of Durulian customs, tapped his forehead back at the foreigner. He smiled in return.

Castor, remembering his teachings from his teenage years on international diplomacy, greeted the Durulian in one of the common greetings of Hem Durul style.

"Gárgrin es góðir," Castor said in a gravelly tone to try and mimic the deep and somber way Durulians spoke. This greeting roughly translated to "Gargrin is good," symbolizing how the god Gargrin survived his ten-day betrayal in the bowels of the underworld. As Castor finished his greeting, the Durulian's eyes shone as brightly as the gems that adjourned his hands and neck.

"Brömli með Þér." the elated Durulian chortled in response. His speech was deep yet full of life, wishing Castor that his god Brömli would watch over his travels.

Castor knew he did not have enough money on him to trade with the Durulian and would not consider haggling with him. Haggling was not a common occurrence with the races of the western continent. Since he was currently tasked with feeding a homeless child, he ended their conversation there and moved through the market.

Across the way from the jewelry shop sat a glassware stall. One of the black leopard Maudians that hailed from the northern jungle regions of Maudif stood across the path. Her booth shimmered with many ornate vases and bottles made of glass and metal. The glass and metalware were displayed across carved wood tables and sat within a few wood chests. Her outfit, complete with a flowing dress of green velvet and a headscarf that covered her entire head down to her shoulders, matched well with her dark fur. The veridian brocade was embroidered with floral patterns in stark black thread. Her outline looked as though it swallowed the bright sunlight entirely with how dark it was. The glass sculptures and chalices came in every color and the range of shapes was nearly endless. As they passed, Atticus could not keep his eyes off the glass containers. Their surfaces dazzled the young boy while small streaks of light sparkled around the booth as he moved around them.

"Watch your feet, Atticus. Do not forget where we are heading." Castor reminded Atticus as they walked past. Atticus's stomach grumbled in agreement, and the boy blushed. As they walked away, Castor nodded to the cat woman as he met her sharp feline stare. A Maudian stare could be entrancing. He did his best to break their eye contact and moved onward.

Castor thought about how rare it was to see a northern Maudian in Anthora. Usually trade only existed between the great Maudians of the southern sands and the tiger-like Maudians from the tepui crags of the Rarnir Khanate. They frequently had wars between their peoples and the Empire of Maudif, which made seeing their peoples peacefully in the same location exceedingly rare. The lynx Maudians native to most of the boreal south of Maudif was also a rare sight in Anthora, as they were very averse to the warm and humid climate. Their Caracal cousins who were native to the warmer regions of the empire were seen on occasion in Anthora, but usually as slaves or cheap labor due to their small size and timid nature.

As they walked down the path, Castor found what he was looking for as he reached the outdoor restaurant of Hana and Clovis. The couple always had their restaurant set up in the center of the plaza. Castor always enjoyed the unique dishes they produced. Hana, with her sleek black hair and straw-colored skin, stood out among the Anthoran crowd. Her Elvari ancestry gave her a height of over six feet tall, which did not help with her noticeable heritage differences.

Hana was an Ainari. Her people lived in the Yasari archipelago before a mass immigration of mainland Elvari to the island chain a hundred years prior. The new feuding matriarchs had formed the Yasari Shogunate, a loose collection of city-states that constantly vied for dominance over one another. After escaping to Anthora a few decades prior following the loss of a local war, she took refuge in the Northwest of Anthora. She met her Anthoran husband on the roads between cities when he used to peddle goods to smaller hamlets between the city-states. They both loved food and decided to open their outdoor restaurant in Thyma after they made enough money. They blended the vegetarian-based dishes of Yasari culture with the fresh and hearty fish and meats of Anthoran cuisine to make a menu of satisfying meals. Castor knew exactly which food would help the hungry boy at this moment.

As they pushed their way through the large crowds of busy shoppers and walked up to the food stall, Hana noticed their approach and nudged her husband to get his attention. As the boy and his prince approached the stall, Hana gave him a slight bow. Her husband, noticing her actions, waved to the young prince.

"Morning, prince. Are you having your typical meal today?" Clovis said robustly as he cleaned off a few ceramic bowls.

"Your manners, Clovis." Hana warned," Do not forget what the young prince has done for us."

Clovis scoffed. "You know the prince is not one for shows of reverence. If he wanted me to bow to him every time he visited, then he would not be the prince that we all have come to love."

She turned back to Castor and bowed a small bow again, this time talking to him directly.

"I bow every time I see him as a sign of respect. I do not bow for the prince, but for the man who saved us from those corrupt extortioners."

Earlier that year during the month of Jade, Castor's century had broken up a racketeering ring in Thyma. The criminals were extorting protection fees from many of the smaller businesses in the markets and industrial districts. Hana and Clovis were among those who were affected by the extortionists and were heavily impacted by the financial strain. Unlike some of the other long-term merchants who traded expensive jewelry or ornate glassware, the couple produced food dishes that were not as profitable. Once the ring was removed from the city, the locals were given much more financial freedom to better their stalls and improve their products. Their livelihoods, and those of their patrons, were appreciative of the city's citizen guard.

"I have told you many times, Hana," Castor said in a polite yet stern voice, "Protecting this town is what I do as a job, and I enjoy doing it. I do not help just to have people owe me favors. If I did, I would not be so different from those who were extorting you in the first place."

"That is true, prince Castor," Hana said in a kind voice. He knew his words did not get through to her because Hana's respect for him outweighed his efforts to be more equal in their standing. She was just that type of person, so he tried to level the field on other terms.

"Just Castor is fine, you know that." Castor reminded her. "I know you are used to speaking with honorifics and class-based societal norms from your homeland, but you need not press yourself to be so polite."

He wanted to get used to her way of speaking but being talked to in such a formal and honored way made Castor uneasy. Ever since he was young, Castor disliked being talked to as some distant being too high and mighty to be spoken to in a casual tone. Unfortunately for Castor, he was one of the heir princes to the nation of Anthora. There were only eleven principalities that made up their nation. As the heir to one of the eleven principalities, Castor was one to be given such honors. While his father, Hecantor, was the current prince of the region of Thyma, Castor knew he would be taking the role of the crown prince soon. Hecantor's ailing health had led Castor to prepare for that day by making himself as worthy of the title as he could be by his twentieth birthday.

"Castor," Clovis asked quizzically, "If I am not mistaken, you did not get married recently, right? You are still nineteen until early next year?"

"You are correct." Castor agreed. He noticed that Clovis was staring at the boy next to him. "Oh, this little one is not my child." He put a hand on the back of Atticus's head. "I am acting as a guardian of sorts as of... well, as of a few minutes ago."

Hana leaned down and spoke to Atticus, who was standing firmly next to Castor during the whole conversation. "Hello there. Who might you be?"

"I'm Atticus," Atticus said sheepishly. His delinquent attitude from earlier seemed to disappear over the last fifteen minutes of walking. The boy seemed to have extraordinarily little experience talking with adults, so being thrown into a situation with all older people must have been far past his comfort zone.

"Atticus here will be joining me for the day," Castor said to the cooks, "and I wanted to make sure he had enough food before we set off for our training."

Atticus looked perplexed at Castor's statement but was not going to pass up an opportunity to get a free meal to fill his belly. He stood quietly next to Castor as Castor continued his conversation.

"I wanted to grab a dish to go," Castor said to the couple, "I know it is not typical to do so, but my schedule has fallen behind this morning."

"Oh, alright then," Clovis said, "That is no issue. What would you like?"

"Do you remember that bowl of rice you made me with the smoked fish and the salty eggs?" Castor asked.

"Ah, yes, the psári gohan." Clovis stated. "It is one of our best sellers in the mornings. Keeps you full all day."

[74]

"Great, I would like one of them, please," Castor ordered the dish and grabbed five obols from his coin purse and handed them to Clovis.

"Right away!" Clovis announced, "You can bring the bowl and spoon back next time you visit!" As they went to their workstations in the outdoor kitchen, the couple got to work on the dish.

Castor grabbed Atticus's hand and moved him into a better position to watch the couple make his meal. Hana had already grabbed a large spatula to scoop a large ball of rice out of their cooking pot that sat over some timid coals. The rice, still steaming, plopped into the bowl and broke apart as their weight moved them into the shape of the container. She cracked an egg from the counter into the bowl and used a spoon they had in a large pile by the front counter to stir the egg into the rice. The golden sticky yolk oozed into the brown rice and coated the grains as she stirred. The steam of the hot rice partially cooked the egg to give it a sticky and coagulated texture. With a small ladle, Hana poured a small portion of Garum onto the dish. The complex fishy solution added a salty and savory smell to the open air.

While she worked on the bowl, Clovis was chopping up the toppings of the dish. He grabbed a slab of smoked fish from a crate off to the side of the kitchen counters and diced it into fine pieces. Once he was done with the fish, he grabbed two small onions and diced the whole plant: bulb, stock, and top alike. He tossed the diced fish and onions onto a grilling plate. The flat ceramic square that sat atop an open pit of glowing coals sizzled under the ingredients. As the fish cooked, he added a few dried anchovies to the mixture. The fat from the smoked fish coated the plate and helped the pieces of onion to caramelize.

Once he was done, he grabbed the bowl from Hana's side of the counter. She had gone to greet a new customer who had walked into the tent while her husband finished Castor's order. He scraped the sautéed fish and onions off the heated clay tablet and added them to the top of the rice bowl. While he finished topping the dish off with a sprinkling of local herbs, Atticus stared directly at the dish like a wild animal ready to pounce on injured prey.

Clovis handed the clay bowl to Castor who promptly handed it down to Atticus. Atticus, clearly allowing his primal urge to eat to take control of his reasoning, started consuming the dish by the spoonful.

"Careful kid," Clovis chided Atticus," You'll choke if you keep that pace up. Chew the fish or a bone will be the end of you"

After a few bites, Atticus regained his senses and properly swallowed his food before talking.

"This is great." He yapped in a happy tone.

"Well, thank you." Clovis smiled warmly at the boy. He quickly went back to his kitchen counter and cut a slice from the loaf of honey bread that sat on top of the counter. He plopped the slice on the edge of the bowl and winked at Atticus. "A little piece of dessert as well."

"Oh right, one last thing." Castor said as he handed a few more obol to Clovis. "One smoked fish for the dog too."

Castor handed the fish down to Atticus' pet and the dog chewed on the fish voraciously. He was well behaved for being so hungry. Atticus smiled and nodded. Castor thanked him and the two left the tent towards the barracks next to the amphitheater.

As Atticus continued to quickly eat the psári gohan, the duo and their dog made their way out of the emporium and towards the northern part of the entertainment district. The buildings that lined the streets in this area of town were all made of white marble and had been built many generations prior. The area was not densely populated with houses like the other sectors. The area held many government, religious, and trade guild buildings. While the capital city of Pynos would house most of the government staff and the largest of the guild headquarters, Thyma was the largest port on the eastern coast of Anthora. It held great significance for trade with the eastern continent.

The temple complex sat on a small hill within the entertainment district. Tall marble columns stood proudly upon the stone plateau it had claimed ownership of. Many multi-story buildings lined the streets with guards or staff at their entrances. As the day was reaching its peak, many citizens were done with their morning chores or work and were starting to fill the streets in search of food, goods, or mischief. The ocean breeze forced its way through the port town's alleys and kept the inhabitants cool in the midday sun.

CHAPTER 4

A Note To Change A Life

19th of Beryl, 453 of the Age of Discovery

eaching the outside of the amphitheater, the boys turned down the eastern street and walked the path towards the barracks. All major roads in Thyma led to the amphitheater, making its location an important landmark within the city walls. The Thymian guard barracks was located only a few buildings down from the amphitheater, allowing quick mobilization across the city in the case of an emergency.

Tall columns lined the front porch of the two-story building. Like the rest of the government facilities, the barracks was made of cut sandstone from the local mountains. A few windows jutted from the front of the building. Bronze lattices were built into the frames to prevent anyone from entering or exiting through the openings. The boys walked up the handful of stairs of the front porch of the building and entered through the giant bronze doors that marked the entrance.

It took a few seconds for Castor's eyes to adapt to the dark interior once inside. The lobby was open to the outside light yet dark enough for his eyes to require adjustment. The only openings to the outside were the front doors and two windows.

"Hello captain." a soldier stood at attention at the far wall of the lobby. It was common for a soldier to stand guard at the entrance to prevent any random citizen from walking into the barracks. Castor assumed the soldier was either new or not normally stationed in the city, as he didn't recognize her voice. After his eyes were used to the dim light, he tried to recognize the woman. He had no luck after an awkward pause.

"Hello there. Are you new?" Castor asked. He didn't mean to offend the guard, but he had not seen her before. The lobby guard duty was usually kept for older guards or captains in need of a break from their typical patrols. She was in neither of those positions.

"I have been working under Captain Acastus for the past two years." She stated, "Oh, but I have not been a lobby guard before. The captain was on duty today and then had pressing matters to attend to."

"Alright. That makes more sense." Castor said. "Did he say he needed any assistance?"

"No, sir." the guard assured him, "He just told me to be on the lookout for a few people, including a man in a bright teal chiton. You seem to fit that description. The captain has always been big on formalities and made sure I greeted you properly if you arrived while he was out of the building. "

"That sounds exactly like Acastus," Castor said. The guard nodded in agreement.

"Did you need some help today?" the guard asked back.

"Actually, yes I do," Castor stated. "Can you fetch me my official wax seal kit? I will also need two official stationeries. I can stand watch while you get those."

"Yessir." the guard, trained on the duties of overseeing the barracks while the other groups were on watch, went off to gather the supplies.

Castor took a seat in the lobby, and Atticus stood next to him.

"Atticus. I do not want you stealing in the streets anymore." Castor said to the boy.

"Ok," Atticus said shortly. He started to stare at the ground near his feet again.

"But I understand your situation. Bullies are not good people." Castor continued.

"No! They aren't!" Atticus agreed in a loud voice, "That's why I do not want to go back there!"

"Do not yell, child." Castor reprimanded the boy. "We are indoors and many people may be sleeping on their time off before their night shifts."

"Sorry." Atticus moped. The boy looked much more like a normal child than a criminal urchin. His curly dark hair held blonde tips from his exposure to the daily sun. He had freckles on his tan skin that were accentuated by the overbearing rays of the Anthoran summer sun. The boy must spend most of the day outdoors toiling without shade.

"With all that being said, I do not plan to let you just go back to your old ways." Castor continued.

A flash of fear shot across Atticus's face, and the misunderstanding of physical punishment was quickly dispelled once he remembered the way that Castor had treated him up until this point.

As Atticus accepted what fate Castor had in store, the guard returned and handed Castor the items he requested. Moving over to the wooden table in the middle of the lobby, Castor started writing on the vellum sheet he was given. The letter was written as follows:

~To those who oversee the Orphanage of Pyrrus in the city of Thyma,

The boy named Atticus who holds this document was caught stealing by the docks. I have taken sole custody of the boy to encourage a proper and fruitful lifestyle. He has informed me of other children at the orphanage who frequently bullied him and stole his food. I do not hold any of the priestesses of Pyrrus responsible for this oversight. I know how busy your days are, with ceremonies and rituals to partake in. I also appreciate all that the temple of Pyrrus does for this city and know how much they add to our stability and prosperity. I ask that you take interest in this topic in the future and ensure the children of abandoned birth are all treated with kindness and respect. Each child's past is expected to be a depressing matter and I hope that those affected by their lineage can overcome their current strife. I believe the children will walk a path closer to what Pyrrus would hope for all of us with your support.

With this all being said, I plan to have Atticus stay at the barracks to ensure he is not bothered by the other children. He will be drafted into the service of the principality and will have full bread and board funded here at the barrack house. I will ensure the proper paperwork is completed once I receive it here at my quarters. I appreciate your attention to this letter and look forward to the outcome of today's events.

~Castor Alexios Daimos
Heir prince to the throne of Thyma

As Castor finished writing his letter to the head priestess of the orphanage, he continued his conversation with the boy.

"I will have you take this letter to the nice ladies who took care of you at the orphanage." Castor said to the boy as he finished his writing, "They will help you gather your belongings and give you paperwork like this to bring here."

"I do not understand...." Atticus said in a worried manner, "I'm being kicked out?"

"No, Atticus." Castor corrected, "I am giving you an opportunity here." Castor gestured to the building around him. "Here, at the barracks. I want you to become a guard in training."

The boy looked confused for a few moments more, then thought of something and looked at Castor.

"What about Trypa?" the worried boy gestured to his dog.

"Trypa cannot stay within the barracks, but he can stay out on the front porch. We can make arrangements for that." Castor considered the benefits of having a fast hound in the future on patrols.

Atticus furrowed his brow and thought about the topic as hard as a child could about state service.

"Is this acceptable to you? You would have your own sleeping spot and food every day. And I can assure you that no one will try to take your food from you. If they do," Castor put his hand on the hilt of his xiphos which dangled on his hip, "you can have them answer to me."

The boy let a small smile crack across his face before regaining his poise. Castor took off his necklace and placed it next to the document. His family crest sat upon the medallion.

"Alright," Atticus stated to Castor, nodding in agreement.

"You will? Lovely." Castor said as he prepared the wax seal. A short prayer to Ignus lit an inch-long flame at the end of his finger, and the flame warmed a small spoon filled with teal wax. The bee's wax was imbued with the dust of broken blue gems and gave the viscous fluid a soft glow on top of its glimmer. As he poured the wax onto the rolled parchment, he pressed his family seal onto the indented area.

The family crest consisted of the letter delta set in the middle of fir branches within a circular imprint. A small amount of energy was siphoned from the gems on his clothing as the seal cooled, ensuring the letter would be untampered and protected from the elements. Castor checked the seal for any defects and, once he was happy with the outcome, handed the letter to Atticus.

"Take care of that now. This little piece of parchment will have a big impact on your life." Castor said to the boy.

Atticus grabbed the roll of parchment from his outstretched hand. He grabbed a little too tight for a normal letter, but the item did not bend under his grip. The spell Castor put upon the item through the wax seal kept it firm and secure.

"Thank you for your help," Castor said to the guard at the doors. She had returned to her seat and watched over the entrance to the building.

"No thanks are needed," she replied, "I am looking forward to working with my new colleague." She smiled at the young boy who was already back to standing just slightly behind Castor.

Castor grabbed a spare rope from one of the tables that were laying in a corner of the room. He drew his xiphos and cut a lashing of about ten feet in length. He handed the bundle to Atticus and told him to tie Trypa to one of the pillars outside. Once the hound was properly fastened to the stone, the two boys made their way deeper into the barracks.

As they left the lobby, they entered the main armory of the city's barracks. The room was two stories in height and had a balcony around the entire upper floor. A chandelier made of intertwined antlers was hanging from the rafters in the center of the room and held thumb-sized quartz crystals. The gems radiated light across the interior of the dark room. The only natural light came in from the thin clerestory near the ceiling.

The bottom floor was rimmed with slate tiles and held a large pit of sand in the center of the space. Racks of blunted spears, old shields, and dented armor lined the walls. The shelves were kept against the walls and out of the way of the walking path around the edge of the room. Each wall held an opening to another section of the building. Castor skirted the edge of the room and entered the hallway on the right.

As the duo continued down the hallway, Castor and Atticus made their way to an open room that sat on the front right side of the bottom floor. Light made its way through clerestory windows at the top of the room. The metal bars on the clerestory kept the room secure but allowed for most of the outdoor illumination to light the room. Wooden beds lined the walls every ten feet. Tall, L-shaped wooden dividers sat in between each bed to add a mental separation between the sleeping spaces. Each bed had a wood chest at the end which allowed the guards to safely store any of their belongings.

"This area is set aside for anyone who wishes to live full-time at the barracks," Castor said to Atticus as they walked up to a bed on the far wall of the room. Each of the claimed sleeping areas had a note outside with the name of the soldier who owned the space and their commanding officer. Out of the fifteen beds within the room, only six others were claimed at that moment.

"Most guards and trainees stay at home when they are off-shift. This room is usually used for those who live in a local village too far to walk to every night or do not have a home to go home to." Castor felt bad for bringing up the topic of families with the orphan boy, but he needed to get everything sorted quickly before he started his training program for the afternoon.

As they entered the second to last stall along the back wall, Castor grabbed the other parchment he had received from the guard at the door and started writing.

"Do you have a family name? And what is your age?" Castor asked the boy.

"I do not know." Atticus looked down at his dirty, bare feet in a dejected manner.

"Alright, no worries." Castor responded, "We shall call you Atticus of Thyma." Claiming the city you hailed from as a surname was a widespread practice in Anthora for those of mundane heritage. Without knowing his origins, Atticus would be known by this name for his near future.

Upon the note he held, Castor wrote the following:

Atticus of Thyma

Age 10

Guard in Training

Member of the Third Century

As he finished writing, he heated the wax as he did in the lobby. This time, he heated the stick of wax directly rather than cutting a piece into the spoon he held in his waist pouch. Once the material was soft, he pushed the melted end onto the area designated for name tags. The section was around Atticus's head height on the divider and left a glob of wax attached to the planed surface. He pressed the letter into the wax and then applied a bit more to the front of the sheet. Pressing his seal into the wax, he channeled a short burst of mana into the sigil. As he removed the seal, he checked for any defects in the imprint. He turned to Atticus once he was satisfied with the results.

"Congratulations, Atticus of Thyma. You are now the youngest member of the guard reserve of Thyma." Castor said in an official and dignified manner. The boy beamed at him, clearly excited about today's turn of events.

Castor walked Atticus to the front doors of the building. Castor was sure the boy was old enough to have spatial awareness and could get back to his bed after being walked through the building twice.

"I need to get ready for the lessons I am teaching at the theater today. I will not be able to join you from here on out." Castor said as they made it back to the lobby. "Your first task will be to deliver that message I gave you to the priestesses and return here with your belongings."

"I do not think I have many belongings," Atticus responded honestly.

"I will need the paperwork the priestesses will give you there, so I still need you to go back one last time and talk to them. Consider it your first mission in the city guard." Castor went down to one knee to be at eye level with the boy.

"Do you think this is something you can handle?" Castor asked him, face to face.

"Yes." Atticus responded confidently.

Castor tilted his head at an angle. "Yes? Just yes?" he asked.

The boy looked puzzled as Castor continued. "You are a part of the guard now. *My* guard, to be more precise. Are you forgetting something?"

The boy's confusion turned to wide eyes. "Yes, sir!" He said proudly.

"There you go." Castor smiled as he patted the orphan boy on the head. "Now run along and make sure you do not give those priestesses too hard a time. I doubt they normally receive royal decrees." Castor pondered to himself for a second with a finger on his chin. "They probably do. But I doubt it is anything this trivial."

Castor turned the boy around with a hand on each shoulder and gave him a light shove out the door.

"On you go." He said lightly. "And take that dog with you."

Atticus made his way over to his hound and untied him from the pillar. The two made their way down the granite steps and off towards his prior place dwelling.

Castor turned back to head upstairs towards his quarters and almost made it into the armory before the guard in the lobby stopped him.

"Castor, sir?" She said to grab Castor's attention, getting up from her chair.

"Yes?" Castor responded quizzically.

"Myra, sir. I wanted to ask you about... all that." She gestured towards the door, seemingly towards Atticus.

"Go right ahead," Castor said.

He was starting to get worried that he would be late for the training he was supposed to teach, but he knew his vice-captain would have started physical training by now. Nikitas, a grizzled veteran in Castor's third century, was known to lead their group in rough training regimens before Castor would take charge of the lessons for the day. Castor's focus on technique and strategy was a nice reprieve from the training Nikita focused on, making his soldiers as strong and durable as possible through brutal training. Castor assumed he would find his group running the stairs of the amphitheater. But Castor did not want to brush Myra off, so he stood and waited for her questions.

"Why did you do so much for that boy?" Myra asked.

"Do you think what I did was all that altruistic? I am sure once he starts his training, he won't be thinking what I chose for him is much better than being bullied in the orphanage." Castor chuckled.

Myra smirked. "Sure, but why a thief? I remember being interviewed before I was allowed to join the guard. Not just anyone is allowed to join. We keep our ranks relatively closed off from strangers to ensure corruption does not get into our ranks. So why did you bring someone who broke the law into our ranks?"

"Does it bother you that someone else had an easier time than you?" Castor asked back.

"A little, yes." Myra honestly stated.

"I do not blame you, and I am sorry if you feel that way." Castor continued, "But then let me ask you this; Why did you become a guard?"

"To protect our people and to ensure everyone has a fair shot at a good life," Myra said.

"As do I. I want our people to not worry about bandits and highwaymen. I do not want them to live in fear of the monsters in the mountains nor the beasts in the sea." Castor said, "But I also want us to aim for bettering our city. Not just to maintain our people's lifestyles but also to improve them."

Castor walked over to the table and pulled some coins from his pocket. He piled them into three separate piles: one obol, two obols, and three obols.

"We used to be here." Castor pointed to the single obol on the table. "After the Maudif rebellions around twenty years ago, our lands had an uprising led by the temple of Vrontir. Now, I was just born when that all happened, but I have heard stories of what all occurred during that time of turmoil. And I am certain that how we live now is better than what citizens had back then."

Castor tapped the single coin on the table. "At that point, we were here. Life was harder and many soldiers worked jobs in the mines and fields to rebuild the communities they fought in. Many citizens were charged with treason for supporting the usurpers and were hung from trees. The population was low and the morale was lower. But over time they built the nation back to where it was and we have been prospering ever since.

He then tapped the stack of two coins. "The last decade has had some hardships, but we bounced back as best we could. Being able to cut the rebellion short by capturing their leader helped quell the discontent before the entire region was decimated. Sure, we still deal with robbers and thieves. We can deal with them effectively with our trained city guards now. Sure, racketeering was proliferating out of control. We were able to find those behind it and end their reign over our citizens. Today we stand better than a decade ago, and I hope those in the future stand better than us."

Castor finally tapped the stack of three obols on the table. "I want us to be at this point somewhere soon. Maybe in Atticus's time, maybe in my time. Regardless, I want us to be here." He tapped the pile and the coin tower topples over.

"I get that, but how does that relate to that boy?" Myra asked.

"Would you hire a petty thief?" Castor asked Myra.

"No. They are scum." She stated flatly. Her opinion of criminals was hard as stone, a common trait Castor had seen often within the city guard. He assumed this was a hard topic for her but wanted to press on to ensure he did not harbor bad feelings towards the boy.

"Would you hire a pompous adult?" Castor asked Myra.

"I guess so." She stated in a dismissive tone. "But how does that change things?"

"Why do you think less of a child thief? Is a person set in their pretentious ways a better representative for the city than a child with a harsh background?" Castor asked as he put the coins back into his pouch.

"One is a criminal and one is just a poorly behaved person." She squinted her eyes and tilted her head as though the topic was hardly debatable.

"That's true. From what I saw today, I had a starving child try to steal from me. He was bullied out of food and sleep. He did not try to steal any valuables except money to buy a meal for himself and his dog. Whereas we never saw the teenagers, or possibly adults, who bullied this child to the point of petty theft." Castor pointed out.

Castor sat in one of the chairs within the lobby near where Myra was posted. The dry wood creaked underneath him as he sat down.

"The point I am trying to make is that we need good people. Here, with us. We need people who have seen the unpleasant sides of this city and chose to be better. An adult is set in their ways. It is hard to change someone's view on life once they are set in their ways. But a child can be taught the right ways to act and improve the area in ways that he was not afforded. That boy has been through a lot but I think he will be a valuable member of our city once he is old enough." Castor reassured her.

"Even if he has already tried to steal from his fellow citizens? Doesn't that defeat the purpose?" Myra asked.

"That is true. We will not know how he will turn out until he is older. I hope that we can teach him to be an honorable man. In the best scenario, he learns from this and becomes a hard-working member of our team. If not, then we lost out on a bit of food over a few years. Luckily for us, we recruited him at an age where he can learn some discipline and manners. I have faith that he will turn out alright." Castor said.

"Well, you are the boss. I'm not going to put my neck on the line to argue with that." Myra said with a smirk.

"If it is any consolation," Castor continued, "I won't forget what he tried when we met. I do not doubt that Nikitas will have some special exercises to break him of those tendencies."

Castor got up and walked towards the armory. He turned before leaving and said, "It never hurts to show a little kindness. I think that's the lesson I want to show with today's event."

Myra nodded in satisfaction. "Yes, I guess it doesn't." She returned to her post, watching the street below the barracks to sate the boredom of her shift. Castor left the lobby and went upstairs to his officer chambers.

His officer's quarters were on the second floor of the barracks. His suite overlooked the main armory from the balcony and gave him a good view of the weapon racks and lobby. He had fond memories from his childhood of looking up towards the second floor from the sandpit below. When he would visit the barracks with his father, he thought of how cool it would be to captain his own century of guards. After a few lengthy discussions with his parents, they concluded that a career in martial training was fit for an upcoming prince. The experience would help him be known for helping others and competing in physical sports. A career in the military was an acceptable path for a prince of the nation, so his parents had no issues with his decision.

Castor removed his medallion from around his neck and placed it against the lock on his door. The lock itself was a cube of bronze that sat at waist height on the doorframe. It had a circular indent in the center of the front surface with a reverse impression of what was on his necklace. As he put the seal into the indent, the delicately detailed grooves slid into the lock and locked into place. The necklace seamlessly fit into the opening as though it disappeared. As the surface was completed, a small, bronze lever shot out of the top left of the mechanism. Castor pushed the lever down towards the floor and the door unlocked. He pushed the lever back into the metal box and his pendant was released from the surface. Its outer edge barely bit into the bronze surface to not fall directly onto the floor. Castor grabbed his medallion and put it back around his neck and entered his office.

The rectangular room Castor walked into was a space he felt at home. In front of him was a small wooden table surrounded by four klines, a type of Anthoran couch one can lay on to relax and socialize. Past the seating area was his desk and chair, which sat in between the two large windows that covered the back wall of the suite. The window only looked into the alleyway between the barracks and the courthouse, but the open corridor allowed for fresh air and light to pass freely into the room. To ensure the building was safe from intruders, the windows up here were also reinforced with a bronze and wood lattice like on the first floor.

Home at last, he thought. Castor loved his family home, but this room was his property. The small suite was secure and housed all of his important belongings. He slept many nights on the klines within it and spent many days reading at his desk. It was good to be back.

Off to his right was Castor's collection of military documents; personal and state books he kept within his quarters. It housed all of his past reports for his soldiers during their performance reviews. The wooden shelves held full paper books while a wooden cross-hatching sat near the ground to hold any vellum scrolls. His century had performance reviews every half of a year. Each of the vellum sheets on the rack was the history of each of the guards under his command. Overall, Castor had around one hundred citizen guards that reported to him across the city. He was one of the four guard captains currently within the region. While the number of standing guards fluctuated around four hundred, they had plans to create a fifth century to compensate for the rapid growth in the region.

Off to his left in the room was what Castor had come for. Training with minimal weight and mobility restrictions would only lead to issues on a real battlefield, so all training was done with full battlefield regalia unless a special session dictated otherwise. Over to the left wall of his desk sat his armor stand and weapon rack. He unloaded his outfit onto his large, olivewood desk and left his mantle on the back of his chair. He rolled his belt into a spiral and put it next to his pouches and xiphos. He took off his chiton and folded it so that it would not wrinkle while he trained. He knew his mother would be upset with him if we returned with a wrinkled or cut outfit, so he knew to wear a chiton specifically for his training regimen. He grabbed the extra chiton from a drawer in his desk and tied it into place before he went over to his armor rack.

On the armor rack sat a panoply fitting of a prince of Anthora. In front of him hung a full linothorax, white in body color with teal blue accents around the edges. The linen armor was a quarter of an inch thick and well reinforced. The armor had full pteruges that hung down onto his legs as well as covered his upper arms from the shoulders. These thick linen tassets were made of the same material as the chest piece and hung openly across the wearer's skin to give better mobility while adding protection to the upper arms and legs.

Castor had this linothorax specially made when he was promoted to the captain's position at age eighteen. He considered it to be one of his best investments to date. The cloth used to make it was mostly layers of linen, but he purchased part of a roll of crystalhair fabric from the Durulian Traders Guild to reinforce the armor. Throughout the body and pteruges, he integrated five layers of the exotic material between the otherwise ordinary fabric. While crystalhair was notoriously stronger and better at heat management than traditionally grown cloth, the material was rather unsightly due to its fibery nature. The coarse hairs of the cave mushroom resembled an unkempt beard and were not suited for being on the surface of the armor. Castor, like many soldiers and mercenaries, found it beneficial to keep his insides on the inside and not on the outside. The layers of crystalhair helped keep that goal a reality.

Along the belly of the chest piece hung rows of scales. The bronze plates shone brightly from a proper polish. Castor was very particular about the state of his armor. On top of wanting to maintain his personal protection, he knew Acco would have something to say if he wore corroded or blemished metalwork. He wouldn't give his brother any more social ammunition during public gatherings than he already allowed. The scales covered from his solar plexus to his hips and up across his shoulders on the straps that held his chest piece and back piece together. The pteruges across his legs bore small square plates of the same bronze and were butted up against one another to cover the whole front surface of each of the large tassels. The same was said for the strips of cloth that covered his upper arms, fully plated to protect his body in a composite manner. Heavy blows could clash against the metal outer surface while the cloth underneath helped dissipate the impact.

He donned the whole garment, making sure to slip the sections around his chest and overlap the cloth on the side where he tied the materials together to ensure full coverage. The armor sat heavily upon his shoulders, weighing close to twenty pounds. While this weight was not cumbersome by value alone, the weight was concentrated on his shoulders and could cause fatigue over time. To remedy this fatigue, Anthorans wore a combat belt, made from metal-reinforced leather, that allowed most of the weight to fall upon the hips rather than the shoulders. His was decorated with a repeating pattern of metal bosses, adding a sense of elegance to an otherwise utilitarian design.

Once his chest piece was secured into place, he was able to grab his greaves. The fully bronze leg armor was not as decorated as the belt he equipped before, but the surface had anatomical details that added to its form. The details were not just to make Castor's calves look more defined, but the accurate locations of muscles in tension gave the greaves a more comfortable fit when Castor was performing combat or training. The inside of the greaves was lined with linen as all the armor he had. The padding helped keep the bare metal from rubbing on his skin as well as allowing for easier cooling. Bronze armor got very warm when exposed to the summer's humid and sunny environment, so a layer to keep your skin from sizzling was always welcome on their training days.

The greaves were painted with a mix of white stucco and tree sap, creating a durable and well-refined canvas for the metal armor pieces. The greaves' design was painted in a pattern that matched the linothorax. This stucco covering reduced how much heat the metal took in when outside as well as gave the outfit a unified style. Castor undid the leather buckles on the inside of the greaves and wrapped them around his shins. He tightened them down to a snug fit before reclasping the buckles. He hopped up and down in place to ensure the greaves were seated properly to his legs before he moved to inspect his helmet.

The dome of bronze that sat at the top of his armor stand was the helmet Castor recently acquired from the bronzesmith. A helmet needed a proper fit, and his last helmet had grown too small for his head. His new helmet was at the peak of Anthoran engineering and had many additions that surpassed older helmet designs. The head protection was a continuous piece of hammered bronze that covered the entire top of the head as well as the back of the neck and down past each of his cheeks. A ridge sat across the brow of the helm as well as across the material where his hairline sat. The ears were unobstructed to allow for unhindered senses during combat but were surrounded by metal to block all but the most accurate of attacks. A thick nasal bar came down the center of the helmet to protect his nose down to his upper lip, and the cheek plates covered the sides of his face down to his chin. While more open than older designs to increase mobility and vision, the selected areas that allowed for the gaps were angled so that most glancing blows would not find their way into his brain cavity. The entire helmet was painted like his greaves. The white and blue theme of the set continued from head to toe.

On each side of the helmet were circular metal hooks that allowed for the attachment of accents and plumes to add flair to the helmet. While Anthorans were utilitarian by design in warfare, their individuality was able to show through in many ways. Core colors for armor were usually white in Anthora to reduce heat stroke during combat, but the accent colors were up to the soldier to choose. Castor's recent gift from Kyros would fit perfectly in these locations and replace the current white chicken feathers he had in their place. His friend knew him quite well, as the orange feathers were a good fit to the teal outfit he wore. He unfurled the metal curls and replaced the chicken feathers. They were worn and bleached from the sun's rays over the last few months of outdoor use, one of the feathers snapping as he was removing them. The sun had degraded it beyond repair.

Castor walked over to the window and dropped the old feathers out of a gap in the lattice. Grabbing two of the harpy crest feathers from his desk, he sat and manipulated the metal hooks around the base of the feathers so they would stay in place without risk of falling out. Pinching the metal and pushing the quill end into the openings, Castor decided the feathers were properly attached after he swung the helmet by the neck guard and knocked it against the ground a few times. The paint that covered the helmet would have chipped or flaked if it was just made of stucco, but the specific mixture used on the armor was made to take light impacts without failure. Checking to make sure the feathers were symmetric on each side of his helm, Castor placed it on the edge of his desk before finishing up his equipment review.

Castor grabbed the reinforced vambraces that sat on the arms of the armor stand. The left arm was made of only leather, which gave some padding when pressed against the inside of his large aspis shield. The right had reinforcements of bronze strips that added some security to his sword arm during combat. He laced them onto his arms and tied the ends into a bow, tucking the extra strapping under the leather surfaces. Castor donned his helmet as the last piece of armor and finalized his garb with a shield, short sword, and spear from his weapon rack. The spear and sword were both blunted for practice purposes but were weighted properly to ensure efficient training wherever the training led. After fastening the sword to his belt and the shield to his left arm, Castor strapped the spear to the inner lining of the shield and made his way out of his room, worried he would be late for practice.

Castor locked his door and replaced his necklace around his neck. The lock slammed into the wood door frame as he pushed the lever back up to its original position. Once it was secured, he waved to a few of his fellow guards returning from their rounds as he walked down the stairs and out the front doors. He felt a strong cool breeze cover his body as he passed into the lobby. The natural draft in the building gave ample airflow and allowed the large and heavy structure to have a pleasant, clean flow in all rooms. The use of clerestories at the tops of rooms created a strong draft within both the rooms and corridors. He appreciated the cool breeze in his heavy gear.

Out the front door and turning right, Castor made it to the front of the amphitheater. The open building was gated on all sides by tall marble walls. The stands of the arena pressed deep into the hillside; their outer walls reflected brightly like a large dish out in the sun. White marble was used for all but the smallest details of the theater. The marble was locally cut in the mountains of the Thymian peninsula and was a well-used material for all high-end public buildings. After removing his helm and stomping his bare feet on the stone road, he walked into the stadium to start his training for the day.

CHAPTER 5

Sparks Scatter On Swirling Shields

19th of Beryl, 453 of the Age of Discovery

ntering through the front gates, Castor walked under the arches that led into the open-air arena. He saw his guards had already begun their training for the day, running up and down the stairs of the hillside. In pairs of three, the teams of fully armored hoplites ran the slopes of the amphitheater with their shields locked. The front surface was a wall of bronze as their shields bounced in formation. Spears were drawn, braced, and sat steadily against the rim of each soldier's aspis. As a group reached the end of a row of seats, they would reposition their formation before starting the next staircase. The soldier on the far right would fold back and lock into the left-most position. This pattern continued as the teams jogged in circles around the seating of the stadium.

Nikitas stood in the center of the orchestra and barked commands and corrections to any who incorrectly practiced their formation drills. As the theater was designed to allow all guests to see and hear what was being performed in the orchestra, every soldier was able to clearly hear the war veteran's raspy commands. As Castor walked closer to his assistant, the former captain of the third century noticed his approach and removed his shiny bronze helmet.

"Ah, Castor. I was starting to think you may have taken after your brother and slept in today!" the gray-haired man chortled as he patted the prince on the back and smiled widely. While the man was not much taller than Castor, he was far more muscular. His years of battle had hardened his skin and physique. Castor was by no means weak for his age, but the heavy pats on his back were enough for him to brace his stance on the sandy ground.

"Thanks for starting the drills without me. I can fill you in on the details later, but I had a run-in with a petty thief this morning on my way here." Castor said. He smiled lightly to ease any doubts his vice-captain had, as Nikitas knew Castor to downplay anything that befell him.

"Was everything handled alright? No injuries to report?" Nikitas asked after he raised an eyebrow.

Castor nodded approvingly. "No injuries. The thief was handled properly. No issues to report. I will introduce you sometime."

Nikitas dropped his raised eyebrow and relaxed his wide smile. "You do get into the strangest situations." He put his hands up in exasperation. "Very well, have it your way. I'll read the official report whenever it gets finished."

Nikitas turned and whistled to the soldiers who were continuing their drills as the captains spoke. The sharp shrill of his whistle shot across every wall in the theater. It bounced around, creating an echo that reverberated a few times before pattering off.

"Captain Castor has arrived! Form to attention!" Nikitas bellowed to the guards. The groups all turned and made their way down to the ground level over the course of a minute. Across the stadium, twenty-two groups of soldiers marched down to the main stage. The last group in the formation had four men to allow for the odd man out to be able to participate in the drills. Including Nikitas and himself, Castor counted sixty-seven guards who had shown up for the extra training session this weekend. Castor was happy with the turnout. The autumn season usually led to less attendance for non-mandatory training. Between younger members being recruited to support the harvest to older members traveling to visit relatives, the overall amount of volunteer training dwindled as the climate cooled for the incoming winter.

While Castor wanted to think his reputation with his century was the reason he had such a turnout, he knew otherwise. He had posted this session as a way to train channeling with the lower classes, bringing fully charged neroines to the amphitheater. As expected, Nikitas had the two carts that Castor had requisitioned in the theater grounds already. The men and women within Castor's division would usually rely on stationed mana pools around the city or on natural replenishment to sustain their channeling on a normal day. Since Castor was a noble with a noble's proficiency in channeling, he understood their interest in such training. The ability to truly test one's capabilities and channel to their heart's content without risk of personal injury or becoming drained for the following days gave this session much more importance than a typical training session.

Castor noticed the audience today had more women than usual within the ranks. While Anthoran women were generally smaller and shorter, they made up for the difference with their naturally larger mana pools. Anthorans were the second smallest race known within the continents of Petrus, falling just ahead of the Durulians. While some women dedicated their lives to becoming powerful combat channelers, most were utilized for their robust mana supply by working as priestesses, scholars of the Great Towers, and artisans within the town's economy. While only men could sit upon the crystal thrones of the Princes' Table, the hands that pulled the strings upon many political advances were not put into motion without a woman's touch. Castor saw great potential in the soldiers in front of him and always kept a mental note of those who seemed to perform above the rest.

Before Castor could start addressing his trainees for the day, a hush across the stadium befell the men and women gathered. As Castor turned to see what the entire group had been staring at, he felt a wave of déjà vu. Coming through the central archway onto the sandy floor of the amphitheater was a raised palanquin with finely detailed murals around the base. All twelve arms of the dais were held by the same great Maudians of the morning prior. The spectacle was led by the emissary in his orange robe and tall, white, hooded headdress. The ambassador bowed his head at the two men and raised a hand to them.

"I can handle this. Your father had prepared me for this event yesterday afternoon." Nikitas said to Castor as the pair walked towards the Maudian parade. As they approached, the attitude of the ambassador was far different than what Castor saw earlier in the day. Whether it be their difference in the hierarchy or a change in the water, the ambassador seemed far more friendly than how he treated the guards at the gates. Be that as it may, Castor was always welcoming to new alliances and saw this as an opportunity to better relations with the satrapies of Maudif. Great Maudians made for valuable allies and fearsome foes.

The emissary walked towards the Anthorans as they approached the palanquin. Standing between the two groups with arms outstretched, he got close to Nikitas. He clasped his outstretched hands onto the Anthoran's shoulders. Nikitas mirrored the tall lion man and they interlocked their arms. As a typical Maudian greeting, the ambassador pushed his head into the side of Nikitas' neck and nuzzled him with his thick dreadlocks. While Maudians rarely greeted other Maudians in the same manner, Castor had learned that they were fond of doing this gesture towards any Anthorans or Elvari they met. What made this abrupt situation all the more interesting was how much Castor knew Nikitas' disdain for cats, house pets or otherwise. It was not as though Nikitas was racist towards the feline people from the eastern continent, but instead disliked the itchiness he felt after greeting them. The physical contact the envoy gave was sure to cause the grizzled veteran to excuse himself for a quick rinse in a tub of water before they started their practice.

Once the greeting was completed and the ambassador stopped purring, their discussion was able to start.

"Hello Castor, heir prince of Thyma. Hello Nikitas, vice-captain of the third century. We are humbled by your welcoming stance towards our exiled prince." the Maudian ambassador nodded his head towards both the men as he addressed them.

"Welcome Cyrus, emissary to the exiled prince. Welcome Mithra, exiled prince of Thrim. We offer support to you and wish good health for your people." Nikitas spoke in a dignified manner to match the mood of the conversation.

Hecantor had prepared him for this meeting the day prior and instilled the proper response with his right-hand man. Castor was impressed. Nikitas was more known for his battle prowess and war strategy than his skills in delegations. He had adapted well to the common way Maudians spoke and their dialect in the Anthoran language. Castor was also aware of Maudian culture, as he was taught in his studies of all major societies and their ways of communication. While he was surprised to see an exiled prince of Maudif here in his city, he made sure to not show surprise. Doing so would be offensive to the envoy. He nodded where a response was necessary and allowed Nikitas to finalize the pleasantries.

Once the greetings were completed, Cyrus spoke directly to Castor. "Hecantor, your father and crown prince of Thyma, has allowed the exiled prince to view your training regimen. My grace will likely not intervene but shall watch from the stands. The crown prince has permitted us to participate if my lord so wishes, but he will likely watch for today."

A deep purring noise could be heard from beneath the layers of thin gauze that covered the main stand of the palanquin. The hum was deep and resonated across the orchestra. A dozen servants lifted the platform off the ground and raised the Maudian to the first diazoma in the stands. They placed it gently on the ground at the cross-section between the diazoma and the last layer of the theatron which was the only area in the stands that fit the wooden platform. Ten of the servants sat within the stands near the platform and drank from leather pouches as two of the front servants walked onto the platform and rolled the cloth barriers up. When they were done, the one underneath could be seen clearly.

Castor was surprised to see the hulking behemoth beneath. A great Maudian with fur the color of amber sat upon an inclined cushion. His mane was long and boisterous with a tint of black at the end of the dark orange fur. It seemed as though the Maudian had never cut his hair in his life. Like the other Maudians, it was in fashion to have the mane pulled back into symmetric dreadlocks. The hair of the exiled prince was pulled back and held together with ringlets of bronze and silver. The entire mass of hair flowed across the back of his head and down over his shoulders, terminating the gray ends near his pectoral muscles. His large ears had the same gray and amber color pattern of his coat with small zig zags of black up the edges. Mithra's eyes were light gray and sat forward on his face like a predator. Both pupils focused on Castor as he looked up at the giant cat man. He was over double Castor's size and easily triple his weight. Castor was impressed with the strength of the servants who were able to haul this beast around on that wood stand all day. Complaining about their task seemed foolish, considering the creature they carried could break bone with the flick of his wrist.

Nikitas nudged Castor to gain his attention as he had been in a staring contest with Mithra for a handful of seconds at that point. The rest of his group stood by and fidgeted nervously before Castor addressed them. Having such a figure watch their practice was not a common occurrence and Castor could feel the uneasiness in his soldiers.

"Right, so today we will be practicing some techniques for frontline defenses." Castor switched into his more professional mode again since he was now addressing his soldiers. He had to reassure them that the exiled prince's presence was not to be a concern. Channeling was a tiring practice with quick and dangerous techniques. He needed everyone to be focused on their training so no injuries would come from a lack of attention.

"I hope everyone is well warmed up because we are going to jump straight into our lessons today. I need four men for each neroine. Haul the carts to each side of the orchestra. Break into pairs and stand across from one another. Today's first lesson will focus on an offensive flame and a defensive wall of water." As always, Nikitas had water drawn into buckets on the sides of the arena. Castor shared his practice plans with him on their last rounds around the city the workweek prior. Nikitas was known for his efficient preparation. As the last captain of the third century in Thyma, Nikitas was ready to retire at the ripe old age of fifty. He was still as fit as a captain of the guard should be but wanted more time to see his grandchildren. His voluntary demotion to vice-captain was the perfect opportunity for him, as he was still able to support Castor and teach him about leading a century without the full working hours and paperwork involved in such a position. Nikitas was usually only seen on a single patrol every week and focused on training the young and eager in the limited time he was on shift. Castor appreciated all the help he had given him over the last year and hoped his support would not wane any time soon.

The soldiers hauled the carts to their proper locations across from one another and two lines formed in the orchestra. One soldier was left at the end of the line, so Castor whispered to the man that Nikitas would join him once he was back from washing his arms and neck in a bucket. He nodded in understanding.

Castor and Nikitas stood in between the two lines of soldiers with their shields glistening in the sun. Their current armaments were dulled for practice. Their shields were unpainted and their weapons were blunted. Everyone had a short sword on them that was in functional order in case a situation broke out during practice, but their equipped spears and shields were designed heavy and blunt to be used during training scenarios.

"This practice is meant as training and you should use this time to focus on the defensive technique rather than multiple layers of protection. Is that clear?" Castor bellowed to the dual lines of hoplites. A loud bark of confirmation came from the crowd in agreement.

"Today, we will be focusing our control on a spear of fire. This ability is an augmentation of a skill many of us use in our daily lives. Has anyone here not channeled a flame from their hand before?" Castor asked the crowd.

No response came.

"Good. This will speed the lesson up. What we are doing today is bolstering that skill and adding more energy to it. Rather than focusing the fire into a small and tight flame, we will instead aim to add as much energy to the flame as we can to lengthen it. With practice, the mana required to maintain this flame will reduce. Watch closely."

Castor said his normal prayer to Ignus and ignited an inch-long flame from his middle finger. He focused more of his thoughts on the flame and the flame grew. Inch by inch, Castor tempered the flame into a foot-long column that was a few inches in width.

"As you can see, this flame is stationary at the end of my hand and under control. As I move my hand around, the flame follows. You may barely notice it, but the flame's tip will follow slightly slower than the flame's start at the end of my finger. "

As his hand moved, what he described took place. The flame was red on the outside and bright orange at its core. It followed his hand as he moved it around with the end of the flame always following behind by a few inches.

"At this length, the effect is not very useful. But what if I extend the flame?" Castor asked rhetorically.

He put his attention on the flame once again and it grew in length. After a half-second of focus, the flame grew to three or four feet in length. The column had not changed width but the length had stretched the fire and distorted the color. Its center had become a brilliant white. The edges crackled and snapped in the open air. Once the cylinder stabilized its length, the mental duress of focusing the energy was lifted. it took a steady trickle of mana to maintain the blade with his level of training.

As his hand moved around like before, the longer flame acted slower. With its extended length, the column chased his hand by over a foot compared to where his hand was at any moment. With small movements, the displacement was minimal. When he moved his hand quickly, the foot of difference snapped back into place at the same speed as his hand, much like a crack of a whip.

Castor grabbed his spear in his left hand and allowed his shield to fall against the edge of the neroine. His spear was made of a single branch of ash and trimmed bilaterally in bronze langets. The langets went the whole length of the weapon, from spearhead to counterweight. Both the head and counterweight were made of polished bronze. Castor tossed the spear into his right hand where the flame still burned.

It took a good amount of focus to keep the flame controlled when he gripped the spear, but his fortitude withstood the test. As his hand wrapped around the bronze, the flame slid up the shaft like a snake and rested atop the tip of the spearhead. His spear was seven feet in length when the counterweight was set upon the ground. With the extra column of flame sitting atop, the entire weapon now stood over ten feet in height. Castor moved the spear back and forth as the infernal whip flung with the motion.

Younger soldiers were taken aback by the show of energy while the guard veterans seemed unaffected. Castor enjoyed teaching training lessons like this for that exact reason. He never knew what skills the audience had. He wanted to make sure that everyone had some intermediate channeling capabilities when situations grew out of control in the streets. The other captains focused on physical capabilities, which was important, but Castor wanted to bolster the city's supernatural training on top of their more mundane skills.

"Some of you have done this before, so you more than likely know where this lesson is heading." Castor extinguished the flame on his spear and walked over to the bucket of water near Nikitas' feet. He quenched his hand, the radiant heat from the open flame had made his entire arm heat up to near cooking temperatures after those few minutes. Once cooled, he used his channeling to pull a fist-sized sphere of water out of the bucket. It levitated a few inches off the palm of his open hand. With the orb of water on his right, he lifted his shield with his left.

"The defender will be using this defensive technique to protect themselves from the flames." Water rushed around his hand as he prepared the proper ideas in his head. He was not used to channeling water, but his noble blood gifted him with natural control over the elements. Without a word of chanting, he was able to use his raw mana to manipulate the water to his bidding.

With the bronze shield on his left arm, he channeled the water around its rim. The current flowed in a clockwise direction. Little ripples could be seen in the stream. Around and around the water went. Castor started to pull on the water with little tugs like the pull of the tide. Each pull extended the water near the top of the shield a little farther out and a little thinner. The water on the other three sides of the shield was unaffected and continued to flow around as though nothing was changing. As the tugs and pull added up, the top rim of water extended like a bubble around the shield, extending its sides farther and farther until it was hovering around the same surface area as the shield itself. At this point, the flat panel of water extended to around a third of the outer edge of the shield and was easily moved as Castor rotated the shield on his arm with a simple movement of his hand. He could move and nudge the water to rotate around the edge of the shield so that it shrank and extended the layer at ease. Once the channeling was complete, maintaining it was as easy as maintaining the column of fire, although the fire felt more natural to Castor. Open palmed, he took a small amount of water from the bucket and coated the openings in his helmet with the liquid. A bubble sized at half-inch thick sat between the bronze plates. The water was crystal clear and did not move, stationary within the openings like a sheet of glass. This would protect everyone's sensitive eyes and ears during the practice.

Healing was capable with mana channeling, but usually on small scrapes and burns. Repairing vital organs was a much harder task.

"This will be what you use to protect yourselves from the flames." Castor said to the crowd, "This water will be your barrier, your lifeline on the frontlines. This conjured surface is very good at deflecting attacks. Even a piercing arrow or flick of a whip of flame could be stopped with this technique."

The men pounded their spears upon the sandy clay that made the base of the orchestra. Only around a hundred guards in the city were capable channelers. Most could hold a flame for a short while or move water from a well into a bucket without the use of a rope. Castor was renowned across the guard as one willing to teach the masses in the ways of channeling. This was something that created issues within the aristocracy across the principality. His citizen-centric ideology found him ire from some controlling aristocracy within his city, but Castor did not care. He saw his abilities as a gift from those much higher than himself and did not believe rich patriarchs and matriarchs had similar importance as the deities who gave the people their channeling abilities. He knew he would have to deal with these issues one day during his reign in the distant future, but today was not that day.

Castor knew some of the guards within the training were much more skilled than others. Castor saw the top guards of Didyma's century within the ranks, no doubt taking every opportunity to record their findings to the Lorekeeper of Thyma. The old crone of the library was one who Castor did not enjoy conversations with. Her sharp tongue and intensive lessons on Anthoran tyrants and civil wars always felt overly focused on the young prince when he was being tutored at the Thymian Library. She fit the position of Lorekeeper perfectly and Castor knew it. No one else could serve the White Oracle in such a selfless way. This did not mean Castor agreed with how selfless her actions were, seeming to force that selflessness to the behest of others. Her position was kept as a guard captain only in name alone. Her connections to the Oracle of the White Tower and her studies on mana rarely allowed her to step foot within the barrack's grounds. Her vice-captain, Thalia of house Othonos, was the acting captain of the second century and usually on countryside patrols to fetch people or materials for the Lorekeeper. He had seen the real captain only a handful of times during holidays or the yearly captain's meeting. Thalia had participated in Castor's training a few times a year, but today she was not around. Her elite guard group consisted of five noblewomen who were at the training session and would relay any information they gathered to her.

The two lines of trainees went to their respective sides of the field near their neroine. The carts buzzed to life as the mages took power from their mana-bearing stones. These carts were more ornate than the cart the farmer had used earlier in the day. Its wooden panels were carved with ornate patterns and reliefs depicting events from Anthora's rich history. The copper wires and bronze slabs were set in symmetrical patterns to keep the various clusters of crystals in the cart organized. Unlike the bland and uniformly green-brown collection of gems and jewels that sat within the cart on the farm, these carts held an assortment of colors. Citrine and calcite spires sat along the edges with amethyst and fluorite geodes in various positions with the center. A tall pillar of quartz sat at the center of each cart and shone brightly as its energy was absorbed by those who required a repletion of mana.

"Make sure your reserves are fully charged," Castor said assertively. "You will not be siphoning off the neroine as we train. Make sure you break your connections before you return to your positions. When you start channeling, make sure any chants are quiet. Silent chanting is preferable. These techniques can be difficult for some and they will need as much concentration as they can muster."

A soft pounding of spears upon tamped clay assured the prince that his command was heard.

As they lined up to practice, the air around them got warmer. One by one, the line opposing Castor started to spark small flames off the tips of their spears. Some were quick to enhance their conflagrations, some took their time. The flame's color was unique to each channeler, as every flame had different outer layers and thicknesses. Only a few got to the white heat that Castor had summoned earlier, but that fact alone gave Castor hope for these warriors. Castor prided himself on his control of flames, his strongest element and the one he had the least worry about improving for the Tournament of the Three Kings the following autumn. Seeing those of the middle-class channel white flames in this situation was impressive to the young prince.

As the other side summoned their barriers, Castor reminded them that all other protection spells were prohibited. Not only would a body augmentation normally drain mana at a noticeable rate, but this group was not trained nor bred for such maintained improvements to the flesh. Some were, like the Koukoulofóroi from the war-loving city-state of Kimpos. Those who bred their citizens solely for physical perfection were known for their great skill in physical augmentations, hardening their skin into sheets of bronze and tightening their muscles like taught bowstrings. Castor shuddered at the thought of facing their warrior prince, Ajax of house Typhonus, at next year's tournament. His reputation was one of legend.

Shields were wetted with discs of water and small chants could be heard from the crowd. While noticeable overall, Castor was pleased with how quiet the chants were. Chanting was the most common method to channel their elements efficiently. As most citizens of Anthora had much smaller mana pools than those like Castor or Acco, the use of chanting to improve performance throughout combat was necessary. Over the centuries, many found chants to the gods to be the easiest way to focus their abilities. Having a patron deity gave even better results with the proper chants. While the differences in endurance were noticeable, Castor was a trained Anthoran prince, and not all had his lineage and training to use and hold their techniques for long periods.

"Ready," Castor said.

Flames wreathed the ends of the opposing force's spears. Bronze tips turned blue and magenta from the growing heat and created a light patina across their surfaces. The defending force braced their shields together into a shield wall, creating a tight phalanx of heavily armored soldiers. The water domed up and covered the edges of those on either side. Every flowing mass of water surrounding each shield flowed in a clockwise fashion, creating a hypnotic effect on those who watched from the front. The water that extended upward was thin enough to see clearly through with small bubbles coming in and out of the liquid as the cool breeze within the stadium flowed around them. Their spears, although not coated with fire, stuck out the top of the formation in a typical phalanx pattern, creating a wall of sharp points aimed at the enemy.

"Steady," Castor said.

Shields locks on the offensive side. Their shields were more spread out, their spear tips hanging out the top-right edge of each shield. Without the water blocking their vision and angles of attack, they were able to get their spears around to multiple spots across the top edge of the bronze wall. Flames flickered as the pillars of flame sparked and crackled on the more novice member's weapons. Those with experience in flame channeling had columns of brighter and less sporadic conflagrations. Each soldier couched their weapon in a comfortable position that allowed for maximum movement. They also had their helmets reinforced with water, just in case any whips of fire were to flick back during the initial crash and cause friendly damage. Both sides were prepared for the drill that was about to begin. The amphitheater became quiet; all local noise dimmed in the calm before the storm.

"Charge!" Castor shouted.

As he shouted the command, the line of aggressors barreled forward with their formation like a solid wall of spikes and shields. They charged the thirty feet across the stadium floor towards the opposing wall of spikes and shields. Any dirt in their way upon the floor that was not packed down was tamped after the charge. When the two walls collided, a deafening clang of bronze upon bronze rang across the area. Those in the street nearby would have thought the city was under siege, as the shape of the stadium amplified the bronze clanging out towards the city. The offensive line smashed into the watery defenses and left no quarter. Whips of flame crackled and sizzled against the saturated surfaces. The defense held strong; their line barely pushed back a few inches during the collision.

A few cries of pain rang out across the orchestra. The right flank of the offense was made up of Didyma's experienced guard and had made a solid impact on the defensive forces. Their whips, longer and brighter due to the training the wizened hag had given them, broke through the weak barriers of the neophytes on the left flank of the defense. Their water barriers, barely flowing around the edge of their shields, could not dissipate the heat fast enough. The columns of flame broke the edges, ripping through their protection. Castor watched as the flagellation smashed against helmets and pauldrons, breaking down the sides and sizzling the arms of the trainees. The damage was not permanent, but the guards in training would have this event as a mental scar in future combats. They would learn from the experience and better their defenses for next time, lest they end up getting branded by scorching lashes once again.

As the left flank collapsed, the middle and right withstood the attacks. Those who were injured dropped to the ground after taking damage and rolled out of the way. By standing to the side, the effects of a weak flank could be felt towards the rest of the line, the middle soldiers turning their formation inward to compensate for the additional enemies. Whips flew and spears pierced. The cacophony of impacts rang out across the group. The water on the helmets helped to deafen the sharp noises, but the sheer volume was still loud to all those in range. Castor barked to some of the recruits that neared the neroines that they were not to recharge their mana during rounds. Those who did go near the carts dropped to the ground and did a few sets of push-ups as punishment for not remembering their captain's orders from earlier.

As the mock battle waged on, more of the defense started to crumble. As they were not meant to attack back other than parries and counters, the offense was near full capacity. A few younger attackers ran out of mana and retreated off the battlefield once they were physically drained. By the time Castor called the end of the conflict, only around a dozen of defenders were still standing with their barriers intact.

"Good!" Castor announced to the crowd as they broke from their formations and returned to their respective standing lines. Castor continued their lessons as he dismissed the spent soldiers back to the neroines to top up their mana reserves. Those with mana left were kept in line. Many scholars in the capital believe reducing stored mana down to a minimum and building it back up was a good way to build one's mana pool. Some disagreed, like Didyma and the other matrons within the council of Thorned Roses, and believed mana pools were stagnant with the only improvements being made to the casting efficiencies. Those who were from her coven here, the Sisters of the Thorns, agreed and aligned with Didyma's ideals. Castor did not care for the arbitrary nature of whether one expanded or another became more efficient. What mattered to him was the improvement of his and his soldier's skills. He wanted to allow everyone to build their abilities as well as their confidence in channeling so their patrols would be more efficient in keeping the region safe. He would rather leave the debates on mana efficiencies to those with more spare time.

The drills continued for a short while. In the next round of combat, the new defenders were able to last the conflict with sixteen guards left in the formation. The battle sisters on the left flank held their ground, with their channeling capability showing well in the group. Castor took note of some of the newer soldiers who were within his division, like Vara and Phineas. These neophytes were barely of age and a part of the guards-in-training. They were the two newest members of his century, not including the child Atticus, and their inexperience was evident. Castor read over every member's background when they joined his battalion. These two had nothing of interest to note. Both children were from a local village and sent by their families to make money in the offseason. Soon they would return for the harvests, but they stated earlier in the week they did not want to miss the chance to use the city's neroine. Mana channeling was exciting for the lower class. Their capabilities with channeling would give them a solid edge over those within their village. Castor hoped his training would help them thrive.

After both sides had taken their turns as the offensive and defensive lineups, Castor mixed the two lines to create a fresh set of teams. Every other member switched sides starting from the leftmost position, and then the ranks were divided at the halfway point. The second half moved to the end of the line, becoming the new first half. This method kept the positions within the formation varied and kept small cliques from dominating one section of their formation. For today's lesson, this helped break up the battle sisters from the second century. They were now pitted against one another as well as spread out, adding their skills across the line rather than within one location.

Once everyone was set on their new teams and a few minutes were given as a respite, Castor started the drills over again. Lines clashed against one another, soldiers dropped, and formations molded to the flow of battle. Castor kept a close eye on the entire situation. His responsibility was to ensure no permanent injuries were to befall the trainees as well as learn about the general strengths and weaknesses of the city guards. Some members within the sixty-odd group were from his century. Fifteen including the decani were present from his group, but other leaders were present as well. Castor noticed the way the soldiers from Acastus' century were able to defend much better than the rest of the unit. The eight men from the first century were all well into their thirties and very skilled with their channeling techniques. While they were just barely comparable in mana quantity to the Sisters of the Thorns within the ranks, they were much more battle-hardened. They took a handful of blows without falling, their pain thresholds were far higher than the younger members of the orchestra.

One group in particular caught Castor's attention. A group of older men that formed at the beginning of the training were well versed in defensive spells. They did not break his command that limited the use of body augmentation. Castor could sense the lack of mana within their muscles and bones. It would be very clear if they did break such a rule during training. Instead, they excelled in the manipulation of the water their shields had created. Unlike the novices within the crowd, these soldiers would pull and push the water as it flowed around the rim to better cover the areas that were being bombarded by flagellation. They would quickly pull the water like a small wave to meet the flame, dampening the columns before they had a chance to get close to their bodies. This ability was something even Castor did not use too often, as it used far more mana to constantly change the motion of the water. He made a mental note to check with Acastus on how they maintained this technique without draining their mana. It was more than likely just experience and muscle memory keeping the movements efficient, but he figured asking wouldn't hurt.

"Raise your shield higher!" Castor barked at Phineas as he got hit for the third time that day. The trainee raised his shield an inch, which Castor pushed up another three inches with the butt of his spear. Phineas nodded and kept the shield up in the next round, deflecting two blows that would have made contact if not for the change.

"Focus your column tighter!" Castor barked again, this time at Vara. Vara visibly squinted as she consolidated her channeled flame a few inches in diameter. The fully dark red flames were brought up to a bright orange at the core once her technique was improved.

Castor made sure to keep his face steeled as he barked commands. He wanted to smile and congratulate them on their improvements, but he had to show himself as a captain of the guard. He knew he shouldn't play favorites within the ranks and overly complimenting could lead to them becoming content and stagnant with their progress. A quick pat on the back was the best reinforcement he could give them.

Lines clashed for about an hour before Castor planned to move to the next stages of the practice. More and more burns and scrapes built upon the practitioners until some were unable to continue in the training. As the midday sun peaked in the sky, Castor went and retrieved an amphora from the battle hall. Within the armory was a shelving unit that held a good portion of the city's Vótanodor supply. This purified liquid was created by the holy fathers at Vrontir's temple. They collected rainwater during thunderstorms and fused it with herbs unknown to the general public. With a lengthy ritual and a transfusion of mana, the priests created a powerful painkiller and healing drought. Not much was needed to heal small wounds. While it couldn't reattach a limb, it could be used to help the hurting and calm the panicked.

Castor sat the vessel within the center of the open stage and poured a few cups each into the two buckets of water nearby. The slightly green liquid dissipated into the water and gave the entire container a glossy texture. One by one, members of the group came and took a handful to apply to their wounds. Channeling was used to disperse the balm over their injuries. Once the wounds were properly coated, a small burst of mana added to the salve activated the healing properties, changing it from its garish green to a glowing ocean blue. The wound then started to heal at a rapid rate, moving through the different steps in the healing process in front of your eyes. In this situation, the burn victims were able to get through most of the healing process within ten minutes. As the training exercise was intended to limit full exposure to the open flames, most burns within the group were first degree.

Castor watched as Vera applied the salve to the wounds on Phineas's left shoulder since he was fully spent on mana and needed to rest for a while unless he risked kindling himself. As the salve activated, it brought fluids to the surface of the skin. Phineas clenched his hands as the pain of the entire injury washed over his shoulder in this short period. The water within the skin bubbled underneath the wound and dissipated outward. The initial area was pink and sore but moved to a dark red as the blood died off and was removed from the outer layers.

Not all were injured, however. Many of the trained guards, like those from the first and second centuries, were able to get through the training without a scratch. They took this time to vent the heat from their armor, cupping water from the buckets into their helms and swaying them back and forth with their arms in the air to cool the heated metal. The Sisters of the Thorns channeled water from the buckets and across their metal armors, sucking the heat away and returning it to the bucket. Nikitas removed his suit completely, dropping his bronze thorax to the sandy floor and taking a seat in the shade behind the stone gateway near the entrance of the amphitheater. He drank from a leather water pouch he had sitting in the shade. Castor informed the crowd of their plans for sparring after a short break and joined Nikitas behind the wall.

"Taking it easy, are we?" Castor teased as he walked up to the war veteran.

Nikitas raised an eyebrow at the boy before realizing it was the captain speaking. He looked away and took another sip from his container.

"That's rich, coming from you," he shot back; his words rather icy cold for such a warm autumn day.

Castor laughed. "Yes, I know. But someone has to check on all of our troops and keep note of everyone's improvements. If not me, then who?"

"Were you keeping an eye on Phineas?" Nikitas asked.

"Yes, I kept track of his progress," Castor said flatly. "I think you were right, but I still want to give him a chance."

"You can't coddle him forever." Nikitas stated, "Three thefts have gone uncaught under his guard. I know you want to give them a chance to prove themselves, but the boy..."

"He is a man, Nikitas." Castor corrected. "He is twenty-five this year."

"I'll call him a man when he acts like it!" Nikitas barked in a gravelly tone. He made sure his discontent was known without speaking too loudly so that the others could hear within the stadium.

"Sorry," Nikitas said in a scoffing manner. He knew he could be open with the prince, but he knew when not to push his ground on common hierarchies.

Castor slumped up against the wall next to Nikitas within the boundaries of the shade. "I know you aren't a fan of random farmers taking over shifts from the upper- and middle-class families, but we need more support from the local towns." Castor reminded him.

"I know. Your father mentions that all the time at our council meetings." Nikitas reminded him. "I am aware of the current state of affairs within the region. I give my advice to your father and he does what he wants with it. That does not mean I have to agree with your family's... egalitarian approach." Nikitas took another swig from his pouch before handing it over to Castor.

"I get it. I really do." Castor said in a compassionate tone, "But we do have a different approach here than in Kimpos. We do not just throw someone out when they do not meet our standards."

Castor knew Nikitas came from Kimpos when he was younger as a Banished One, an *Exorístike*. In Kimpos, living as a citizen came with its two main drawbacks; strict social standards and difficult trials before citizenship was granted. Those citizens who did not meet strict standards in the city-state were not allowed to stay. Many of their citizens passed these tests and became full citizens once becoming an adult, joining their citizen guard which made up eighty percent of the citizen class. Those who failed to undertake their trials of adulthood were forced into the class below citizens, which consisted of traders, artisans, and bronzesmiths. Nikitas made it to adulthood in the city and worked in their military as a full-fledged citizen for five years before applying to become a Koukoulofóroi. For every opening in the Koukoulofóroi ranks, three citizens were allowed to try for the position. The two who did not succeed in the competition were exiled from the city, forced to roam the lands of Anthora as Exorístike until they found a suitable master or community to welcome them. Many became mercenaries across the seas, while some stayed on the mainland and used their contacts to build a new life from scratch. Nikitas was welcomed into Thyma by Hecantor a few decades back, becoming a guard captain immediately after finalizing his citizenship within the new region.

"Well, as long as you see why I want to test them, then I see no issue here." Nikitas mulled as he shut his eyes and stretched his arms in the cool shade, "Keep staying soft on them for all I care, my prince."

Castor nodded, remembering his princely duties coming within the next year. Having to participate in the tournament and sitting in on the assembly of princes was exciting and terrifying to him at the same time. Claiming the feldspar throne at the Princes' Table was a task he knew he would eventually have to fulfill at some point in his life. He did not expect it to be as soon as he became an adult. He was glad his father was still around to run the city but wished he was healthier to keep up his title in full until Castor had at least five more years of experience within the city. His right to the throne seemed to require his attention sooner than he wanted.

Castor took a swig from the canteen and fought the urge to spit the liquid onto the floor. Greenish liquid dripped from the rim of the container and across the cork that hung from the side on a leather loop.

"Did you spike your water with Vótanodor again?" Castor asked, fighting the urge to choke on the viscous liquid, "And why is it so... minty?"

"Well, that's clearly because I added some mint leaves to it," Nikitas said flatly. "Mint and a little lemon zest."

"If you need to add a bunch of spices to enjoy the flavor, what is the point of adding it in the first place?" Castor asked.

"Do not blame me. Blame my upbringing. It is not my fault they fed us this stuff when I was a child." Nikitas shot back, "The stuff can't be that bad for you. It is the third most common drink for Kimpian citizens, behind wine and water. You won't let me drink wine while we train."

Nikitas sat on the ground, looking up towards the sun overhead. His hair was dark and cut short, as this length was the maximum regulated length during active duty. He was retired now, and technically did not need to abide by such standards but did so to set a good example. His sideburns came down below his ears and tapered inward, forming a point towards his mouth. A little bit of gray had started to form near the tips of his sideburns, showing his age was starting to take hold. His face was clean-shaven except for a goatee about an inch in length. It was tapered to a point, which seemed more stylish than Castor gave Nikitas credit for. As Castor stood there, Nikitas put his thumb and pointer finger under each eye and pulled downward, wiping away the sweat around the edges of his facial hair. *Ah*, Castor thought, *that is why it looks like that.*

"Water is an option you just mentioned, yes?" Castor reminded him, realizing Nikitas noticed his constant glare.

"It's boring. And doesn't cool you off as easily." Nikitas retorted.

"Just try not to take too much from the supply. I would rather we heal all wounds before you start chugging the stuff." Castor said as he handed the pungent liquid back to the burly man.

"Sure, sure," Nikitas said, getting to his feet. He put a hand out and helped Castor off the ground. He seemed unbothered by Castor's weight and gear, supporting his full weight with one arm. Although he did not become a fully-fledged Koukoulofóroi, his training in their elite phalanx hardened him beyond normal Anthoran standards.

Once re-equipped and cooled off from their first bout of training, the captains walked back into the amphitheater and prepared for the sparring exercises they planned for this afternoon session.

Almost as if listening in on the return of the captains, Castor was startled by the Maudian diplomat standing on the other side of the wall. He was far enough away to not be heard, but close enough to surprise Castor who was under the impression that they were alone on this side of the orchestra.

"Hello, heir prince of Thyma. I have come to talk to you. Is that alright?" Cyrus asked in a pleasant tone.

"Sure thing. What did you need?" Castor responded. Nikitas elbowed Castor in the side, reminding him of the diplomatic weight their encounters had. Castor continued, "Is there some way I can be of help?

"Thank you, I appreciate your time." the Maudian purred in agreement. "The exiled prince has noticed that your group plans to participate in... sparring drills."

The *sp* sound was difficult for a Maudian tongue to speak, but his point got across to Castor. "The son of the sun wishes to participate with you in the drills of sparring."

"That would be perfectly fine," Castor stated. "I do not believe our armor would fit him, however. These bouts can be rather dangerous without proper protection and blunted weapons."

"That is not a problem at all." Cyrus assured him, "We have prepared the bright one's armor in anticipation for this event. We should only take a minute to prepare him for you."

As they spoke, Cyrus whistled up to the group huddled in the stands. As soon as the command was given, the palanquin bearers moved into action. They retrieved sections of armor and various clothing bits from hidden compartments within the sides of the wooden mass. Sheets of bronze scales came from various openings and were sat on the stands, leather straps connecting the sections. Mithra rose from his pillowed bed and walked out onto the granite stands. He stood at least eight feet tall at the peak of his mane, which now flowed within the windy amphitheater.

The banished prince stood on the stairs as his servants worked around him. Using the extra height of the seats that lined the edges of the stairways, the servants attached his armor pieces to his body as they put sections together. Bronze scales glittered in the sunlight and chalky white bones protrude from edges. The armor looked defensive, with most of the body covered in scales or plates. The bones that sat on edges or were intricately engraved and attached as ornaments were not in areas that would be at high risk, but their hard, brittle nature would help defend against crushing blows if need be. A circlet made from gold and inlaid with dark red rubies was placed upon his head. The yellow metal stood out on the full suit, its surface different in color and status compared to the rest of the outfit. Mithra shook his armor around to ensure all pieces were comfortable and stepped back to his pillowed throne. He grabbed two bronze katars from his personal area, the push daggers connecting properly into the slots on his wrist guards that allowed for ease of movement when he was not holding the weapons. Rotating them back onto his wrists, the blades fit nicely into the surface, giving the vambraces a bladed edge across the top surface.

"Those look sharp," Castor commented on the katars he had grabbed. "Does he have any weapons that aren't as ready for war as those? I would prefer no one got seriously injured today."

The dignitary nodded and gave a short bow to Castor before returning to the entourage. The lithe creature sprinted up the stairs, taking two or three steps at a time. Cyrus got up to the area his comrades were working and talked to Mithra in a hushed voice. He could hear the tonal change in their conversation, the soft purrs and short hisses of the Thrimic dialect of Gurebhsi just barely noticeable from their distance away. The exiled prince seemed irritated, no doubt because of the limitations on sharp weapons. All of the sudden, after a few minutes of discussion, Mithra ripped the metal push blades from his wrist guards and tossed them up towards his lounging bed. A few hisses later, Cyrus backed away in a bowing motion, understanding that the situation had irritated his master not of his own volition.

If Castor had learned the language of the Maudians, he was sure the words being used were not ones he would speak to his mother or Lydia. He did not need to translate the stubborn anger in his voice to realize the exiled king had a hot temper like the rest of the ruling Maudian clans. He knew they had a history of quick decision-making and snappy reactions, but Castor assumed an exiled prince would have a better attitude after wandering foreign continents following their exodus. Castor, knowing Maudian culture and the way traveling bands tended to work, assumed Mithra had either skipped his lunch or did not have the proper mid-day break that Maudians were known to follow religiously. After a few seconds of consideration, he recalled this time of day would correspond with the typical siesta time in Maudian culture, he chalked this behavior up to something like a child not getting its way; temperamental but without hatred.

Mithra turned and spoke to the servant closest to him, a few trills and spits in Gurebhsi could be heard at this point with his raised voice. Although loud, he got his attitude under control. His orders were sharp and clear, and the servants moved in an orderly fashion to complete the commands. They retrieved a collection of large bones, in the shape of femurs, which were broken in the center. Their fractured tips were sharp and their blunted club ends were as thick as a forearm. The servants removed the vambraces that Mithra wore and attached cloth straps to their now bare surfaces. Wrapping and twining the layers of cloth, the normally weak material was bound around his beastly arms and created thick padding. Another servant helped hold bones steady as the head servant wound and bound the bones into their proper places. The osseous protrusions stuck out from his wrists like the push dagger, three bones to each hand sat betwixt his furry knuckles, the concave openings between his knucklebones fitting smooth with the convex surface of each bone.

Moving his fingers back and forth, Mithra flexed his hands into fists and then relaxed them. While the push blades required the grip of each hand, this archaic setup was not bound by such limitations. His hands were free to perform some tasks, like grabbing an ornate silver bottle to drink from. The entire outer surface was engraved with the head of an elephant, a favorite animal amongst Maudian aristocrats. The trunk of the elephant was integrated into the spout of the container, giving the silver storage vessel an anthropomorphic feel. He wet his palette and handed the bottle back to the head servant, who returned it to the storage containers.

After looking at his hands for a few seconds, Mithra seemed to realize the sharp ends of the bones were not much different than the bronze katars he had prior. He thought for a second and decided on a solution.

The solution he chose was violence.

Jumping over to the wall that sat at the bottom of the epitheatron, the giant Maudian started to press his claws into the stone surface. Using his other hand as leverage, he started to snap off the points of the bones. One by one, tip by tip, bone fragments shot out of his paw as he broke the sharp edges down to sit flat at the end. As these bones were the size of an

Anthoran femur, the sheer force this creature had to exert to break the bony protrusions with his bare hands was astounding. Once each of the six bones were properly snapped and their ends set to a relatively flat surface, the great cat started scratching the walls. Scratch left and scratch right, the colossus rubbed the blunted ends on the gritty surface, its hewn texture ground the bones into dust. White lines started to appear across the surface, osseous matter building on the coarse granite chunks. Back and forth, up and down, the once pointed bones became rounded and soft. Their hollow internal cavity which was once used as a blood channel was not just another sanded pocket. Once happy with his results, Mithra flexed his hands one last time to ensure his bindings did not loosen during this arduous process.

Turning quickly, whether it be in anxiety or short temperance, the beast leaped off the diazoma and down the theatron. His stance was like that of a cat, his movements were crisp and became more quadrupedal rather than bipedal. He landed in front of Castor, Nikitas, and Cyrus, who at this point had returned to the orchestra while his master finished his changes to his claws.

He turned and looked at his emissary. His bellowing voice was not angry nor irritated, but deep and distant like a disappointed parent. "Happy?" He asked, which received a violent nodding from his first in command.

"Hello Castor, heir prince of Thyma." the exiled prince spoke in a calm yet firm tone. His gaze was strong and focused, like a wild animal seeking prey. He only turned away to look at Nikitas, nodding and blinking at him as a sign of recognition towards those under his societal class.

"Hello Mithra, exiled prince of Thrim." Castor returned, "It is nice to meet you."

"I would like to fight with you." Mithra continued, "I want to fight *you* in particular."

He scoffed under his breath, the Anthoran language was both difficult for a Maudian palette as well as the language being something new the exiled prince recently learned. Once he was able to control his tongue again, he continued.

"It would not be fair to fight with one who has already shown his skills and techniques in front of a crowd without reciprocating the process. There would be no..." Mithra turned to his diplomat and spoke the word 'aftkhar' to him in the Maudian dialect.

"Honor, your grace." the diplomat said gently to the prince. The prince nodded and turned back. "No honor."

"Allow me to fight your strongest warriors, show my skills, and then fight me," Mithra said. "You can choose your weapons and your...." He thought for a second before agreeing on the proper word, "champion."

Castor considered who he would pit against the creature. Nikitas was a skilled warrior and would be fine, but he was not as young as he used to be and was more used to wielding his maces rather than a spear and shield. He considered one of the Sisters of the Thorns in the crowd, but also considered the ramifications of relying on another century to represent him. He could not rely on the trainees who were barely able to recover from their wounds before the afternoon session. Castor even considered skipping the formalities and taking the beast on himself, taking responsibility if he was to lose quickly to a cheap trick. He did not know the exiled prince's intentions, and hoped they were not nefarious.

The outcome was put on hold before Castor could decide on his champion to participate. The heavy ringing of the city's guard belltower started to clammer from the barracks next door. Through the arches, Castor saw citizens running away from the docks. A soldier, covered in sweat and blood, stumbled into the arena. He pulled himself off the floor, blood dripping from his thigh. Castor ran over and held the man up, who was turning pale from the loss of blood.

"My lord, help me." He said before losing consciousness.

Castor called a guard over to tend to the wounds as he started sprinting for the barracks, the rest of those accompanying him in tow.

CHAPTER 6

Splinters Of Wood On The Water

19th of Beryl, 453 of the Age of Discovery

 whirlwind of soldiers passed through the street as Castor propelled himself towards the guardhouse. While only a quarter-mile down the road, he knew every second would count in an emergency. Preparations had already been made from what Castor could see, as stands of spears and swords were sat upon the porch of the barracks. One bare rack was left to the side, meant to hold any of the blunted practice weapons they were bringing back. Myra stood at the top of the stairs, waiting with a few spears in hand to arm those with the captain.

"What is the situation?" Castor asked quickly, switching his blunted spear out with a sharp one on the stand. He tossed his blunted spear onto the empty racks, barely catching one of the prongs and staying upright. The men dropped off the wounded scout against the wall of the building. Myra huddled over the man who was passed out on the stone behind them, blood pooling on the fabric from the large gash in his leg. It was wrapped tight and the bleeding was staunched, but the bitter smell of blood was already across the patio. Myra gained Castor's attention by standing upright in front of him.

"Emergency down by the docks, sir!" She said as he made his way to the porch. "Some large creatures are attacking the townsfolk. I---" Her voice cracked before she got ahold of herself. "I ran up to ring the bell in the tower and saw the things. They are huge."

"Alright, alright. Any other information you can give me?" Castor asked, focused on her to keep her talking.

Yes!" she yelled, "They look like giant turtles!"

Castor was taken aback. "What?" He said dumbfoundedly. "Like the Atropethian turtles from the marshlands in the southern wastes?"

"Yes! ...Maybe?" She looked confused, as she was not versed in the wildlife from across the continent. "I assume so!" she stammered. "They... they are really big!"

"Alright, I understand, thank you." Castor turned to the crowd around him gathering proper weapons and placing their practice weapons away. Nikitas ran past them as Myra explained the situation, running inside and towards the staircase that led to the captain's quarters.

"Everyone, listen up!" Castor shouted at the crowd, "Our enemies..."

He looked over to Myra and whispered, "Enemies? Plural? How many?"

"Oh...." She racked her brain, the surprise of the situation jostling her memory. "A handful, maybe? That's all I could see from this side of town. No more than a dozen across the bay, from what I would think."

Castor called out to the crowd and split off half the soldiers he trained with from their combined group. He stationed them at the guard house with Myra. Their abilities to channel would serve the incoming patrols well. The remaining soldiers assembled in front of the barrack stairs after they retrieved their weapons.

"We are under attack by a dozen Atropethian turtles, large reptiles from the southern marshlands!" Castor called out to the men and women in front of him. It seemed silly to even say that statement out loud, as the Atropethian snapping turtles were not from anywhere around this region. These waters were far too salty and warm to keep the behemoths sustained for an extended time. Castor did not have time to wonder whether this was a ploy by a rival family or a rival nation, or merely a trick of nature.

Castor continued, "These beasts are attacking townsfolk and we need to stop them. No doubt the current patrols are overwhelmed, maybe some are dead as it is. I know this isn't the practice I promised you today, but our duty to our city come first and foremost. Steel your hearts, as your friends may die today. I do not know what awaits us at the shores but we will do our duty to defend our home!"

A sturdy battle cry erupted from the crowd as sharp spears propelled in the air from the excitement that came forth. Castor saw Atticus running out from the building, a dozen xiphos and falcata bundled in his arms like a stack of firewood. He ran out and dropped the blades on the rack, oblivious to Castor's presence. He ran back in, no doubt trying to grab another armful of blades for the next group of soldiers that passed through after them. Castor smiled, glad to see the boy putting himself to use.

Castor noticed many citizens running away from the ocean as they formulated their plans. He knew every second counted as they worked their way to combat.

A large paw sat atop Castor's shoulder as he noticed Mithra joined the crowd. He had run off towards his palanquin as they left the stadium and Castor assumed he would leave, but the sharp blades of his katars that sat atop his wrists seemed to say otherwise.

"I will join you, prince of Thyma. It has been a while since I was tried in combat. May the blood of our enemies fill our glasses at tonight's banquet." Mithra growled.

The deep voice combined with the utterly primal statement the man-beast had spoken gave Castor both a reassuring sense of security as well as a shiver down his spine.

Castor nodded to the Maudian. "I appreciate it. Are you fully prepared? We should head out as soon as possible."

"I am. Lead the way." Mithra said.

"Everyone!" Castor shouted, "Form two formations of a loose phalanx, three rows of five. Form up and prepare to march!"

The group split into two equal sizes, each taking half of the participants. The spears and shields were set on shoulders and forearms, ready to march. They were close enough to protect their comrades within spear reach, but far enough away that running down the street would not cause anyone to trip over those in front or behind. The left formation held both the Sisters of the Thorns and the veterans from Acastus' century. Knowing they were the strongest of the soldiers here, he split their forces. Taking two of the sisters and four of the first century's veterans, he swapped the front lines and formed the group quickly yet efficiently. The two formations, now balanced with those who held combat experience, stood ready to follow the princes to the shore.

Nikitas left the front of the building, fully kitted out in the panoply of his hometown. He wore a solid bronze muscle cuirass painted in Kimpian colors and matched his overbearing Kimpian war helm. Instead of a typical spear and shield, he held his war maces; the very ones he used during his trials to become a Koukoulofóroi. Dual-wielding the heavy chunks of bronze and silver, he swung the weighted metal cudgels which glinted in the sun. The pure silver cores of the mace heads were in bright white contrast to the coarse windings of spiked patinated bronze that encased the partially exposed cores. The bronze twirled and wound its way around the solid silver cores like the roots of a tree. The spines only accentuated the brazen style and the core altogether looked as though the man was wielding the gnarled root ball of a great, metal pine tree. Castor remembered trying to wield one of the maces and recalled their weights were astounding. Only using proper Kimpos war dances would one be able to adequately control such a heavy weapon as an Anthoran. Castor assumed even Mithra would have trouble wielding such weapons without proper training.

"I am ready, my liege. Lead on." Nikitas said to his captain. Castor nodded in approval.

Castor moved to the front of the formation as the two phalanges followed. Nikitas and Mithra each claimed a side, their armaments ready for the first sight of conflict. The group moved through the streets of the town, hewn stone buildings within the entertainment district giving ample room for the small formations to move between. Occasionally some citizens would run through their group, splitting Castor up from the others for a few seconds before moving back into formation. The streets in this area were wide enough for three carts to pass one another, so keeping the loose formation together was no issue. The entertainment district led into the harbor district as the stone buildings regressed to wattle and daub designs. Large warehouses and an industrial layout kept the streets wide, but the roadsides had crates and barrels piled high from the crowds that fled. More and more people ran away, breaking down alleyways as they failed to break through the formations of the soldiers. Most stood to the side as the phalanges passed through the streets, many faces looking a little more relaxed after seeing the citizen guard deployed into combat.

A crowd of people, all fleeing at the same time, stormed up the road. The crowd was far more than what the passage could handle. Wild and thrashing, the mob moved forward in a sporadic and feral manner. Castor, seeing them from a distance, worried they would break against the front phalanx and cause harm to his men or his citizens. He knew a wild mob would have no logic, just moving like a flock of birds; each individual following the flow of the greater path. Castor, Nikitas, and Mithra moved to the side, hugging the coarse wall to avoid the crowd.

Castor called out to the phalanx and commanded "Form a circle!"

Like many other formations, the circular phalanx was a shape the soldier had practiced many times before. Usually used to defend against a cavalry charge or a pack of beasts, this formation was useful in binding the soldiers together and dispersing the forces from the front line to the rest in the shape. Each soldier folded in on himself and turned a little to the side, the edges of the formation turning inward and connecting in the back. Some from the centerline moved outward and only a few from the backline filled the center of the circle. Castor, Nikitas, and Mithra were safe in their location, using barrels and crates to avoid the mob. Back-to-back with shields interlocked, the stationary group stood their ground and braced for the surge of limbs and bodies.

Like a mindless horde, the crowd broke against the shields. They passed around like flowing water across smooth stones in a babbling brook. No shield budged and the phalanges stayed put, barely bothered by the clash of the crowd. As the panic moved on, the group moved back into a loose formation and continued down the path.

After passing the warehouses, the group made their way to the stalls overlooking the docks. Many stands laid open; their goods once stuck behind sealed glass containers were stolen from those taking advantage of the situation. Most stalls within this area were bulk goods traders, so their margins for loss were low, but the idea of someone looting during such a serious situation disgusted him. He could see many locked chests in the stalls though, so Castor hoped the merchants had time to lock away their valuables before fleeing for safer grounds.

Castor focused on the crystals that sat within the metal of his belt end. He summoned their stored power and focused on his body, feeling the mana flow over him. His muscles tightened, sinews binding and flesh hardening. His eyesight became focused, razor-sharp, and ready for combat. He chanted to himself, a faint hum of a prayer he always enjoyed as a child. It was a song his mother sang to him before bed, a prayer foretelling the gentle nature of Pyrros. The rhythm was slow and easy to recall. His humming continued as he focused the mana into his bones, making them tougher and reinforcing the ligaments like metal wires. He felt the mana surge from the gems during his channeling, and a slow drain came from the glowing facets as they continued down the path.

Castor kept the soldiers on the main road and walked to the edge of the wall that looked down to the port's waters. Right over the edge, a cacophony of violence and death spread across the open plaza. Many were already dead, with more to come.

Children screamed as their mother was torn apart by a pair of giant snapping turtles, their bulking shapes stationary as their heads moved like lightning. A cask of wine was broken across the stone roads which looked no different than the pools of blood that were spilled right beside it. People ran, cowered, or stood in shocked horror after seeing their friends and family dropped in front of their eyes. A few guards were spread around the area, fending off the half-dozen of monsters that stormed the beach. A total of four giant turtles sat within the lower area on this side of the peninsula. A few merchant marines laid lifelessly on the pavement, no doubt giving their lives to buy time for the wealthy merchants or traders that employed them. Yelling could be heard from the other side of town, but nothing more was in view from this vantage point. All that was left in the lower landings were fools and corpses. Castor took a deep breath and walked back to the soldiers behind him. He started to bark orders to the soldiers, planning their attack as safely as possible.

"Group one!" Castor pointed to the front phalanx that stood closer to the entrance of the staircase leading to the port. The stone stairs were spotted with drops of blood and muck from the fleeing crowds. "Follow Nikitas and move down the ramp. Hold the right flank. I do not want us to be ambushed by any more of these things."

"Group two!" Castor pointed to the front phalanx in the back, getting everyone's attention by walking around the front group, "Follow my lead to the left, we need to hold those beasts in place while the civilians evacuate."

Spears hit the pavement as confirmation for the tasks given. The first group moved out, pushing down the stairs and forming a tight wall of spears and shields once the formation made it fully to the bottom landing. Nikitas led from the front, holding the rightmost position in the phalanx, maces ready to find a weak spot on the creature. Castor started down the stairs with group two and Mithra in tow. He looked towards Nikitas, seeing him slam his foot onto the stone tiles and launch from the ground. The floor rumbled under his command. The stone below propelled him twelve feet into the air, maces overhead, before Castor turned out of view and focused on the beasts that stood ahead.

In front of Castor were the remaining three turtles on the leftmost side of the bay. One creature had an arm hanging from its beak, the last remains of the mother who valiantly protected her children from the creature. The children, petrified in fear, stared blankly at the sea. The phalanx charged in and raised their spears towards the maws of the creatures. The two turtles closest to the stairs focused their gaze on the yelling crowd.

Beaks clicked as they moved their lumbering bodies closer to the formation. Castor, moving left to distract the farthest turtle and gain its attention away from the group, barely stopped himself from running directly into a nude Kyros standing in the plaza.

Dripping wet and covered in pungent liquids, the unclad warrior fended off a powerful peck from the giant turtle with his hoplon. Bruises covered his arms and legs, but no blood seemed to be coming from the man. Small scratches and knicks covered the face and neck of the giant beast, and rivulets of blood dripped onto the floor. Kyros noticed Castor and locked shields, creating a larger surface to block the oncoming attacks.

"Hello there!" Kyros said quickly to Castor before moving his shield upward to deflect a strike from the turtle.

From behind, Mithra leaped into the fray, striking at the extended neck of the creature. His katar shot across Castor's vision like a streak of light, fast and accurate. The turtle recoiled at the quick movement, pulling its neck inward to hide within the thick, knobby shell. The extended blade glanced off the rim but struck true, piercing the fleshy skin that bundled at the border of the neck and shell.

Castor took the opportunity to grab the two children that were standing petrified in front of the horrors they had witnessed. He took the younger boy under his shield arm and tucked him against his side as he grabbed out at the little girl next to him. Neither reacted to being lifted off the ground and whisked off the battlefield. They just hung there from Castor's arms like ragdolls void of emotion. He put them down on the stairs fifty feet away. They sat there still like marionettes, as though the puppeteer that controlled their lives was absent in this stressful moment.

Another stream of blood started to flow before the whip of the neck crushed into Mithra's chest cavity. The blunt force tossed the giant aside, far enough to be out of reach for a few seconds. Castor jabbed with his spear to take the creature's attention. The pair moved to the opposite side of the beast's vision, flanking the creature and making its attention spread between the split forces.

"What happened to your armor?" Castor asked loudly.

"I was bathing! Damn things came out of the deep and started biting people into pieces!" His breath was exasperated. Castor noticed two guards were flung dead across the pavement.

"I tried to help," Kyros said glumly. "Had to grab my weapon first. I was too late."

Castor knew his friend's panoply would not hold out. Kyros' shield was cracked at the edges, the wooden layers delaminating from the barrage of impacts it had taken. The prince noticed that the shield he was holding was not even Kyros' shield. His was clad in a sheet of bronze and would have stopped such damage from occurring after a short battle. Castor assumed he claimed it from one of the dead guards.

"I can spare you some time," Castor said aloud. "Get their armor on. You can't defend yourself if you are completely unclothed." Castor broke from the small formation they had set up and took a step forward, putting himself between the creature and his naked friend.

"Much obliged," Kyros said quickly, turning on his heels and running towards the fallen body. Hand on a shoulder strap, he dragged the larger of the two guards out of the center area and near the stairs. A streak of crimson followed the body. Castor's vision was distorted as a large beak broke against his shield, a loud ding ringing through his head.

Tugged forward, he was thrown off his feet by the pull of the massive maw. He instinctively jabbed his spear forward, piercing the creature's cheek. He caught his balance as it recoiled away, but his ankle fell upon rugged terrain, rolling over and causing him to fall. He threw his shield in front of him and tucked his leg to reduce as many chances as possible for the creature to grab him again. Mithra leaped forward to strike once more, taking the opportunity of the lack of attention to get to the same location he stabbed earlier. This time, the turtle expected the move and swung its tail around, using the hardened ridges that lined its long tail to batter the cat man and crush his left arm. If his katars were not connected to his vambraces via the strapping system he had wound around his forearms, they would have likely been tossed across the plaza and into the sea.

Boats swayed in the bay as waves built upon the water's surface. The wind in the area had picked up, making ripples of light dust dance across the stone platform. Castor could see some people on the boats poking their heads out of the deck to see the battle. *Most likely travelers or merchants*, Castor thought to himself, *since they had not tried to help nor protect their goods*. His gaze made a few heads duck back under the wood decking of their triremes. He dismissed the onlookers, disregarding them and focusing on the battle ahead.

Castor jumped forward and struck at the exposed neck of the creature. It was quick, and it retracted, his attack missing by a few inches. He leapt back as the creature swung its head around to try the same move on its second opponent, but Castor was prepared and deflected the blow with his aspis, striking upward as its head glanced across the bronze. It winced in pain, giving him some room to breathe. The monstrosity's focus was set back, giving Mithra a second to recover.

The creature's eyes were bulging. It looked panicked. Castor had not the time nor willpower to care for the monstrosity. He had watched it tear a woman in half. No mercy would be given to such a beast, even if it did seem like it was forced into this situation.

Castor channeled his mana from within, reciting a few lines from the first hymns of The Laments. Mana coursed through his veins as his focus fixated on the tiles below. His steps were calculated as he pressed his bare feet onto the cool granite. He stomped the ground, finishing a line from The Lament as he did so. A pulse of energy shot through the stones a few feet away and a block of granite launched through the air towards the lumbering beast. It squirmed as the edge of the brick made contact with the creature's forehead. As tough as its skull may be, a chunk of hewn granite hurled at its skull was enough to have it take a step back towards the sea. It pulled its giant neck back into its shell and bobbed its head as more blocks, one by one, started to fly at its vulnerable spots.

Castor continued his chanting as his feet moved to the rhythm of the song. Step by step, he started launching stones as each verse was completed. Each verse, around five seconds in length, gave a guttural pulse to the floor as he landed his foot on the last note. In his core, he could feel his mana pool being spent as each pulse rippled across the floor away from his point of contact.

The rugged yet refined dance he performed slowed his mana expulsion. Stone by stone, the wave of rocks launched towards the target. The large, bony head bobbed and weaved as it could, but a few more stones made contact with their prey. The clashing of stone on bone let out a deep thud on contact. Mithra took this time to recover his stamina and check his push blades for damage. Crossing paths with a stream of stones and an angry beast was not something even a foolhardy exiled prince would consider in mortal combat.

The beast pushed back into a metaphorical corner and lashed out at its attacker. Head fully tucked into its shell, it charged forward at Castor. Each step rumbled the plaza. It moved quite fast for such a lumbering monstrosity. Its muscles were built for short, quick bursts. Stones continued to hurl through the air until the creature was upon him. He tucked his shield and braced his stance, knowing he took too long to dodge the charge.

The head collided with his bronze aspis and the force launched his entire body off the ground. The physical augmentations he applied to his skeleton and muscles kept his bones from breaking, but just barely. He felt his humerus within his shield arm deflect in a way that would not normally stay together if he had not applied the augmentations to his bones. The impact could be felt across his body as he was sent careening through the air. After a few seconds of hang time, he landed on a vendor stall, ripping through the yellow shade cloth that covered the shop. The tear that formed caused the support structure to unbalance, and the split fabric collapsed onto him.

The fabric folded and bunched around him on the ground, clumps of light material forming and overlapping layers trapping him beneath. He gripped and pulled the flowing sheets left and right to no avail. Some areas sat off the ground, suspended from the chests and stands of now crushed fruits that were placed around the stall. He could see some openings, but none that were easily accessible. As he considered his options, the indent of a large testudinal face flashed across the fabric before embedding into the tile below. The movement took place a handful of feet away from Castor's body.

The irregular shapes beneath the cloth must confuse the crazed animal, Castor thought to himself during this momentary respite. He knew he had little time to recover from this situation before a massive beak would impale him. He was too far from an opening to escape without being caught and the blinding material made striking back at attacks all but impossible. He considered his options.

After a few seconds of dabbling, he assumed his best choice was to use the fabric to his advantage. He grabbed a melon that sat broken on the pavers to his right. Using a small burst of wind, he launched the fruit at a crate farther off under the fabric. The collision made the display stand of apples and pomegranates sway and collapse, creating much movement on the right side of the collapsed shade cloth. A few seconds later, a strike lands near the impact. The creature lashed out at any noticeable movements it could see. Castor took this opportunity to remove his shield and spear from his hands and prepare for a large burst of channeling. He tapped into the stored energy within himself as well as those within his silver bracelet, the deep blue sapphires emanating a now dim light. He formed the idea of what he planned within his head and gave as much detail to the image as his mind could muster.

As the head was still in contact with the ground, Castor shot forth a massive blast of wind from either side of himself, encompassing any fabric that laid upon the ground. The wind whipped through the small gaps in the textile and enveloped the mass as his mana steadily drained. He manipulated the winds once they completed their initial task and pushed outward. The tattered cloth propelled forward, wrapping around the beak of the turtle and swaddling the entirety of its neck and head.

The beast stumbled back, dazed and confused. Castor's vision was returned as the area around was exposed. He could see the children still sitting in awe on the stairs. Kyros was garbed and working with Mithra to push the blinded turtle back towards the water. It seemed their strategy was working well. Little by little, they were whittling down the crazed beasts.

Thirty feet away, the phalanx held its ground against the two turtles they were pitted against. The pair of gigantic creatures focused their attacks on individuals within the formation, but the firm wall of wood and bronze held against the oncoming attackers. High attacks were met with spear tips, low attacks were met with bronze greaves. The interlocked shields dispersed the impacts to not wear a single person's stamina down. A few in the backline had extended columns of fire past their spear ends, increasing their lengths and frightening the wild animals.

From behind, Nikitas launched through the air. Another attack from above gave him ample time to plan his swings. As one who has attempted to join the ranks of the Koukoulofóroi, his technique and prowess with his dual maces were unparalleled outside of his home region of Kimpos. As he maneuvered atop the stone block that had set his aerial attack in motion, he performed his battle meditation. Eyes closed, his body started to move in the wind like a spinning top. Building momentum, one rotation after another, his body moved in inhuman ways. His arms looked as though they were limp, pulling the maces around him as tightly as possible. His speed only increased as he sailed into the sky and his arc started its downward span. As he fell his speed picked up, even more, wind propelling him around, quicker and quicker until his whirling resembled that of a windstorm.

The turtles, now interested in the flying object, broke their relentless attacks. One focused on Nikitas as the other continued to attack the formation. It tucked its neck in and prepared to strike. Tension built within his giant neck; a muscle larger than any on an Anthoran body. The tightened tendons snapped like a bowstring, launching out at breakneck speeds and aiming for the Kimpian soldier.

It was too slow.

Across the open plaza, a loud, deafening crack was heard. Nikitas had manipulated his downward speed as he fell with the wind he had been using to increase his gyrations. The beast missed its mark, and Nikitas took the opportunity to deliver a devastating blow to its vitals. The beast was massive in comparison to the smaller bipeds that they were in combat with, but the size of the warriors mattered not. One mace, now extended at maximum rotational velocity, pulverized the top of the giant turtle's head. It's hard endoskeleton caved in on itself as the ball of twisted metal passed through the skull of the creature. Bone snapped and skin ripped as the gnarled ball eviscerated the giant creature. At such speed, the ball of twisted metal barely slowed as it sent a section of the beast's head off in a sailing arc. It finished its path of destruction as it passed through the creature's lower jaw, splitting it asunder. As quick as the strike had taken hold, the thunderclap of the impact was heard across the area. The giant, lifeless body dropped to the floor as the last moment of its life passed.

Nikitas, slowing to a halt after the act was complete, dropped unscathed to the ground. He retreated behind the phalanx and sat, his action taking a toll on his stamina and mana supply. Such a feat was nigh impossible for someone average at his age and completing such an act was worthy of a quick break during combat. With the number of opponents halved, the formation held easier and had no issue giving refuge to the tired hero.

Castor was about to run across the platform to check on Nikitas before he noticed a group of soldiers on the docks. A few merchant marines appeared at the end of one pier, no doubt coming from one of the triremes that were harbored there. They wore colors loyal to a merchant family from the island city of Cleotidus. The orange and gray armor they wore was painted brilliantly. They were paid well enough by the family to protect their cargo during maritime travel. Their armor was much like what Castor wore currently, light and breathable, yet defensive enough to protect the wearer from most impacts. Their head protection was of an older, heavier design, and was made of two plates of solid bronze riveted together down the ridge of the helmet. The javelins they lofted and the pelta shield that hung from their other arm were lightweight and more suited for marine combat. They held a single short spear in their main hand and had four more held in the off-hand behind their large crescent shields. Their family crest was painted vividly on the center of the pelta, the orange fish painted in bright detail on the gray background. The seven of them jumped off their trireme and onto the wood docks that jutted out across the water in the bay.

They were able to make it to the stone landing before the turtle attacking the second phalanx took interest in them. It turned and stomped towards them. Its tail whipped around and narrowly missed the front line of the second phalanx. It shot its neck out at the peltasts, nipping and biting at their smaller shields. They dodged out of the way, their light armor allowing for much more mobile movements. One peltast rolled away from the stampeding creature and threw his spear with the forward momentum, driving its shaft into the back of the beast's knee. It whipped its tail around to push the men away, but they easily pushed themselves back. Some channeled the air around themselves to propel their bodies back, making their movements akin to leaves in a heavy draft. Skilled with their acrobatics, the men spread themselves around the creature and prodded it to find weaknesses between its thick outer armor.

Castor smiled, happy to see progress being made. But his happiness was short-lived. The blinded turtle that was still enveloped with cloth was no longer being pushed back. It seemed the small stabs and cuts the katars and spears had given it only pushed it towards an animalistic rage. A dry, raspy hiss came from the beast, and it stampeded forward. Its head was well protected by the layers of cloth, and its shell was fully intact. The behemoth barreled into the loudest source of noise that was near it: the leftmost phalanx. Their attention was fixated on the second of the turtles so their flank was exposed. The lumbering brute pushed into the phalanx and pressed its advantage. Limbs snapped as small arms were pressed into the ground by giant, stubby flippers. The skin was cut and blood flew as sword-sized claws ripped through the lines. Some tried to face the beast but were met with pain and sorrow. The formation was broken, many losing their will to defend from multiple sides.

The second turtle took the opportunity to single a guard out who was fleeing back to the stairs. Phineas had let his guard down, turning his back on the enemy in full retreat. A large beak pierced through the air and crashed into his left calf. The bronze greaves dampened the blow and stopped the attack from tearing his leg clean off, but the metal crumpled under the pressure and dug into his flesh. He yelped in pain and fell to the ground. The sharp bill of the turtle retracted and assailed again, this time aiming for his shoulder. He tried to block but was too slow. His shield came up too low and the beast impaled his muscle with the top point of his bony mouth. Phineas howled in pain and dropped his shield, clawing and gripping at the source of the anguish like a wild animal defending himself. His small fingers made no difference to the giant snapping turtle and its osseous jaw. The beast lifted him into the air and shook his body, stunning and disorienting its prey. Over a few seconds, Phineas' hope of survival disappeared.

A few Sisters of the Thorns still held their ground against the beast and together they struck at what little areas they could to distract it. A few spearheads met their marks and stuck into the thick skin of the creature's neck, but none were strong enough to draw blood. Upon the irritation of those below, the turtle released its grip at the vertex of its whipping motion, throwing the limp body across the plaza and causing it to splatter against the back wall. The human projectile barely missed one of the soldiers from the first century who was rallying the fleeing troops. Phineas bounced lifelessly against the wall next to the staircase and his limp frame slowly tumbled down the stairs, becoming completely still as he dropped off the last stair.

Unacceptable. These were wild beasts. Castor thought as rage filled his mind. Phineas was his soldier, his life was within his hands, not the hands of fate. What terrible stroke of luck would befall one of the weakest of the group at such an inconvenient time. Castor knew no clemency was found on the battlefield. He knew violence only begets violence. But he knew Phineas was only here to train and earn money for his village. He aspired to be a potter, not a soldier. Castor was the soldier. He was the prince. It was *his* duty to put *his* life on the line for *his* people, not the other way around. Castor suppressed his rage, as he knew it would only cloud his judgment. He rose from the ground with a little bit of extra energy begetting his steps to avenge his fallen man.

The wrapped turtle continued to recklessly plow through any group that made noise around it. When the Sisters of the Thorns took their chance to distract the beast from continuing to violate Phineas' body, the creature stomped through their line. They were some of the most novice members of the Sisters of the Thorns and their experience in combat the complete opposite in status of the Matrons of the Thorned Roses like Didyma. They were not a part of the upper echelons of the Thorns, so their skills and capabilities were still limited. While they tolerated the barrage of attacks from the unhindered turtle and the sporadic charges of the blinded turtle, the attrition of battle could be seen in their slowing responses. As a turtle stampeded through their line, one was crushed under the webbed foot of the beast.

The weight was incomparable to human standards, as though a boulder had fallen on the woman's chest. Her bronze cuirass, although hardened and chiseled to deflect forces, was not much more than a temporary abatement as the full weight crushed the armor and her chest cavity. Blood launched out of her mouth as her organs were crushed and her bones were broken. Her life bond stood next to her in the formation as life bonds were bound to do. After the beast moved through and she noticed what had occurred, she quickly knelt next to her dying love as the beast continued to plow across the courtyard. She tried what she could to help her, small bouts of magic to try and staunch the bleeding, but the damage was far too much to recover from. The fallen warrior gurgled blood, trying to take a breath that had no lungs to go to. She smiled at her best friend before her eyes glazed over. The tense muscles in her arms and neck went limp, and she passed. The kneeling Sister hugged the lifeless body gently, caressing her and rocking back and forth. The others tried to keep the beast distracted as she was forced to pull the body of her life bond across the cold, damp stones and gently lay her against a wall away from the action.

Castor knew the life bond of a Sister of the Thorns was important to their order. These women, either infatuated with others of their gender or having poor relations with men, were a strictly female order who mainly interacted with other women. They were bonded together at a young age with a single significant other and never left their side so long as both lived. The relationship did not need to be romantic, as many of the Sisters had platonic loving relationships. Castor knew the life bond was the most important person in one's life as a Sister. Losing your life bond, and at such a young age, would be devastating. Castor knew to stay clear of the Sister as the battle continued. He heard of stories of the unbonded Sister going into an unbridled rage when such events took place.

As the scene unfolded, such an event did take place. The Sister, now blinded by her hate and agony, flew at the beast. The cloth on the turtle's eyes and head had fallen by this point and its vision recovered. The extra senses it had now bolstered its accuracy, but it seemed to not affect the Sister. Her movements were crude and lacked grace but were easily on par with Mithra or Nikitas. The mana she was consuming was far exceeding what Castor could maintain at one time from his mana pool. Women were naturally more skilled in controlling mana, but this usage was due to her mental state.

Like a broken flood gate, the mana she kept inside her was washing through her body and was being consumed at a rapid pace. No longer did the Sister wield her shield, but instead replaced it with her sidearm, a bronze kopis around two feet in length. She stabbed at the creature and deflected its retaliations with the flat of her blade. A hefty strike from her kopis landed on the beast's eye, cutting deeply and blinding it on its left side. Her intensity did not falter with her successful attacks. Her speed was on par with the beast and her strikes were able to land with impunity as she danced around the creature's front half. Her anger was felt across the area, with no one, not even her fellow sisters, to try and dissuade her from this wonton barrage. Castor only hoped they could finish the fight before her mana was spent. With how she was now, he worried she would start to kindle her own body to continue her fight. The damage the kindling could do to her would not be something she could recover from.

Mithra ran over to Castor as they tried to lead the partially blinded turtle away from the fleeing crowds. The peltasts had joined them, leaving the unblinded turtle who killed Phineas to the other Sisters and the remaining veterans from Acastus' first century. The veterans had taken the front line and augmented their shields with water, much like how they had during their practice session. With their lives on the line, they held nothing back. Their bodies were augmented and their skin was hardened. The water swirling around their shields was glistening with small particles of sand and stone floating along the currents. The Sisters behind, looking inspired by their fallen comrade, spent their mana as well and channeled fire to the tips of their spears. Short columns of fire, condensed and focused into a tight hot beam, extended less than a foot from the ends of their spears. The formation moved against the bloodied beast.

"Son of Thyma, I have a request," Mithra spoke gruffly to Castor as they led the beast across the plaza with feints and jabs.

"What is it?" Castor asked shortly, his stamina still recovering from his time under the broken cloth tent.

"I plan to attack the beast from behind." Mithra explained in vague detail, "I request that you keep your soldiers here and distract it from the front."

"Alright, I see no issue with that," Castor said. "I doubt I would dissuade that Sister from attacking the creature head-on anyway." He saw the Sister continuing her attacks on the beast. Her movements were more controlled now, the wear of constant mana drain showing its taxation on her body.

"Do not relent. I will not need support." the Maudian purred. He advanced towards the blind side of the creature, stalking around on all four limbs like an animal. Great Maudians were very mobile and flexible creatures who were feared on the battlefield. Their sharp claw blades were known for their accuracy and gruesome injuries. While not the best weapons against large creatures such as these, the katars Mithra wielded were tough enough to be used efficiently in the right situation and thick enough to last through the battle ahead.

Mithra ran to the aid of the berserk Sister, striking at the beast's back left leg and drawing blood. The beast whipped its tail around to strike the cat man. Mithra dodged the strike, dropping to one knee and arching his back. Like a compressed spring, he built up forces in his already reinforced back muscles. As the stubby tail flew over his head, he struck upward with his katars and sunk the foot-long blades into the beast's meaty flesh. They made contact between the armored ring segments and cut through the fletch until they were deep enough to come in contact with the tissues surrounding the tail bones. The thick tail flexed and the beast bade a deep roar, clearly in pain from the metal's incisions. The tail flexed and turned, locking his push daggers in between the segments of hardened keratin.

It whipped the tail back and forth to build up momentum. At first, this barely impacted Mithra, as his arms were pulled and strained his shoulder muscles. As the forces increased, he started to lose his footing. The beast twisted its body and continued to get more and more momentum built within its tail, trying to dislodge the attacker. Mithra also tried to remove his blades from the meaty tail, but neither was successful.

Their discordant attempts only furthered the katars deeper into the muscle and sinew. The creature reacted suddenly as the blade made contact with the bone. The pain must have been excruciating, as the creature reared up on its hind legs and dropped to the ground, bringing its entire weight down on the bay stones. Tiles cracked around the clawed feet of the beast; the impact sent stone chips flying in all directions.

The momentum of the beast falling to the ground whilst whipping its tail launched Mithra into the sky. His katars dislodged from the hard carapace rings as the creature flexed the muscles in its tail while it fell. Mithra sailed through the air, completely free from the beast. His launch was unpredicted, but he found a location to land as he used small air currents to steady his course and slow his impact. He narrowly dodged the end of a wooden crane that was used to lift cargo from the boats. A bronze pulley struck his head as he passed by. His large body made contact with the stone side of a tall guard tower. He collapsed the wall and the upper floor collapsed around him. Dust filled the air as the stones piled on the second story.

"No!" Castor yelled. The damage looked excessive. Castor was not sure if the cat man was capable of augmenting his body to protect himself from such blunt force trauma. He saw many gems faceted to his armor and crown but was not sure to what extent he could channel the mana stored within. He hoped he was properly trained and the gems were not just for decoration. He had a good chance of surviving if so.

He did not have the time to check on the exiled prince of Thrim. He hoped he had survived.

Castor and Kyros held a small formation as the turtle continued to fight the three of them, the Sister leading the assault and the two hoplites filling in when she tired. She had been bitten in the torso by the turtle's beaked maw, but the tip of his beak was not strong enough to pierce the bronze carapace that she had worn. Try as it might, the vain attempt to pierce her armor once it had bit down only gave her time to cleave at its head with her kopis and leave a large gash above its left eye. The strike nearly met its mark, but the creature was still able to see.

The battle had far exceeded what Castor had planned for the day, and his mana reserves were nowhere near full. He had cut his augmentations from his chest and legs, just bolstering his arms at this point to reduce any potential bone damage from the blunt impacts of the turtle. He still had a decent amount left and what was stored within the gems of his sword, belt, and torc. He had to make sure he kept enough in case a dire situation arose again.

From the east, screams filled the air. The phalanx at Nikitas' disposal was now met with the attacks of three turtles. While one was dead on the ground by the edge of the water, two more had shown up from down the coast. Castor said a quick prayer to whoever was pitted against the beasts before, as their lumbering presence here meant they had failed. The phalanx had taken a beating, with chunks taken out of different shields in the front lines and spearheads snapped off after lodging into hard areas on the turtles.

Nikitas was on his feet again, recovered after a short battle hymn on the ground. His shining silver and bronze maces swung through the air and collided with one turtle's beak, cracking the keratinous surface and sending small chips to fall to the rough floor. He led the formation from the right side and protected their unshielded flank. He stood a few feet away to give himself enough room to swing his weapons without risk to the other soldiers.

Castor looked at Kyros and saw he was tiring, but a smile never left his face. He knew the mercenary was well skilled in fighting monsters and hoped they could all continue with his level of calmness.

"Do you have any ideas on what to do?" Castor asked Kyros as they defended against another strike of the turtle's beak.

The turtle's head bounced forward again, but this time Castor could feel the weight behind the strike. His lack of augmentations was noticeable, and he hoped they could keep up with the beast.

"I think the Sister is doing a great job at whittling it down." Kyros explained, jabbing his spear in a feint towards the creature's remaining eye.

Kyros pointed to the turtle. "Look."

Castor noticed the creature had slowed considerably since the beginning of its fight with the berserker. Its blood had pooled on the hewn tiles, making the surface slippery and wet. Its front right leg had slid on the spilled red goo and it had lost its footing before recovering. While the humans and Maudian within the courtyard were tired, they were not as bloody as the beasts. The only creatures not fully worn down from combat were the turtles that had moved in from the eastern flank.

"Alright, split from me." Castor said." Support the Sister."

"Oh? bossing me around now, are we?" Kyros joked as they broke their shield wall. "I'll have you know that I am still under contract by the trade guild. So I am not sure if your command even holds weight right n---."

Kyros was pulled forward by the bite of the turtle and the shield was twisted. He turned his body with the motion and recovered his poise. Releasing his spear, he drew his xiphos and held it in a reverse grip. He stabbed upward and skewered the beast in the jaw, causing it to release its locked jaw.

"No time for jokes, it seems." Kyros frowned before winking and charging the creature. He stood far enough away from the Sister that he wouldn't be within spear reach. Their attack kept the creature at bay.

Castor moved to the left side of the beast, which was focused on Kyros and the Sister. He started to use the remaining power in his belt's gems to channel into the air around him. He ran at the turtle from its centerline and leapt. The wind carried his armored body through the air and he landed with a thud on the large shell.

The turtle was surprised and tried to buck him. It bent its knees back and forth, creating an undulating pattern. Castor steadied his stance and focused some mana into his thighs to give him better balance. The beast swung its tail back onto the shell, but it was not long enough to reach where he was standing. It could not bite backward. It was caught in a stalemate.

This momentary distraction allowed Kyros to stab the creature in its now unguarded neck. The bronze pierced the underside of its neck skin and severed some muscles. It croaked in pain. The Sister vaulted forward and hacked at it with her kopis while keeping her spear blade in the creature's jaw. A few strikes in short succession let a torrent of blood flow from the beast. It struck back, but its blood loss was taking a toll on its reactions now.

The attacks on the ground distracted the creature from the person who rode upon its hard shell. Castor stood above its front portion now, his feet straddling the areas where its head connected to its body. He grabbed his xiphos with both hands. His shield hung from his arm near the elbow, connected to him but not in the way of the blade. He channeled mana through the blade with the gems he had stored in its pommel. The energy flowed down the core of the weapon and focused on the tip. He said a small prayer to Ignus and a bright white flame shot from the end. It enveloped the top five inches of the weapon and the handle was getting hot, the fire burning as hot as a fully lit forge. The beast's fate was sealed before it could react to the searing heat.

He plunged the blade down into the beast's neck. At first, the blade did not sink far into it. The bright flames sizzled as he pushed down and the hard knobby skin shrunk as the flames bit at the exposed surfaces. Liquids bubbled as he forced the sharp metal deeper into its neck. The creature tried to turn, tried to flee into the water, but it was too slow. With a bellowing shout, Castor forced the blade to its hilt and severed the creature's spine. The thin piece of sharpened bronze slid through a disc between vertebrae and severed its spinal cord. The beast dropped instantly to the ground as its brain lost connection with its body. With the heated edges still cutting through flesh and tendons, Castor pushed left with his top hand and right with his bottom hand and the blade turned within the neck. The movement parted half of the creature's neck with a swift motion. His blade was freed and the skin sizzled as it came to open air. He steadied

[157]

himself on the now fallen beast before confirming the creature was dead. It was.

The Sister screamed, overcome with emotion. She stormed off towards the other turtles and ran past the second phalanx, which had rallied the retreating troops and started to leave heavy damage on the turtle it had been in combat with since the beginning of the encounter. She joined the first phalanx on their left flank and started to attack the leftmost turtle.

As Castor landed on the ground, Kyros grabbed him and steadied his balance. He expended a lot of mana up on that shell and needed to take a short break before joining the combat again. He watched as the others fought valiantly against the beasts. The second phalanx, battered and bruised, held their ground against their last turtle. Three guards were on the ground, either dead or passed out. One had been stepped on after falling and had her legs broken. The others dragged their fallen comrades out of the area as they could, either when the beast retreated or when the peltasts had distracted it with a volley of javelins.

A brief catching of breath gave Castor the energy he needed to continue. Kyros had torn a piece of fabric from a fallen civilian and bandaged a cut on his right leg. The wound was just above his right knee, missing the delicate area by only a few inches. He had a small pouch of Vótanodor, the healing drought, tied to his belt. The little bottle popped open with ease and he put a bit under the bandage as he tied it tight. The pressure and trickle of mana from his reserves sealed his wound and kept him from further damaging the area. The battle raged on as Castor and Kyros made their way over to the second phalanx.

The turtles had started to push the formations back. The single turtle facing off against the second phalanx had taken its toll on their numbers, with half the group either dead or injured. It seemed most were injured, as he could see a few people on the stairs tending to each other's wounds. Vara was slumped against the wall next to Phineas, who was covered with a cloth at this point. The mangled mess was not something she could stand to see, as her injuries were bad enough on their own. Seeing a lifelong friend die in front of you was a horrible atrocity that Castor hoped he would never have to deal with.

The far flank was also being pushed back. The enraged Sister was slowed and was barely deflecting attacks at this point. Her kopis was bent halfway down the blade and turned outward a few inches by the tip. Nikitas was holding his ground while he quietly hummed his battle chants. He could not hold all the enemies back though, and the first phalanx was trying to hold the enemies back from all sides. Their numbers only dropped a handful by this point, as they were stagnant in the formation for most of the combat, but the constant holding of a tight formation was taking its toll on even the least expended. Castor examined the battlefield and considered their options.

Kyros was not such a tactician and ran into combat on the eastern front. He saw an opening by the exhausted Sister and pressed his advantage. The Sister held her ground a few paces back as the creature pushed forward. Suddenly, she collapsed. Her body dropped to the ground slowly and with arms extended. Her exhaustion had caught up to her. One of the soldiers in the back of the first phalanx broke formation and dragged her away from the battle, her weak grunts and moans in protest to leaving the combat. Kyros filled the gap and held off the northmost turtle in her stead.

He stabbed upward as a turtle bit out at the flank of the first phalanx and made contact with the skin under its chin. The extended blade glanced off a patch of hardened carapace and shot upward. The turtle reacted with the twitch of its neck and bashed into Kyros, sending him sprawling across the floor. He rolled with the motion to dampen the blow and came up to defend himself with his battered shield. Castor was making his way over to the fray before the creature focused its barrage on the mercenary.

Thump, went the creature's head against the wood shield. *Thud*, went the hardened beak against the splintering wood. He was building his stamina for another attack. The constant fatigue and loss of blood had dulled his senses, but he continued. Kyros prepared for another strike before a third impact made contact with his shield.

Crack.

The shield splintered under the forces of the large beak. Pieces of wood fragmented and launched through the air. A large shard broke off and embedded in his elbow, piercing the skin and damaging his joint. The beak now slowed, pushed through the shattered shield and into his arm. It opened its mouth and chomped down onto his bicep. Tissue severed as the giant maw tore a chunk out of his flesh. Kyros yelled in pain as the retracting head brought ripped skin with it. Blood pooled down his arm as he grabbed at the open wound.

Leaping off the ground and with great speed, Castor flung at the beast's head with his xiphos fully extended. He continued his attacks, keeping his shield close and focusing his mana within his body. He pulled all the stores he had left. He was not planning to lose anyone else in this battle, much less his best friend.

His attacks were quick and accurate. Each strike continued into the new swing. A strong stab was met with the beast flinching. He took this time to continue his flurry with a heavy overhand strike. The thick of the blade cut deeply into the forehead of the creature. It tried to retreat its head, but Castor shot forward with a gust of wind. His shield pushed into the creature's face and blinded it from his continuing attacks. He rotated his shoulder and drove the blade upward into the underbelly of its neck where the skin was thinner. It cut a great gash in the monster's skin and blood pooled. He did not relent.

He pointed his middle, ring, and pinky finger outward away from his sword hand. They stood straight out, perpendicular to the blade. With a soft breath, he chanted to Ignus for strength. His was as follows:

Ignus, who has lit the darkness of the world,
May you find my prayer, though unworthy,
among your graces.

May you pour into me your light unshadowed,
that I may sing your flame's perfect praises.

His sincere request was honored with a purging flame, three feet in length and bright orange. The conflagration was focused out of his extended fingers and lit the area around him. His sword, still within his grasp via his pointer finger and thumb, bobbed around in the wind that came from the flame's torrent. He aimed the fire at the creature's head, and it recoiled. The bright flame cut through the creature, boiling blood and bubbling flesh. He struck it with an overhand strike across the brow and the flames burned the creature's eyes. It quailed in fear of the primal flame that struck its soft tissue.

Castor's anger, his pent-up rage, boiled over into his bloodlust for those that maimed and killed his friends. He cared no longer for the circumstances that brought them to his town. No matter how accursed their situation, such defilement of those who were dear to him would not be taken lightly.

Castor did not relent. He continued to burn the flame into the creature, step by step, as he let the heat soak into the creature's skull. It tried to recoil, tried to pull back before it had nowhere for its head to go. Its head was as recoiled into its shell as far as it could be. Slowly the creature lost its animosity and overheated. As seconds grew to a full minute, the turtle's life gave into the inferno that seared it.

Skin sizzled and heat built as Castor came back to his senses. The creature laid still; a crevasse sat where its brow once was. He became lightheaded as the blessing he received started to wear off. He fell to the ground and sat. His shield was held over him, but he was still an easy target for those around him. Three turtles still stood in battle, and their stamina was running low. Castor could hear Kyros grunting behind him as he tended to his wounds, but he had not the energy to turn around and support him. He barely had the energy to sit up and keep his bronze aspis in front of his vitals.

The first phalanx had many more wounded pulled from battle and the second phalanx all but collapsed. Only a few held their spots. All hope was lost before a rumbling came from above the docks. Castor saw a turtle turn its attention to him and his wounded friend, the blood from Kyros' arm showing weakness to the frenzied beasts. He tried to get up, but his legs would not follow orders. His final fight had drained his mana pull to its limits. Even the gems across his outfit were run dry. He tucked his legs in and hid behind the bronze shield, expecting the impact to toss him across the platform. The bloodied Atropethian turtle recoiled its neck and prepared to strikeout. Some of the soldiers noticed and tried to shift the formation to block the incoming strike, but they were too far away to do so. Castor braced himself for the attack.

But none came.

A large shard of ice shot across the open platform and crushed into the turtle, striking right near the base of its shell near its neck. It pulled back, surprised by the barrage. Another bolt of cold crystal impacted the creature near the same spot, this time striking into the hard skin that was below the rim of the shell. The chunk of ice exploded on contact and small pieces of frozen water skittered across the stone tiles.

As Castor looked to the top of the wall near the platform. Standing atop were the reinforcements for which he was hoping. A few soldiers and mages stood near the rim. At their center was the current prince of Thyma, Hecantor Daimos. Castor knew they had been saved.

CHAPTER 7

Dust Falls Onto Crooked Boards

19th of Beryl, 453 of the Age of Discovery

eaning upon his gold cane, Hecantor stood at the top of the stairway. The soldiers behind him rushed down the steps and onto the battlefield. The fifty or so soldiers he had run into on his way to the docks followed him instantly when they saw their lord out of his office. He adjusted his weight and shifted his stance, surveying the open area and the carnage that had taken hold.

His gray beard and curly hair were matted from his walk to the shore. He leaned heavily on his cane, which sparkled in the sunlight where the rays caught the many facets of his masterfully cut gems. Cabochons and cushions bedazzled the gold inlays on the collar of the handle. The plum wood that made the shaft of the cane was gnarled and the grain was bold. The ferrule came to a dull point and stuck into the ground, gripping the hewn stone tightly. His outfit was as regal as expected from the highest-ranking official on this side of Anthora. His flowing robe was the color of honey and his mantle was a dark orange, closer to the color of rust or apricots. The entire outfit was embroidered with geometric shapes in repeating patterns that added a pleasing style to the prince's attire. His eyepatch matched his outfit, no doubt made to pair with his official garbs. The scar that went from his upper brow to his jawline was partially covered by the eyepatch and its embroidered leather straps.

Before the attack, Castor assumed Hecantor was either partaking in official government meetings or was at the courthouse for a trial. Those buildings were far away for the maimed prince to travel by foot, but Castor was happy to see him, nonetheless.

Next to Hecantor, wings tucked and feet stationary, sat his pet eagle. Apopsi pecked at stone bits scattered across the ground. Hecantor called the bird to his arm, and it perched on the patterned leather wrapping he wore on his left arm. As it landed, its attention seemed to focus, and Hecantor closed his eyes. A light flow came from the gems on Hecantor's cane and the bird started to survey the area. Castor was always impressed with his father's natural gifts with animals, but the ability to overtake his pet's senses was astounding. The bird's glare focused on Castor before Hecantor opened his eyes and the eagle dropped to the ground and went back to pecking at anything it found interesting. As he overlooked the courtyard with his remaining eye, he saw his son and pointed. A few guards were called over with the flick of his wrist.

Hecantor wore his prince's crown upon his brow, which was something Castor did not see his father wear too often. The splendidly detailed gold diadem along with their leader added morale to the wavering troops, which was further bolstered by the phalanx reinforcements and magical support. As the main unit reinforced the phalanges, the few soldiers that Hecantor had spoken to were bee-lining it straight for Castor. They dodged the raining ice shards and incoming javelins that flew across the battleground.

When he shifted his weight, the movement caused Apopsi to shift away, scuttering sideways to bump slightly into Didyma. It stepped on the hem of her flowing blue cloak. She looked down only for a second to ensure the bird had not damaged the white fur trimming, and then returned to viewing giant turtles. Her focus was broken for only a fraction of a second, but her glare focused back on her injured target. Bolts of ice shot across the square and punctured the Atropethian turtles between their bone plates and hardened skin. As she dialed in her aim, the barrage of frost flew more viciously across the way.

Didyma Pentalon was a sight to behold. As one of the Matrons of the Thorned Roses, she had an air of importance to uphold in public. For a woman in her sixties, she was majestic. Her upturned nose and dark brown eyes were fashionable for Anthorans, and many men fawned over the chaste Sister of the Thorns many decades ago. The wrinkles on her face only added to her wise and dangerous visage. She wore a long indigo dress with a tall collar. The ornate collection of gems that she wore within her baroque necklace was large and stylish. Many patterns were seen within the folds of her clothing, all of which would normally clash if worn in any other combination. But Didyma did not allow such details to cause her problems. She made sure all aspects of her life, including her outfit, were designed with the intent she wanted.

She continued to hail shards of frost upon the enemy before her beastly target finally fell. The single turtle facing the second phalanx was her main concern since it was the closest to the stairs and the injured soldiers. As she honed her attacks, she had started to increase the length of the crystals whilst making them come to a sharper point. At this point, the turtle had been skewered six times prior by her bolts of ice. It had opened its mouth to bellow in pain. Didyma sent one long splinter of rime directly into its open maw and pierced it to its core. The beast could not react fast enough as the ice drove its way into its head cavity and out the back. The creature dropped dead to the floor, blood pooling around its head and neck.

Castor at this point was being lifted by the two soldiers his father had sent. At first, they tried to lift him and carry him away, but he rejected their support and only allowed them to help him to his feet. He had caught his breath at this point and, although in no shape to continue fighting, focused his attention on Kyros. His usually smiley friend was in a state of shock and seemed only focused on his torn bicep. Muscle was missing from where it should have been. The skin was torn from the area and blood was pooling down his arm into his clothing. Castor directed the soldier to help Kyros off the frontlines and helped direct them to the stairs where most other injured were.

As they pulled him against the wall, Kyros yelled out in pain. Castor tried to calm him, but Kyros was not dissuaded from his fit. The blood loss would be catching up to him soon and Castor knew they had little time before more permanent damage would occur. At that moment, Castor saw a small boy carrying a jug of Vótanodor down the stairs.

It was Atticus.

Most likely prompted by those within the barracks, the young boy had carried a large amphora down the city streets towards the battle and delivered the payload to the front lines. Castor got off of his knees and walked briskly to the boy.

"Here!" Atticus said, lofting the container into Castor's arms. With how weak his body had become, the container almost slipped out of his grasp had it not been for the handles that were built into the sides of the storage vessel. He let it slowly slip to the ground and let it softly make contact with the hard stone. Castor had tears in his eyes, as he knew what this supply could mean for the wounded and dying.

"Thank you, Atticus," Castor said, choking back tears. The boy looked worried, but Castor rubbed his short curly hair with his hand that was less bloody and reassured him. He called over a few of the soldiers that were tending to the wounded and told them to divide the salve amongst the wounded.

"Do not worry." Castor continued to Atticus, "You did great. What you just did saved many lives. I am very happy that I met you today."

The boy beamed but looked concerned after examining Castor. To Castor's surprise, he was bleeding heavily on his left leg. It looked as though, either from fragmentation from damaged equipment or a glancing strike of the turtles, a large open gash was visible on his thigh. While the straps of leather that hung from his belt protected him from nine out of every ten attacks, this time it did not. Castor grabbed a handful of the salve from the container and slathered it onto his wound. With the little bit of mana he had left, he channeled it into the thick goo to catalyze the healing process. The now glowing blue salve started to seal the wound as Castor wiped the excess blood away.

A soldier handed him a strip of fabric. He saw a wounded guard next to him, pierced through the chest, who had his tunic completely ripped from his body to give the impromptu medics more visibility to the wound. The cloth he wrapped around his thigh was clean from what he could see. Tying it off, he tried his weight on both, and then one, leg.

"Atticus, listen to me." Castor grabbed the boy by the head with his hands. He made sure to focus the boy's attention on his words.

"I am very happy with what you did. But I need you to leave this area."

"But I can--!" the boy started but closed his mouth when he saw how serious Castor had gotten.

"You did a great thing, bringing us this salve," Castor said again in a stern voice, "but I need you to get away from this area. It is no place for a boy your age. This is in no way a punishment for me looking down on you. But I need you to listen to me. Do you understand? I need you to run back up that street and return to the barracks. See if they need any more help up there if you are still eager. Do you understand?"

"Yes." Atticus said confidently. He nodded every time Castor asked him if he understood. He had no reason to argue with Castor, as Castor was the only person to truly look out for him in recent months. He nodded the last time and ran back up the stairs, only looking back once to make sure Castor had not changed his mind. Castor's face was steeled. Atticus turned back and continued up the road towards the barracks.

Castor let out an audible sigh. That was one less thing he had to worry about. He turned his attention back to his friend, who was now surrounded by three soldiers. One had been salving and binding his wounds as the others held him down. The pain must have been great, as he had not seen Kyros act like this before.

After the procedure of cleaning and binding was complete, it seemed Kyros had calmed a little. When Castor noticed, he got up from binding another soldier's wound and checked on his friend.

"That was not fun." Kyros stately flatly. His long blonde hair was matted with blood and dust.

"I am sure it was not," Castor responded. "How are you holding up?"

The mercenary's smirk faded as he got into a more serious mood.

"I can't feel my left arm, Castor." His tone was somber and nothing like what his friend was used to.

"You are just in shock right now," Castor reassured him. "Muscles do not always respond when you lose so much blood. Your senses will come back with time."

He could see the damage that had been done. Kyros had lost a lot of blood. While the wood fragments had been pulled and bandaged, the damage from his multiple injuries had piled up. He had four wrappings on him at that time, with two of the injuries being life-threatening up until a few minutes prior.

"Try not to strain yourself," Castor said in a calm voice. "The last thing you want to do is make any of them worse."

Kyros nodded and subsequently winced at the pain such a movement caused. He had no witty remarks for that one. Just a somber nod.

"I am going to check on my father and see if he has any plans. Do you need anything before I head up there?" Castor asked.

"No. Nothing right now," Kyros responded. His intention in watching the battle play out was clear. Castor let him lay against the wall and watch the rest of the soldiers finish his fight.

Castor, back on two feet, climbed the stairs and walked towards his father and Didyma. They were still overseeing the battle from the top of the wall. Hecantor was talking to two soldiers as they noticed Castor's arrival.

At the top, he found Nikitas kneeling in front of his lord. Helmet down and on one knee, he bowed his head as though he was asking for mercy.

"I am sorry, my lord." Nikitas said in a husky voice, "We did not act swiftly enough and lost multiple civilians. Even some of our ranks were killed. I did not act quick enough to save them. I wish I would have."

Apopsi, who had returned to perch upon Hecantor's shoulder, looked over at Castor as he approached the group. Didyma paid him no attention and continued her shallow chanting and icy barrage. Hecantor did not turn his head but knew Castor was there.

Hecantor frowned in an overtly comedic way. Rather than yell or reprimand, he instead started to wrap upon Nikitas' bronze helmet with the gold ferrule of his cane. Each blow shook the helm and made the ringing of a bell.

"Come now, friend." Hecantor protested in a silvery voice, "I know I have told you a thousand times. We do not do that groveling here in Thyma. You have customs from home that you abide by, but our customs are not so authoritarian. Now get off the ground and go lead those troops. I'd rather you spend this energy saving another life than up here on your knees with me."

Nikitas rose from the ground and saluted his leader. He nodded to Castor before leaping over the edge and back into battle. Once his retainer was gone, Hecantor focused his attention on his son.

"Ah, my boy." Hecantor walked to him with a stiff gait. His cane shone as he moved. Hecantor embraced his son in a tight hug. For a legally blind man with a limp leg, his war veteran father was still capable of nearly breaking ribs when performing a bear hug.

"I am glad you are alright." He said as he released his grip. "I heard you were one of the first to charge into battle."

"It has been one tough day, to say the least." Castor smiled.

Didyma cleared her throat. "Hecantor, we have a pressing situation to attend to."

Over the edge, three more turtles joined the fray from the east, either scared toward this side of the town from reinforcements on the eastern front or frenzied here from the smell of fresh blood. The turtles, now numbering six in total, were spread across the plaza to the right of where they were standing. Since the second phalanx was now freed of their attacker, the two groups had lined up together to hold the path against the giant beasts. Totaling around sixty soldiers, the thin lines of hoplites held the formation against the beasts. The peltasts, which were able to restock their throwing weapons from the fallen, had been commanded by Hecantor to take up position on top of the wall and shoot down onto the beasts below. As the phalanx held their positions, the peltasts continued to barrage the beasts with the spears of their victims. A quarter of the spears found their marks and the turtles started to take attrition from the prolonged combat.

"Ah, I have someone I need to check on," Castor said to Hecantor as they watched the combat unfold. Castor pointed to the now partially destroyed tower across the plaza. "A great Maudian that had joined us for practice was thrown through that wall. "

Hecantor looked surprised. "Are you referring to the exiled prince of Thrim?"

"Yes," Castor responded, "Mithra had joined us for practice and then for this combat. He would not take no for an answer."

A smirk shot across his father's face as he finished that last line but continued to look quizzical. "I am very surprised he was put out of action so quickly. The exiled prince is renowned for his feats in the Maudian Sand Pits. I know he mentioned he was exhausted from his travels, but I did not expect him to fall so easily."

"Well, he did hold a turtle off by himself at the beginning of combat. But I did not see him use his channeling during our time together. Maybe his mana pool was depleted?" Castor asked.

"Could be." Hecantor agreed. "Regardless, you look like you have been through a lot. Do you think you can handle that?"

Didyma nudged Castor between her casting and reached into the many layers of cloth surrounding her body. She pulled out a bronze amulet four inches in diameter. Its elliptical surface was jeweled with an assortment of rubies and topaz cut in Trillion and Radiant patterns. The ends of the amulet had a hanging connection of metal that held a large round opal in the engraved claws of a bird. The object was hefty, but Castor could tell its craftsmanship was of the highest quality.

"You look like a mess, boy." Didyma harped, "Use this to restore some of your mana and complete your task. We can't have the next prince of our town passing out on the floor at the end of combat. It would be terrible for appearances."

Her speech was short, but that was all the time she gave Castor. Her focus went solely back to the new threats looming in the east. More icicles propelled themselves towards the lumbering brutes as she continued her attacks. As she focused her gaze on them, she looked as though she was completely oblivious to everything else around her.

Hecantor chuckled. "Well, you heard the matron. Go check on the exiled Maudian while you can. Keeping our foreign dignitaries alive is generally helpful."

Apopsi poked at Castor's feet. He leaned over and petted the bird, it cooing under his hand. It was always strange to Castor that this bird was older than him, and by at least fifteen years as well. The brown bird rubbed its golden beak into Castor's palm.

"Very well. Take care." Castor said. His father nodded and shifted his weight once again. Apopsi flew up to his shoulder and focused its attention on the frontlines.

Castor walked down the stairs and looked over the wounded. Many were in stable condition now, with only around a dozen bodies being covered up. This included the guards and citizens that had already fallen across the docks before Castor's party had arrived. The wounded leaned against the wall and were resting. Only a few soldiers stayed to keep them company, while the rest returned to the phalanges.

He continued past the battle and walked past the fallen turtle that blocked the path towards the guard tower. He held the amulet in his left hand and tightly gripped the pommel of his sheathed xiphos in his right. As he walked, he siphoned mana from the amulet into himself as well as into the gems on his body. Her amulet held a very large volume of mana due to the pristine quality of the gems and the patterns in which they were inlaid. The opals at the ends of the jewelry were exceptionally well polished and shone like small moons in his hand. He kept his guard up as he passed the turtle, but it stayed still. It was dead.

He came up to the tower and looked inside the first floor. Most of the furniture and fittings were in place except for a few stones that had rolled down the stairs and broke a wood table with an oil lamp placed on top. The oil spilled across the ground and the wood splinters covered the floor. The way up to the second floor was blocked by the cave-in, so Castor looked around outside for a way up.

Luckily for him, a merchant had stacked a few barrels and crates next to the tower before the battle had started. Castor moved one barrel and stood it on its end. The crates of merchandise were stacked on top of each other and gave Castor access to the hole in the side of the second story of the building. He climbed on the barrel and lifted himself onto the edge of the crate. Tossing his legs around, he propelled his weight up to the next level. His leg began to burn as he extended the torn tissue and the wrapping he was wearing turned slightly pink. As he carefully got himself to the second layer of crates, he focused a trickle of mana into the wrapping and activated more of the healing salve that was not completely used up yet. The pain subsided after a moment.

He focused his mana on his feet as he attempted to control the wind around him. During the heat of battle, the adrenaline rush coursed through his veins, amplifying his physical capabilities. He also had an ample supply of mana to bolster his potential. Now, with the rush gone and his mana pool dwindled to a single amulet, Castor found his body not responding as it once did. He took his time to ensure his hands and feet were placed firmly on the ground as he climbed. One bad grip could cause him to fall to his death if he wasn't careful. The remaining mana could stop the fall, but just like in battle, anything can happen when someone is fatigued.

With a short burst, a gust of strong air wrapped around his body and forced him up to the ledge of the second story. The extra three feet that the wind had propelled him exhausted two of the remaining gems within Didyma's amulet.

With a firm grip, he hauled the majority of his body through the opening, stopping only to catch his breath. The piled stone and tower rubble lay still in front of him. He could see a foot covered beneath by the shadow from a section of mortared bricks that had fallen into the pile. The leather boot was massive, fitting only a large Elvari or a great Maudian. As Castor did not know of any other Maudian princes visiting the continent of Anthora, he assumed it was the boot of the exiled prince.

"Mithra?" Castor called out to the pile. He cupped his hands around his mouth and focused the sound towards the area where the cat man would be lying based on the position of his foot. He assumed the foot was still attached to his furry body. He hoped it was.

"Mithra, can you hear me?" Castor started to remove some of the stones that were perched atop the pile. He could have removed them quickly and efficiently if his mana was not at its limit. Instead, he picked chunks of broken rock manually and tossed them to the side. The pile was large, more than what Castor thought he could completely move by the end of the afternoon, but he had to check on their foreign guest.

A small rumble shook the tower. Castor threw a chunk of granite to the side of the heap as he heard a deep growl from within the mound. Calling out once more only returned silence. But he now knew the Maudian was still alive, and that was a relief. Dust started to build within the cavern as the igneous material continuously hit the ground. Each chunk he moved was less weight on Mithra's body. Castor was surprised he was not dead from the ton of pressure, much less his impact with the solid stone wall. It seemed he had underestimated the durability of a great Maudian. The reputation that preceded him was more accurate than Castor had imagined.

He made sure to lift small lumps of the broken wall as he worked. Rather than straining himself, he took this time to replenish his stamina and give his body a rest. The battle outside was quieter now, as though it was coming to a victorious conclusion. He was glad his soldiers were able to hold out for the reinforcements. Not all were lucky enough to survive, but the civilian casualties were low. He did not want to think about what could have happened if one of the Atropethian turtles had made its way into the city center. If its flanks were protected and it charged down a street or corridor, he was sure the casualties would have been more than their entire combat earlier. The soldiers they had lost today were not in vain.

As the stack of rock dwindled, the deep humming could be felt again. This time, however, the vibrations did not falter. The stone around the room lifted as energy swirled around the mound. Like an ironhusk beetle emerging from the soil after a spring rain, the stones started to split from the center of the peak and rolled away like a hill separating from an eruption. At first, only the small stones and pebbles moved from the centerline. As the vibration increased, larger and larger chunks of rough rock started to disperse from the area.

Castor had backed away by this point. He stood near the opening in the wall where the cat man had broken through. Off to his left was the blocked stairway that led to the bottom floor. As the vibrations moved the heap above Mithra, so too did the stones on the stairs move. The mana permeating the room seems to affect all earth, rock, and soil in a way that Castor had not seen before. It commanded the hewn rock to move like the flow of water that fell to the lowest point in the room. It seemed the idea that Mithra was weakened or out of mana was false, as the energy within the room easily disproved such accusations.

The vibrations were clearer now; the gentle thrumming moved towards more of an undulating reverberation. Castor braced as the pulsations grew in strength. All of the sudden, the pile exploded. It sent debris and dust across the room. Mithra rose from his early grave and propelled forward. The forces he used on himself must have been more than he anticipated as he was on a trajectory to fly right out of the hole he came in through.

Castor moved his body in between the flying cat man and the rough entrance. He used a small channeling around his feet to anchor himself onto the hewn stone that lined the opening. While the second-story flooring was wood, the bottom foot of the now exposed opening was still connected by mortar to the rest of the building. Bracing his right foot against the ledge and dropping to one knee, he shot a strong amount of wind toward the Thrimic noble. The turbulent forces slowed his advance, but still, he went. As they collided, Castor pushed back and allowed the wall to bear much of the weight of the impact. Small bits of stone crumbled off the wall as Castor stopped the giant Maudian.

Mithra looked as though his eyes were glazed over. He saw Castor in front of him, but Castor thought something was wrong. His attention did not stay on the same object for too long, instead looking around as if to realize where he was. The steel gaze Castor remembered from earlier was instead replaced with a pallid glare.

"Mithra?" Castor called to him, "Are you alright?"

After a brief moment, Mithra's attention focused back on Castor.

"Ah, yes. Hello, son of Thyma." Mithra seemed distant.

A short delay of silence was all that sat between the worried Anthoran and the confused Maudian.

"I am alright." Mithra continued. He rubbed the back of his head.

"Are you hurt?" Castor asked. "You took quite a hit breaking down this wall."

"I have been thrown through many walls in my time." Mithra scoffed. "I just need a second to rest."

The Maudian sat on a large chunk of stone that was now laid upon the wood floor. It was too large for Castor to sit comfortably, but it was the proper size for a creature over eight feet in height. He continued to rub the back of his head. While he rested, Castor checked his body for puncture wounds and broken bones. It seemed he was unscathed from the front. Only a section of matted fur with a gray tint covered his exposed areas. The dust from the collision and the sweat of battle hardened his fur into thick clumps. His mane, although mostly intact, was matted near his ears, neck, and face.

"Are they dead now?" Mithra asked as he got his senses back, "Did everyone else survive?"

"Most did. We had a few casualties." Castor did not want to think about the people he lost today. He was still recovering as well and needed to give his mind a break from the onslaught. "Reinforcements came. They are finishing the remaining creatures now."

Castor confirmed Mithra was fine from the front and sides and moved behind him to check his back. When he did, he almost let out an audible sigh. Blood coated the fur around Mithra's head and soaked into the back part of his mane. His hand, which continued to rub the wound, was only adding to the flow of red liquid. Castor moved his hand down and out of the way. He bumped the wound directly as he pulled the paw away and was met with a deep growl. For a second, the sharp focus that he had seen earlier in the day had returned to Mithra's eyes.

"What are you doing?" Mithra hissed.

Castor moved to his front and looked the giant in the eyes. Castor was standing straight and was barely taller than the large cat man when he was sitting. He knew he needed to take care of the injury sooner than later or else he could be maimed for life.

"Mithra, do you remember anything else from before you got stuck under those rocks?" Castor asked. He grabbed a cloth from the broken tables in the room and cleaned it with his water channeling. While not ideal, he used some Anthoran wine that was within the tower's storage bin to clean the dust out of the ripped rags. He wicked and dried the bandage, leaving only the cloth fibers behind. After the bandage was cleaned, he applied some healing salve to the center of the strip and rubbed the viscous liquid into the fibers to ensure they were properly soaked.

"I did not expect the creature to throw me like that. It..." Mithra pondered the word he was looking for, "The hard tail end grabbed my blades and threw me. That foul beast threw me across the landing. I dodged the crane and came through this wall. I woke up a few times. But you calling out kept me awake. Thank you."

"No worries, friend," Castor said to keep his focus off of what he was doing. He had started to wrap the cloth around the wound, all while the great Maudian was staring arrows into him. The makeshift bandage stopped the blood from flowing and kept more dust from getting to the gash. The angle at which the wound was cut through his skin made it hard to tie off. The open wound was five inches long and went from the middle of his head to the midpoint of his neck. The impact barely missed an artery in two spots, which is probably why he was still alive. The damage around the area was still serious, and the blood loss from the wound was surely the reason his consciousness was waning. Once wrapped, Castor channeled some mana from the amulet into the wrapping and allowed the Vótanodor to work its magic. Its pain-relieving qualities seemed to work well in this case, as the clenched muscles of the tall Maudian relaxed.

"I think you weren't as lucky as you thought you were with the crane, Mithra." Castor said as we returned to the front and stood a few feet away.

"Ah." Mithra trilled. He now noticed the blood in his hand and continued to trill in the back of his throat.

"Do not worry, you will be fine after this," Castor reassured him, "The bandage I applied had a healing salve on it. We will properly clean it and sew it shut at the day's end. We have great doctors in Thyma. You will just need to rest for a while after today."

His trilling slowed, then stopped. He seemed calmer after he was done.

"Thank you," Mithra said again, this time his glare was less sharp. "Not many in my life have helped me as you have. Without compensation expected. Many have served, not many have helped."

A short respite of silence filled the room as Mithra adjusted the wrappings around his head and Castor reapplied the salve and bandages to the wound on his leg. The clump of fabric he had used before was soaked a reddish-brown with dried blood.

"How many were lost?" Mithra asked as he stood. He almost lost his balance by standing too quickly, but he braced himself against the edge of the opening.

"Less than ten, I would expect," Castor said solemnly. "A half dozen had fallen before I left, and I expect a few more by nightfall."

Mithra put a giant paw on Castor's shoulder. "I am sorry." he said.

Castor pushed it off and patted him on the arm, only able to reach the middle of his bicep.

"Do not be," Castor said in a steady voice. "They were soldiers. They signed up for this and made their city proud. Many others were spared because of their sacrifice."

Castor kept his composure, but inside he was hurting. He knew some were exactly like he explained, but not all of them. He knew Phineas was just a kid, like himself. He was raised as a common farmer and did not want to become a soldier. Such situations were not common, but there was not much that could be done when a village had too many hands and not enough land to be worked. He hoped he could do something for them. He did not have the time right now, but he knew he had to prepare something for his family that Vara could take back.

Mithra nodded, not pushing the subject.

He put a hand up to scratch at the wound on his head, but Castor stopped him by grabbing at his elbow.

"Do not!" he barked. "I know it is itchy, but you will only make it worse. Let the salve do its work. It will help greatly."

Mithra snarled, a natural reaction to being yelled at when you live your life as a spoiled prince. He had learned how to live a mundane life since his banishment, but his instinctive reflexes were not something he was able to control. After seeing Castor flinch from the aggressive behavior, he shrugged his shoulders and continued away from the stone pile.

They started to walk towards the opening in the wall before noticing the staircase down had been cleared during Mithra's channeling. The stones had piled at the bottom of the stairs and dispersed onto the bottom flooring. The duo made their way across the loose stones and ensured they had proper footing as they walked. The last thing either of them needed was another head injury from stumbling on rocks after the battle. Within the room underneath were the typical lodgings for a guard tower. A table and a few chairs littered the ground. A small desk and a few other chairs had fallen over due to the collision, their contents sprawled across the floor. The rest area on the second story had been demolished, but the first floor was still in decent shape. Only a few beds and wall repairs were needed. *Repair costs will be high,* Castor thought to himself in a vain attempt to lighten his mood.

Castor grabbed an apple off of a table. He was famished after all the fighting and channeling. Not only was he constantly taxing his body with physical exercise, but it also took calories to restore his spent mana. Mithra grabbed a pear which was sitting next to the apple and ate it while they left the tower.

They both put their hands up as the bright outdoor light blinded them for a second before their eyes adapted. They could see the battlefield a hundred feet away. Only one turtle remained, and a barrage of ice from Didyma was making good progress in changing that. As they left, Mithra leaned against one of the granite pillars which lined the front porch of the stone tower.

"I am fine." he growled before Castor could ask about his condition. He pushed himself off the carved fluting and continued down the stairs that led to the foundation of the building.

As they walked across the stone plaza ahead, Castor saw the crane that Mithra had been thrown into. The top of the crane and its wood mechanisms were broken off, leaving two support struts hanging in the air from their fastened ends. Castor pointed and Mithra slowly looked directly at his hand. He snapped to gain the Maudian's attention and jerked his finger forward. Mithra looked up and saw the broken section of wood and brass. He put his hand up to rub his head. He caught himself, however, and put his hand back down slowly to play the action off as a stretch. Castor smirked when Mithra turned towards their destination.

They reached the temporary medical area and saw eight bodies covered with cloth. The fragments of torn tents they had used made the line of fallen comrades more colorful than a typical battle mortuary. With so many large beasts and such a last-minute attack, Castor felt torn between applauding so few losses and deprecating his lack of control over the situation.

The last turtle fell with a large pillar of ice piercing his left knee. Its right leg had given out already from three javelins that were lodged between the thick skin and scale hide. Nikitas finished the beast with his bronze clubs. His actions were swift and his attack was accurate. The blow caved the creature's skull in like the one earlier, only this time being much closer to the ground. It was dead instantly.

The phalanx broke as all attention went to healing the wounded. Nikitas started his way towards the other turtle, ensuring its demise with swift strikes to the foreheads. Soldiers took rest upon the stairs or on piles of cloth around the entrance to the plaza. Vótanodor was applied to many cloth bandages made from the ripped tents of the harbor market. One of

[183]

the uncovered stalls held a cheese merchant. All of the damaged goods were liberated for the city and the healthy guards fed the smashed cheeses to those who were recovering on the ground before helping themselves. The lack of mana within the soldiers put the group at risk if another wave of the crazed beasts were to make landfall. They ensured their stamina and mana pools would recover faster by eating as much of the ruined wheels of cheese as they could.

Castor checked in on Kyros, who was resting against the levy wall and munching on a block of deformed feta cheese. The acidic smell of the goat cheese hit Castor as he got closer.

"Looks like you are recovering well," Castor said as he approached. Kyros' left arm was fully wrapped and splinted. While he did not move it, he did not seem to be delirious from the pain any longer. His right arm was completely fine and held the block of cheese with ease.

"Free snacks. Can't turn that down." he raised his chunk of solid milk to the heir prince, bowing his head in jesting mockery. "I am so glad our lord was uninjured in the battle."

Castor raised the leather straps of his pteruges like an exotic dancer at night, showing off the bandaged wound he had received.

"Maybe luckier than you, but not as lucky as you think," Castor responded. "And Mithra had it much worse. I think he had his brain shaken when he was thrown through the crane and wall."

Kyros noticed the giant cat man standing next to him and saw the bandages around his head. Mithra stared at Kyros, saying nothing. For a second, it seemed like he had taken a disdain for the mercenary, but he quickly grabbed onto the wall and steadied his hulking form. Castor assumed a wave of nausea had hit him because of his injury and he just could not continue the conversation. Kyros looked like his muscles eased as the great Maudian looked away.

"I am going to take him to my father. Hopefully, we can get him to see a doctor soon and he can get this taken care of before it becomes permanent." Castor informed. "Do you want me to get you set up with an injury trainer too?" Castor looked at his left arm and Kyros shifted his weight from the glare. His tone became less fun and more serious.

"No, I do not think so." Kyros responded, "My father is good friends with a well-known physical trainer in town." He used his right hand to move his left arm, wincing from the pain of the movement. "I think I will stay in town for a while. I won't be able to complete any contracts like this. I will probably cover as a private guard or a tutor for a while until I get this taken care of."

"It looked bad, but I am sure you will recover," Castor said as he gently patted his friend on the back of the head. Kyros smiled, knowing he was right. They both knew this injury would take a few months at the minimum to heal, but he would be able to fight again one day.

As they talked, they were approached by the Sister of the Thorns. Her battle frenzy had finished and her bloodlust seemed to be quelled after she had woken up. She came over to the group and walked directly up to Castor.

At first, Castor thought she was angry. He had killed the beast that had struck down her life bond. He was worried she was going to start drama after the battle ended. But that was not her intention. He tightened his muscles in response.

She instead wrapped her arms tight around him and gave him a big, soft hug. She squeezed him firmly but not in an aggressive manner. He was very surprised. Not many would come so close to an heir prince, especially one of her following. Some Sisters of the Thorns were notorious for their misandrist behavior. Instead of being stunned, Castor instinctively reciprocated the show of affection.

His worries seemed to drift away, if only for those few seconds. He just had a mentee die under his command. Many others, including citizens of his city, were brutally killed not even thirty feet from where he stood. His best friend was maimed and a new foreign acquaintance was just concussed. The day, which started well and good, only ended as one of the worst days in his life. He needed to keep his confidence high on the outside to set a good example for others. On the inside, he wanted to cry. He was only nineteen. Seeing so many deaths at once while fighting for your life was not an event he had experienced before. He knew he would learn from this day. Right now, his focus was on keeping everyone else safe.

The Sister pulled out of the hug and put her hands on his cheeks. Her hands were cold, as though they were sucking the energy out of the area around them. The cool feeling was a nice reprieve from the heated bloodshed he had just experienced. Luckily, they were not near the main group and a broken tent hid them from the triage area, or else this scene would have drawn more attention than Castor would have wanted.

"Thank you," she said quietly. "You killed the one that took my Myrine from me. I thank you for your help."

Castor was blushing by this point. Such honest affection was not so common for an heir prince, much less a noble's son. Boys were not allowed to marry until their second decade of age and most did not marry until their mid-twenties when they secured a stable career. As much as he wanted to hide his rosy cheeks, his natural response was enough for her to put her hands down to her sides. As a Sister, physical interactions with men were usually not acceptable.

"You are welcome," Castor said, trying to dissipate the awkwardness. "I would have preferred the situation not to get to where it did. But as it is, she will be remembered honorably."

"I hope so." she mewled. "I will have to report this to the Matrons after everything is sorted here. I did not think my time as a Sister of the Thorns would be so short. I do not think I am ready to become a Thorned Rose yet."

Castor learned of the basic practices of the Sisters when he was under the short tutelage of Didyma in the library.

"It may be hard," Castor comforted her, "but your blooming pilgrimage after this can take as long as you like. You do not need to return after a year, which is just the minimum. If it takes you half a decade to come to terms with this, then so be it. Just know you will be welcomed back here in Thyma whenever you need a place to rest."

A small tear rolled down her cheek, an emotion not commonly seen among those of her order. She nodded, turned, and returned to her fallen lover.

Castor took a second to catch his breath. The day had been a surprise he could not have expected. Many had fallen. Even more were hurt. He couldn't remember the last time he had such an eventful day. After taking a second to relax his mind, he slapped his face, took a deep breath, and trotted over to the medical area to continue medical treatment on the wounded.

CHAPTER 8

Orange Leaves On A Bleached Skull

37th of Jasper, 453 of the Age of Discovery

he crisp autumn air bit Castor's cheek as he hauled an amphora into the storeroom. Autumn had started and a cool wave of dark clouds had moved into the region. Earlier than most years, the chilly weather and darker days made it all that much harder to get out of bed in the morning. Castor pulled on the wool mantle he wore and tightened the brooch near his neck.

"Didn't expect to start our autumn preparations with such weather!" Castor exclaimed. He stuck his right foot out in front of himself and pointed his toes upward. Bending over, he extended his leg muscles and relaxed his lower back. The wound from the turtle invasion a few months ago had healed well and only a slight ache lingered where the skin was overextended.

Acco dropped a crate onto the ground near the entrance of the dark room. He wore his wool tunic and dark himation tightly against his body to trap in the heat.

"Nerea betrayed us this year," he remarked in a guttural tone. "Should have been warm for the rest of the month! Now I am stuck here, with frozen feet and ears, all because what? Vrontir probably got caught chasing another woman and Nerea takes it out on us?"

Castor put a hand to cover his mouth and pushed it outward, then repeated the process with his heart and his belly button. This symbolic gesture was a way to ward off evil and the ire of the gods. He did not want to be smitten just for being near his brother when he spouted such blasphemy.

"You better watch yourself," Castor joked, "She may not be predominant in this region, but the words you speak would get you a stern lecture from the priestesses in town."

Castor put the pointed base of the amphora in the small hole he had dug before they started hauling the items into the shed. The bottom sat around a foot into the ground and stood steadily on its own once he patted some dry soil back around the base. That made five pots on the back wall, and another fifteen spots were already dug.

"Luckily, I rarely ever go into town now. With the new forging job Aretha got me out of Tyressos, I won't have to work for those ghouls here anymore!" His smile was bold and cocky. "It even pays a whole stater more a month."

"Do not forget the travel costs of passing over the mountains." Castor reminded him, "You will want to go with a caravan. Traveling alone and without knowledge of the area is very dangerous."

He scoffed. "You do not have to remind me. I'm no fool."

He lifted a crate onto the one he had placed on the floor before. For its size, the box was not too heavy. It was only filled with dried fruits, so its density was not too high. It was still bulky and large enough to make stacking it within the shed awkward for someone of Castor's size, so he left the heavy lifting to Acco.

"Are you planning to start your other mosaic before you venture out for Tyressos?" Castor asked. "You leave after the new year in the middle of Quartz, right?"

"Ya, I will have some time." Acco agreed. "My current issue is finding a good plan and pattern for the next piece. Do I match the colors of the one I already designed for the great hunt? Or do I change it up? I have even considered asking father if I could create one outside my room. That way I wouldn't be limited to any specific colors or patterns if I had it in a new room. Maybe I can ask to start one in the chapel."

"I like that plan!" Castor agreed. "Heck, I would even commission you to make a great mosaic of Ignus. If you made the mosaic on the floor, then you could have each god with their own design."

Acco scratched at the stubble on his cheek. While his beard was not as long as someone like Nikitas or Hecantor, It was still growing nicely for a nineteen-year-old.

"That's not a bad plan," Acco pondered, "but I would have to start with Pyrros first. Patron god of our people and all that. I am sure you understand."

Castor had brought in a sack of grain from the cart outside. He slumped it on the wooden rack that held the grains off the ground. The cloth loop at the top of the bag slid over the wood hook that was built into the rack and the bag swayed gently after Castor let it go.

He shrugged. "Ya, I understand. And I expect your second mural to be of Brömli since he is your patron."

"Yes, that would be great." Acco assented. "I hope I can get to it. If we do go ahead with this plan, I would like to finish it before I leave for Tyressos. His guidance would be greatly appreciated. I will be doing proper smithing there, not just supporting as an apprentice smelter like I was here."

Acco tossed another crate onto the stack he was forming by the door. Now three tall, the pile was about as tall as he was.

"Besides, I still plan to go and help with the start of the winter kilns at the beginning of Moonstone. It is easy money for someone with my smelting experience. And we still have the Arietia for the next week, so I won't be able to even get this project going before we are part of the way into Azurite." Acco said, shrugging his shoulders.

"Ask dad about it before we start the hunt," Castor advised, "and he can think about it as we are out. And since it would be in the chapel, I am sure he would want to choose the colors and materials. It'll save you from paying for everything and everyone gets to see your work. With luck on your side, it could lead to possible future jobs if you have the right guests to see them."

Acco scratched his beard again. Castor noticed he started to do this whenever he contemplated a topic. Whether it was to mock Castor for his lack of facial hair or merely a subconscious movement, Castor tried to not let it irk him. He knew his brother enjoyed teasing him. If he allowed himself to give in to the temptation and call him out for doing so, he was sure he would see much more beard-stroking in the future. Instead, he turned his back and moved to grab another sack of grain from the cart.

Outside, a few friendly faces were arriving to greet him. Perseus the house boy was pulling a wood cart up the sloped road with Atticus and Maya on his flanks. Atticus waved to Castor cheerily as they got closer. Maya had her bow slung over her shoulder and the coin purse from their shopping ready to be handed over to Aretha inside.

"Welcome back!" Castor called out to the group. Castor clasped arms with Maya, who took her bow off her shoulder and held it in her offhand.

"Those merchants drive a hard bargain." she said jokingly as she placed one end of her bow on the ground. She rubbed the side of her head with her hand after their greeting was complete. "Nothing to report other than some bad deals and a lot of arithmetic."

After placing a foot through the belly of the bow and tucking the start of the lower limb behind her left knee, she twisted her right foot into the end of the limb. She slowly pulled on the end of the top limb and popped the string loop off the top nock. The taught wood and horns that made up the limbs of the bow bent under the pressure, flexing silently as she unstrung the well-crafted weapon. Once the limbs were relaxed and the string was off, she placed it in a small pocket on the quiver she had dangling from her right hip. White and brown feathers stuck out of the end of the quiver, properly cut to shape and bound to the end of her arrows.

"That's good to hear," Castor responded. "The practice you three got from this was worth more than losing a few obols along the way. "

"Obols?" Perseus muttered, "Ha! You would be lucky if she didn't lose less than a few decadrachma in those deals!"

Maya glared at the house boy, who faked a whistle and looked away as he started to unstrap the cargo within the cart.

"Watch it, boy. I could make you disappear if need be." She said dryly at the sixteen-year-old attendant.

"I'd like to see you try." Perseus goaded back. "You are only twenty one, so who are you calling a boy? Without me around, who would haul these carts? Atty? He's a child. And I didn't see you lift a finger besides to pay and lift that one crate onto the back."

"I'm not paid to haul." she said while turning her head away, thinking herself above the conversation. "I am paid to protect. And my services lie within what lady Aretha asks. If you were older and more capable, I would not need to join you in the first place."

"Atty isn't paid at all, and he still pulled the cart when I got tired after a mile of pulling it." Perseus shot back.

"I did a pretty good job at it too!" Atticus said proudly, aimed mostly at Castor.

Castor patted Atticus on the head. "I want to clarify that Atticus gets a monthly stipend through the city guard as a trainee. I consider this a part of his training; physically with the cart hauling and socially with talking to you two. That includes watching your conversations with the vendors and each other."

His passive-aggressive comment put both of them in their place, their attitudes quelled to more friendly banter.

Castor leaned in and whispered so that Atticus could not hear. "Your bantering is...cute," he jested to the two of them. "but let us try to help Atticus learn proper manners at his impressionable age. When he isn't around, feel free to fight all you like."

They nodded in agreement, taking the young lord's request seriously.

"Do you want us to handle this now, boss?" Perseus asked. He had taken an amphora in his hands and started moving towards the door of the storage shed.

"That would be great. Thank you." Castor said. He turned to face Maya, "If Aretha has different plans for you, you are welcome to go find her inside."

With a bag of grain across her shoulder, Maya smirked.

"Well, after what this boy said earlier, I have to redeem my honor." she said spryly.

"Understood." Castor smiled. He patted Atticus on the head once more before retrieving Acco.

He ducked his head inside the shed and called out to his brawny brother, "Hey, let's go help with the decorations up front. These three said they will handle all this."

Acco adjusted one crate so that it lined up exactly with the box underneath. He nodded and walked out of the dark and dusty room.

Handing a small amulet to Perseus as they passed, he said, "Make sure to lock everything up when you are done."

Perseus nodded. As he was the one to usually handle these resupplies, he was used to using the crest lock on the door. Like the door to Castor's barracks, the shed was equipped with a sturdy lock that required a precisely cut family crest and a pulse of mana to activate the internal mechanisms. The boy was well versed with the device and would have no issue locking the building back up when they were done.

The storage shed sat within the estate walls, hugging the northeastern corner of the family's land. The villa, which sat in the middle of the plot, was only around one hundred feet away. The main street of the town they lived in ended at their manor and sat flush against the estate's southern border.

During the time of the Arietia, citizens around the region of Thyma move their shrines of Beltunia to an outdoor location. The goddess of the hunt welcomes the change of season and many hunters worship her for her protection during the autumn months. Her shrine was usually adorned with offerings from any creatures caught during these times, with gifts of offal and jerky being predominant at her feet.

Castor and Acco walked around the villa and made their way to the front of the house, where they were greeted by a group of diverse friends. Hecantor and Xenia were around the location of the shrine, which was placed near the southeastern entrance in the estate walls. The shrine was placed so any passerby would be able to see the statue, offerings, and other assorted decorations during the festive season through their wrought bronze fence gate. Xenia was arranging a bouquet of autumn flowers while Hecantor placed the offering bowl near where the statue would be placed.

Xenia, looking up after finishing her detailing of the arrangement, saw her sons and smiled.

"Look dear, the reinforcements have arrived." she said to her husband.

Hecantor, sporting a gray wool robe with purple embroidery, turned to the boys and nodded.

"Perfect timing, you two. We just finished with the lighter stuff. Now it is time to put your muscles to the test."

"Oh sure," Castor shot back, "leave the hard work to us."

"Well, why do you think we have you, dear?" Xenia said in a sarcastic tone. "Children are the most expensive servants you can have, but they tend to be the most loyal."

"To be fair, you didn't have me." Acco said gruffly with a smile, "I'm here against my will."

Hecantor grabbed his cane and pointed it towards the open gate.

"I do not see that gate being locked." He said with a raised eyebrow and a cheeky grin.

Acco walked next to the aged man and put his hand to his chin, pondering at the gate.

"Hm...." he said. "I guess you are right. I can't believe I never noticed that."

Hecantor let out a short laugh before turning back to Xenia. "Do you think it is time we get the collection out?"

"I already have the proper people tasked with that." Xenia said in agreement, "They should be done unpacking soon. As Beltunalia is an Anthoran holiday, I figured this would be a great opportunity to get Mithra inundated with our ways."

As if on cue, Mithra came through the front door of the home with the marble statue of Beltunia on his shoulder. The massive chunk of carved stone dug into his long yellow robes. The thick silk textile flowed around him, giving off a slight shimmer in the autumn's dimming sunlight. Pink water lilies were embroidered across the long dress and a hem of matching colors kept the edges reinforced.

Castor only saw Mithra wear this outfit one time before when they met with the high priest of the Temple of Ignus in town. Seeing him wear his intricately designed formal gown reinforced the idea that Mithra was taking their holiday seriously. It gave Castor some confidence in their hunt that started in a few days. Mithra was in his hunting party and he felt relieved that everyone in the party was within Beltunia's good graces.

"Hail, heir prince, and adopted son." Mithra declared in a deep voice, walking over to their parents. "I have brought your idol. Would you like it placed upon this stand?"

"Yes, that would be great, Mithra. Thank you." Xenia said. She knelt and put fingers on each side of where the statue would be placed to give Mithra some guidance on its position. She did not want to have to move the marble statue once placed, as her arrangement was already in the position she exactly wanted it. She had to make sure everything looked perfect before the festivities started.

He hefted the bulk of shaped stone and placed it gently onto the area outlined by Xenia. His mane was puffed out and helped insulate him against the cold temperatures, but also acted as padding on his shoulder where the statue had sat. As he got up, a few hairs caught the flower arrangement and pulled from the glass vase they were set in. With a quiet snarl, Mithra pulled the flowers from his furry neckline and put them back where he thought they came out.

With the smile on her face never wavering, Xenia quickly moved in front and replaced the two flowers he had incorrectly put back. Since it was not a major deal overall, Xenia was not about to make her guest feel bad for something he had tried to fix. She felt obligated to ensure the arrangement was perfect. Beltunia was the patron deity of her home city of Delhenion. The lakeside town was surrounded by rolling plains and lush meadows, which made the region a major purveyor of furs and meats due the vast amount of ranching and hunting that took place in their verdant hills. Her family had connections to the head priest of Beltunia's temple in Delhenion, which made the perfecting of her shrine during her celebration all the more important.

Mithra had not noticed her impulsive behavior and instead turned to see his servants coming to join in on the decorating. Aretha led the group with the skull and antlers of a large deer in her arms. The Maudian servants followed her with an array of items from their storage cellar.

These items were well preserved and kept in the safety of the home because of their importance to the holiday and their value. While some servants only held the support stands and poles that would house the trophies of past hunts, the others held the trophies themselves. Skulls of various beasts slain by the Daimos house were carried out to the front of the estate. Some trophies were from times past with their shapes browning with age. A few red tail deer skulls were large in the Maudian's arms, as the largest antlers spanned five feet. Others were from the current family members, like the skulls of a pair of harpies and a griffon skull taken by Hecantor back in his younger years. The collection of trophies was placed on the ground while the group got to work fortifying the poles into the ground.

Xenia approached Castor and poked him on his cheek. Her long fingernail was sharper than he imagined, but she did not intend to hurt him. She then put her arm around his shoulders and hugged him tightly.

"Dear, are you sure that the letter you got from that farmer was detailed enough to show you where to stay?"

Castor retrieved the letter he received two weeks ago from the pouch on his hip. It was a message from Glaucus, inviting their family to stay at his brother's house the night before the start of the Arietia. Normally they would travel to the village on the day the weeklong hunt began, but this year they were invited early to not be tired when the celebration started. The first night of the Arietia was when the rules were read and the contestants from around the region were set to gather. When Castor mentioned the situation to Hecantor, he was happy to accept, as this was another way for Castor to build his network of friends within the region.

"Yes, I think it will be a nice opportunity to get away and relax before we venture out on the hunt. Our party plans to travel far for this hunt. We do not want to get stuck on this side of the Sideros like many other parties do." Castor said in a hushed tone. His siblings were on a competing team and he did not want them to hear about their plans.

"Honey, you only have ten days to complete the hunt. It will take at least three days to just get to Tyressos." she insinuated her doubt behind a reassuring voice.

He tapped the side of his nose. "Oh, do not worry, mother. I have a quicker route planned."

Her eyes squinted and then relaxed, coming to the same conclusion as her son.

"Ah, through there." she emphasized. "Look at you, using your brain. Do be careful, though. While it is generally safe to travel on this side of the mountains, there has been talk of bandits and other foul beasts farther up north."

"We will be." He assured her. "Kyros is an experienced mercenary and Mithra is, well, a giant lion man. With the three of us together, I wouldn't worry too much."

"Very well, I will leave your fate up to Beltunia." she smiled and kissed her son on the forehead.

She went back to preparing the shrine, directing the Maudian servants on the spacing for the wooden pergola that was to be placed over the statue to protect it from the elements.

"Ah, Castor, I forgot to mention before, but take a look over here." Hecantor said as he walked over to an object covered by a cloth canvas. He bent over and used his cane as leverage to unveil the object underneath.

The sheet gave way to a large, bleach white Atropethian turtle skull, fully intact and cleaned to sanitary perfection. The sharp beak looked as though it could rend through a wood table with ease. Giving the skull a thorough review, Castor understood why their battle went so poorly. The head of the creature was almost completely bone. Except for the openings for the ears and eyes, every inch of the creature's head was a thick sheet of hardened bone. Their spears and swords simply were not designed for such naturally reinforced defenses.

"As a reward for defending our city a few months back, I went ahead and had the most intact specimen prepared for today," Hecantor said, tapping the wood box that sat next to the skull. "This is for you as well. Well, you and Mithra. You both led that group of trainees into combat and experienced minimal losses. For that, the city of Thyma thanks you."

Castor's heart fluttered for a second as he remembered the faces of the dead at the battle. Seeing them, covered in cloth and led to the temples after for their funeral rites, made Castor queasy. He swallowed and assured himself that his dad's words were true; they truly did save more lives that day than they had lost. He did not let his self-depreciation show. He steeled his nerves and thanked his father as he looked inside the box.

He found a full leather belt, with pteruges included, on the top of the pile. The thick leather strips were hard and scaly, no doubt made from the brown, mottled hide of the giant turtle. He found a linen lining with smaller pteruges to the right of the belt. These strips could replace the epaulets he had connected to his linothorax and give his upper arms more protection during combat. He appreciated this item, thinking about the issues Kyros had been going through over the last two months.

Under his items were two pairs of sandals and a pile of various leather cuts from the leftover hide. The sandals were different sizes, with each pair made for Castor and Mithra, respectively. Castor set them on the ground and switched his current footwear. The leather was surprisingly supple on his feet. His socks gave warmth and padding to his feet but the leather strips fit well around his toes and ankles. After placing his items on the ground on top of a slab of prepared leather, he grabbed the box and handed it to Mithra to inspect.

"Exiled prince of Thrim, your service that day was well-noted and we appreciate your bravery for our citizens. We want you to use these gifts however you please. The sandals should be to your dimensions, and I had worked with Cyrus to prepare them. After a discussion with him, we felt it best to leave the prepared leather to you for future use. Cut the strips into your arm wraps, fashion clothing or jewelry with it. It does not matter to me. I hope this gift helps offset your personal sacrifices on that battlefield."

Mithra snarled. "Bah! I was a fool to jump so readily into battle. I was ill-prepared and had a hot temper from my prior travels for that past week."

The mood around them grew awkward, with his words seeming like a confrontation. Mithra noticed the shift in the air and corrected the words he had chosen.

"My mana was low from the constant running, and I foolishly tried to take glory for myself. Had I not been exhausted from our exodus and searching desperately to quell my vanity, I would have saved all of your citizens. But instead, I was thrown through a wall, and..." He tapped his clawed fingers on the side of his head as he searched for the word from his memory, "concussed."

Mithras stood by Castor and patted him on the head. "Had it not been for this boy, I am not sure I would have made it. The doctor you had taken me to said I was very low on blood. Had Castor not tended to my wounds that day, I may have very well died."

He nodded to Cyrus, who had finished his work on the wood poles, and the emissary walked to the side of his lord. His parents walked closer and stood a few paces back, which had Castor confused.

"Castor, without expectations of reward nor payment for a debt owed, you saved my life. For this, as is per Thrimic tradition, I owe you a life debt. Your life will carry the same weight as my own, and I will do what is within my power to pay back the life you have spared. Do you accept this life debt?"

Castor was stunned. He had no notion of what was to transpire. He hastily looked over at his parents who smiled back. Their lack of worry reassured him, but the gathered crowd of Maudians made the situation all the more tense.

A hushed voice appeared behind him, and said, "Your response should be 'I accept this life debt and hope the sun shines upon both you and me.'"

Castor recognized the voice as Cyrus, the emissary of their group. He was always a helpful fellow and Castor appreciated his support during this spontaneous ceremony.

"I accept this life debt and hope the sun shines upon both you and me," Castor repeated the phrase told to him.

"So, it shall be." Mithra bowed his head and handed a metal amulet to the emissary. The Maudian chanted for a few seconds in Pârsi, their native Maudian language, and a bright flame extended from his thumb and pointer fingers. He focused the flames on the amulet, which lit red hot under the constant heat.

Mithra held out his left hand, which had his claws fully extended. The gray nails were filed to sharp points. Castor did not know whether he had sharpened them for this occasion or if it was customary for Maudians to keep their nails sharp.

"Your hand," Cyrus said.

Castor was taken aback but understood the situation after a second of thought. He put his hand in the Maudians paw and looked away. It was not every day an Anthoran teen was branded. But given the situation, Castor knew this to be a rare situation. He had read of the life debts of Maudian culture before. He had not seen one in person, however, and never expected to earn one himself.

Without hesitation, Cyrus stamped the seal into Castor's right hand, sizzling the flesh at the base of his thumb. Castor flinched instinctively in pain and focused on the distance. There was a brief moment that Castor considered pulling back, but his nerves were stronger than he gave them credit for. The small imprint only took a few seconds to leave its mark. After Cyrus applied the seal to the same location on Mithra's left hand, creating a symmetric marque on the lion man's paw. The smell of burnt hair filled the area and was more unpleasant than the branding itself.

Cyrus handed the seal to one of the other servants and put a hand over each of the burned areas. He continued his chant in old Maudian as he finalized the ceremony. Mana flowed through the marks and relieved Castor of the throbbing pain he felt in the area. Once the chanting was complete, Cyrus removed his hands to unveil a glowing orange imprint of the sun on his skin. This sun symbol was the crest of Mithra's family back in Thrim before he was exiled. His family crest was one of many depictions of the sun. The symbol was now branded onto Castor's skin below his thumb.

The glow subsided and Castor was surrounded by two of the Maudian servants. They wrapped his hand in bandages. To ensure the pain had subsided, one of the servants channeled mana into the salve they had applied to the gauze. The dark gray liquid was like the Vótanodor of Anthoran invention but felt warm to the touch. When the cat man forced energy into the greasy liquid, it did not glow but instead warmed his skin, giving a sensation of a heated rock. While the mark was small, Castor knew it bore a great weight in Mithra's eyes.

"Thanks," Castor said meekly. "I do not know what to say."

"There isn't anything left to say." Mithra corrected him, not understanding the context of what he said in Anthoran, "The ceremony is over."

Castor nodded, not wanting to correct the Maudian after such an important occasion. "Hopefully, we do not need to put this life debt to test during our hunt next week."

"Worry not, for I believe luck will be on our side." Mithra purred. He stretched his fingers back and forth, getting used to the brand that sat beneath the wrappings.

Acco tapped Castor on the shoulder and looked at Mithra. "Do I get anything for being Castor's brother?"

The Maudian was taken aback, confused by his question.

"No, you were not there that day and did nothing to earn such a mark," Mithra responded with his brow furrowed.

Castor lightly punched Acco in the shoulder. "Do not mess with our guests like that. You know Maudians do not understand our sarcasm."

Acco rolled his eyes and turned away, "Fine, take all the fame and the glory. I'll just get back to setting everything up for this holiday. Do not mind me."

Acco and Castor walked over to the Atropethian turtle skull while Hecantor and Xenia clarified the joke Acco had made.

Their preparations for the coming month of hunting started with their home's decorations. Castor and Acco lifted the skull of the turtle onto the end of a pole and fastened the jaw to the wood with knots and rope. Together they lifted the skull into the air and fastened the bottom portion into the holes that were dug prior. The skull hung in the air ten feet off the ground, easily tall enough to be seen over the estate's outer perimeter wall which was at head height.

The others continued their preparations while the brothers worked on Castor's trophy. Aretha and Cyrus prepared the red-tailed buck antlers to a post, which needed extra support to reinforce the old bones.

The rest of the servants prepared the posts and tamped the dirt around the finished trophy stands.

The assembly of skulls above their walls was an impressive sight. Many of the other families in their town had their trophies up already, the pole proudly displaying their family's past hunts from decades past. There were domestic skulls of red-tailed deer, griffins, and harpies. A basilisk and a mountain drake took the most predominant trophies they could see. A few exotic creatures like the skulls of a Sangmartan spider brood and a desert serpent were above the walls of the Karaklopos family a few houses down. They were a wealthy family with a wide trade network around the largest ports of the three continents. Their children became either merchants or monster hunters, either way expanding their connection with exotic goods and materials. As their father was the head of the Thymian Traders Guild, their family played a part in most foreign trade in the town.

Upon finishing their decorations, Xenia gave the entire assembly a once-over. Her position as the matron of the estate gave her an excuse to ensure the entire area was prepared properly for her matron deity. Once she gave the go-ahead, the group returned inside, ready to celebrate the Beltunalia in the inner courtyard.

The doors to the courtyard were closed off this time of year to keep a draft from pulling through the house. Painted wood doors closed the gaps with only the door to the kitchen being left open. Lydia and Penelope had worked in the kitchen and greeted the guests as everyone huddled inside. The windows were closed and Penelope ensured every guest had enough coverings to not be cold for the celebration.

While they were servants, the house staff of the Daimos estate were allowed to participate in the celebration and enjoy the food given. They still completed their tasks of cooking and preparing the celebration, however, and they had done a great job in doing so while everyone was working outside. They had even tended to the stone altar in the center of the courtyard, the glowing orange embers popping occasionally as new wood was fed to the inferno.

Once inside, everyone settled in around the altar. Xenia spoke up, clearing her throat and starting the night's speech that would kick off the Beltunalia.

"Tonight, we celebrate the ending of autumn. Cold weather will once again cover our lands and life will seem to fade from the landscape. It seems this year, the cold settled in a little early. But fret not, friends and family. Hunting season is upon us. While we rely on the crops of our fields during the summer, the autumn will still yield a great harvest. As our fields fallow, our land is yet ripe with life."

Xenia raised her glass as she spoke.

"We celebrate tonight to honor our matron, Beltunia. We ask for her guidance during these coming weeks. We are honored to have such an extensive amount of wildlife in our region. We pass on this tradition to our children, and them to theirs. We honor the lives we will take, as their sacrifice will give sustenance to our peoples over the harsh winter months. Let us give thanks that we have this opportunity to harvest these lands in the name of our goddess."

Xenia gestured to Lydia, who brought a platter holding the hearts of the two animals used for tonight's meals.

"Tonight, we honor Beltunia and give to her the lifeblood of our sacrifices for tonight's celebration. May she accept our offerings and bring us good fortune in the coming weeks."

Xenia tilted the silver platter and dropped the hearts into the glowing coals of the center altar. Smoke billowed as sparks shot across the open air. The Anthorans in the room put their hands over their mouth and heart and lifted them away, symbolizing the chasing of evil spirits from the area. Mithra saw their actions and mimicked their gestures with his servants following suit. As the starting ceremony had drawn to a close, the guests moved their way over to the main event; an authentic Anthoran feast.

The cypress wood table held the cuisine for the night. In the center, many different cuts of pork and mutton were sautéed and baked on multiple platters. The meat was cooked in various ways, such as being glazed in garum or roasted over a fire with a covering of dill and cheese. Some spicy, some savory, and meaty meals were a great boon for everyone at the party. A few snack dishes, like honey-glazed wheat puffs and the sesame honey oat bars, gave a sweeter option to the otherwise savory main course.

The guests grabbed food to their liking onto their plates and the servants ensured a glass of spiced wine or fruit juice was put on each of the lounging couches. Each of the couches had a blanket draped over their seats in case the partygoers were to get cold as the night progressed. Everyone grabbed their food and settled in for the start of their celebration.

CHAPTER 9

The Start Of The Hunt

40th of Jasper, 453 of the Age of Discovery

astor sat on a bench with Glaucus in the crisp autumn air. They were just outside of the shepherd's brother's home. As their family was away on a pilgrimage to the high temple of Pyrros in the holy city of Pharmais, the guests had the estate to themselves.

"Thank you again for inviting us to stay here at your brother's house before the hunt started." Castor pulled his himation tighter around his body. They had woken up less than an hour prior and Castor felt the early morning chill still in the air. They each enjoyed a cup of warm wine while watching over the pastures below.

"I am glad you were able to make it up here a day early!" Glaucus responded. His tone was much different now than it was when he first met the young lord. Knowing the heir prince was a happy and agreeable fellow made his timid nature easier to quell. They sipped on their mulled wine and waved to one of the townsfolk that passed along the roadside.

Glaucus continued after he swallowed the warm beverage, "When I told my brother about our conversation, he was elated to have the royal family stay in his abode." He giggled to himself under his breath, "You should have seen the way they cleaned before leaving for their pilgrimage. The entire house was turned upside down."

"It really wasn't necessary. Honest." Castor chuckled lightly. "It was nice enough to be able to arrive a day early. The trip up the roads around here is not the easiest path on our steeds. I remember the trip from last year being overgrown, but after this trip we plan to get Olynthia connected better between the towns. I plan to talk to the engineer's guild and set proper funding for the project for next year."

Glaucus' eyes widened, "You do not have to worry about us, my lord! It was not my plan to bribe you in any way to do such a thing!"

"Glaucus." Castor said in a monotone voice, "You gave us housing and hosted the royal family. We shared the same roof for a night. You do not have to talk to me so formally. I am not the crown prince of our lands yet. I am merely the heir apparent. You are welcome to be formal with my father, but I would prefer you treat me like you treat your neighbors."

Glaucus nodded. He was about to apologize, but Castor scolded him for doing that too much, so he caught his tongue.

"It's my job to find ways to improve our nation." Castor comforted Glaucus, who averted his eyes away from Castor like he did when they had first met. "While we all are here to celebrate the Arietia, my job as a guard captain and heir apparent does not simply get put on hold. I want to help where I see that I can."

Castor pointed down the rolling hills to the stream at the bottom. In the distance, the tanner's lodge was nestled in the point bar of a meandering brook. The wood structure sat next to many circular vats. While they were far enough away to not smell the pungent scent of the tanning hides, Castor imagined the smell and put his drink down on the bench to his left.

"That there is one of my reasons for improving the roads. Tanned leather would be of great use in Thyma proper." Castor pointed at each of his hands, showing off the sheepskin gloves he brought for their trip. "This area of the peninsula is well known for its leathercrafts. It is not just Olynthia, but Oia and Amida as well. The smaller towns around here could benefit greatly from shorter travel times and the city could barter for better leather trade contracts. Everyone would benefit."

A look of understanding passed over Glaucus' face as he nodded in agreement.

"Thank you for seeing us in such a good light," he concluded.

Hecantor made his way through the front door and greeted the two men on the bench. The gems on his cane sparkled across the gold inlays.

"There you are, I've been looking for the both of you." He said, walking closer with the help of his cane. Each step he took with his left leg lined up perfectly with the swing of his cane, making it seem like his right leg was a middle leg when he walked. He had been using the cane for over a decade at this point and became quite skilled with it. He held an item in his left hand which was covered with a cloth. Apopsi sat on his shoulder and looked off into the fields, observing the smaller herd animals with a focused glare.

"Hello, my lord," Glaucus said, standing to bow to his visually impaired prince. While Hecantor may have been injured during his past experiences in wars and rebellions, he still held a great amount of prestige with the common people of Thyma. His tax reforms and improvements to trade incentives revitalized the region after the Vrontian rebellions a few decades prior.

Hecantor smiled gently. He always emanated a kind and polite aura. Castor tried to learn from his father, but the way he was naturally so friendly to anyone he talked to seemed difficult to the aspiring prince. It seemed like his persuasive attitude came with his mellowed manners and calmer nature now that he no longer had any participation in the military or town guard.

"I have something for you." he said, sitting on the bench just far enough away from Castor so that Glaucus could sit between the two of them. Apopsi hopped off Hecantor's shoulder and perched on the armrest of the bench. It pecked at Hecantor's arm. Hecantor smiled and patted the bird on the back of its head. It let out a soft whistle as he did so.

Once his pet was taken care of, Hecantor removed the cloth on the mystery item and revealed a large brass dodecahedron. The chassis of the item was angled brass bars supporting clear glass sheets on the surfaces between. Within the framework sat a large double terminated quartz point. The multifaceted jewel was suspended within the center of the device with smaller channels of brass which kept it centered and upright.

"Have you seen one of these before?" Hecantor asked Glaucus while he rotated the object in his hands. As the light hit the glass panes, it reflected across other sides of the polyhedron and sparkled in the early morning sun.

"I have not, my lord." the shepherd was mesmerized by the lights that came around the device. Hecantor waved his hand over the top of the object and the crystal inside illuminated. The now brightened lamp cast light from each of its openings and created a kaleidoscopic effect as part of the radiance refracted internally.

"This is called a fotovolo. I use these quite often when I have paperwork to fill out in the late evenings. As it is now, it will light a room for a few hours after dark. Someone with a sense of channeling can control it. On or off, dim or bright, it can be used for work or leisure. If you do this..."

He pulled on the top section of surfaces and the brass edges inverted their positions. Three of the five surfaces that were attached to the top pentagon now stuck upwards like the petals on a flower. Hecantor angled the shape so that the morning sun was caught by the petals and focused the light inwards towards the quartz point. As the sunlight concentrated on the gem, it radiated a brighter light.

"Well, if you do this, it will help charge the device during the day. You can charge it through channeling, of course, but this method lets you save your reserves for more useful tasks during work hours."

Hecantor folded the extended pentagons and extinguished the light. He moved it in his hands once more, back and forth, before plopping it in Glaucus' lap.

"And now, it is yours." he put his hands back in his lap but was again bothered by Apopsi's incessant pecking. He played with the bird as Glaucus got ready to object.

"My lord, there is no way I could take such a fine gift from you!" Glaucus objected.

"No way?" Hecantor asked, "But I have already given it to you. Clearly there is a way. It was the way I just did it!" Hecantor feigned his rebuke with clear amusement on his face.

Before Glaucus could argue again, Hecantor pulled up his hamation and revealed the belt that bound the robe around him. On it, three identical dodecahedrons hung from his belt on leather straps. Unlike the one in front of Glaucus which was a half foot wide, these were an inch in width at their max. At their centers, well-cut pristine gems hung from their silver enclosures. The gems within these fotovola were at a higher level of raw quality and craftsmanship than the brass one in Glaucus' lap.

Hecantor detached one and held it up. He waved his hand near it and activated the tiny gem that it held within. The crystal exuded a vast ray of light that emanated in all directions. He reactivated the large device, which shone the same. While it was much smaller than the brass fotovolo, it emanated at least the same amount of light.

"I think I plan to keep these three, but I think you may have better luck using that one. You would be doing me a favor. It is hard for me to carry such a heavy device around, with this bum leg and all." Hecantor patted his right knee and smiled, his comment reassuring the shepherd of his worries.

"My lord, thank you for this kind gift." Glaucus said, bowing his head and almost headbutting his hegemon in the process, "My only concern is that I will not be able to use it to your fullest expectations. No one in my family can channel mana. The only people within the village who can are my brother's youngest daughter and the tanner down by the water."

Hecantor put the lights out once more and tucked his himation back into the edges of his belt. "That's quite alright. It only takes a second to activate the gems. And even with a limited pool of mana, the daily sun will recharge them to their capacity. I expect this one could run at full brightness for two or three hours. I recommend having your niece turn it down a bit. Maybe let her play with it under your supervision. It would be a fantastic way to foster new channeling skills."

Glaucus nodded with a smile. "Very well, my lord. I will do just that."

As they finished their conversation, the front door flew open and out came the rest of the guests. Mithra tried to catch the door before it slammed into the wall but missed the handle by an inch. He was focused on not hitting his head on the head jamb as he was far too tall for a door in a rural Anthoran village. Luckily, the village leader's home was made of mortared stone, so the wood door bounced off harmlessly.

"Seems like someone is overstaying his welcome." Kyros teased the great Maudian as he exited the building.

The exiled prince hissed gently as the mercenary. "You humans have such meek frames. Doors in Maudif are twice the size of this one."

Kyros threw his hands up and called over in a monotone voice to Castor. "Protect me, my lord. The emissary has gone feral!"

Mithra rubbed the top of Kyros' head with his large paw, ruffling his blonde hair into a tuft of fluff. His gaze was unnerving for Anthorans, as the stare of a great Maudian can feel as though one is being viewed as prey. But Castor had started to learn the nuances of Maudian etiquette. Mithra was a great guest in their home.

"Stop teasing our guest, Kyros." Castor shot a squinted glare at his friend, his arms folded in front of him. "I know I have told you a few dozen times now that they do not understand our sarcasm. It doesn't translate into their language. And is it wise to tease someone that is over twice your weight and a good two feet taller than you?"

"If I wanted to make someone disappear, I would not rely on my large size, mercenary of Thyma." Mithra purred while still playing with Kyros' hair. "I would wait for an easy time to dispose of the evidence and create a valid alibi, like a warfront or a hunting expedition."

His glare grew tighter on the mercenary, who, for the first time in his life, felt small in comparison to his current company. The vertical slits in his eyes narrowed in on Kyros as he looked the mercenary up and down. Kyros' sarcasm was subdued under the pressure the beast man gave off.

After a few seconds, Mithra looked to Castor and said, "Was this a satisfactory use of your sarcasm? I believe I performed it as well as we rehearsed."

While expressions were not common on the faces of great Maudians, Castor thought he saw a small smile from the exiled prince. Maybe it was a reflex of being around Anthorans for so long, maybe it was a trick of the light. Either way, Castor noticed the deep purring of satisfaction from the cat man as he walked over to the roadside and away from the quickly growing crowd around the door. He used a waist-height stone wall to start his morning stretches a few paces away.

Castor grinned; happy they were able to get the upper hand on Kyros for the first time in a long while. He loved his best friend, but Kyros' quick wit made him a master at messing with Castor. While Castor was glad that Kyros never treated him as the heir prince of the region, his pranks and sarcasm were sometimes more than what Castor wanted to put up with. Events like these helped balance that out.

"Well, that just goes and proves my statement from before. Attempted murder? Bah. I will be avenged!" Kyros said with a wide smile, trying to play the situation cool after being intimidated a minute prior.

"Do not lecture me on such triviality." Mithra yowled as he bent his left leg into backward shapes to stretch out his hamstrings. "It was just premeditation. No such attempt was made yet. If such events were to arise, I doubt anyone would be yelling about it so early in the morning. Besides, I do not plan for such an event to occur, as my time will be focused on bringing down the mightiest beast on this hunt."

"Bold words from someone not from the winning group in this competition," Acco said as he walked over to the mounts stabled in the open barn stalls next door. Castor could hear the aurochs moo as Acco fed them some hay from the bales inside. Their chariots sat in the yard next to the barn.

"Ah, adopted son Acco, you are ready for our morning drills, yes?" Mithra purred, eager to train before the competition started.

"Yes sir." Acco said, "I just need to feed our mounts and ensure they are ready for the journey. You can keep stretching and I can join you in a few minutes."

"Splendid." Mithra purred, his eyes closed and his face scrunched up like a Maudian kitten.

The Thrimite had gotten close to Acco over the last few months. He had taken an interest in his mosaic work around the estate and Acco appreciated the attention. When Mithra found out about Acco's skill with channeling earth, he took the opportunity to foster a martial relationship with the burly teen. While not close to the same size, Acco was the best fit in the Daimos family for magical and physical sparring bouts. Castor stayed as his cultural and etiquette trainer, but Acco's more muscular frame and free time before his apprenticeship allowed him to train with the Maudian behemoth. At first, he was hesitant, as he needed his mana reserves to work at the winter kilns in the coming months, but Mithra offered a wide array of mana crystals to regenerate his pool after they fought.

"May I remind everyone that this hunt is not a competition," Hecantor said as he made eye contact with everyone while he got to his feet. "We are here to celebrate the goddess of the hunt and to share prosperity with this village. Do not look to sate your vainglory during this event. Enjoy it while it lasts and uses this time to unwind from your daily tasks."

Acco and Mithra moved to the dirt path in front of the home to spar with stone chunks they had taken from the knee-high wall near the far side of the road.

Castor and Kyros finished the preparations for their departure as Hecantor said their proper goodbyes to Glaucus. While they fastened the saddles and reattached bags to the stocky beasts of burden, the entire party had congregated in the front yard of the home. Clumps of hewn rock whistled as the two hurled the flagstones back and forth. Maya exited the house and spoke to Glaucus with Hecantor. Aretha sent her in her stead for this year's Arietia since she had a few important business meetings to attend during this week. While reluctant to leave her side, Maya left her boss in the capable hands of her coworkers and focused on the hunt, hoping to bring home a worthwhile trophy for the Isadora Trading Company.

Nikitas and his sons, Nomiki and Paeon, had finished tidying the home before the group made their way to the campgrounds. Paeon was joining Acco and Maya on their hunt for the next week while Nomiki and Nikitas were around to escort Hecantor back to town after the celebration started. Nomiki's youngest son, Teris, waddled out into the front yard and watched Castor as he finished up strapping the aurochs with their tethers and ties. The six-year-old boy watched silently from the edge of the stables, as he always did. The boy was not very talkative and Castor had only seen him speak a few times in the past.

"Hello, little one," Castor said to Teris as he pulled on the auroch's strapping near its yoke. It shook its head and the chariot shuttered. The boy nodded and took a few steps back as the towering oxen moved closer to munch on some supple grass by the boy's feet.

Nikitas had finished his discussions with Hecantor and left his sons over by the entrance to grab his grandson and toss him onto his shoulders. The boy giggled and patted his grandfather on the head.

"Is this boy giving you any trouble, my lord?" Hecantor smiled as he steadied Teris on his shoulders.

Castor laughed and agreed, "Oh yes. Very much so. I think he deserves some tickles as punishment."

"Very well, my lord," Nikitas said, turning his head to Teris. "You heard him; it has to be done." And with that, he grabbed the boy off his shoulders and held him upside down, tickling him in the process. The boy laughed some more. He always seemed to open up to his grandfather no matter how many scary adults were around. Nikitas put him down on the ground and the boy scampered off to his father across the way.

"Are you two ready for your trip?" Nikitas asked, leaning his head in closer. "Do not worry, I haven't told anyone of your plans. I think it will be cutting it pretty close, but I wish you the best of luck nonetheless."

Castor nodded and thanked his mentor as the three of them brought the draft oxen to the front yard. They finished their discussions as they all prepared their animals for the days ahead. These draft oxen were a taller, more lithe breed of their field-bound cousins. The Anthorans bred this type of cattle specifically for mounted travel. As the only animal that was large and docile enough for such a task, the local populations created these beasts over past centuries of selective breeding. The mounts they used today were made for off-road adventures.

The group departed their temporary home with their oxen and started their way towards the campgrounds that were situated by the forests on the other side of town. Glaucus joined them for the trip, as his home was by the forest's edge. He owned the grassy hillsides near the campgrounds as the village's only shepherd. Glaucus and Hecantor sat on the backs of aurochs as everyone else walked.

The village was homely, with their properties spread out every few acres. Castor always liked the space a smaller town gave to its citizens. The same amount of land within a city like Thyma would be used for an amphitheater or a market. No individuals would own that amount of land within city limits for personal use only. That's exactly why the Daimos family had set their estate out on the western hills of the city's outskirts.

While the line of princes was important in a region, taking such a blatantly excessive amount of land within the city's walls would be seen as an overstep of the local government.

The homes were large but not built to the standards of the city proper. Many were made of sun-dried mud bricks while others had rough-hewn stone packed in between. Some outer walls were coated with stucco to defend against the region's inclement weather, but not all. Wood beams protruded from edges where the structural support of the building was showing through. The roofs were lined with ceramic or wood tiling to keep the rain and snow from getting into the homes during times when Vrontir took spite on the Anthorans. Having stayed in a village home the night prior, Castor felt their living situation was a lot better than the rumors that spread around the city. He would personally choose to live out here in the mountains rather than in a city apartment, so long as war was not being waged within the lands.

As they walked, Castor took in the quiet and relaxed lifestyle of the village's residents. A local bronzesmith worked in his front yard, hauling charcoal to the forge that sat on the side of his abode. A small wisp of smoke billowed from the main smelter's chimney. A group of women weaved linen cloth within the atrium of a home. They waved as the party passed the front yard. A few village girls ran around the trees, playing games while the older women worked.

They continued down the streets and past the village center. Overall, about a hundred people lived within the village proper. Out of all the homes on the village streets, only two were left abandoned. The population was down right now, as the Vrontian rebellion of years past had impacted the region's headcount by a fair margin. Things were looking up though, as a newlywed couple planned to move into one of the abandoned houses in the coming month.

They eventually reached the end of the road where Glaucus' house sat. It was a meager villa but made up for its lacking size with the attached barns and stables that sat nearby. Glaucus bid the party a final goodbye.

"Thank you again for taking us into your village for a night. I am sure the hunters appreciated the ability to relax before they started their adventures." the crown prince said gently.

"No worries, my lord. We were humbled that you would spend time in our village." he said in a confident, albeit humble, manner.

The others turned to give their agreement to the town's hospitality, including Mithra. Acco, being a bit away from the conversation due to the training he and Mithra were performing on their walk to the campgrounds, did not realize that Mithra had turned away and put his attention on the farewell conversation. Thinking their training was still being performed, Acco slung a coconut-sized block of stone at the Maudian, who had stepped out of the way to join the conversation easier. The projectile launched through the air and was on a collision course with Glaucus, who stood in the fence gate on his property.

Kyros, who stood nearby, tried to reach out and block the stone, but he quickly winced in pain from overextending his maimed arm. He dropped to the ground and grabbed at the spasming bicep muscles to quell the convulsions. Castor saw the object fly across the road but was too far away to react properly. The shepherd, seeing the boulder careening towards him, instinctively jerked his hands up to block the impact.

A few feet from colliding with Glaucus' head, the stone halted its movement as though it had been snared in an invisible net. The stone fragmented from the instantaneous stop and each of the small pieces of shrapnel halted their course a few inches past the main section of stone. Apopsi, perched upon Hecantor's shoulder, stared directly at the incoming objects. On his cane, Hecantor had lifted his pointer finger from its resting place and a few of the brilliantly cut gems along the collar of the handle gave a dull glow. The stones held their place in the air for a few seconds before the invisible net released its grip. The now stationary stones fell lifelessly to the compacted dirt road.

Turning to his son, Hecantor glared with his functional eye. "It is generally bad manners to strike down the host of a party before the day has finished."

While strict, Hecantor showed control in his tone as he was certain that his son had done so out of carelessness rather than out of spite. Acco had rushed over to Glaucus, patting the man down for injuries and apologizing profusely. Besides the mental trauma of seeing one's life flash before one's eyes, Glaucus was completely unscathed. The barrier Hecantor had around them had stopped the rocks in place and nothing had gotten through. While he may be maimed and partially blind, the crown prince of Thyma was still a force to be reckoned with.

Castor checked on Kyros as the others had given their attention to the terrified herdsman. He hid his pain under a well-placed smile. Castor knew the mercenary had lingering pains within his healed arm, but he usually was not physically hindered by it. After ensuring both Kyros and Glaucus were alright, the party said their final goodbyes and moved into the woods towards the campgrounds.

After passing the edge of the woods and hiking across the forest trails, they came across the meadow that held the campgrounds of the Arietia. Some parties had already gathered, but the area was not as full as it would be in a few hours when the hunt was finally underway. A painted wood arch on the opposite side of the clearing signaled the start of the hunt, which would officially begin at noon. A few groups stood around their aurochs and discussed their plans for the upcoming week. A wood and cobble pavilion held the overseers of the event. A wood table held the sign-in sheets and information about the hunt. A large bonfire roared in the center of the clearing.

As the party waited for the rest of the participants to meander their way into the campgrounds, the group broke up into their respective groups. Castor, Kyros, and Mithra stood by their two mounts while Acco, Maya, and Paeon huddled their party a hundred or so feet away. Hecantor, Nikitas, Nomiki, and Teris spoke with the overseeing priests of the event. Many participants gathered around Hecantor's group, hoping to make small talk with their regional archon. Gaining the favor of the regional leader could be a great boon for one's employment and social standing. Hecantor went back into work mode and greeted the citizens as politely as he always had.

Castor and Kyros ensured all their gear was in the proper places on their mounts. On top of their gear, Mithra's belongings were shared between the two draft oxen. His main bag hung off the wood frame of Castor's chariot. Great Maudians never rode on steeds, instead choosing to travel their whole lives by either foot or palanquin. Most Maudians preferred to walk rather than ride, but great Maudians were particularly obstinate with this cultural ideology. Being as prideful as the rest, Mithra was no exception. Since he was to take this adventure without his servant guards, he elected to travel by foot. Luckily, great Maudians had naturally high stamina so his pedestrian ways would not hinder their travel speeds.

"Is everyone still in agreement with our plans for this trip?" Castor asked, ensuring there was no faltering in the current proposal.

Kyros nodded and gave Castor a thumbs up. Mithra squinted and purred, petting Castor on the shoulder, neck, and back. The non-verbal communication of Maudian culture was something Castor had gotten used to over the last few months and understood this action as agreement.

Over a few hours, groups of travelers made their way to the clearing. A group of three siblings stood near Castor's party and waved when they recognized him. The two brothers and the elder daughter were Castor's neighbors, belonging to the Periankor house. They were also government officials, overseeing the entertainment district.

Castor never liked the children of their house growing up, as they grew spoiled and ostentatious. The parents ruled their district with an strong fist and focused their attention on their work, only giving their offspring petty contrivances and any material worth they desired. Pyrrosleion, the older of the two brothers, wore his ornate hunting bow slung over his shoulder for all to see. Gold inlays traveled down its limbs and coiled around the grip. While the metal may help somewhat with channeling on his arrows, such a volume of a fine metal was only there to show off to others. Castor waved back and acted as politely as he usually did when dealing with such people.

The sun grew in the sky as the hunting week grew to its start. The area had around forty parties prepared with gear and mounts. Some bystanders talked to the groups while locals came to see the adventurers before they left. Castor had seen Glaucus with his son from a distance speaking to Hecantor and the overseers near the pavilion. It did not seem as though the shepherd saw Castor from across the filled meadow.

The overseer of the event walked in from the wood arch and gathered everyone's attention. His long gray beard waved in the crisp winter air. He stood off to the side of the arch on a small wooden platform right behind a stone sundial. He swung his wood walking staff in the air above his head as much as an elderly man could. The large quartz crystal that was fastened at the end of the staff lit up, gathering the attention of the groups that had not seen his approach. Once the clearing of one hundred and fifty-odd people fell to silence, he started to discuss the upcoming week-long hunt.

"Welcome, everyone. If we have not met, I am Sander, high priest of the Temple of Vrontir in Thyma. The priestesses of Beltunias were not able to oversee this holy hunt as they have another Arietia to attend to in their home city of Bythe. As the head of the largest temple in our region, I have been asked to oversee the hunt this year."

The old man spoke loudly and clearly so that everyone in the clearing could hear him well.

"The Arietia has been celebrated in this region for over two hundred years. Our ancestors started this tradition during a time of famine to help feed the hungry and bolster the winter granaries. Times have changed and our region has flourished. Pyrritrios Drakos, Father of Polybolas Drakos, helped raise our region from poverty and supported the common citizen. His legacy lives on in our traditions as we celebrate Arietia, the great deer hunt, for the two hundred and thirteenth year in a row."

The crowd applauded and cheered. While the original hunt was started many generations in the past, the local villages still felt the economic and social impact of hosting the Arietia. Olynthia was chosen this year and expected many benefits like the improved road systems that Castor had mentioned earlier in the morning.

"For those of you who have not participated in an Arietia before, I will discuss the rules now." the old man bellowed, pulling a scroll from his vestments. He wrapped his arm around his staff and propped the large vellum up onto a knot in the wood branch.

"This hunt is not a competition. You are encouraged to fall the largest prey in the land. But do not hinder or injure any other parties that are out hunting. You win nothing other than fame and glory for bringing back the largest beast. You have exactly ten days as of high noon today to pull your catch back through this gate. If you just bring trophies or are late, you are disqualified. The creatures you bring after are still welcome, as all meat harvested by the hunt will be donated to support the local economy. The harvest will be split into three: a third to the hunters, a third to the state, and a third to the local village. We will finish on the tenth day by butchering and preparing the meat that is harvested and a small celebration will commence upon the tenth night. Does anyone have any questions?"

No noise came from the audience. Most of the groups here came from families that had participated in the hunt for decades prior. Castor saw a few new faces, but they either learned of the event or had experienced party members that had taught them beforehand.

Castor got a shiver up his spine. It was either from his excitement or the chilly wind that blew through the forest. This was the first year he was old enough to go without his family. He relished the idea of traveling with two of his friends for a week of camping, hunting, and relaxation.

"Very well. Then..." Sander moved to the sundial and watched as the shadow crossed the main stem and signaled the middle of the day. "Good luck and have fun. You may begin."

And with that, the parties moved through the wood arch and began their hunt.

CHAPTER 10

Welcomed With Wrapped Arms

40th of Jasper, 453 of the Age of Discovery

he late day sun was just starting to descend behind the tallest of the plateaus as Castor, Kyros, and Mithra made their way over the crest of a hill. Kyros wobbled back and forth from the deep stride of his mount. The heavy beasts were well weighted with gear and supplies. Mithra matched their pace, his long legs and digitigrade posture allowing him to walk as fast as the animals moving on all fours. They had been traveling for six hours since the start of the hunt and Castor had not noticed any fatigue in the Maudian. For someone who frequently traveled on a bed of pillows, the exiled prince was surprisingly athletic.

"I meant to ask you, Mithra. Why did you leave your nation in the first place?" Kyros requested as they rode down the grassy slope. "What caused you to go on your exodus?"

Small patches of thorny bushes littered the landscape. Their mounts lumbered around the dry bramble.

The Maudian hummed deeply in the back of his throat, "You ask that as though I had a say in the matter."

"You didn't?" Kyros asked, perplexed.

"Being exiled is not always the same as participating in an exodus, hairless one." Mithra yowled, "The decision of becoming exiled was made within the royal family."

The two Anthorans looked on, expecting more of an explanation from such a revelation.

Seeing their inquisitive stares, Mithra continued. "You see, my father ruled our nation as a satrap under the Empire of Maudif. Our nation prospered for many years before we were taken by the empire, and we prospered more under their rule. The king of kings, Druther Nink, brought the empire into a golden age. And my father followed suit, under his leadership."

The cat hissed, "I was the firstborn, the rightful heir to the throne. Through combat, I would have won that right as all kings of Thrim had earned in our history. But my bastard brother Rashn had other nefarious plans. That perfidious dog. That tepid hyena. He bided his time at my father's side until he earned his trust. I warned him of his disloyalty. He was the runt son of a prideless consort. He was a no-mane. He was not even a mark on our history. It should have stayed that way."

Mithra caught himself hissing at his words and controlled his emotions. He was not someone to show their feelings outwardly. His body language was still showing his anger, with hairs on end and his mane puffed up. But he continued his story, nonetheless.

"The betrayer struck a deal with Alborz, heir of the empire. They plotted and killed my father. They pinned the death on me and my two younger brothers. Now the satrapy of Thrim is ruled by a traitor and the true bloodline is banished from our lands."

"The plot was never found out?" Kyros asked, "Even with the three of you testifying against one bastard son?"

Mithra roared. "Ha! Testify? There was not even a summons, much less a case to the courts."

While Maudians had different words for their sounds, Castor could only describe the noise he made as a scoff.

"No," Mithra continued, "Nothing was done. Nothing could be done. The rule of the king of kings was the law of the land. So is our tradition. And that amnesty falls upon his family as well. The king of kings Druther Nink would not put that hyena at fault. If he did so, then his only heir would be at fault as well. That was not what our ways would allow. So we left. The decree of our exile was announced the following day. We had gathered our valuables and our closest companions and left on our exodus. Our family and the families of all our supporters, friends, and compatriots traveled to far-off lands to avoid political execution."

He growled once more. "Not that leaving changed much. We travel often and we travel light. We all tried staying in one location at the beginning. In the coastal nations of the Elvari, we lived on the Bright Isles of the Yasari Confederation. We were able to stay contently on an island where they kept their foreigners as we planned our future. Unfortunately, my brother was not done with us and assassins found their way to our island. My mother and my youngest brother were killed along with many of our supporters."

A short silence fell across the party. It was not intentional, as Mithra had paused from sharing his story to drink a bit of water from his leather waterskin, but the silence was just about palpable from where he left off. Once he finished his quick drink, he continued his story.

"Since then, my last brother Izad and I have stayed separated. I have dyed my mane this bright white to gain some..." he paused to look for the right word. He settled with, "Anonymity. I am known as the night-maned elector back homeland because of how dark my mane was, even amongst my family of dark maned kin. Izad has probably done the same. With our manes discolored, we can pass off as unimportant nobles that were exiled with my family. I do not even know where he has ended up. It is for the best. This makes it harder for them to find us again."

Castor had pulled on the reins of his ox and moved close to the giant cat man. He wrapped his arm around his giant head and rubbed his mane where he could reach. He knew Maudians appreciated physical communication over verbal, so he thought this gesture to be more fitting for the severity of the conversation.

"Do not worry about me, little prince." Mithra purred deeply. The rumblings of his throat vibrated Castor's arm as he stroked his mane. "I had made peace with my mother and my brother many moons ago. They were true Maudians. I have no doubt they have joined Ig'Natas on the eternal hunt."

They continued their journey, passing up and down hills of light green grass like a small canoe on the open ocean.

As they peaked the precipice of yet another small knoll, the outline of a town was seen nestled within the mountainside. It sat at the base of the first mountain on this side of the Sideros Highlands. Small strands of smoke wisped their way into the clouds, the small hovels barely noticeable in the gray haze formed around the village. Castor recognized the plumes of acrid smoke as the town he planned for them to settle in for the night. The town of Flegomena was their destination for this day.

"That's the village Aretha mentioned back during the summer solstice?" Kyros asked Castor, bringing up a discussion they had during the celebration of the mid-year. "It seems a lot smaller in scale than what was described in the past."

"Ha," Castor chuckled, rubbing the side of his eye. "There is more to this city than what meets the eye. Just wait until we get inside."

"It is...pungent," Mithra chimed in. The great cat sniffed the air and gurgled after finding a scent he did not take a liking to. "Are we resting here for tonight?"

"We are." Castor confirmed. "No other village is within a dozen miles of here, and we would be backtracking for a few hours to find ample lodging for all of us."

The aurochs munched on the tall grass that covered the top of the hill. The smell of lavender filled the air as one took a whole plant in its jaw and ground the plant down for consumption. While not a full mountain range, this collection of tall hills and fjords was not easily traversable with carts and wagons. They were lucky to have such durable steeds within this area, as their mounts were native to these hills. Though not from this specific area, the Anthoran aurochs were renowned across the eastern side of the continent as strong, agreeable mounts with little stubbornness and strong legs. They traversed the steep hills of this landscape with ease.

Getting closer to the town, the scent of the acrid smoke could be smelled in the breeze. The once gray fumes were now tar-black and billowed into the sky. The occasional clanging of large hammers could be heard from this distance alone, the sounds bouncing through the fjord. The town itself was not too large, maybe thirty large buildings in total, surrounded by a wooden palisade atop a head-high wall of cobblestone.

As they got closer, Mithra started rubbing his nose more and more often.

"I do not like this place," Mithra said. "It smells of pollution and decay."

"You smell something?" Kyros asked. "I do not. Just the lavender in the fields. Castor?"

[230]

"I do not either, but Mithra is not wrong. The ferric ore they smelt in their village is quite pungent. I am sure you and I will notice once we are closer."

Mithra grunted. "I noticed from here. Let's hope it doesn't get worse."

"Oh, Mithra, I almost forgot!" Castor pulled a large pouch from the storage on the side of his auroch. He handed the package to Mithra, who pulled the drawstrings to unveil a large amount of charcoal and flowers.

"My sister knows how smelly this area can be, so she prepared you a satchel to escape from the smells when you need it. The charcoal should cut the fumes and the cyclamens blooms should smell pleasant."

Mithra inhaled deeply into the bag and purred. "It is nice and gentle. I will put it to good use. Thank you."

"Ya, no worries," Castor said. "Oh, but make sure you keep it closed when you aren't using it. It'll lose its effect after a while. Once we are into our lodging, you should smell it less. We are downwind now, so you are going to get the worst of it before it gets better."

Mithra held up a small glass ball with his long claws and the small, sealed container glinted in the sun. A light pink solution moved back and forth from within the ampoule and an elliptical bubble of air bounced across the top of the surface.

"Be careful with that. Break that container and you will be unable to smell for a short while. She had that packaged away in case you needed it during our trip. Considering your upbringing, she was not sure if you could handle the smell of a butchered corpse or a punctured gut."

Mithra purred and nodded. "I am well situated with the smells of death, but the... sentiment is much obliged."

"Your sister didn't prepare me a satchel as well? I am hurt!" Kyros grabbed at his heart and kicked his legs up, faking a heart attack. The auroch underneath dodged a dry bush and almost knocked Kyros to the ground before he grabbed the reins.

"Oh no," Castor retorted, "She had seen you after returning from your mercenary adventures. She knows you are basically nose blind."

"You wound me, sir." Kyros shot back with an exaggerated frown.

"If only I could." Castor rolled his eyes and chuckled.

The town grew larger on the horizon as they crested each consecutive hillock. The village was surrounded by a wood palisade around twelve feet high and was sharpened at the top foot of the poles. The wood was tinted gray from the sun's harsh rays. The walls and gatehouse were plain, clearly focused on function over form. Mithra occasionally breathed through his charcoal bag on the way over the hills.

As they got close to the gates, a face appeared on the gatehouse. It was not a normal, fleshy face. The face they saw was a face covered with a bronze visage. The mask was brightly polished and molded with the details of an Anthoran face but set deeply in the lightly colored metal. Their head was wrapped with white cloth, pulled tight and unwrinkled around their shape.

"Who are you?" the masked villager yelled, "Where do you hail from? Who do you represent? We had no payments nor trades planned for today."

The voice traveled down to them, but the lack of expression from the mask of metal made the questions all the more accusatory.

"Hello!" Castor yelled back, "We hail from Thyma. My sister does business with you frequently. I came today on her behalf."

"Who is your sister?" the bronze visage called back, the tone of their voice matching the inanimate plate of bronze. The voice was feminine, like that of a grandmother or a widow. The face leaned closer, although Castor could not see her eyes. She was no doubt trying to get a better look at the riders that had approached their home.

"Aretha Daimos of Thyma is my sister." Castor responded confidently, "I am her brother, Castor Daimos."

"Oh!" she shrilled, as though her control over her vocal cords gave out a mild exclamation. As quickly as the head had popped into view, so did it disappear. Scuffling and shuffling could be heard behind the gate, and then an audible click. The log gates swung inward and revealed the smelting town's central square.

A town built around the smelting of ferron was in front of the traveling hunters. Small rivulets of mountain water ran between and under buildings. Some streams were crystal clear while some ran a murky orange liquid downhill. The buildings that they could see were mostly made of wood and cobblestone, most likely stones taken from the mines and put to use over being thrown in a landfill. Black smoke slowly rose from the tops of buildings. Off to the left of the gates, within a stone wall, sat many mounts of clay that held the smoldering remains of a charcoal kiln within. The piles were almost identical. They stood twenty feet in height and released acrid smoke from any cracks that formed during the heating process.

Although not much different than the other villages around the region, the town here felt less alive. It was not as though the town was devoid of color, but the streets were empty and the buildings were not decorated from the outside. Aretha warned Castor of this, as this was the way of the citizens here in Flegomena. She made sure to tell Castor that the locals were a lot nicer than the village would seem once you got to know their customs.

On the other side of the gate, a group of ten or so people stood around the edges of the wood gatehouse. They all sported the same white robes and headwraps. Each and every face was covered with a bronze mask, the details now much clearer than when Castor had originally seen one from so far away.

Before Castor could walk into the village, one of the larger villagers threw a white cloth sack through the gate and near their feet. The pile jingled as it rolled on the ground and fell into place. Castor, dismounted at this point, opened the bag to find three bronze masks and three stark white himations. The masks covered the entire face from forehead to chin like those worn by the villagers, but the ones within the bag were not as detailed as what he had seen so far. The masks in the bag looked generic, like something he had seen in the theater in Thyma.

"Welcome, our young prince and his guests." An older man said from behind his own mask, bowing with arms extended. "Lady Aretha had sent a letter about your arrival, but we were not sure when it would be. We are very happy to welcome you to our village for the night. Preparations have been made on the other side of the mountain and your outfits have been prepared for you. Normally we would not take such precautions with our guests, but given your status, we do not want to risk infecting you with our curse."

Aretha had mentioned to Castor the details of their curses a few nights before they left. Everyone within the village of Flegomena was deformed, the illness spreading across their skin and leaving behind terrible lesions. Whether it be by poor luck or the spite of one of the gods, the accursed had horrible welts and wounds across their bodies that made them both shunned by their peers and a risk to other communities. While the way the curse is spread was not exactly known, many people within the village were the first to acquire it within their original homes and were banished to this town to live the rest of their lives. Outbreaks of their curse were seen across Anthora, so villages of the cursed were not uncommon.

"We won't force you, my lord." the old man murmured hesitantly, seeing Castor had not donned his given clothing for some time. He was not rejecting their kind offer, but instead focusing on the masks. The town only mined ferric ore and processed it into bars of ferric metal. The dark gray metal was not nearly as abundant nor as useful as brass and bronze. It hindered the effects of mana channeling when held and put channelers at a disadvantage. Usually used in the construction of military buildings or defenses, ferric metal earned the nickname of 'dead metal' as it seemed to be both a hindrance to channeling as well as a formidable way to deafen the healing effects of mana.

Castor assumed they traded for the metallic brown alloy with their ample supply of ferron. The masks they were given, while not detailed to the human likeness of the villager's mask, were ornately designed and the quality was surprising for an item they threw on the ground so willingly. Castor distributed the masks to the two others and allowed each to grab their himation.

"No, it is quite alright!" Castor said. "I appreciate the effort to ensure our safety. I was just admiring the work you put into these masks."

A few of the villagers bowed when Castor complimented the visages, no doubt taking responsibility for the fine craftsmanship.

They entered the town now wearing their new garbs and brought their animals with them on leashes. Mithra held his mask in his offhand and remarked before entering about how his people were immune to the Curse of the Hairless, the name that Maudians gave to the skin curse that plagued humans, Durulians, and Elvari. As Castor had read in a book before that no Maudian had ever been seen with the curse, Castor did not push the topic. He knew Mithra was well-traveled and trusted his companion's decision.

"Thank you for housing us tonight," Castor remarked to the older man who had addressed them before. "We are grateful that this opportunity works so well in our favor during our hunt."

"We are glad we were able to be of use." the elderly man said. "Your sister has helped us where others would not even consider. The least we could do is return the favor."

While every person in the town was veiled in identical white cloth wrappings, the individuals could be told apart by the details in their masks and any other items they wore. The old man, with a hunched back and a simple wood cane, looked at Castor with a tilted head. The bronze mask he wore was so detailed that it seemed like a face covered in bronze-colored paint was looking back. Every wrinkle was etched in the shiny surface, a few sunspots stained on the veneer like a patina. The work they put into their only identifying feature was breathtaking.

"I hope the accommodations are to your liking." the man continued, "We have prepared rooms for you three on the other side. We will take you there after we visit the town's matron if you are alright with that."

"No worries," Castor continued, trying not to stare too long at any one face. "Let us abide by any customs you have here in your town."

Now that he wore his own mask, he felt as though he fit in alright with the crowd. Only Mithra stood out, trying to fit the human-sized himation over his bulky head and fitting the surfaces around his broad shoulders. By the time he was done fidgeting, the cloth looked more like a shoulder cape. Having tied their aurochs into the stables near the front of the village, they carried what they needed for their meeting with the village matron.

Walking through the streets, they noticed the town was very well off in terms of public facilities. The streets were completely paved with stone slabs and buildings were almost all mortared stone on the first story. A bathhouse was near the right side of the village and had clean mountain water diverted into it from the stone channels that passed between buildings in the alleys. No dirt or mud was seen in the streets, no doubt kept clean for the sake of all residences. Having their curse meant a lot of personal maintenance, so keeping their town clean was crucial to survival with such an ailment.

They arrived at another palisade gate that led to a higher section of the village. When the villagers opened the area up, they were surprised by the wide array of colored flowers that grew across the soil landscape. While the main portion of the town was paved with stone as much as it could be with little land open to the natural ground, this area felt different. It felt natural. As they walked into the higher courtyard, it was as though they were back in the fields they had been riding across before entering the village.

They walked by a boy sitting on a wood bench. His legs were bound together, most likely past where they could be useful to the poor boy due to his curse. He hummed a gentle tune and seemed to not be deterred by his physical limitations. He sat by a small patch of yellow flowers and appreciating their late-season blooms. The vines the flowers grew on had also crawled up part of the bench and made the boy look as though he was a part of the garden himself. He waved to the group that passed by. His head was covered by a cloth cap over his head wraps and the edges of the covering were tucked into his bronze mask.

"Hello there!" the boy called out. His voice was raspy like an old man that smoked too much but the way he talked sounded like a child. "Do you have some time to play?"

Mithra knelt by the boy, who did not flinch or pull back after seeing a being easily five times his size. Mithra purred and set a giant paw on the armrest of the bench, making sure not to touch the frail child.

"What do you like to play?" the cat man asked.

"It doesn't matter to me." the boy said. "If you do not have anything in mind, we could always just talk about the flowers! Did you know these are called Erysimum?"

Mithra purred as he sat on the bench. "I did not." He picked a small flower and examined it closer.

The boy giggled and put one of his arms up in front of him. The wrapped arm was bent and gnarled in a way that was not normal. Castor felt bad for the boy, although the child's kind attitude did not seem to need his sympathy. After a few moments, his arm began to shake from holding it in such a position for so long. Before he put it done fully, a butterfly gently landed on his hand. The wrapped hand was small and his fingers were all wrapped together like a mitten, but the boy did not seem to be held back. The butterfly was brown with bright blue dots along the edge of its wings. Mithra put his paw out and extended a finger near his hand. The butterfly lightly danced over to his finger and perched on the flower he had picked.

"It's alright to pick a couple, but do not pick more than that! If you do, then the garden will disappear!" the boy exclaimed, "Those are called crystal winged butterflies. They live in the cold months to help the flowers that bloom late like these!"

"I understand." Mithra purred. "I am Mithra, son of the sun and slayer of the great snake Azikesh. What is your name, little one?"

"I'm Marcus." the boy said, "But the others call me Marky. You can call me that too!"

The beautiful rows of well-maintained plants made the area smell as wonderful as it looked. Unlike the industrial buildings billowing smoke below, this little refuge seemed like a small place of rest from an otherwise dirty and soot-covered environment. A few buildings were scattered within this area of the walls. The group of veiled villagers led the trio to a cobblestone longhouse near the top of the sloped plaza.

"I will stay out here for a short while," Mithra announced to Castor as they approached the longhouse, pointing to the wisps of smoke overhead. "The smell here is pleasant and a nice break from that...stench."

"Suit yourself." Castor shot back. "We shouldn't take long."

They entered through the open doors and found a large room filled with color and decor. Unlike the outside, the interior of their building was full of life. A handful of people lay on the floors near small fires, keeping warm in the winter weather. A woman, garbed like the rest but wearing a silver mask, sat at a table full of vellum scrolls and tablets of clay. A map of the area was well painted behind her desk and small pins stuck out of it. They marked different spots in the mountains. The woman, most likely the town matron, stood and bowed when seeing Castor.

"Hello, my prince." Her gaze was towards him and, although he could not see her eyes, he could tell she was examining him and his companions. She walked up to them and stood in front of Kyros.

"My, your sister said you had grown, but you seem a lot taller than what she described." the woman said, looking up at Kyros. She was short, even for an Anthoran woman, due to her age. Her demeanor and voice made her sound as though she was in her late thirties or early forties. The details in her mask confirmed his assumptions.

Castor started to put up his hand in protest, "Um--" he started.

"I know, dear. I am only joking with you." the woman paused before turning her head towards Castor. She sidestepped and set a slight bow as she addressed him. "You walk like your sister. I could tell you were related as soon as you walked in."

She put her hand on her hips. "Welcome to our town. Aretha's family is always welcome here. I heard from her of your plans to cross the mountains through our mines. It is a smart plan, if I do say so."

"Thank you..." Castor said, not knowing who he was addressing.

"Mavra. Mavra Kapela." She performed a small curtsy as she introduced herself. "I know it is customary to shake hands during introductions, but considering our...circumstances, such actions are generally refrained from."

Castor did a small bow with his hand on his chest, the only acceptable action for a prince to have towards his citizens, and fully introduced himself, Kyros, and Mithra. Once introductions were out of the way, Castor grabbed the wood chest that Kyros was holding and put it down on Mavra's desk. With the help of one of the other villagers, they opened the chest together and looked inside.

"My sister asked me to bring her normal gifts in her stead this month. She said she has too many meetings to visit like she normally does but wanted to make sure she was able to get you what she normally sent."

Mavra let out a gentle chuckle under her breath as they took out a few bars of well-crafted soap. Made from olive oil pressed in Thyma and scented with various perfumes from Aretha's personal collection, the bars of light green cleanser filled the chest to the brim.

"Your sister has always taken good care of us." Mavra placed the bar back on the pile and closed the chest back up. "I know some of her goodwill is to keep our trade deals flowing through the mountain, but she really has been a gift from the gods these last four years."

She chuckled to herself, "And we would know a thing or two about the will of the gods." A few others chuckled with her, making light of their otherwise serious affliction.

"One thing I was concerned about was our mounts." Castor said, bringing their focus on their plan to pass through the mountains in the morning, "I was not sure if they would fit through the tunnels."

"Oh, yes." Mavra waved her hand in front of her face as though the point was moot. "Our main corridor is wide enough for two of our aurochs side by side. If you travel in a single file, then you will have no issues passing through."

"I will say, though," Mavra continued as she walked over to a brazier next to her desk to warm her wrapped hands, "I have never heard of hunting being done on the mainland for the Arietia. Are you sure it is allowed in the rules?"

"We checked with a priestess of Beltunia in the city before we left." Kyros answered. "Well, I did, since I had so much time on my hands these last few weeks. She said so long as we are back by noon on the tenth day and we slay our prey ourselves, there is no rule as to how far we can go."

"It is a creative endeavor, at the very least." she said, "It seems luck is on your side as well. The main corridor was only fully mined to the other side of the mountain last year. If we never found that cluster of amazonite and a few other feldspar deposits, we never would have mined through to the other side."

"Maybe Beltunia favors us on this hunt then," Kyros suggested. "Her or Gargrin. But do not tell Acco about that. He may get jealous."

"Yes, I doubt my brother's patron deity was our benefactor in this." Castor chuckled. "Although the idea of claiming that and seeing the look on his face would be very fun."

Castor reached out and extended a smaller present he had brought to Mavra. Before he could finish telling Mavra about what he had brought, a side door to the longhouse flew open with a few masked villagers bringing in a smaller person. An elderly villager was laid on a straw bed near one of the walls, wheezing in a weak fashion.

"Excuse me." Mavra uttered as she removed herself from the conversation. Castor, while keeping his distance, went over near the crowded area, seeing Mavra and another masked Anthoran huddled over the older woman on the floor.

The duo unwrapped the woman's torso to reveal large swaths of warts and lesions. As soon as the bandages surrounding her torso were released, her wheezing subsided. Her breath steadied further as they poured their mana into healing the older woman.

A few of the villagers standing in front of Castor realized he had gotten close and put their hands up to keep him back.

"I'm sorry, my lord." A man murmured from behind his mask. "We do not want you to be put at risk. Can you please not involve yourself?"

Castor could hear a wet cough start, which was followed by a few muffled gasps. Blood soaked the wrapping around the poor old woman's neck and shoulders as she coughed up blood. The mana the duo was applying to the ailing woman was not as fast as was needed to suppress her pain. Castor could sense the flow of mana within the room and he knew their skills in channeling were not sufficient.

"Hold her here," Mavra instructed another in the crowd to apply pressure on the new clean gauze she was pressing into the open wounds. "And keep the guests back. She is spreading the curse right now. Castor, get out of here!"

Castor was young. He cared about his people. He had not fought in wars nor was a victim of a violent crime as a child. He was raised in a safe environment. But seeing his men die in Thyma changed him. He did not like seeing people he cared about die. He could tell this woman mattered to the people around him. Maybe she was a mother, maybe she was a widow. Maybe she was new to the community and didn't matter at all.

But Castor couldn't stand and watch her die like this. He had training from the temple of Nerea on how to seal internal wounds. He had a supply of Vótanodor on his belt sitting patiently to help aid the ailing. His body moved on its own, pressing through the ever-growing crowd and aiming to get at the meek elderly woman on the floor.

Mavra, seeing Castor do the opposite of what she said, called out.

"Are you a fool?" She said with a bit of anger in her voice, "Get back! We have seen countless others fall to the curse when someone is in this state. Get back! Get away!"

"I can help," Castor murmured, moving closer. He was in an almost trance-like state. It was not as though he lost his mind, but he was merely moving like a soldier would; reactively.

Mavra called out again, this time to some of those in the crowd.

"Get him back!" She yelled. " I won't put our community on the line for one person."

She aimed her gaze back at Castor. "If you get infected, our way of life would be snuffed out. This region and the country as a whole would blame us. We would be lucky not to be executed. Do not put us in that situation!"

The coughing got worse, this time blood and phlegm pooling onto the floor near where her shoulder pushed into the straw bedroll. The color and smell were gut-wrenching.

"She doesn't have to die! I can save her!" Castor yelled, almost tearing up in the process. He didn't know what had come over him. He was usually very good at controlling his emotions, especially under pressure. Maybe it was his anxiety for the trip, maybe it was the lack of sleep he had gotten recently due to all the holiday events. Either way, he still tried to push forward through the forest of white limbs that tried to hold him back.

"You fool!" Mavra drew a pugio from her belt and held it to the old woman's throat. "Is this what you want? Do you want me to end her suffering now? If you continue this and get infected, she will die anyway. We all will. You can fix this! Give us our space! I beg you!"

The woman, who was slipping in and out of consciousness due to her condition, awoke from a bout of drowsiness and saw the blade at her throat. She screamed a blood-curdling scream, no doubt seeing the pool of blood at her side and a knife at her throat.

"I won't let any of you die! You are my people. Not one, not some. I would put my life on the line any day to protect even the weakest of you!" Castor called out.

His progress forward was halted by this point, although he was still trying to move towards them. Enough of the crowd had pushed back. Little, white, wrapped fingers jutted out from swaddled arms like branches in a birch forest. No one around him gave their ground. Either scared of the foreseen future or out of respect for their lord, the crowd kept Castor back regardless of his cries to help.

"Let me help. Let me help." Castor said with eyes full of tears. He tried to resist the pushing crowd but could not. Mavra had focused her attention back on the woman, trying desperately to calm her convulsing body and staunch the flow of fluids.

At this point, the front door had opened quickly and Mithra had entered the room. He had listened to the conversation and surveyed the situation. He heard what was being said as he walked up to the door, choosing to come back inside when the injured woman screamed out in her delirium. He saw Castor standing a few feet away from the scene being held back by a mob, a knife at a crying woman's throat, and a puddle of blood. He called out and Mavra explained the situation as curtly as she could considering her focus on the woman's open wounds and fluid-filled lungs.

He pushed through the crowd, the small and decrepit humans merely parting in front of the giant beast man. He was almost double the height of the average villager and had no issue pushing through their ranks. He snarled as he got close, grabbed Castor by the cloth on the back of his neck, and tossed him backward out of the crowd.

Castor, gasping for air from the impact with the solid floor, looked startled at the Maudian's response. The rush of the pain he had taken was enough to shock him to his senses, although it took Kyros with two hands on his shoulders to keep him seated.

"Stay down, little prince." Mithra snarled. His serious tone was enough to scare away any of the villagers from his immediate vicinity, leaving a circle of open space around the half-covered cat. "Use that brain you are known for. In your love for your people, you put them at risk. Keep your wits about you and let me handle this."

Mithra turned and moved toward Mavra, kneeling in front of them and relaxing his foot paws as he relaxed on the ground. He grabbed a large standing pillar of ruby around four inches in height and an inch in width. The hexagonal spire was raw and uncut, but the rough surfaces were smoothed as though they were slowly lapped on hard rock. While Castor had not seen Mithra hold this crystal before, he held it with high regard as he carefully took it from a fur-padded pouch from his belt and gently set it near the woman.

With Mithra at her side, Mavra was able to calm the woman and heal her wounds. Mithra channeled his mana and the stored energy from

[245]

the pillar's pool into the frail old woman and helped close her wounds and empty her lungs. The fluid was vile and malodorous, but Mithra was not allowing it to affect his concentration. No one could smell the exudate since Mithra had popped the ampoule from Aretha's care package and allowed the vapors to nullify his sense of smell.

If one could describe the effects of the liquid, it was as though anyone in the area could smell to the same degree as someone looking through a thick fog of gray smoke. The scent they sensed was neither bad nor good. They had their sense of smell still, but it was as though they could not distinguish what the smell was. For Mithra, losing his sense of smell was very strange, but without it, he was able to focus on the task at hand.

Mavra pointed to different areas and Mithra followed with a flow of mana. Bandages were replaced and wounds were stitched together. The area was cleaned with an ample supply of cleaning rags, bowls of hot water, and a few detergents. At one point, a villager grabbed a bar of soap from Aretha's chest and used it to clean the liquid that had raced downhill across the floor.

Seconds turned into minutes as they worked through the process of saving the old woman. Her breath steadied and she calmed to a drunken stupor with the help of some herbs and a copious amount of distilled liquids. As they cleaned up, Mavra retreated to her desk, replacing the wrappings on her limbs with clean clothes. A small hamper sat against the wall behind her and she had placed all spoiled clothes within the bin.

"I am sorry," Castor murmured, not standing and taking in the situation better. "I... I would like to retire for the evening."

"I understand, my lord," Mavra said in a raspy voice. Her vocal cords were shot from yelling out commands for the past half of an hour. "I will have someone escort you to your quarters for the night."

"Thank you." He croaked. His eyes were still glazed over, ashamed and confused at how he acted earlier. He and Kyros followed a masked individual out of the building and through the rows of flowers outside.

Mithra stood near the basket behind Mavra's desk, wiping foul liquids from his arms and legs. His sense of smell was still hindered but he knew the matted fur would stink in the morning.

"Thank you for your help," Mavra murmured. "I believe Delia would have perished without your support. You have my thanks, Maudian."

"Your thanks are received well." Mithra yowled. "I would like to exchange your thanks for a hot bath. I cannot travel with my body covered in this disease, even if it would not affect me. My companions would be at risk."

"I completely understand." Mavra agreed, wrapping her scarred left forearm back up with white linen and tying the end off at her elbow. "I will have the others who are too dirty for simple wrapping to escort you to the bathhouse. The water should be clean and warm."

A man standing near Mavra spoke up as he rebound his own wrappings near the hamper. "If you would like, I can have your kandys and sirwal washed while you bathe."

Mithra looked down at his robe and pants. The light green and blue patterns were marred with streaks of red. The sanguineous stains were still wet from the past half hour of surgeries and would likely come out of the clothing if properly laundered.

"I would appreciate that. Thank you." Mithra purred. He put a hand up to rub the side of the man's head and shoulders, like Maudians usually did to show agreement or affection, but he stepped back out of reach.

"Sorry," he stammered, "It's a habit around here."

[247]

Mithra nodded in understanding.

Mavra chuckled, the first sign of a light-hearted mood returning to the room. "I am glad you were able to keep a cool head through all this, Maudian." She was clearly hinting at Castor's behavior during the commotion.

"I knew the little prince was ailing from his recent losses, but I did not know it affected him so deeply." Mithra rubbed his mane slowly, the closest thing an Anthoran could see in regard to a Maudian expressing sadness.

"I won't pry into his past, and I am sure his intentions were well. I did not want to put him at risk. Our curse is not reversible and always leads to an insufferable end." Mavra felt strange talking so improperly about the heir prince and her benefactress's brother, but she feared the potential outcome of a cursed ruler.

"I am sure he understands," Mithra said as he removed the himation above his personal clothing that was caked in ooze. "I have not seen him act that way since I met him, but seeing his soldiers die in front of him left its mark."

At that point, Mavra noticed the bag that Castor was carrying sitting beside her desk. She picked it up, and considered giving it back to him, but knew he mentioned it was for the village. She opened it to find a wide array of children's toys. From farm animals with wheels for feet to paddles with wood balls attached, the sack was filled to the brim with colorful wood trinkets and baubles.

"Yes, he mentioned he wanted to bring some things for the children here," Mithra confirmed as she laid the items across her desk. "He had not seen any in town so far so he was worried that you didn't have any around anymore."

"We do," Mavra confirmed. "Less than I wish we did. The children work in the mines with their slender frames or go out foraging for food in the local forests, so they just had not returned from their work for the day yet. I am sure they will be delighted to see all this."

She turned away as though to hide her face, which was unneeded as her face was covered with her silver mask. "It is hard around here as it is this time of year. This gift will serve to keep the spirits high through the upcoming months."

She turned back to Mithra, facing him directly. "Please give our kindest regards to the young prince. He probably does not know what these gifts will mean to our people, but I hope a fraction of our appreciation is set upon him."

"I will make sure to convey the feelings well." Mithra purred.

She turned away again. The masked man next to her had finished his wrapping and led Mithra to the bathhouse for a much-needed evening of relaxation and cleansing.

CHAPTER 11

Sharp Teeth Gnaw At Night

2nd of Azurite, 453 of the Age of Discovery

s the events of the afternoon made Castor a little uneasy, he retired to his lodgings for the night. He and Kyros led the aurochs through the mineshaft of the mountain and to the area set up for guests at Flegomena. The mountains were steep and perilous but traveling through them made a multiple-day trip around the peaks into an hour walk under them. The area they stayed for the night was well made out of dry-stacked stone blocks and kept far away from the village to reduce the spread of the curse. Castor left the town around twenty-two o'clock and calmed his nerves until twenty-three o'clock.

Mithra returned, freshly fluffed from the baths, around twenty-three o'clock and brought their dinner with him. His large frame and extraordinary stamina made carrying a bunch of boxed meals basically effortless. The three of them sat down for dinner and ate the variety of dishes they were given by the villagers. There were smoked freshwater fishes, two dozen hard-boiled eggs, and a salad of freshly picked winter flowers. An amphora of local wine was easy for Mithra to bring along as well, as he just tied it with string to his belt and let it hang as he walked. The trio enjoyed a relaxing evening before they continued their trip.

There was enough food to fill their bellies and have extra for the road, which was a nice touch since they had only brought staple grains for stews and porridge for the trip and relied on daily catches of wildlife for their meat supply. They kept a few of the smoked fishes for their future week of travel since they would be perfect to add to a hearty stew.

Castor's earlier outburst still weighed heavily on his mind, but he knew he didn't have much time to think about it at that moment. He was on a rather limited schedule for their hunts to work out well. It was twenty-four o'clock at this point, the sun already set behind the mountains. He spent an hour praying and meditating at a makeshift altar he made out of a rock cairn and a small statue of Ignus he kept with him for the trip. He found solace in his thoughts and in his god. He aimed to better control his emotions in the future.

By twenty-five o'clock, he was ready for bed. The lodgings were split into a few rooms and allowed each to sleep separately. After spending some time washing up with the use of his water channeling and a natural wellspring on the side of the mountain's slopes, Castor retired to sleep for the night.

The morning kicked off around five o'clock with the sun coming up in the distance and leaving a red haze on the horizon. It was distorted in a thick fog that laid across the northeastern slopes of the Sideros. The landscape was much more verdant on this side of the mountains, with trees and bushes and vines growing sporadically across the sloping hillsides. While the creeping vines and spiky bushes would have made travel harder by foot, the use of the aurochs as steeds nullified the issue for the Anthorans. The Maudian they were with was held up at some points due to these new hurdles but overall did not slow the caravan down. While his homeland of Thrim was a dry and arid steppe land, Mithra was well-traveled due to his exodus. He had been through much worse situations in the past.

The group had scaled down the remaining slopes of the Sideros and made it to the flatter lands by midday. Midday in Anthora was at fifteen o'clock since their days had thirty hours. On average, the sun shone for around twenty of those hours and the night held ten. Since they were closing in on the winter solstice in the next few months, it was closer to a split of eighteen and twelve.

The land here was warmer than on the southern side of the Sideros, as it was situated between two mountain ranges on the continent. The Sideros chain sat in the south and the Nidaros chain in the north. Their goal was the Nidaros chain, which was still a few days away, in order to hunt for their ultimate prey. The herds of female red-tailed deer would be migrating north to meet with the males that spent the year vying for territory. Their aim was one of the males that held up in the woodlands north of Tyressos. The widely crested males had antlers as tall as an Anthoran and stood taller than Mithra. They were behemoths of the northern plains and were notoriously well adapted for defending themselves and their territory. They were not only quick and agile, but they could blend into their natural surroundings with ease due to the shades of their fur. There were regional beliefs that the spirit of the Nidaros forests took the shape of one of these deer and defended its territory against unwelcome guests. While the spirits had been spotted throughout history, Castor still found it hard to believe without seeing for himself. He hoped this trip would not be the trip he did. Their plans did not involve coming into contact with a demi-god.

They spent the rest of the day traveling north towards Tyressos. They stopped for the night around the twentieth hour to give Mithra's feet a break. Castor and Kyros went hunting and with their javelins and magic captured two wild chickens for the night's feast. They had warmed up some porridge for breakfast and lunch during their short breaks and added some of the leftover flowers and some molasses. While nutritious and full of energy, consuming the same gruel for days on end would be bad for morale, so the chickens would fill that gap.

They roasted them over the remains of an open fire and added some of the spices Castor had brought for the long journey. He slathered some honey onto the skinned chicken carcasses and drizzled a little bit of garum onto the outside of the birds. A mix of pepper, cinnamon, and ground sage was sprinkled onto the sticky surface. They had the chickens tied to a rod and let them roast slowly above the carefully tended coals. For drinking, Mithra channeled water out of the humid air and into the metal cups they brought for the journey. While taxing on his mana supplies, it was a safe and easy way to acquire water for a long trip without having to lug it around with them. With freshly roasted chicken and pure rainwater, the meal was enjoyed and the men went off for their nightly prayers before sleeping for the day.

The trip continued like this for the next day. On the third day, they passed Tyressos. The port town was almost as large as Thyma but not nearly as dense. The city's sandstone walls stood tall enough to hide what was inside, but the smoke plumes betrayed the hidden city. It was known for its smelting and forging operations of bronze and brass. The air was much more pleasant here, not smelting ferric ores or constantly producing charcoal. They were able to use dried wood for their heat supply when their forgemasters weren't using their channeling to maintain the temperatures, so the smoke that was over the town was light and fluffy compared to the acrid clouds over Flegomena.

They passed the city and continued their journey north, making it officially to the mainland and off the peninsula by the time they stopped for the night. They picked back up in the morning and continued north for the fourth day. Since they had ten days in a week, they planned to hunt on the fifth and sixth day, giving them ample time to return home if they caught a beast this far north. If time was getting close to the final day, they could use their mana to travel faster by cutting the wind in front of them and reinforcing the muscles of anyone that was traveling, man or beast. But with their current plan, finding a crested red-tail deer would not be too difficult, as they were into their mating season and were not hiding out as they did for the rest of the year.

The fourth day also passed uneventfully and they traveled along the edges of the forests south of the Nidaros mountain chain. They caught a glimpse of a deer, but it was one not crested so they cut their pursuit. They found a clearing that would make for a perfect place to camp for the night and set up their cloth tents in the open area.

"I swear, I am not leaving home without a padded cushion for a long journey again!" Kyros exclaimed as he grabbed some dry branches off of an old oak tree. The withered wood would work perfectly for their campfire that night.

Castor grabbed a few boughs of live pine branches and brought them to the site for their bedding. The fine needles would make for a nice barrier between the earth and their sleeping cloth and would keep them warm during the winter night.

"I fully agree," Castor said as he pulled the boughs towards the center. "My calves are killing me. I really wish they invented something for longer trips that made travel more comfortable."

Castor's answer was quieter than his normal self. Kyros had given the Anthoran teen some space since his breakdown at the village a few days earlier. He had recovered since the outburst and had acted normal in most conversations, but Kyros could tell he was holding his emotions back. Kyros was older and had seen two of his friends die. But the Anthoran prince had his first bout with death in such a concentrated manner that he was not surprised his best friend was having issues with it all. They had a polite discussion the night prior about it, so he wanted to give him a full day's rest from discussing the topic.

Kyros dropped a stack of branches onto the ground and rubbed his thigh muscles. "Exactly! I've done such trips before on oxback, but it is not common for us to ride on such rugged terrain."

"That's only because we are trying to minimize our travel time." Castor pointed out as he moved a bough of pine needles under his oiled cloth tent roll. "If we had an extra day, we could have taken the longer routes on state roads."

"You humans complain too much about such a meek adventure." Mithra said after he had stacked rocks in a circle and ignited a healthy swath of flame into the dry bramble in the center. The purring he was creating tipped Castor off to his joke.

"Well, I for one would like to see you ride one of these beasts, Mitty." Kyros jested.

Kyros had chosen to add Mithra to his list of people he frequently teased. Maybe he had an obsession with tempting fate or really did enjoy the idea of corporal punishment, but Kyros found a lot of important and affluent people on his list of those he enjoyed messing with.

"Watch your language, mercenary." Mithra hissed. He bared his fangs, a sign of anger and conflict. "You are not of kin nor king. You are not of high enough importance to use such names."

Kyros knew the exiled prince did not like the pet name he was being given. Birth names in general were not frequently used in common conversations and with common people. It was far more common to address someone by their titles and feats rather than by what their daily names were. Such a nickname would be strictly reserved in Maudif for his parents or his king. As Kyros was neither of those positions in Mithra's eyes, he frequently reminded the prattling human about where he stepped over bounds.

Kyros knew when to pick his fights. He may be strong, but not nearly as strong as an eight-foot muscular cat athlete. Even when he thought an obsolete custom was just getting in the way of idle conversation, he digressed when necessary.

"Very well, rightful heir of Thrim, exiled prince of the Land of Trinities, satrap to the great king of kings, the night-maned elector, slayer of the great snake Azikesh. I will abide by your customs." He bowed a clearly mocking bow but did so with such grace that Mithra was not upset. "Am I missing any titles?"

The great cat man grunted a deep grumble, accepting the apology in doing so. He ignored the question and answered what he had been asked earlier about the oxen.

"Not possible." He twilled, "Maudian royals are forbidden from riding mounts. Only a Maudian may carry a Maudian prince, whether that be their own person or others."

"Very well, then. You are welcome to your own customs." Kyros shot back, now out by the edge of the clearing to gather some larger sections of wood to feed the fire in the deep of the night. "We are blissfully aware of how you get carried around the city. It is a rather pompous method of travel; do not you think?"

"Hmph." the exiled prince exhaled, "That's not just done for my benefit. My retainers use those trips as training for their muscles and stamina. As nice as it is for me, it is not an entirely selfish idea. The palanquin also holds our supplies and hidden weapons."

His steely gaze shifted off to the right and back to Castor. "Do not tell your father about that last part."

Castor, who had been focusing on binding branches together with twine to make a temporary windbreak for their camp, focused his attention when he saw the direct stare of orange, slitted eyes.

"Oh, uh, yes. You have no worries from me." Castor chuckled, his mood bettering as they settled in for their hunt. "We have no regulations on being armed within city bounds so long as weapons aren't readily drawn."

The camp they developed for use over the next few days was primitive yet utilitarian in design. The windbreaks were set up in cross-hatching patterns around the tents to block wind and vision in case a wild animal were to move into the area while they slept, allowing the hunters to keep their concealment. A bonfire sat within the center of the campground. It was ringed with large stones with one side housing a stone pillar. This design allowed the fire to burn more efficiently and reduce smoke, further concealing their position. With the reduced smoke and windbreaks set up around the tents covered in pine boughs and dead branches, their position was masked from the outside. A slight fog rolled into the clearing while they worked but did not impede vision anywhere within the meadow.

They had arrived early enough so as to have time for both shelter-making and hunting for dinner. On their way to the meadow, they had found the forest was inhabited by many different types of small game. While they had not yet seen any larger animals, the forest was still littered with wildlife of the smaller variety. They were met with wild hares bolting across the forest floor, a bouquet of pheasants within a few tall trees, and a team of ducks out on a small lake they walked by while hiking into the mountains.

Castor had no issue channeling the lake water to capture two of the ducks while Mithra used his earth channeling to trap a large hare in an earthen snare near the roots of a great pine. Kyros, who had little control over his channeling, stuck to his more physical skills by shooting down two of the pheasant with his recurve bow.

Unlike the pompous neighbors of Castor, Kyros' bow was not ornate nor ostentatious. It was a style of recurve bow that was adopted by the Anthorans centuries prior from Maudif that curved at the ends to deliver more power to the arrows it fired. The compact shape made it much easier to use when mounted and was originally developed by the sand Maudians to combat their fearsome relatives whilst mounted. The great Maudians were expert fighters in close quarters but were outpaced when hordes of sand Maudians rode away from them on the backs of antelope. Sand Maudians were much smaller than their lion-like cousins and could not rely on their strength to overcome their adversity. Their technological advancements for smaller species were well received by the Anthorans, who were not much bigger than the Maudians of the sand steppes.

When the hunting party was done hunting their game for the night and returned to their campsite, they were able to finally have a proper rest after days of travel. Their rationed and bland food had taken a toll on their morale over the course of the thirty or so hours of travel and except for the occasional chicken they caught, the Anthorans had not eaten much protein recently. Mithra had his supply of dried meat he kept in his storage bag, but he needed that meat for himself as Maudians were notorious for eating a predominantly meat-based diet. Castor did not mind the porridge and molasses, as it was very high in energy, but eating the same thing day in and day out was not typical for an Anthoran royal.

They sat by the fire, enjoying the roasted poultry as the hares were smoked far above the open flames. A broken-up branch from an apple tree they found near the outskirts of the meadow was soaked in water and placed on hot rocks, smoking the hanging meat above. Kyros prodded the smoldering wood with a stick, pushing the unsinged section onto the rocks to let them also smoke. The hares would supply them with food during their hunts the following few days while the well-seasoned poultry was a nice boost to their team's spirit for the night. It seemed to be working, as Castor was in a far better mood than before.

"I meant to ask, Mithra, why do you use your real name if you are trying to stay undercover?" Castor asked, bringing up their prior conversation with a bit more enthusiasm.

Mithra purred. "That is not an issue, little prince. Names are different in my land than they are in yours, as we have discussed. Titles are what distinguish a person in Maudif. My given name pertains to me, as a person. Mithra. Son of the Sun, Arbiter of Justice. It is a name saved for those of royalty. Within Thrim, I am the only Mithra that I am aware of."

The Maudian took a large bite out of the tender pheasant, tearing a chunk from its leg and scarfing down the meat without chewing. "The people within your family and those chosen to be family are important to us. So any who serve or support my right to the crown is a part of me, Mithra. They are also a part of my identity as Mithra since they serve the son of the sun and help me arbitrate justice."

He petted the back of Castor and Kyros' heads, showing physical affection as he always does. The young Anthoran men were the size of children to him, even though Kyros was larger than the average human and Castor was almost fully grown.

"I use my name because everyone uses my name." Mithra continued. "All my followers who were exiled with me use the name of Mithra as their own. It gives me more freedom in my movements as well as keeps our legacy alive under one banner."

"Oh, so then with your mane being this lighter color and your identity not being much different than the others, they would just assume you were a pretender or merely a vassal of yours," Castor asked and tilted his head, showing a little confusion as he tried to wrap his mind around Maudian names. Anthoran names were unique to each person and used in official matters so that such mixing of names would not be ever considered within Anthoran culture.

Mithra paused for a second to consider what Castor said before saying, "Yes, in a way that is true. I wouldn't call my allies pretenders, though. They honor me by using my name as their own. And anyone I associate and agree with is allowed to use it. You could too if you wanted." Mithra purred at the two boys, clearly showing his respect to his companions.

"I appreciate the offer and would take you up on it if I was allowed," Castor said, fully aware of the power of names within Anthora. Especially among the noble families, names were not to be used lightly. Claiming to be of another house could make political enemies or get you arrested if not done correctly.

"Kyros Mithra. Now there's a name I wouldn't expect to hear." Kyros jabbered on. "Or would it be the other way around? I'm not sure how my parents would take it, but I could use a name like that when working on a tr--."

Kyros was cut short as an arrow sprouted from his chest, the impact knocking him backward and the duck breast in his hand falling to the dirt floor.

Castor, mouth agasp from starting to reply to Kyros, quickly ducked behind a windbreak after tumbling to the ground in shock. He instinctively grabbed for his sword, which hung at his side, and drew his blade. The crystal pommel shimmered as he pushed his offhand outward and let loose a plume of flame. It was instantaneous and did not linger long, but the extremely bright light should at least disorient their attackers for him to check on Kyros.

It was not necessary though, as Kyros was wearing his linothorax under his winter wraps. It was standard to wear a light set of armor when traveling on long excursions for exactly this reason. The arrow, while long and heavy for what he was used to seeing, had a stone tip and did not pierce through the glued linen sheets protecting his chest. He was panting for air though, as the blunt force was enough of a surprise to knock the wind out of him.

Mithra snarled and shot up, leaping onto all fours and scanning the outskirts of the meadow for their foes. He drew two curved daggers from his waistline in a fluid fashion and continued off into the field without delay. His expression was terrifying and Castor was taken aback for another second when seeing such a fierce visage.

Castor crawled on his elbows and untied his supply bag on the ground a few feet away. He looked into his bag and grabbed the light bronze helmet he brought in case of an emergency. It was less of a helmet and more of a cap, as its protection was nothing like the professional headwear he wore in the guard. It was enough of an improvement from no headwear at all though, so he quickly tossed it on before looking over the wooden wall to scout out the foes.

Castor expected bandits. Human bandits within this region were not unheard of and would take an opportunity to strike at travelers even during holiday events. They did not care for the scorn of the gods as they had probably earned enough sins to cost them many lifetimes in the underworld. Another thought that crossed his mind was assassins. Given their recent conversations about Thrim and the exodus, It was not unreasonable to assume the attackers were from the rival faction tying up loose ends. But what Castor saw was much, much worse.

A vile force of small figures danced in the darkness, skipping between trees and hiding their pale bodies. Castor could see their size and hear the sharp snickers from the fog. While they were distorted in the evening shade and mist that eluded their bodies, he knew what they were; goblins.

One of the creatures was closer to the camp and he could see it very clearly in the fire's dim glow. It had sharp teeth and a flat face with two slits for nostrils. Long pointed ears drooped off its bald head and its scrawny frame was pale gray like an old snowfall. Its hairless torso portrayed a gaunt and emaciated child that seemed too skinny to survive. Its lower half was covered in shaggy fur and its tail was long and nappy. Cloven hooves skittered across the dirt when it noticed Castor's gaze. Its pitch-black eyes were unnerving, and it bared its teeth in a spikey grin.

Its large hands had sharp black nails and held a wooden spear. Castor realized the oversized arrow in Kyros' chest was not an arrow at all, but instead a javelin. The lanky creatures were the size of human children, so their throwing spears were the size of human arrows. Kyros had removed the embedded javelin from his linothorax and tossed it into the fire, arming himself with his bow afterward.

Mithra was out into the middle of the field holding a goblin down with one of his knives. The creature tried to swipe at his face with the gnarled nails that grew from its spindly fingertips, but the lion man brushed them off with the turn of his head. His mane was far too thick to be pierced by its fingernails. His khanjar, however, were much different than the little hands of the forest demons. The knives of his homeland were well-designed tools of war and were made specifically for dispatching foes in close quarters. One strong swipe of his offhand put the foe down for good. He roared out, making many small shadows near his position scatter like bugs under a recently lifted log.

A few javelins came into the camp, missing the hunters by a good distance. Their tactics worked best when they were concealed and in large numbers. With a great Maudian as their foe, they were not organized enough to push an advantage.

Castor saw at least a dozen of the primitive creatures jumping between the trees, their small frames hard to spot in the building mist. He channeled a burst of flames once again and sent it out, singeing the ends of some pine branches at the edge of the clearing. The shadows scurried once more and javelins came towards them once again. Two of the throwing spears came directly at him, so he sent a burst of wind with his left hand to deflect their trajectory. They bounced off the cushion of air and flopped to the ground.

Kyros had started firing off some arrows towards the shapes he could see, but the trees blocked his shots from where he was bunkered down. The small campground was both a sturdy defense as well as a hindrance to their attacks, being so far from the tree line that they were unable to impact their assailants. Seeing their situation at a standstill, Castor moved out to aid Mithra in the fringes of the field.

The Maudian had finished off another creature the same way he caught the first, pinning it to the ground and slicing the throat with the offhand. Castor noticed some of the goblins had tied bones or sticks to their bodies as some sort of primitive body armor. It was not of much use in this situation, as the sheer difference in power between the evil little creatures and the great Maudian prince was significant.

A group of the short monsters charged forward from the tree line at the two hunters from their flank with pointed wooden spears aimed at their vitals. A short blast of wind from Castor's hand disoriented the two on the right side and Mithra followed through with a whip of flame. The burst of mana made his bejeweled belt shine from between the dark layers of winter clothes. Castor could hear a humming from the cat man's throat, no doubt a battle hymn for some spell he planned to use shortly.

Castor bought him some time by charging the goblins in front of them. The plume of fire singed the shaggy imps and sent one into a panic. The other three were able to continue their attack together with spear tips all aimed at Castor now. He deflected the rightmost spear towards the center, blocking the vision of the two on the left. Using the sword as a guide, he maneuvered his left hand to keep the spear away as he struck the rightmost goblin with his xiphos. In and out, the leaf-shaped blade pierced into the gremlin's side and skewered it through its lungs in a single motion. It choked up blood as it grabbed at the sharp pain with its tendril-like fingers, but it was not long before it dropped to the ground dead.

The other two swung around and pushed forward, taking short jabs at Castor. One spear poked into his chest but was only a sharpened stick and bounced off the hard linen armor. The other goblin had a stone blade attached to the end of its spear, so Castor had to worry a little more about that weapon.

By this point, Mithra's chant was finished and his prayer answered. His Khanjar started to glow; a bright luminescence permeated from the curved bronze blades. As though recently taken from the belly of a bronzesmith's forge, the daggers shone bright orange, brighter than what a bronze bar would normally glow to without melting into a viscous puddle of molten metal. Rejuvenated by his blessing, he leapt forward like a predator on prey and cut into the unsuspecting goblin nearest him. The flesh sizzled like meat on a well-kept fire and yelps of pain emanated from the barely sentient imp. His motions were quick and precise yet seemed to hold such strength and anger as he cut down his foes. Castor stood back as the remaining goblins were removed from the combat in a dozen fluid motions of whirling, glowing blades.

From behind, Castor heard Kyros call out as he turned to look. His friend was hurdling over the windbreak and started running towards the others as he abandoned their encampment. Across the way was a horde of the little whelps, easily numbering close to a hundred. Castor was astonished to see so many, as goblins usually stayed in small tribes and attacks were usually only seen between ten and fifty imps at once. There were at least a hundred just in the clearing itself and he could see shadows dancing in the fog all around him. He understood why Kyros gave up their camp. There was no way they could take this many of them.

"Run!" Kyros said, snapping Castor and Mithra back to reality as they saw the foes around them increase every second. "Up and to the right, past the great oak tree!"

Castor could see their oxen dead on the ground under a few goblins. The creatures had slaughtered their quickest way to escape. They planned to trap their prey within the forest. Luckily, the northern flank was not holding up to the same cohesion as the southern side, so they were able to start their retreat into the mountains. Castor thought that maybe that was their plan all along, but given the circumstances, he didn't have much time to think about it. Once the last two remaining goblins were dispatched with an arrow to the chest and a xiphos to the skull, the three ex-hunters ran from the new hunting party.

Castor remembers the chants he had done a few months back with the farmer on the way into town. He started reciting the laments, each line helping to calm his breath as they ran up the hill into the trees. As a verse ended, he felt a pulse of energy within his step and he was propelled forward. Earth beckoned to his call as he lamented the trials of Gargrin. He could hear snickers and cackles from behind them. At one point, the footsteps of the imps got closer, following behind closely but not fast enough to close the distance. Kyros and Mithra were in front of him, their long legs and better physique giving them the advantage in the long-distance they were traveling.

Castor could hear a few getting too close for comfort. Kyros turned quickly as he ran and fired an arrow off. It flew by Castor's left side and a shriek was heard from behind. He didn't have time to look but he could tell it met its mark. Using the attack to his advantage, Castor pressed forward a few steps and unleashed the energy his chants had given him. A heavy step upon the ground urged the earth to rise up, raising a wall of dirt to flow like a wave of water towards the pursuing warband. The earth had sunk and rose like a sideways S. The mound wall of dirt was low in the front and tall in the back, making it difficult for the small creatures to traverse the soft soil.

Water poured from the ground as Mithra channeled mana from his daggers, the well-cut gems glistening across their gold inlays. The water pooled in the dugout moats and made the ground difficult to traverse. They could see a few goblins hop the ditch only to fall backward and sink into the mud.

The group kept running but caught their breath when they realized the goblins had to travel around the mound to continue their pursuit. They panted to catch their breath and drank from their waterskins as they walked, keeping an eye in the southern direction for any tricks or surprises. They saw the rough cliff faces of the mountain approaching from the northeast. They had the choice of traversing the rock faces or continuing into the tree line and finding somewhere to end the pursuit.

"Thoughts?" Castor asked as he pointed in the two directions they had at their disposal.

"Mountain cliffs will be difficult to climb for us, but also difficult for them," Kyros said quickly.

"I am not knowledgeable on your lands, Anthoran. I will digress from either decision." Mithra roared. His temper was calmer than it was in the meadow, but his bloodlust was still visible on his twitching face and clenched fists.

"The cliffs may be dangerous." Castor mediated, considering both options. "The forest may allow us to double back."

"Our mounts are dead and our gear was stolen. I have little use of what those critters left for us. Did you hide anything useful?" Kyros looked at the mound and shot a goblin off who was making progress up the muddy slope.

"I tried," Castor replied, carefully overseeing the southern front as he responded. "A few charged gems and the rest of our gear were buried under our bedding. But they may have gotten to it."

Kyros pointed to the rucksack he had strapped to his back. "I have enough supplies for a few days, so we should be alright if we can get away from these brutes."

A javelin flew near their feet as the horde started to make its way past the barrier they created. The stone hillocks that kept the creatures from flanking their position were finally meeting their match with a few climbing up the stony surfaces and onto the layer they were on. From the west, a large section of the hillside Castor built blew out and dirt sprayed into the clearing.

Goblins poured through as a tall figure walked into the clearing. A single goblin stood out from the crowd. It was a bit taller than the rest and stood with a large, gnarled staff in its hands. The creature was ugly and deformed. It was missing an ear and its tail was clipped short, either from a past battle or a disease. The staff it held carried a large chunk of raw quartz tied into its hollow with what looked like sinew or twine. It wore a patchwork hide robe with bits of different types of fur and skin sewn crudely together to make the outfit. Little bits and baubles of stolen Anthoran jewelry glittered across its arms and neck. The staff top shone brightly as the malformed imp stumbled into the field and smiled a crooked smile at the hunters.

It was a good thing the group of hunters was far enough away because the time it took them to process what they saw was long enough for goblins to get far too close for comfort. Mithra was the most focused in the group and funneled a large plume of fire forward as the other two sprinted east towards the stone cliffs. The gems on his daggers glinted before fading, their mana reserve running dry after their prolonged use.

"That was..." Castor stuttered. They continued up the hill and onto the loose ground.

"Impossible." Kyros finished his sentence. The open field of gravel and pine trees overlooked a canyon below.

Goblins were not able to channel mana. There had been no accounts of goblins being able to channel in Anthoran history. The impish species lived on the fringes of the continent with very little contact with human societies. They were brutish and dull, relying on violence to acquire shiny objects. Castor had never heard of their society being able to channel or any sort of class system, but in front of them was a war leader with a large crystal plowing earth asunder with the flick of its wrist. Castor channeled mana into his muscles and skin, feeling even more uncomfortable from this whole situation.

The party moved up onto a bluff, gravel falling down onto the sloping cliffside below. The path tightened to a few feet wide as they made their way across the stony area. The tight passage would block the advance of the imps, but also impose a risk to themselves at the same time. The stone cliff that made up their left side had clods of moss and small plants clinging to its surface. The green spongy material gave little support before falling away as Castor grabbed onto it. They would have to rely on their balance alone to get across the passage.

Their pursuers did not slow down. A crowd of goblins grew near the top of the bluff. Their leader smiled his wicked smile, standing a few paces behind the front line. The creatures cackled and shrilled as they tried to poke and prod at their prey. Mithra had surpassed the two men at this point and moved to the front of their formation, his mana reserve dwindling during this ambush. One javelin hurled from the backline of the group and pierced the shoulder of its fellow goblin. It clawed at its wound before falling into the ravine below. Kyros made up the middle and fired off an arrow into the crowd of approaching creatures. His shot struck a bolder imp in the leg that had approached Castor in the frontline. It yelped and toppled over. The gravel under its hooves gave away near the edge of the cliff and the creature also tumbled into the misty abyss below.

The creatures continued to prod at the group as they backed their way across the slope. The narrow pass gave them cover for the incoming projectile. Any thrown javelins that were not directly in line with the hunters had either bounced off the cliff above or fallen silently into the fog below them. As they traveled, Castor pulsed a few bursts of wind outward when a javelin got too close for comfort, knocking a few of the imps off the edge as a result. Mithra was having a specifically difficult time in the stony channel since his weight and height made stepping near the edge of the path dangerous. The gravel gave out multiple times as he walked, causing him to leap back towards the cliff face.

Their attacks slowed as their numbers fell. The leader's smile dulled into a half-hearted grin as it paced in the backline, no doubt thinking of a plan for their next trap.

Castor stepped forward and stabbed at a goblin that got too close. It tried to push his blade away with the end of its spear, but Castor feinted the attack and came around with a sweeping strike to its head. The impact killed the creature instantly and it fell limp onto the cobblestone path. The goblin behind hissed and shrieked, clearly upset at the death of its comrade. It wasn't too upset, as it pushed the dead comrade off the edge with its foot and into the valley below.

The weather had turned for the worse as the situation unfolded. A light spitting of rain fell across the landscape. Dry dirt turned to mud as the rainwater continued to batter the mountainside. Castor held off the front of goblins as they made their way up the sloped pathway. It was only a few hundred feet of unsteady ground, but the worsening conditions made travel difficult.

Castor noticed that the war party's leader was smiling again. He could see it moving its lips, but he could not hear anything over the rain, wind, and other shrieking imps. A few more goblins stabbed at Castor as they made their way to a wider section of the path, and one spear made contact with his skin. His thick wool pants protected him from most of the impact, but the sharpened stone spearhead slipped through the fabric and pierced his thigh. The attack grazed him and the wound only tore through his skin, but the pain made him flinch.

Another goblin tried to follow up on the unfocused prince, but he was able to see the attack coming in from his right side and deflect the blow into the rocky cliff face. The tip of the wood spear got caught in a nook and the charging goblin rebounded over the stuck weapon, falling to the ground at Castor's feet. Before he could react, an arrow shot forth from below his sword arm and pierced the creature through the neck. It gurgled as Kyros lunged forward and pulled the arrow out for reuse. It tried to swipe with a flint biface knife, but its small arms and short blade length left it far out of range of Castor's body.

They had made it close to the end of the pathway. The area opened up to another bluff a few dozen feet ahead of their position. Even with the rain and fog, they could see the area had many paths for escape, both up and down the mountainside.

Suddenly, a rumble came from overhead. Cackling echoed from the path they just walked as the goblins retreated a bit back towards their malformed leader. Its smile was wider than Castor had seen yet and he began to worry. His worry was for good reason, as the creature tossed its decrepit hands in the air and then towards the ground. The rumble deepened as small stones and pebbles started to fall from overhead. The size of the rocks continued to grow as they tried to escape the falling debris. Castor raised a bubble of air around their position to deflect the avalanche while they tried to run towards the end of the path. Mithra had also raised an air cushion and together they pushed through to the end.

Unfortunately, their luck had run out. A large boulder crashed across the upper sections of the ridge and towards their position. A rhythmic chant could be heard from the goblins, who had backed far enough away to avoid the rockslide. The rock fell towards them and Castor braced for impact. They were only a few feet away from getting to the end, but the freefalling chunk of craggy chert fell much faster than Castor could run. He saw Mithra and Kyros had just made it to the end of the path, but it seemed he would be too slow.

A large paw reached out and yanked the boy forward, tossing him off the path and through the air towards the clearing. Castor's reflexes heightened and time seemed to slow down as he realized the exiled prince had leaped forward to save him from being crushed by the boulder falling towards the group. He couldn't stop the boulder, as it was far too heavy to be slowed with what mana he had left. His only option was a quick burst of wind to push Mithra out of the way. He activated his mana and blasted his friend backward, launching himself towards the ground in the process.

The exiled prince of Thrim narrowly missed the giant boulder as he was propelled back into the cliff pass. He caught his weight and stumbled, trying to catch himself on the wall. A chunk of moss gave way just as his foot slipped off the edge of the path. As he grabbed out, a small rock launched past Castor's vision and collided with the cat man's right leg. The force pushed it too close to the brim of the path and his weight made the stone give way. Mithra plummeted downwards into the foggy valley below with many chunks of hewn earth following close behind.

CHAPTER 12

A Descent Into Darkness

4th of Azurite, 453 of the Age of Discovery

astor watched as the son of the sun tumbled down the slope into the foggy ravine below. Rocks flew by as the avalanche slid down the cliff face and collided with where they just stood. The goblins shrieked and squealed as one of their prey fell headlong down the rust-stained incline. Gnarly, lanky limbs flapped about as they celebrated the first of the victories they expected that day. Their enthusiasm made it seem as though they orchestrated the entire event up until this point. The ever-grinning goblin chieftain continued to stare down its prey on the other side of the passage.

The rockslide had damaged the pathway, taking much of the remaining cobble path with it down into the canyon. Castor saw an opportunity and signaled to Kyros to run. They continued up the path as the goblins hopped over the remaining cliff towards the upper bluff.

The stony outcropping was littered with bones and smelled of death. They sprinted across the clearing, dodging the remains of many travelers, villagers, and lost pets as they ran. Goblins that were on the cliff face with them had already made it to the clearing with the rest of the warband not far behind.

A few bodies were near a lonely juniper tree on the northern side of the bluff. Castor let out a prayer to his patron deity as they ran past when he noticed the bodies were those of armed men. While decrepit and weather-beaten, Castor grabbed the unadorned wooden pelta off the arm of the deceased traveler. No bronze, silver, or gold was left on the bodies, but it seemed the impish scavengers left the remains if they did not shimmer or shine.

Kyros did the same, finding another wood aspis near the edge of what looked like a cave. At first glance, the opening seemed to just be a dozen feet deep, like that of an alcove by the ocean, but gave way to a dark tunnel near the back left. Soft dirt and moss were piled near the mouth as though it was recently opened. Kyros and Castor, armed with their swords and fitted with battered shields, stood their ground as a dozen goblins charged toward them.

A single goblin led the charge a few paces ahead of the others. Brave or mad, the fiendish beast screeched as it ran to impale one of the two Anthorans. The pointed branch it held struck out at Kyros as he parried it away with his kopis. The hefty blade stuck into the pointed stick, leaving the imp pinned to the ground as he stepped on the branch to release the blade's edge from where it caught. He tugged the blade out and with the momentum of the tug, arced the blade over his head and cleaved the goblin's head into halves. He pulled back as it dropped to the ground to join the victims of prior days.

The main group of goblins came in a wave and pushed on the two as they stood their ground. One goblin held a bronze dagger, no doubt stolen from an unlucky traveler in the region. It tried to sneak the blade around Castor's defenses and through the open area of the crescent-shaped shield. He reactively struck at its hand when it passed into his personal space and cleaved a few fingers off in the process. Without respite, Castor pushed forward and stabbed at the confused goblin, piercing it through the torso. It wheezed as its chest cavity collapsed. Castor tucked the stuck blade into the opening of the pelta and pried it out by pushing with the shield and pulling on the sword. Two goblins lay dead on the chert bluff with many more to follow.

The two worked together in an impromptu shield wall to fend off the first wave of goblins. If one struck out between the pair, the other would deflect the blow. If a blade got close to someone's exposed limbs or neck, they pulled back and parried the attack. Without the use of mana and with bellies full of roasted meats, the pair of Anthorans held out against the incoming horde of imps with their backs against the chert cliffside. Javelins and rocks came overhead, but their combined shields easily deflected the projectiles. As their blades dropped more of the hideous creatures, another pair would make their way up the ramp and onto the bluff. Without the leader organizing their numbers, they fought like wild animals. The bodies piled as they cleared a few dozen of the beasts. Their bodies started to pile in front of their position, making the assault even harder on the incoming attackers.

The tide of the battle seemed to turn in their favor until they saw the goblin leader slowly crawl over the edge of the cliff and onto the plateau. It was panting from the exhausting ascent to the upper area, no doubt more exertive than what the war leader was used to. Its patchwork robe was ripped in parts from the sharp stone surfaces and the jewelry it wore was covered in mud. Its typical smile was just a straight line across its face now. Only four little fangs stuck out from beneath its grayish-blue lips. It lashed out at a goblin near it and stuck it in the back with its four-fingered hand. Another goblin came up and handed the creature its staff. It seemed to have some issues with the ascent and had another carry its gear.

While the goblin language was primitive and crude, the sharp trills and guttural barks the leader made seemed to snap the rest of the group into a more organized state. Rather than just charging head-on, some of the goblins tried flanking the two from the sides. Each Anthoran now had to defend against a larger angle ahead of them. Kyros did not have much more of an issue since his aspis was large and covered most of his body, but Castor's pelta was smaller and crescent-shaped, designed for short skirmishes rather than the front lines of a battle. At a few points, Castor had to pulse a burst of wind outward to deflect an attack that was out of his reach. His mana was still dropping as the battle progressed, but the battle was not lost.

Even with a wound on his leg and the numbers against them, Castor wouldn't let the odds get him down. Castor and Kyros were trained professionals. Kyros spent the last decade honing his skills as a mercenary and gained copious amounts of battlefield experience. Castor was the heir prince of Anthora. His days consisted of combat training and strenuous exercise. Even as an officer of their guard, he made himself train like everyone else specifically so that he would be ready when the situation turned dire.

Castor noticed the goblin was smiling again. Having caught its breath, it started to chant and Castor could feel the area start to shake once more. They were pinned against a cliff with over fifty imps in front of them. Retreating was not an option. Even an escape into the tunnel they noticed earlier was still too far away from a safe course of action, given how the goblins had organized their formation across the bluff.

The rumbling continued and their chances seemed to dwindle as screeching could be heard from above in the fog. As fast as Castor noticed a dark figure flying down through the fog, it disappeared again. From high above. screaming could be heard. It made the crowd of goblins silent. After a few seconds of an awkward stalemate, a loud splat was heard a few dozen feet away from the Anthoran's position. Castor turned to see the distorted body of a goblin strewn across a red-streaked stone slab. The creature that dropped it from an immense height landed atop the lone juniper tree across the bluff.

"Oh, not those again," Kyros muttered, pulling on Castor's shoulder to huddle closer in their formation.

"That's a harpy?" Castor gasped, stunned that a creature could be uglier than the imps they were fighting. He stepped back and locked their shields tighter, using a section of the rock ledge to cover their flank as they tightened their formation.

The flying beast was unsightly, perched at over five feet in height even when hunched over as it assessed the area below. Its face was like that of an old woman, its skin wrinkled and features sharp. It had no lips but showed a grisly visage of stark white teeth. They tapered across its head to two buck teeth that made it seem like it had a beak. Its face and clawed hands were the only uncovered areas on its body with the rest of its surface covered in mottled brown feathers. Drabs of folded skin and down feathers covered its front, which gave the appearance of the craggy skin of a wild turkey. The bird was hunchbacked and moved in awkward directions as it analyzed the creatures that had invaded their land. Its neck protruded outward at one point when it vocalized to the rest of its clamor. They flew overhead, masked by the fog and rain. It was a terrifying sight, the noise it made not much better.

A pair of goblins had the bright idea of throwing their javelins at the bird, narrowly missing where it roosted. The war leader hissed and snapped at the goblins who had realized their mistake too late. The squawks and caws of the harpy signaled the threat to the rest above. After the creature took off into the mist, the underworld itself broke loose.

The terror birds dropped at a breakneck pace into the visible area of the plateau and struck goblins down with their giant claws. As the goblins were mostly nude save for a few individuals that had stolen wrappings or crude patchworks, their talons cut through their targets with relative ease. Javelins were being tossed across the platform but rarely came close to contact with the birds as their hit-and-run tactic was working well on the disorganized mob of imps. An occasional spear struck a bird out of sheer luck from the volume being thrown about, but only one harpy laid dead on the ground within Castor's vision. The two of them sat back as the goblins chose between attacking their prey and stopping themselves from becoming prey.

Castor surveyed the area and tried to think of a plan to turn the battle in their favor. He saw the harpies swooping down and the goblins organizing into small clusters. The bird beasts would fly into the fog and use the weather to their advantage. The imps were seeming to adapt to the diving attacks. Castor saw their leader barking orders by the cliffside to keep his troops together and to fight off the aerial swarms.

"I have a plan. Can you cover me?" Castor said to Kyros. He pointed at the goblin leader squealing in the back lines. Kyros nodded and took a step forward, propping his shield up to fend off incoming attacks.

Most of the goblins had diverted their attention towards the sky, leaving only a few to keep the Anthorans pinned. Kyros kept their attention, driving his shoulder forward and stabbing at their openings. Castor flanked around on their right side and sprinted for a gap in the goblin's formation. He got as close to the goblin leader without alerting it to his presence and started to chant.

Vrontir, high lord of the clouds and skies,
father of the veritable four winds,
hear my prayer.

You, who strikes at the roots of the land,
and keeps the heavens at a distance,
hear my prayer.

Save me, ancient lord, I pray you,
deliver me from these evils of the mortal coil,
hear my prayer.

Castor whispered his chant to the god Vrontir, a popular god among Anthorans. His control over the wind and weather would allow him to enact the coup de grace he thought would finalize their safety in this dire situation. Ducking out from behind a boulder, Castor channeled some mana he had left in his blade's hilt and pushed a column towards the goblin mage. The spout of fire quickly exploded into a cloud of steam in front of him and concealed the entire area he was near.

Goblins squealed and screeched as they lost vision of their leader and their foes. The only sight Castor could make out in the direction of the goblins was a white beacon among their horde. Seeing the top of the mage's staff, Castor focused the blessing he asked for towards their leader. He stepped around the boulder and secured his back against it. He dug his feet into the ground and braced himself as best he could.

Castor let forth a giant burst of hot steam from the center of his clenched hands. The storm god, being as haughty and excessive as he is known to be, gave Castor the ability to focus a giant plume of hot air towards the goblin formation. The force was enough to push him back, digging his back and calves into the giant rock behind him. The confluence of vaporized water launched toward the goblin leader who could not see Castor through the fog. Being taken off guard, the small and malformed creature was thrown through the air and scalded by the column of steam. The gust blew the ugly imp clean off the bluff and, without a slope to catch himself on, he plummeted to the valley below. All that was left was a quickly dimming beacon near the edge of the cliff.

The goblins panicked due to the loss of their leader. They had expected to just take out a few travelers like they had done many times in the past. The attack from the harpies ruined their plans and many more goblins died that day than they were expecting. When they saw their leader's staff by the edge of the cliff, they completely lost their cohesion and their formations were broken.

Castor ran back to Kyros' position by the cave's mouth as they watched the panicked goblins and injured harpies clash across the stone bluff. Rocks continued to fall down the cliffside as the quantity picked up with the prevailing winds. The imps had gone feral and swung wildly, injuring harpy and fellow goblin alike. Ironically, their wild, unpredictable movements caused more damage to the agile bird beasts than when they held their formation defensively. Some of the goblins attacked Castor wildly as he retreated, but his blade led them to the afterlife with a few calculated cuts and jabs.

Once back, Castor and Kyros considered their options. The bluff was chaotic and could be dangerous to traverse with the different factions waging their war. Castor noticed a trickle of blood on Kyros' arm, but he brushed it off as a graze. Castor did not want to put Kyros in danger again. He was still recovering from his heavy wounds over the last few months and was not at his peak performance yet. Any more injuries and he could risk becoming maimed.

The rocks above them started to shake with the mountain as they saw a half dozen giant boulders coming for the landing from the high cliffs above. They could feel the vibrations far before they could see the flying hunks of stone, but they quickly retreated into the cave's mouth to avoid any collisions. Maybe it was their waning stamina or a trick of the light. The boulders ended up being much larger than they originally thought as house-sized pieces of the mountain fell into, and through, the bluff. Castor and Kyros stood by as half the area was swept away from the collision of a few giant chunks of stone. Goblins, harpies, and skeletal remains alike were completely obliterated as the stones tore through the plateau and shattered the bluff.

The Anthorans took a few steps back into the cave and hid from the onslaught of plummeting boulder chunks that filled the area. A mob of feral goblins tried to charge them, seeming to only want blood at this point. There were around fifteen of them, and they were moving faster than they had seen before. The humans did the wise thing and sprinted into the cave system.

Castor lit the three fotovolo on his belt and handed one to Kyros. The devices lit up the caves so they could see where they were running towards. The caves wound down into the earth as they followed their natural bends and turns. After a few directions split into their retreat, they waited to see if the creatures were still following. They could hear the pattering of cloven hooves on hard stone, so they knew their aggressors were still in hot pursuit.

They made it to a large cavern that was illuminated in blue light. Stalactites clung to the ceiling and held small glowing nodules at their ends. Glowing caves were not a surprise in Anthora, as the glow worms that created the bioluminescence were found in many coastal regions across the continent. The duo made their way across the glowing cave's shallow ponds of water and up onto a mound of compacted clay. They could see the goblins enter the chamber and spread out in a fan pattern to keep their prey from escaping.

Behind them was another passage, but Castor noticed it looked different. It was more geometric than the rest of the cave passages. The entrance was rectangular and seemed to be only partially opened as though a door was missing from its frame. Ancient ruins were also not uncommon in Anthora, but they were quite uncommon this far underground. The pair made their way through the opening and into the hewn halls, continuing down a corridor to find a means of escape.

Castor realized after a few hundred paces that their pursuers were no longer hobbling across the stone floors. Castor was confused and looked back to see no goblins. He stopped Kyros and, handing him the fotovolo from his belt, snuck up to the edge of a corner they had already turned and looked towards the opening to the cavern they previously passed through. He saw a few goblins standing near the doorway, but none entered the hewn halls. They snarled and hissed, seeing their prey peaking around the corner.

Goblins had incredible night vision, so seeing the reflection in Castor's eyes only seemed to irritate the creatures more at the doorway. Their shallow growls and pacing attitude made Castor think something was wrong with where they went. Maybe the creatures were just scared of ancient ruins. Maybe they knew of something that lurked within. Without another plan, Castor defaulted to exploring the ruins for a safer way out.

The duo continued down the corridors, passing a few open rooms along the way. The doors were not attached to what looked like the frames of the doorways, but Castor was not sure where they went. When looking inside, they did not find much, just tables and chairs made of what looked like stone or very soft metal. It wasn't bronze or ferron, but it felt softer than any stone Castor was used to seeing. His brother had taught him a great many things about stones, minerals, and crystals because of his mosaic hobby, so he knew a thing or two about earthen materials.

They passed a few other rooms with open doorways and found what seemed to be sleeping quarters. Alcoves in the walls seemed to be where people could rest, with stone coffers built into the wall underneath each bed. They searched the cavities but nothing was there. Either the ruins had been pillaged in the past or the original residents did a good job of clearing the place out before its abandonment.

They took a break at one of the tables in the sleeping quarters. Kyros retrieved a bag of dried oats from his rucksack and poured the items into two small bowls he had brought in the sack. They took a few minutes to take care of their wounds with some of the Vótanodor Castor kept on his belt and some strips of cloth Kyros had in his bag for emergencies. Their wounds were not too bad, but the blood loss was still something to consider for the rest of the day. With their lifeblood levels lower, Castor's mana pool would refill slower too. Their food break was to sate their hunger during this stressful time, but more importantly, it should help him keep his mana regeneration higher so they could maintain their light sources to traverse the otherwise pitch-black halls.

After they were done with their wound care, Castor poured the remains of his waterskin into the cups and channeled the humidity in the damp air to refill the vessel. With a short prayer, Castor lit a column of fire from his hand to warm their oatmeal, but Kyros made him cut off the spell.

"We are too far into the mountain," Kyros said in a hushed voice. "If you do that for too long, we will have an issue breathing."

Castor was confused, and his face showed it. He trusted his friend because he had much more experience on adventures but did not ever see an issue with breathing around an open flame.

Kyros responded to his look. "The air only has so much life energy in it. It is not a problem on the surface but it is much less in the bowels of the earth. If you let the flame consume it and make its own heat, then there won't be enough left for our hearts to create our body's vital heat."

"Well, alright then." Castor digressed. Kyros wasn't one to make claims without a good reason and although he was no doctor or wizened mage, he believed him. "As long as you can put up with cold oats."

Kyros nodded and poured a bit of honey into the mixture. They ate in the dimly lit room, only allowing one fotovolo to stay on as they ate. Castor was worried they would eventually run out of mana to maintain the light. His personal stores would fuel them for a good while, but he wouldn't be able to keep refilling their reserves for days just on his passive regeneration alone.

"We will be alright. Do not worry." Kyros said to Castor as they ate. He saw the forlorn look on Castor's face. He had been deep in thought when eating, considering all their options and what their next steps should be. All his years of tutoring, weeklong trips into the wilderness near Thyma for survival training, and hands-on experience in the guard did not prepare him for the events that unfolded today. Magical goblins, a clamor of harpies, rockslides, and an underground temple complex were never events he considered to be prepared for.

"I just can't figure out who made these ruins," Castor said glumly. "I mean, how have we never seen a place like this so close to home? This isn't the deadlands or some buried temple in the northern desert sands.

We are two days north of Tyressos. It is too close to a major city to just be found."

He noticed a few sets of symbols that were repeated in different rooms. He figured the symbols were from an ancient language or far-past culture that had been forgotten through the annals of time. He traced the glyphs with his finger after handing his bowl back to Kyros for storage. Having no other equipment on him, he looked for a way to write the symbols down for study later in case they made it out of the cave system alive. It could be a major discovery if a new civilization was found.

"Do you have a notebook or a way to trace these?" Castor asked Kyros, who was rummaging through his rucksack for any food packages he could find. He looked around and shook his head. He would have to rely on his memory if he wanted to review the symbols at a later date.

The two packed up their belongings and wiped the bowls they used with a towel Kyros had tied to the side of his sack. They both took a second to offer a prayer to their patron deities for surviving the battle and having the opportunity to have another meal. They avoided the topic of Mithra, as they knew that discussing it would only put them in a bad mood. They continued on in silence.

The halls turned and twisted through the mountain, making the complex seem bigger than they could have imagined. They came across large rooms with multiple doors on their way, with some paths being blocked by the strange stone slabs they considered to be ancient doors. They could not read the symbols around them and found no means to unlock the passages. After Kyros tried to pry a door open with his hunting knife and snapped the tip of the bronze blade off in the process, they continued down corridors they could get access to. Castor knew he could manipulate the doors with his mana, but he figured they should spend the time they could with the unlocked passages and save his mana for a more dire situation.

He scoffed at the thought of a more dire situation, as they seemed pretty dire already. Kyros patted him on the back, reassuring him that their hope was not all lost.

"We were able to find a way in pretty easily, we will find a way out as well." he remarked. "We will look back on today as an amazing experience in a few months. So do not fret about it just yet."

Castor could tell Kyros was forcing his responses. He knew just as well as the young prince that their hopes down here were pretty low. Their last resort would be a bloody path through the remaining goblins after they had run out of food supplies. But considering the effort that Kyros was putting in to keep his younger friend in good spirits, Castor grinned and pressed on.

They came before a pair of doors that were oddly positioned at the center point of a hallway. The end of the hallway terminated in another closed port, and their trip back to the central hall was a couple of minutes' walk back. They took a second to examine the two doors with markings they could easily identify: shapes.

Most of the doors and halls had symbols that were worn over time and hard to make out. Without a way to read them, the duo had been ignoring most of them if they didn't see anything that stood out. These doors, however, were different. They were not nearly as worn as the rest of the doors and were a slightly different color. Given the difference, Castor stopped Kyros and the both of them reviewed what they saw. Rather than glyphs and foreign letters, they were met with a grouping of shapes. The left door had a circle, triangle, and two rectangles carved into the flat, stone surface. The right door had the same circle and rectangles, but the triangle was replaced with a square. The Anthorans were well aware of basic geometry, as Anthora was the birthplace of basic mathematics. Castor looked over the combination of shapes, trying to figure out if they had some rhyme or reason to their order or locations.

"Maybe we should try touching them?" Kyros asked as he pressed the shapes in on the left door. He touched the corners of each shape, counting the three on the triangle and the four on the rectangles. Nothing happened. Castor did the same with his door, outlining the shapes with his finger and looking for a response. Nothing happened again.

Kyros outlined his letters and expected nothing to occur. He bashed his fist against the circle, losing his patience with the futile situation.

"Sorry." he murmured.

His palm was pressed in the middle of the circle. The shape sank into the door and started to glow white. The two of them stepped away from the door, startled by the automated movements. The light passed across Kyros' body and shifted to a ruby red once it returned to dimmer luminosity. The button went back to its original position and the ruins returned to their inactive state of dormancy.

Castor was stunned that this temple had mana left in its locks after such a long time. He didn't know of any records of a city here in Anthoran history, so the place had to be at least a few hundred years old. Being that the structure was in the mountains and had unknown runes across its walls, he considered it could be a forward outpost of the Durulians from the western continent. To hide such a massive structure underground in a relatively dangerous mountain region so close to an Anthoran city without anyone noticing would be far-fetched.

"It seems that door is still locked," Castor said as Kyros repeated the process with the same outcome. "The original owners must not want us getting in there."

Kyros repeated the motion, but this time on the right door. After the light passed across the hall, it lit a light shade of blue, like amazonite or sapphire. The door creaked as the slab of stone disappeared into the wall to the right.

"You think that means they want us in this room then?" Kyros asked with a grin. Castor laughed and shined his fotovolo into the dark and damp room the opening had revealed.

Before entering, Castor shot his head left to the end of the hallway. He heard a noise.

They entered a long, multi-chambered room with alcoves lining the sides of the main corridor. The central corridor held many stone benches and countertops within the areas that did not let into the alcoves. The alcoves had lines cut into the walls that made the image of many overlapping rectangles. Whether it was a choice of form or function, Castor could not tell. They went through the rooms and tried to touch different shapes for a response but received none. It seemed the trip inside was a waste until they made it to the last alcove and found a large hole in the wall.

"That's a bit foreboding," Kyros said, looking down the hole as far as he could with the light from his fotovolo. The tunnel in front of them wasn't clean-cut like the rest of the facility. Either they built the complex around a tunnel system that was already in the area, or the hole was dug by something.

Castor glared hesitantly into the opening. The complex was abandoned thus far so he had no reason to expect any other surprises. But something felt off with this area. He could not put his finger on it, but Castor felt uncomfortable in this area of the ruins.

Kyros shrugged and started walking into the hole. He didn't even look back, saying "Well, after today, I doubt it could get worse" and continued into the hewn tunnel system with his sword drawn.

Castor followed, swallowing his instinct and helping to illuminate the surrounding walls with a steady supply of mana into his fotovolo crystals. The clear gems glistened as the mana spilled into their crystal lattice, storing the mana for later use.

The tunnels wound around much more than the hewn hallways of the prior level. Rather than being led down flat corridors or properly cut stairways, this new section elevated and descended at a whim. The passages split at a few points, but they continued to follow the rightmost path to try and find a way back into the ruins. If they were able to find another hole in a wall, they may be able to get access to the areas behind the otherwise sealed doors they found over the course of the last few hours.

As they got deeper into the tunnel system, the grayish red stone started to turn white as though a mold had grown across all the surfaces. Castor touched the cave wall and felt the gritty, spongy texture that seemed to give more than a stone wall should. The other reason they kept to the rightmost path was that Castor kept feeling terrible when they delved farther into the powdery white tunnels. It felt like everything in his head urged him to stay away from traveling deeper into the mountain.

They continued for a short while until they came to another opening and were stunned. In front of them was a cavern that opened to a long ravine. The open area was easily a few miles long, as they could not see the end in the darkness. They could see small holes in the rough stone cliff faces. The white mold they had seen earlier was still around, cropping up around the openings in the walls of the ravine. It was sporadic and made the cavern look as though it had an infection of some kind. Moonlight trickled in from a far distance overhead.

How far underground are we? Castor thought. Two hundred feet? Four hundred? He could not tell how far the ceiling was, as their lights only illuminated a hundred feet up. The streams of moonlight that jutted through the otherwise pitch-black darkness were too varied in shape and size to give him an idea of depth. Castor felt the hair on his neck rise. He didn't like the feeling of being so much in the open. He felt like he was being watched.

"Um, Castor?" Kyros drew his attention forward, where he saw an odd-shaped pillar. The mound of stone sat in an open clearing, and atop its hard surface was the most brilliant gem he had ever seen. A crescent of dark, milky pearl protruded from the stone surface. As though out of a story that Castor had read as a child, the jewel pillar glistened in a shaft of moonlight. It was gently cut from the feldspar vein below it.

"What is-" Castor began to ask, but Kyros cut him off.

"Labradorite." He said quickly. "At least, it looks like labradorite. Remember the guy I was working for a few months back? This looks like what we were hauling across the countryside to Bythe. At least, we were hauling much smaller versions of that."

Castor walked up and touched the stone. Its cool surface emanated primal energy and calmed him even as his senses were tingling from being so exposed. The crescent of the opalescent mineral was a dark, cloudy glass with speckles of the rainbow within its surfaces. The refraction of the moonlight gave it a sparkling appearance.

"Are you sure?" Castor asked. "I know you had experience with it from that trip, but from what I see, everything about it looks like a moonstone." He paused for a few seconds. "Except it doesn't."

He traced his finger across the outer edge of the crescent gem. It was almost two feet in length and around six inches wide at its maximum.

"See the dark color? That is like labradorite. But the striations within the crystal aren't there. Which means it is more likely a moonstone. But the texture shifts and layers of colors are more like labradorite."

Kyros shrugged. He was staring at the gem the whole time without breaking eye contact. "Well whatever it is, it is a beauty. Grab it and put it in my bag."

Castor put his hands on each side of the gem and pulled it out of the muddy mound it was fastened into. It came out with a noise that was a mix between a pop and a crack. As the pier of glistening moonlight was pulled from its resting spot, a stream of crimson flowed down the edge. Castor dropped it instinctively when he noticed how deep the outer edge had cut his hand. It bounced off the outcropping of orthoclase it had grown from and plopped onto the muddy floor.

"Careful!" Kyros exclaimed, handing Castor a wrapping of cloth he had grabbed to wrap the crystal in. Everything was fine though, as the gem was still in pristine condition. They expected it to at least take a scratch where it had hit the rock cluster, but it was completely unscathed.

They packaged the pile carefully into a wrapping of used linen and bundled it away in Kyros' rucksack. Castor mended his hand as his feeling of uneasiness washed over him again.

"Well, that was a lucky find," Kyros said with a gallant look on his face. "That thing could easily fetch us a thousand staters! I'd expect we could even ask for a few hundred denarii with how well preserved it is!"

Castor thought of how much gold and electrum that would be. They could fill a wood chest with that amount of money and still have some leftovers. He could buy a whole house in the city with that sum.

Kyros' smile fell to a neutral pose and then became a look of terror as an overwhelming wall of dread punched Castor in the chest. He instinctively rolled forward and came up closer to Kyros who was still frozen in what looked like absolute fear. Castor regretted looking in the direction his friend was looking into the ravine, as he saw what he couldn't process with his mind at the time. He stood there and viewed what seemed like hell for the young Anthoran man. He was scared.

There were things in the dark. They were vile things. They were abhorrent, detestable, and repulsive. They made Castor's mind feel foggy just from looking at them. Oh, he did not want to be near those gross, foul things. He was scared from the event earlier in the day. He hated and feared the goblins. He was bothered but happy the harpies showed up when they did. But these things, these abominations, made Castor feel less. It made his mind feel like a soft putty. He averted his gaze and he was able to feel the sense of dread that was so vibrant before washing over his senses again. He turned Kyros away by a tug on his shoulders and he snapped from the delusion. They ran.

They continued to run. They ran as fast as their bodies would allow them. Castor may have enhanced his body with magic during his panic, but he was not aware enough to realize if he did. He noticed Kyros had not kept up with him, but he was not sure if it was from the weight of the rucksack or his lack of mana.

That wasn't important. What was important was to run. To get away. To retreat and live. He felt only death from what he saw. He pulsed his mana backward, sending rock chunks crumbling down after they entered a tunnel. The white mold was back. It was suffocating. It made the mined shaft feel small and cramped. The creatures made him feel closed in too. They made his mind feel closed in. They were like the mold, spreading and moving ever closer. Castor was terrified. He had no thoughts other than fear and wanting to get away.

They continued down the tunnels, and the noises from those things seemed to decrease substantially. They did not care. They kept running. They were exhausted. They were panting, sweating, and running. They ran so much. They could still hear the things, though. Down the tunnels, through the mold. It was always there.

They made it to a tee, but the decision did not matter. They went on the right path as they had done so many times before. As long as it was away, away from the things, Castor was alright with the decision. He saw Kyros, who had sweat dripping from his face. He seemed just as scared, although he was never one to show his emotions outwardly. He nodded, giving Castor the okay to lead through the right tunnel.

Castor started down the hall and continued to run. A few feet forward and his feet stopped running. There was nothing to run on.

A cold sensation struck his left thigh as he looked down. His lower half had fallen through the floor. The stone that was abundant everywhere around was not under him. His fotovolo was above the gap and obscured by some dirt, so he couldn't see downward. He was exhausted and losing his grip on the stone around him. His leg, barely in the view from the glimmer of the fotovolo from Kyros' waist, was red all over. Blood poured down his thigh and dripped into the cavern below.

Kyros tried to pull him up, but they were too tired. He couldn't get a good grip as blood dribbled from a cut on his hand. When he tried to pull Castor out, his hand slipped and was punctured on the sharp rock of the floor. Castor's mana was depleted. He couldn't pull himself up and he couldn't use his mana with his mind so clouded.

Kyros stepped away. They heard the things coming. They snapped, gurgled, and chirped. They skittered across the walls and stridulated across the floor. Castor felt panicked but had no way to do anything. All his energy was to keep himself from falling into the abyss.

Kyros closed his eyes, took a deep breath, and nodded.

"Good luck, my friend." he said in a somber tone. Castor looked wide-eyed at him, confused and dazed.

Kyros retreated to the tee in the path and took a step down the other direction. Blood dripped onto the floor and saturated the dry dirt. He called out as the noises got louder. Castor could see his best friend call towards the abyss, sword in hand, staring death in the face. He called again, this time much louder, and slapped his sword into the stone wall.

He sprinted down the left tunnel. His light faded as he got farther away from the tee in the path.

Castor panicked. His best friend just abandoned him in a cave with unspeakable things. His mind felt even more clouded as his grip weakened. He fell.

He fell only a few feet, landing hard on a stone pile before dropping fully to the ground. His leg felt like it was on fire and blood exuded from the open wound. He could feel his leg, but it was too weak to stand on. He couldn't pull himself up to his feet either.

His light was available again, no longer covered in dust and gravel. It looked like he fell into a tomb or crypt. Sarcophagi lined the walls, each closed by a large stone lid. He noticed he fell onto one. It was dark and covered in dust. The whole room felt old, but he noticed it had the same designs as the ruins they were in before.

He felt the dread closing in again. He crawled across the floor, trying to get away from the hole in the ceiling. It was the only opening he could see around him. He didn't want those things coming into this room with him. He only wanted to run away and hide.

He noticed that one of the sarcophagi was open. Its lid was propped up and allowed access to the cavity inside. A single strand of hope was laid before him. He could tell the blood loss was affecting him as much as the fear. He continued to crawl and grovel and writhe over to the open container. He pulled himself inside. Blood dribbled down the edges of the hollow as he took a deep breath. He sat up and pulled the lid over him. It didn't budge.

They were here.

He had little energy left to panic. He just felt the fear this time but was barely able to respond to it. His vision was dimming, but he could see shapes moving in the dark. It felt like the white mold had moved into the room with him. The light shapes peered through the opening in the ceiling. His grip on the lid strengthened from the pounding in his ears. He let the panic take hold this time. He pulled and pulled and eventually the lid gave way. It closed over the top of him.

He heard scratching outside the sarcophagus. It was a light noise. The walls of the casket were thick and durable. He could barely hear the noise. The inside was not spacious but he felt less cramped than in the white tunnels. He felt safe. His light was dimming. A pulse of white light seemed to come from below him before dimming also. He wasn't sure what he was seeing. Was it real? Was he imagining it? He felt a prick on his leg, but he had no energy to react. His legs felt cold. Actually, his whole body felt cold. But at least his panic was gone. He felt a bit at peace as he fell asleep.

CHAPTER 13

A Respite Of Euphoria

0th of Quartz, -1249 of the Age of Discovery

His vision was blurry. Warmth returned to his legs and he could again feel the tips of his fingers. He wiggled his toes. They felt a soft sensation, like that of grass. He did not think that he was in a field or on a knoll. He remembered the dark and damp walls of a cave or building. He looked down at his feet.

There was grass.

He was lying in a field of grass. It was a sprawling hillside. Nothing grew except a meadow of clover and short turf. He felt a bit itchy but was not aware of anything that would cause him to itch. Maybe it was the grass? He wasn't sure.

He heard clicking and other noises behind him. He looked around but couldn't pinpoint where they came from.

"Hello?" he called out. He was able to stand, so he did. His leg didn't hurt anymore. Was there a reason it hurt before?

"Hello there." a deep and mellow voice echoed from behind him. He turned around, panicked.

He turned to see nothing. Just grass. He was surprised. The voice felt like it was pretty close. He heard some scratching off in the distance.

Something clicked in his memory. He remembered where he was just now. Those things were still here. Where was here though? It didn't matter. He had to get away.

He was about to start sprinting down the hill as a cool wave settled over his mind. Like the trickle of a cool creek across a campfire, the panic and fear were quenched and he felt at ease.

"Easy now, friend. You've only just woken up." the same deep voice spoke again from behind him. He turned again, this time seeing an older man standing a few paces away.

He reminded Castor of his father in a way, with a walking cane and fancy clothes. His gray beard was the exact opposite of Nikitas, with hair all over his face except for his chin. That wasn't a style of facial hair he was used to, but it seemed to fit the eccentric older man.

"Where am I?" Castor asked. He was wary, as he could still faintly remember being terrified a few moments ago.

"Well, right now it looks like you are standing with me in this meadow." the old man croaked. "Does it matter where we are? Would somewhere else make you feel more at ease?"

The answer was strange to the nineteen-year-old prince. He wanted answers, not riddles. He thought he would be more irritated with his dodgy response. After all, something had just occurred. He couldn't remember what it was, but it left an impact on his mind.

"Come now, do not be so standoffish." the old man continued. "Why don't you join me at my table for some tea."

He gestured behind Castor as he hobbled over to a little wood pergola that was behind him. He must not have noticed it before. He shrugged and took a seat across from the older man and looked over the verdant hills towards the mountains in the distance. He could see a little plume of smoke on the horizon. Maybe it was Tyressos? It probably wasn't Thyma, considering how far they traveled. Where again were they traveling to?

"This is one of my favorite blends." the old man poured a cup of warm, tan water into a small bowl with a handle. His was of some foreign fashion, but Castor's was a very well-made kylix. The Anthoran drinking cup was elaborately detailed. It had an image of small fish swimming at the bottom of the bowl and dolphins painted on the handles.

"This blend is something I have enjoyed for quite a while." the old man said after taking a sip from his mug. He took a bite from a small pastry that sat on the wood dish next to his teacup.

"May I?" Castor gestured to the little stand of sweets, sipping from his teacup.

"Most certainly!" the man guffawed. His smile was beaming as he squinted behind his saggy jowls. "I think you'll find them to be quite close to what you would find in your cities today."

What an odd thing to say. Castor thought to himself as he took a bite from the pastry. It was a fried ball of oat flour with a drizzling of honey and cinnamon on top. He heard this type of treat came in from the western side of Anthora near the capital and the mountainous city of Bylessos.

"Oh, was it?" the man asked inquisitively with a tilted head. "I do apologize. I haven't had a guest in quite some time."

Castor looked towards him cautiously with partially squinted eyes. The wave of coolness swept over his mind as he took another sip from the tea. It had a sweet aroma and a flowery flavor. He could see little flowers swirling in the liquid of the glass teapot. He was amused by how they were still moving so quickly after being put down a minute or two ago.

"I am not sure if this blend is even available in your lands anymore." the graybeard continued as they looked over the rolling hills. "I believe this flower went extinct quite a while ago."

"Is it native to the western lands or Maudif?" Castor asked. He was quite fond of the flavor and wouldn't mind finding a contact that could import some for him. With its fruity scent, he could use it to spice his yearly wine barrel made with his family in the upcoming spring.

"Oh no, it was only grown in the mountains north of here. I would expect it has been quite a while since the last flower bloomed there. After it became a desert on the northern side of the Nidaros some years ago, I do not think the matronberry was able to adapt."

Castor was a little confused. The records he had read in their city library all conclude that the northern side of the Nidaros was a desert. He never saw a single account of that region being anything more than a barren wasteland. Maybe the old man was getting his geography mixed up. He did live underground.

Underground? They were clearly in a grassy knoll. Why did he think the man lived underground?

The man read from a book he held in his right hand. He didn't see him holding it before, so he assumed it was within his long, silvery robes. They weren't too ornate or overly designed. They did seem rather well-tailored though, as they held to his body quite well and seemed to be comfortable. He never saw the man adjust his clothing while he was sitting there, which was uncommon since it didn't seem like the fabric shifted at all since sitting down.

"Oh, well no matter." he said, shutting the book within his right palm and placing it on the table. "Would you like to come inside? There are a few things I wanted to discuss with you."

"Inside?" Castor asked. They were clearly in a field.

"Yes. Inside my house." He said nonchalantly with a hand gesture aimed at where they were sitting. Castor turned to see a well-built stone home sitting in the field on the other side of the hill they rested on. He must have missed seeing it before since he was preoccupied with the view.

"Oh, yes. That would be fine. And thank you for the tea. I am glad I was able to try such a rare treat." Castor finished off the rest of his tea and placed the kylix on the serving plate that held the pastries. They walked out of the pergola and up to the home.

"My name is Alexander, by the way." the man said as he held his hand out to Castor as they walked. He shook Alexander's hand and nodded.

"It's a pleasure to be your acquaintance, Alexander." smiled Castor.

The house was made of natural clay bricks and stood upright without any stucco or mortar on the outside of the home. Although it was two floors tall, the atrium was completely covered, making the front hall feel closed in. Alexander led Castor through the front doors and off to the right, where the main hall opened up into a two-floor library.

Castor was amazed. Such a large collection of books was very rare in Anthora. The volume of encyclopedias and compendiums that lined the wood shelves of one man's home was rivaling that of the Thymian library. Full books crossed the walls of the building and free-standing racks of scrolls were housed on the open floor.

Alexander stood in front of a shelf that was placed near an open window. The view of the rolling green hills was very pleasant. Castor could easily live here if he had the chance.

He heard scratching from outside, so he peeked his head out of the window. After looking around the foundation of the building, he didn't see anything.

"Ah, here it is," Alexander exclaimed, taking a book off the shelf. Castor brought his body fully inside the building again and looked at Alexander inquisitively.

"Wanted a little more information on you and your people," Alexander explained, gesturing with his left hand to the open pages he held in his right. "I figured understanding you and yours would allow us to talk easier."

"Oh!" Castor said, surprised. "I didn't know anyone had written about us."

"It's good to keep a record of your accomplishments and use your experience to make better situations in the future," Alexander stated as he walked over to a comfy-looking chair in front of a stone fireplace. It was inviting enough for Castor to join him, sitting across the open space on a reclined bench covered in cloth pillows.

They sat in silence for a few minutes as Alexander skimmed over the contents of the book. Castor took the time to relax and enjoy the scenery. The library was beautiful, with many different colored books sitting side by side across the shelves. They made a rainbow pattern across the walls, like the shimmering scales of a fish.

Castor watched as Alexander tabbed through the pages with his thumb, raising his eyebrows at parts that he took an interest in. He didn't take long on each page. Castor was curious as to what the contents were, but it was nice to just sit back and relax. His feet felt warm prompted up near the fireplace.

"Well, I think that covers everything I need to know," Alexander said as he closed the book. He plopped it onto the table next to his chair and crossed his legs.

He looked directly at Castor with a serious look. It didn't make Castor feel uncomfortable but he felt the conversation take a more serious route. He sat up a bit on the recliner couch and shifted his body to face Alexander.

"So let's go over some things if you do not mind." the older man stroked his beard as his gaze shifted to the fireplace.

He had nothing to hide. If anything, he had as many questions as answers. "Sure. Ask away," he said.

"So, your friends. Do you know what happened to them?" Alexander asked.

"I..." Castor almost started to speak as memories washed back over his mind of the day's events. He remembered Mithra plummeting down the cliffside, most likely to his death. He remembered Kyros being chased by those... *things*.

His blood raced in his veins. His heart was pounding and a light sweat built on his brow. The very thought of those things made Castor react in such a primal way that Alexander reached out to calm the boy.

The cool sensation he felt before calmed his thoughts again and he felt more at peace. Alexander frowned, not from disappointment, but rather from surprise.

"Well, then. That will limit how far our conversations go today." he said flatly. He took another look at the book he was holding, reading the last few pages again within its bindings. He nodded as though he found something he missed the first time reading.

"Alright. That is not the end of the world." He grunted and caught himself. He was amused at some sort of inside joke he was making. "So let's go over some of the things we need to discuss before we are done here."

Even in his calm state, Castor felt agitated and confused. He had remembered the horrific events of the last half dozen hours and still could not understand what was going on. Considering everything he went through, he even considered he had passed to the next world. But they were not at the god's great table. This man was not his patron deity. He expected a lot more food and wine and companions to greet him in the afterlife.

"Oh, do not worry about that," Alexander said. He took a few seconds to ensure his next statements were crafted to convey what he needed to get Castor to understand. "I am not here to take you to the afterlife. On the contrary, I am the reason you aren't going there. Consider me as an oracle. Or rather, a harbinger of fate. My job is to ensure the canvas of our lives keeps flowing forward. If a thread or two gets snipped here or there, the canvas is still in one piece. Some threads are more important than others and require some tending to."

Alexander pointed at Castor. "You, my dear little prince, are one of those important, stubborn threads. I may not control the flow of the canvas, but I can at least help keep it in one piece. Based on my..." he hesitated and looked in his book again, searching the last few pages for something. Once he found it, he nodded and closed the covers again. "From what the gods have conveyed to me, you are needed to play a part in some very important events to come."

Castor was surprised. He was an important social figure in Anthora, so being someone of status wasn't new to him. But to have someone he never met before, in a palace he didn't even know the location of, after being chased by goblins and harpies and other nasty things, come and say he was a chosen of the gods? That was even hard for him to believe at such short notice.

"I think it is more important to understand the risks and sacrifices this position entails." Alexander had gotten up and replaced his prior book with a scroll he claimed on a shelf near their sitting arrangement. He unfurled the vellum page and carefully looked over the details inside.

"You will go through many trials and tribulations," Alexander stated in a deep and serious tone. "You, and your family, and your friends, and your people will suffer greatly. This world is full of sin and decay. Whether it be in your city or your country or a faraway corner of another continent, the impacts of what is to come cannot be stopped. There will be many events in the coming years that will tear this world asunder. You alone do not have the power to stop fate."

Castor was irritated. The scratching he heard earlier was still around him, like a gnawing sound in the distance. The man he thought was helping him was now telling him his fate was sealed to a path of pain and suffering.

"Why are you talking in such riddles?" Castor demanded. "Are you reading the prophecy from that scroll? Let me read it. If my fate is already sealed, let me be the arbiter of it. If it will affect my family and friends, let me do what I can to help them."

Alexander released his tension on the scroll and it curled back into its circular shape. He placed it back on the rack among the dozen other sheets.

"Your selflessness is an appealing trait, young prince. Do not lose that tenacity." Alexander said after sitting back in his chair. "My role is not to prepare or aid you on your journey other than help you onto your feet.

You are an acceptable candidate to become what you would call a hero of your age. I have the authority to deem it so. And I do."

He leaned forward and looked directly at Castor. His stare was as strong as Mithra's gaze; steely and focused like a predator on a hunt. But there was a kindness there. Some sort of empathy or sympathy. Castor wasn't sure which one.

"What you went through the last few days, and even the last few months, was no easy feat. It will have a toll on someone of your age and status. Staring death in the face and surviving is not a task one comes to often. Those who do are not always lucky enough to come out the same."

Castor agreed. He felt that last statement in his chest. Feelings rushed around as images of those things came back to his mind. He had blocked them out before but he was seeing them again. The cool sensation washed back over him and he was able to face the fragments of the memories he had of that cave.

Alexander nodded and leaned back. "Yes, I think you will do just fine. So the rest falls onto you. I can leave you here. You can spend the rest of your days in this beautiful, warm, and peaceful limbo. You would not have to face death again for what would feel to you like thousands of years. I could teach you about the past and show you what we expect to be in the future."

Alexander had his hands out in front of him, gesturing his open palms like the weighing pans of a scale.

"Your other option is to be sent from this place and live the struggle the gods have set before you. Many will die. They would die regardless of your choice, but this way you will have a hand in their deaths. Either by ignorance or choice, many will suffer under your command. But you are fated to save the rest. You can be the one to spare this world of its eternal cycle. Is that something that interests you?"

Castor kept his head aimed at the fire like he had since the last time he spoke. He felt out of place here. For the first time, he felt like his position wasn't that of the upper hand but rather like a peasant at a royal feast. He felt uncomfortable. This man was spouting what would be seen as nonsense if he was met in a street or alley in Thyma.

If the man was telling the truth, then what he said worried Castor. He did not want to cause pain and suffering to others, especially those he cared about. He did not like the predicament he was thrown into. He had one question to ask before he continued to debate his internal conflict.

"Answer me this, Alexander." Castor pried, looking for more information without dedicating it to one of the binary paths he was given. "What if I wanted to just leave and not partake as a hero? What if I just lied and said I would, and then continued with my life as if this never happened?"

Alexander tapped the side of his head and pointed at Castor with a smirk.

"See!" this is why I want to choose you as my champion! Quick wit and quicker on your feet!"

Alexander took a deep breath and his tone became serious once more.

"You are welcome to do so. But it won't change the strings of fate." the pallid man stared into the fire as he spoke. "Regardless of your choice, most of the people you know will die."

Blood rushed to Castor's head as he took in the impact of their situation. He did not like what he was being told but there was nothing he could do to change the current events.

"It won't just be people you know." Alexander continued. "There will be many, many people that will die. It will be the worst event of your age."

He took a sip from the teacup he had on the little table by his side. He let his words sink into Castor as he let the dramatic pause take hold.

"But you will have the ability to dampen the damage. You will have the ability to save some. There's even the chance that you can stop the events from happening altogether."

Alexander looked over at Castor to weigh his response. Castor was staring at him intently, trying to pry as much information out of the scruffy old man as he could.

"I wouldn't get your hopes up, young man. I cannot promise you a happy ending. The fates, as they are, do not work in ways that are convenient to us. But with the gods on your side, you may just stand a chance."

Castor had sat up fully at this point and faced the caretaker of this realm with intent.

"I accept your terms," Castor said directly to the man.

"As easy as that, eh?" Alexander said. "You are sure? There will truly be struggles beyond your current comprehension. It is not a bad choice to stay here. I can show you what the fates have in store."

Castor did not hesitate. He pressed forward, not letting the man's silver tongue press its way into his mind.

"If I can save even a single one of my people, then that is a fate which is fine with me," Castor said confidently.

He lost enough people just in the last few months alone. After the attack in the port, he had to deal with two more deaths of deceased relatives who had passed from the heartache of their losses. On top of them, there were reports of more travelers going missing in the region and even reports of a small village in the north disappearing altogether. Whether those events are tied to what Alexander had just explained was not something he knew.

He figured he would not get an answer from the mysterious man either, as he seemed just as happy trapping him here as he would letting him go. He wanted to ask specifics about it, but it seemed his curiosity could sway Alexander from letting him become the hero he claimed he could become. To Castor, it did not matter. He would not change his answer if he knew how stacked the odds were against him. He was committed to his people and he could not abandon them.

Alexander sighed. It seemed as though Alexander was regretting his decision. Whether it be because his visitor had chosen to leave or because of other reasons unbeknownst to the young prince, he did not know.

"Very well," Alexander murmured. "I do wish you the best. I really do. I can't say for sure how difficult your road will be, but I am sure there will be times you regret your hasty decision."

Castor caught his wording as odd and tried to press him on the topic as the man got out of his chair and walked to the back of the room.

"Was it that hasty? Did you expect me to take much more time to decide on my path forward?" he asked coyly.

Alexander rolled his eyes in thought. It seemed he was looking for the right selection of words to not tip the boy off any further. He put a finger up as he stopped walking and corrected himself.

"Hasty, maybe not. But I can tell you that the others before you took longer to decide. Maybe you are the bravest, or maybe the dumbest. I cannot tell you even if I did know. But you did give me the most confidence, so that is a good mark in my book."

As he continued to walk, he cut Castor off as he began to open his mouth.

"And no, I cannot tell you who came before you. That information is not privy to you at this time. Whether you find that information in the future is on your shoulders. I have probably said too much as it stands."

Castor closed his mouth and nodded. If this was the path the fates had decided, then he accepted it. He considered the ramifications as Alexander had retrieved something from a shelf behind him. As Castor stared into the fireplace, Alexander brought Castor a large bronze amulet that he sat in the boy's lap.

"This one seemed to call out to me when I was sifting through my drawer," Alexander said with a smile.

Castor held up the solid bronze symbol. The symbolic sun was of his patron deity. Its center held layered rings that overlapped and created an undulated effect. The wavey coronas that came outward were finely engraved with repeating geometric patterns that made the object feel lifelike. It was far too detailed and slightly different than what he was used to on his shrines and in his sacred texts, but the object he held felt very important to him, like a lost child.

"The sun of Ignus," Castor muttered, tracing the pattern with his finger.

"Ignus. Ig'Nataz. Ez Nakhasht. They are all the same to me. Call him what you will. What matters is that he calls you too. Hero, chosen, son. While his body left your lands many years ago, his will lives on. And it seems he has found an interest in you."

For the first time in his bizarre encounter with a mysterious man in a place he did not know, Castor was speechless. To know you are seen by the gods is a feat in and of itself. To have your patron consider you worthy of their direct praise was something entirely different. He felt a mix of euphoria and warmth, like an adopted child feeling the love of a foster family for the first time. He thought of Atticus and wondered if this is how the boy felt when he took him in.

"You are welcome to take your time to appreciate your patron's care for you, but I do need to continue our conversation with our limited time together," Alexander said in a caring tone. He wiped a few of Castor's tears from the leather arm of his sofa, making sure they did not leave a mark.

"Thanks," Castor said as he composed himself. He took some time to appreciate the detail of the ancient symbol of his patron deity, making a mental note of the differences between it and the symbols he was used to seeing.

"As I have told you before, I cannot tell you everything I know, as that would go against the very nature of your world. Since you have chosen to stay within your lands and help as you see fit, I do not plan to keep you here. You will be free to go back and participate in the canvas of fate. Whether you end up building upon the fabric with your strands or knotting it will be up to you."

Alexander had brought over a scroll and sat at the end of the couch Castor was prompted up against. He unwound the scroll and held it up for Castor to see.

"The only thing I am allowed to share with you is this," Alexander said as he reviewed the painting of an object. It was a drawing of a tall pillar. He felt as though he had seen the object before but nothing crossed his mind when he thought about it. It felt familiar though.

"You will need to find this," Alexander explained. "When you do, you will be on your first steps to becoming what you aspire to become. I would not go out of your way to find it, as you most likely will cross paths with it because of your decision here. But you will need to stay ever vigilant for when you do.

Castor made sure to get as good of a mental image of it as he could. Unfortunately, the scroll was not in the best shape with the image having watermarks and tears along the edges. Regardless, Castor focused on what it held.

The object looked like a large stone scroll with ornate colors around the edges. It was very flat and he could just make out a few letters around the edges. He could tell it was a large scroll, as he could see a few beeswax candles on the ground near it which paled in comparison. The drawing was made from the top down, so the angle made it hard to discern any details of objects around it.

"When you find this, and I am sure you will, you will need to find its keeper. The keeper of this thing will guide you on your journey. At least that's what should occur. Hopefully, we aren't too late and the keeper is already long past."

Castor raised an eyebrow but Alexander shrugged it off.

"It should work out fine. I wouldn't have accepted you as a candidate if there was no option to fulfill your duties in the first place and I knew the keeper was dead. I would be more worried about getting the keeper to believe you. The keeper may not be the most trusting, as I am sure this role has essentially become this person's entire life."

"That seems fair," Castor said. He thought back to the epic tales in the stories he was read as a child. "You wouldn't want to pass the fate of the gods off to a stranger on a whim. I assume I have to pass a test or a trial?"

"Oh, no." Alexander disregarded the notion. "Nothing of the sort. I have some phrases you need to say, and the keeper should believe you."

"Just like that?" Castor raised his eyebrow again. Alexander reached out and pushed his eyebrow down with his pointer finger.

"Just like that." he said. "All you need to do is tell the keeper you are ready to start your journey. Once you do, he or she will probably disregard you as not important. You need to convince them you know about what is to come. I think the easiest way to do that would be to tell the keeper 'They are coming again and we must prepare.' If you do that and continue to do that until the keeper listens, then you should have an easy time with your journey."

Castor squinted at the burly man. He didn't seem to be lying, jesting, or generally joking around. He seemed to be telling the truth. He had no reason to think otherwise. Alexander responded to his stare with a wide grin.

"Hey," he said, "Do not look at me like that. I didn't make the rules. I fulfilled my job by acquiring a suitable candidate. Anything past that was not my choice."

Castor nodded with a smile. "That's fine. I won't shoot the messenger."

"It's very much appreciated!" the older man announced, reading from another book he had taken off the shelf. They sat in silence as he read, and a perturbed look crossed his face. Alexander realized he had become too enamored in his reading and he turned his attention back to his guest.

"Sorry. Yes, let's get you going then, shall we? No reason to keep you here any longer."

"Ah, alright then." Castor was surprised by his quick change of mood. He held out the emblem of Ignus to return it before he left.

"No, I think you'll need that. Hold it to your chest, like this." Alexander said. He crossed his hands over the center of his chest and tucked in his fingers. "Oh, but lie down first, it'll make you feel a lot less."

Castor nodded and did what he was told. He laid across the padded kline as he pulled the amulet to his chest. A wave of cold water passed across his body, flowing out of where the holy symbol made contact with his sternum. He panicked for a second, feeling like he was drowning in a deep, dark pool. But his mind calmed as the flow of peaceful energy emanated through his limbs.

Like passing through a cool, autumn stream, Castor felt the chill of the flow numb his fingers and tighten his toes. He felt vulnerable, but he persisted. His eyes felt too heavy to open, so he traversed the stream in utter blackness.

It was good to feel again, though. He did not feel much when he was visiting his friend in that other land. He was just there, existing, allowing the will of the gods to transpire. He did not mind, but he was glad to get back to what he was doing. What was he doing before this, again?

CHAPTER 14

An Amulet Of Carved Onyx

4th of Azurite, 453 of the Age of Discovery

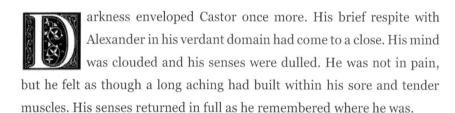

arkness enveloped Castor once more. His brief respite with Alexander in his verdant domain had come to a close. His mind was clouded and his senses were dulled. He was not in pain, but he felt as though a long aching had built within his sore and tender muscles. His senses returned in full as he remembered where he was.

He grabbed out in the darkness and clenched his thigh in his grasp. He remembered the cool flow of blood seeping across his leg before he entombed himself. The floor had given out and the sharp edges cut his body. His hand was also cut by that crystal they found in the deep caves. There was something else there too, right?

His attention focused on his wound, or rather the lack thereof. He poked and prodded and could not feel the blood in his clothes nor the slickness on his skin. Everything felt dry. There was a gritty texture on his fingers, like the residue of boiled oats after leaving one's dish out overnight. He remembered the texture from a few nights prior when he had to wash his bowl with sand and cloth because he did exactly that. His fingers felt gritty as he wiped them on his pants to clear his skin.

His muscles were sore. His body ached, but not from the wounds he had prior. Instead, it was an aching one received after a long and arduous journey or a backbreaking day's worth of physical labor. He remembered this soreness when he was younger. He felt this way after his first long day of guard training when he had turned fourteen. His muscles felt tight and ached a deep ache for the following two days. He hoped this ache would dissipate sooner than two days.

His linothorax sat heavily on his shoulders. His helm had fallen off during his sleep and rolled down the casket to his feet. His toes could feel the cold blue paint on the bronze helm and little pinpricks shot up his legs. It was a good sign though, as he was worried his injuries could have caused permanent damage.

The gods had spared him, and he knew it. Whether it be his unwavering faith in his leonine god or sheer luck, his life was exchanged that day for service to a higher power. The messenger of the Kalotrapia had given Castor a great boon that day and he was very grateful for his support. His mind felt calmer and he could tell his emotions were far more under control than they were during the pursuit some time ago. His head hurt a little as he remembered what the pursuit was.

Oh, right. He thought. *Those things.*

His heartbeat quickened as he remembered the hideous, terrible sight of those things that dwelt within the mountain. Those grotesque things made him feel many emotions at levels he did not feel comfortable with. Fear, anger, hatred, pain.

He remembered the fall of Mithra. The lion man surely saved Castor's life at that time and he was confident his gods would see his debt repaid in the next life. He remembered Kyros running down the other hall

[315]

as those things chased him like ravaging wolves closing in on an injured hare. He felt weak and small. His friends had most likely given their lives for him. He was not able to return the favor if they were dead. His anger and self-pity wallowed in his head before a cooling sensation returned to his body.

He remembered this feeling from his trip to the messenger's land. It felt cool and calming like the caress of a babbling brook on his brain. He knew where it emanated from. The center of his chest felt like a natural mountain spring, allowing the cooling effect to sweep across his body as it burbled forth. He tried to grab at the cool instinctively, but he could not as the linothorax covered his chest. It wouldn't matter though, as he could tell the spring of calming was deeper than the skin layer. It was something within him that was cooling.

As if spurred on by the feeling welling within his chest, the casket lid creaked open and no longer held Castor into the tombs' unforgiving embrace. He barely caught himself as he fell to the ground. His helm clanked against the hard stone floor and bounced a few paces away. He must not have realized before that the sarcophagus was sitting at a steep angle. Or maybe it was moved while he slept?

He did not know, nor did he care. He was thrown from its safe internals and cast onto the hard ground. He had to focus his mind and get a grip on the reality of the situation. He was still stuck miles underground with deadly creatures and no source of food or light.

Wait, that wasn't true. He did have light. He passed his hand across his belt and groped blindly at the various bits and baubles he had tied to it. As he passed over his leather money pouch, he felt the cold bars of his fotovolo. He focused on his mana well within his chest and passed the flow along his arms and into his fingers. The trickle of energy ignited the glowing gem and the room lit with a crystal-clear radiance. He could see again.

It took a few seconds for his eyes to adapt to the sudden influx of brightness that now bombarded his retinas. The room was lit and he could again see his surroundings. They were plain and covered in dust. He could see the hole in the ceiling that he had fallen through. The door to the room was engraved on the farther wall opposite his current position. This room's door was sealed shut like many of the others within this underground ruined temple complex.

Castor released the strings on his armor and let the coverings fall to his waist. He checked his body for any wounds or bruises but could not find any. His leg wound was healed and only had a scar in its place. His hand was healed as well and recovered fully. His time convening with the messenger of the gods seemed to have more of a physical effect on him than he expected.

After lifting his shirt, he found the largest change in his body. In the center of his chest where the cool feeling was emanating from was a large imprint of the sun. It was identical to the amulet he was given by Alexander of his patron deity. The details matched so well that he could trace the raised skin on his chest and recall the same features from his dream. He felt the raised surface on his skin with the ends of his fingers and traced the eight-pointed sun from top to bottom. Surely this was the mark of his god. He had become a god-kissed.

He had never heard of a god-kissed having their mark on their chest. All god-kissed in history had the mark proudly portrayed on their faces or necks. To have it somewhere else made Castor feel confused. Was he not worthy of openly representing his god? Was Ignus ashamed or contrite of his decision? Or was there a deeper reason for it, one that made his journey for his patron more covert, and a furtive indication was required for his trials ahead?

He had gotten to his feet and rebound the ties on his linothorax. He did not have time to dwell on it now. Between the running and the crawling and the hiding and the dying, the bindings of his linen segments required attention. He retied the leather straps and made sure all the connections were in order. He went to fetch his helmet but felt nauseous.

He was hit with a wave of vertigo as though he was falling forward. He realized that it wasn't a feeling of falling, but instead the actual act of falling itself. As he grabbed his helmet off the ground, he felt the room tip ever farther towards the back end. A small panic lit within his heart. He did not know the best course of action. Was he falling? How was a stone room falling?

The cool sensation fell across his chest and he felt safe once again. His panic turned to a burning desire to survive. He steadied his stance and allowed his body to move with the new point of balance. He could feel the foundations shifting as a high pitch screeching was heard below. It was not an organic noise, but instead that of nails on a chalkboard. Castor could feel the hairs on his skin stand on end as he focused on his center of balance.

The ever-moving floor started to shift more rapidly as the back wall fell away. He had stepped back towards the higher end of the room at this point, anticipating such a collapse ahead of time. He could see a deep black ravine outside of the open wall. The light of his fotovolo only expanded so far and lit the walls nearest him outside the room. It did not give any view of the deep beyond, however.

The room continued to sink down and out towards that black gap below. He could not get a sense of how deep it was. Maybe this was another cavern below the one they were in prior, maybe this was something entirely different.

Castor made his way to where the opening in the ceiling was. He stood on one of the sealed sarcophagi and propped himself up towards the broken opening. The edges were sharp and a bit of dark brown stained one side. He had grabbed a rock off the floor and started to bash the sharp corners down. Each thrust of the blunt stone chipped away at the edges until two of the sharp points were blunted down to flats. The stone shattered on the third point, so he had to grab another stone off the ground and continue his hammering.

Just as he cracked off the last of the sharp edges as the room started to cave in. He propelled himself upward and pulled his body through the gap. With his armor tighter and energy put into tightening his muscles, Castor forced his way through what formerly was the way he was to die and instead made it into his only chance for survival. He made sure not to use his mana to manipulate the air, as the cave was on the precipice of collapse as it was. As he crawled out through the opening, he pressed forward on his elbows and crept into the tunnel system he had fled through earlier that day.

Castor could feel the pull of cold air behind him as he narrowly escaped the collapse. He could not see behind him into that black void. The angle of his fotovolo did not allow for the light to extend past the leather tassets of his waistline and the pitch blackness below stayed as dark as it had been for the past eons. He could feel the cold air and the exposed area. It made him uncomfortable. He could not see what could lie within the swale of darkness down in that hole. It was an open void that could house horrors beyond his comprehension. Or there could be nothing. Both ideas had Castor crawling just that much quicker across the ground.

He trusted the flooring after he could see the tee in the path again. He knew the extent of the collapsing tunnel would be behind him now. He tested the flooring with a few jumps, prepared to propel himself with mana if need be. But the need did not arise. His feet kept to the hewn stone walls of the earthen tunnel.

He looked back and only saw darkness. The light did not extend far into the void, and his vision only went as far as a few paces into what seemed like a pool of black tar. His curiosity tempted him, but he knew better than to put his face near that opening on the floor. There were dangerous things in these tunnels and going anywhere that could put him in danger would not be worth the risk. His friends sacrificed too much for him to throw his life away.

My friends! He thought as a light burst into his mind. He remembered that Kyros may very well be alive. Mithra could have also survived the fall, but his more immediate goal was to find his closer friend. His lifelong friend had lured those things away before and could have outrun them. He may have been injured, but Kyros was at his peak physical performance in his life. Without his reliance on mana and channeling, he was unmatched within the mercenary guild when it came to physical prowess. He was sure he was able to outrun them.

A shiver went through Castor's spine as he thought of those things. He was able to keep his emotions in check now with the cooling sensation keeping his mind in one piece, but the thought of those... *things*... still made his skin crawl. It was weird to have an animal make him feel so vulnerable, but they did.

Castor went past the tee in the path and looked in both directions. He knew Kyros had traveled down the right path and upwards into the mountain. The way they came was behind him and he remembered the caves it led into. He could see that white powdery mold built on the walls where they had come from. It was chalky and dusty and odd. He did not feel comfortable around it. He was thinking of scoping out the downward path before traveling upward into new territory, but he just did not feel comfortable going any further. The walls were not covered like this when they had run through before. After a swig of water from his waterskin and a bite of crisp and degraded ox jerky, he figured it would be best to just carry on. He proceeded up the leftmost path.

The halls wound around the mountain's depths like they were dug by giant worms. The vacillating tubes of cut earth seemed to have a mind of their own. He continued onwards, ever upward, and came across very little on his way. He walked into a small chamber that felt more squarish than what a natural cave would seem, but nothing came of it. There was only the way he came in and the way forward. He passed through the room with no resistance. He came to another long room that was the size of an atrium. There were two exits this time, but the rightmost one collapsed after a few paces in. The stone roof seemed to have given way, either during Kyros' escape or eons prior. He could not tell. With no reason to go farther in or consider clearing the rubble, Castor shrugged to himself and continued his journey through the tunnel system in search of Kyros.

His walking made him parched and he finished off the rest of his water supply. Luckily, his time resting in the tomb gave his mana reserves time to replete. He had no issue taking water from the damp air and condensing it into the waterskin. The water tasted weird, but not in a way that worried the young prince. He put up with the strange taste, as his parched lips overstepped his standoffishness to the slick liquid.

He did realize that their adventure was putting a strain on his physique. His armor was tied tighter than he had it for a year prior, leaving a lot of excess leather straps to tie upon his shoulders. With his constant depletion of mana, little rest from physical exertion, and lack of food,

Castor could tell his body was smaller than when they left a few days ago. While he felt healthy enough to continue without worry, he knew he would need to eat a lot when he got home. His trip had taken a lot more out of him than expected.

He made sure to eat what was left of the jerky in his pouch as he walked. Maybe it was from his time in the damp caves or the general state of his body but the jerky seemed to taste off. It tasted old and dry and cracked easily in his grip. He did not have much of a choice of sustenance, so he kept eating, but he made a mental note to forage for some fresher food once he was out of the mountain and into the wilderness again.

As he walked, the path opened up again and seemed to be larger than the deeper dwellings. Rather than feeling claustrophobic, he had more room to move around and the air seemed to get easier to breathe. His spirits needed the boost as he felt lighter and sprier. His walking continued until he found himself in a large cavern.

The ceiling was around thirty feet high at its peak and extended a few hundred feet at its longest. Stalactites were extending from the roof and stalagmites building upward. A few outcroppings of stone jutted from the landscape and gave the cave a more natural and wild feel. A still pool of foggy water reflected light from his fotovolo and the soft blue glow of the cave fungus made the scenery look magical. The dark waters of the underground lake gave no hint of their total depth. The ground had drippings of the blue fungus and outlined a few natural paths through the cavern's interior.

He noticed a disturbance on the floor and immediately stopped. He saw that the blue fungus that grew naturally in the cave was disturbed along the rightmost path. When he squinted, he could see the lack of blue across the floor in a straight line that cut behind the one stone outcropping. This cave was not commonplace for foot travel. *Maybe it was the way Kyros went,* he thought. He drew his sword and kept it at the ready, knowing he found the trail of his lost friend. Whether he was in good shape or not, he had a plan forward to search for him.

Unfortunately for the young and tired prince, his journey was not a long one.

He cleared the edge of the outcropping and felt a hot sensation build up in his throat. The site in front of him was not what he expected to find nor was it what he wanted. Strewn across the floor were bones. Human bones. Chunks of torn leather and linen were tossed about. The fine dust that covered the cavern floor was disturbed around the remains as well as across the floor and walls of the outcropping. The bones were mostly piled in a divot in the rock wall with part of the remains launched around. It was as though a pack of wild dogs found the remains and picked them clean.

This cannot be Kyros, Castor thought to himself. *This had to be someone else.*

Castor was not just being stubborn. He genuinely could not wrap his mind around it. He had only been out for a few hours, a half of a day at most. There was no way these stark white bones could be his best friend. It was human, that was a given. The shape of the skull and the size of the remains indicated so. As Castor rummaged through the area and tried to clear his ever-clouding thoughts, he found the one thing that he did not want to find.

In a nook of the stone outcropping, he saw the rucksack that Kyros had brought into the cave system. It was the same size, same color, same style. It was covered in a stagnant layer of dirt and was not disturbed. As he walked over, he saw an item glinting on the ground from the light of his fotovolo. It was Kyros' family necklace, the green onyx amulet partially covered in a piece of ripped cloth.

Castor hunched over and dry heaved. He couldn't do this anymore. Everyone he cared about was dying. Was this what the gods had in store for him? He remembered the cautious words of Alexander before he accepted the journey he was given, but he thought it meant suffering that he would have to go through personally. He did not want others to suffer because of him. Especially not his best friend.

Castor felt cold and alone. He grabbed the amulet off the floor and held it tightly to his chest where that cooling feeling was. He cried on that cold ground, and he did not stop crying. His best friend's remains were scattered like trash across the floor of some cave across the continent. He was not there for him in his time of need. He did nothing but drink tea and rest by a fireplace as his friend was slaughtered some half-mile away from where he rested. He knew deep down that he did not have the opportunity at the time to save him, but that only made him feel worse.

The back of his throat felt dry and gripped his tongue as he tried to swallow through the tears. His eyes hurt from the dust that stuck to the tears on his face. He felt dirty and hated everything about this all. He did not want to believe his best friend and mentor was just... gone. That was it. There would be no more stories of Kyros Delkínitos, the mercenary of Thyma. No more inspiring stories of fighting harpies, no more fateful reunions in the town square. He did not even have a body to bring home to his family. Sure, he had siblings. He wasn't even the eldest son, so his family's trade would stay open and their bloodline would continue. But his best friend would not. Here in this damp, dark cave, the tales of Kyros Delkínitos had ended. There would be no more pages written for him in the annals of history. His string of fate was cut.

Castor searched around on his hands and knees with his eyes clouded with tears for more... closure. He searched for something that would make him feel better or at least feel less, but nothing helped him.

He saw gnaw marks on the bones, so he knew that those things that killed him also consumed what was left of him. His outfit and armor were torn to shreds, so he knew he went down with a fight. His sword was bent in half, so he knew those things were strong. None of this information made him feel better. He expected the fact that he died a warrior saving the life of his friend would meet some sort of requirement for feeling alright with his death, but it just did not. He did not feel better, he just felt more alone. A dozen died in his battalion a few months back, his new friend Mithra fell to his death a day ago, and now his best friend was torn to pieces within the few hours he had been sleeping within the tomb.

For a second, he felt angry. Angry at the gods for allowing him to survive when so many others could not. Angry at his patron for letting his friends die, and angry at the fates for deciding who was worthy to live on. He did not doubt that Alexander knew of Kyros' fate, so he was angry at him too. He just felt mad and overwhelmed and his emotions were running wild. The only thing keeping him grounded was the cooling sensation from his chest.

Castor spent a few minutes gathering what remains he could of his late friend. He grabbed pieces of his armor that were thrown about and slivers of cut cloth from the floor. His shirt that was underneath his linothorax was somewhat intact. Maybe it was ripped together with the linothorax or the linothorax hid the clothing underneath. Either way, he used the large piece of cloth and wrapped his friend's skull in the tattered linens. He held it in his hands. He felt weak and tired and angry and sad. He did not know what to do. Should he bring it back with him? Should he bury it here in this cave? This place wasn't his homeland and it was damp and dark. He also did not see anywhere with enough soil to bury the remains. He wanted his friend to have a proper burial at the very least. He carried the skull with him to the rucksack and prepared it for travel.

He searched the backpack and looked for anything that he could use during his travels. He found a supply of oats and the wood bowls they ate from before. He found the cloth scraps and some fire-starting supplies. He had a few days' worth of food for one person. He also found the large crystal they discovered in the main cave system.

It shimmered in the dim light of the cave. The blue hue from the walls made the dark and opulent pillar shine with an pure radiance. It was dark and mysterious but showed bright refractions of blue, green, pink, and purple. It surprised him how well defined the crescent of moonstone was. For such a large piece, there were no cracks, slips, or fragmentations along its surface. Unlike many other feldspar gems, the internal space was not marred by the natural cleavages that would occur within its crystal structure. Acco had discussed crystal theories with him before and he knew an amazing specimen when he saw one. The sharp edge on the crescent and the lack of damage after it fell earlier that day made it all the more mesmerizing.

Castor wrapped the crystal in cloth and placed it back in his bag. He did not have the time to admire their findings right now. He felt conflicted about the gem too, as it was the last find of Kyros. Should he keep it? Should he give it to his family? Knowing his family's business, it would probably just get sold to the highest bidder at their auction house. He figured it would be best to keep it a secret for the time being, given the gravity of today's events.

He tied the cloth off at the ends and made sure it sat flatly at the bottom of the rucksack. Considering its heft and size, he made sure to keep other items between the crystal crescent and his friend's remains. He would not risk damaging what little he could bring along on the return journey.

The cave felt cold and dreary as he packed Kyros' remains away. The rucksack was getting full and felt heavy on his shoulders. He packed as much as he could grab off the floor and in the indentation of the stone outcropping. He had everything tied down and packed away. He held the Delkínitos family amulet in his hand and looked over its details. The onyx was well cut and worn from many years of use. Kyros got the amulet for his thirteenth birthday and probably wore it ever since.

Castor put it on. He tightened the leather strap around the back of his neck and pulled the slip knot tighter so that it sat comfortably on his collarbone. He would not let his friend be forgotten. He wore his new necklace with pride. He could return it to his family when he was home. For now, his focus was on getting out alive with his friend's remains.

As though the universe was listening in on his thoughts, it seemed the fates had one last challenge for him that day. He heard the eerie noise of hardpoints on hewn stone. The cavern had a ticking that was easily heard around him. Castor drew his sword and prepared for those things once more.

He turned around multiple times, trying to focus his vision on where those vile things were. He could hear their clattering, but it felt distant. They must have been following him. He heard their scuttling by the cave opening he came through into the cavern. He turned quickly but saw nothing. The doorway was open and unobstructed. All he felt was a cool breeze.

Castor's instincts flooded his mind as he jumped out of the way and landed on his knees in a small puddle. He was only a few feet away from the pool of clear water. A ripple came across the pool as he saw some dirt falling from the ceiling. Castor looked up and swallowed deeply.

Above him, clung to the high walls of the cave, were two of those things that dwelt deep in the mountain. They were hideous and his mind was abuzz with emotions. He felt panicked and terrified and angry all at the same time. These things are what killed his best friend. He had no doubt. The cooling sensation in his chest that emanated from the tattoo he now owned was barely able to keep his mind focused. Every fiber of his body told him to run away as fast as he could.

But Castor was tired of running. He was tired of crying. He was tired of feeling small and useless. It was not like him to let his emotions cloud his judgment. He was the heir apparent of the Thymian peninsula. His mind changed from panic to rage.

Castor's face distorted into a curled grimace. He was not controlling his expressions anymore. He let his unbridled anger show. He put a hand out toward the creatures and focused an uncontrolled plume of fire on their location.

The column of flame was much larger than what he was used to channeling. He felt like his control over the flame was immensely higher than earlier that day. Was it a side effect of his new heroic status?

Flames bristled his exposed skin as the fire bellowed upward towards the ceiling. The whole chamber was illuminated in bright orange light as the flames scorched the ceiling surface where those things were just at. They scattered out of the way and dispersed like insects across the walls, the sharp clattering of their many feet dancing across the hewn stone.

They were vile and horrid things. Castor felt sick to his stomach just seeing them in full light. Their pale white skin undulated like a grub. The ringed segments of their bodies moved in unnatural ways. Their limbs were lanky and spindly and did not seem to hold up their fetid, bulbous bodies. As quick as the light lit, Castor had to expel it. The air in the cave simply could not support such an outburst. He felt lightheaded as he gasped for breath.

One of the creatures skittered in towards his location across the wall and onto the floor. Its body oscillated on its center axis like a snake across the sand. It moved in such a revolting and loathsome way that Castor reactively moved his hands in its direction. He channeled the earth around him, picking up loose stones and chunks of fallen cave debris. Parts of the stones were glowing blue from the cave mushrooms that were brought up along their surfaces. Castor shrieked in anger at the creature and his commanding voice focused his stone into a singular strike. The stones all flew forward in a pulse of raw earth and pierced anything they came into contact with. The thing on the floor shifted its weight and leapt out of the way but was not fast enough to dodge all the stony hail. The tirade of earth barreled into a few of the thing's legs and pierced its large carapace. It made no noise that Castor could hear but he could tell the creature was injured from the strike with the dripping of black blood onto the floor where it had just stood.

The force of the strike surprised Castor and even threw him back a few feet to equalize the reaction. He was lucky it did, as a set of mandibles had struck where he was just standing. His senses were heightened after he realized how close he had just been dancing with death. The other thing had snuck around on his flank and tried to kill the boy from his blind spot. The furtive monstrosity slinked back and reposed itself after its near-miss.

The room smelled awful. He did not know if it was from the newly opened wounds, the disturbed remains, or these squalid things in general, but Castor was having an issue with keeping his food down. It was foul and felt like a plashy swamp air had been driven into his nostrils. His stomach twisted in his belly as he composed himself in front of the vile terrors.

Castor doubled down on his closer attacker, sending a burst of wind towards the creature. He had not said a single word of prayers or hymns. All of his power was coming directly from his mana pool and he could feel himself draining in stored energy. His magic felt stronger and heftier but at the cost of quicker spending of mana.

He could feel a surge of energy from his rucksack. The giant gem of shimmering darkness they had found earlier was bristling with stored mana. Castor, being sensitive to the flow of mana, could feel it feeding his channeled attacks in equal amounts to his mana pool. While he would normally feel the power draining just from his chest and out through his arms, he now felt like he had a second heart. It pumped life energy into his core and through the same channels of mana in his limbs. The flow of mana was weak, as the object was not in direct contact with his skin and sat between many layers of cloth and leather. Regardless, the extra trickle of energy bolstered his strength and confidence. He felt powerful and unhindered. It was the first time he felt well in days.

The burst of air blasted forward in a violent zephyr. The air cut through the open cavity of the cavern and impacted the ugly white thing in its thorax. Its undulating sections partially caved inward as the external forces shoved it back into the wall. It reacted smoothly and was able to spread out its emaciated limbs to dampen the impact, but Castor heard a loud splat as its main body impacted the wall. He tried to follow up with another barrage of stones, but the creature was too fast. It skittered away after a few seconds of stunned confusion.

The creature that had retreated earlier seemed to see its opportunity and got closer to the leftmost thing. They had climbed the wall again and kept a fair distance between them and Castor. He was limited to moving on the ground where they had the whole cave ceiling and walls to traverse. Castor rotated his hips to allow his light to show their location. He knew his reach was limited so he thought up a plan to even the fight.

He took the opportunity to channel a stronger spell as those things clicked and clacked on the high walls many feet away. He remembered the pool of opaque water that sat a few paces away by the glowing stalagmites. He had very little experience with any gods of water. While Keanas was the matron deity of Thyma for its coastal industries and Nerea was well-loved within the continent of Anthora, he did not personally have a strong connection with the watery goddesses. While it would not be the most efficient way to curry favor, he figured his best bet was to rely on the gods he did know well and ask for their guidance with an element not favored under their pantheons. Since he was just converted to a god-kissed of Ignus, he figured he would try his luck with his patron for his next channeling.

He dug into his memories of past readings of the letters from the temples of Ig'Nataz. Ignus' homeland of Maudif had a stronger following of the Radiant King both in terms of quantity and quality. Castor had found writings from Ecardis in the Thymian library many years ago and memorized the ancient scripts that related to his god in his Maudian form. He thought for a few seconds before reciting the chant.

Hail, Heart of the Gold Crown, King of the Light.
I have come in refuge to the land of the Radiant King.
You are the heir of the sun.

Hail thee, holy one, shining of the daily star.
Hail thee, holy one, shimmering coat of luster.
Bring forth your might for he who deems you beloved.

Hail the old soul, mighty is your valor.
I have come to hide with you.
Deem me worthy of your sacredness.

[331]

Castor felt a deep radiance within his chest, far deeper than the skin. It felt like his soul was being warmed by an outside source. The brand of his god had warmed on his chest and his skin felt prickly around the edges. He never thought his time spent delving over old texts would have an impact like this later in life, but he was very glad his younger self spent so many hours in the library translating old scrolls to his homeland's language for many an evening.

Castor's plan flowed into effect in front of his eyes. He used one hand to channel the water of the pool into the air and swirl it around in a gyre. The bulbous clumps of gyrating water spun in the circular motion and built speed. He focused his mana in his right hand and started to add heat to the maelstrom. Rather than creating a torrent of flames, he channeled his mana to heat rather than burn. He felt the symbol etched into his chest warm up under his linothorax. His mana pooled around his central cavity and circulated into his limbs. He could feel the remains of his mana dwindling. He knew he was not fighting at peak condition. He was tired and hungry and sad and angry. His emotions and lack of food kept his capabilities limited.

Regardless, he felt capable enough. His renewed faith in his patron and his utter hatred for these vile beasts fueled his composure and allowed him to press past his normal limits. He could feel his body wanting to give out as he superheated the cave water into a piercing spear of steam. This was different than when he fought the goblin leader. He was not just heating the water to make a cloud of fog. This time his goal was to scorch and boil his foes alive.

A tight column of hot, pressurized steam jettisoned from the ever-encircling mass of searing waters in front of him. He struck forth with the vaporous rivulet. It cast across the cavern and struck the ceiling. The creatures skimmed across the hewn surfaces and away from the point of contact. The steam struck the cool walls and sizzled what it touched. Vapor and heat spread across the higher surfaces of the cave. The water crashed down the sides of the space and wet all the surfaces.

Castor watched as he chased the creatures with his whirlpool of hot vapors. They leapt and jumped, skittered and scampered, but the column kept its chase. He continued to pour heat into the water and the cycle continued as he coated all the surfaces with the superfluous torrent.

Second after second, he felt his power waning. The water coming from the pool reduced in volume and the heat from his right hand reduced in intensity. He had enough heat left to keep the volley up for a little while longer, but his strength was dwindling. Luckily for the young prince, his plan had worked. He watched as the two things fell one after another onto the floor below. His constant torrent of heated liquid made the walls overly heated and coated in the slick cave water. With the surfaces too hot to touch and the wet slickness of the glowing blue mushroom mycelium making it too hard to grip, the creatures lost their ability to climb freely on the vertical surfaces.

Castor had backed himself into the exiting tunnel that sat opposite the way he came in. He knew he did not have the energy to continue this fight. As much as he wanted to avenge his friend, he knew he did not have that ability today. After carefully sidestepping to get closer to the exit, he made sure to keep the creatures at a distance so that he could collapse the tunnel entrance and escape from his pursuers.

His plan had worked too well. The surfaces of the cave started to shake as he looked around. The water had soaked into nooks and crevices that had not been wet before in the lifetime of the mountains. The cave creaked and shook, and Castor felt afraid again. He knew something was wrong and he was in danger.

Looking down, he realized his fingers looked burned. He was not careful that day. His mana was running thin. His fingertips looked singed, like the embers in a smoldering fire. He was cindering.

He quickly cut off the flow of mana in his body. He felt lightheaded and his fingers ached. He knew he pushed himself too hard but just did not realize it until now. Without mana to pull from, his mana channels had started to consume his body rather than take from his now dry mana pool. Castor rubbed his fingers into his palms, which was met with sharp and agonizing pain. Little streaks of orange and red danced along his fingernails and under his scarred skin.

How could I be so foolish as to cinder my hands? He chastised himself as he ran into the tunnel ahead. His rage had kept his mind clouded during the duel. He knew he should have been more careful. He was still tired and hungry and his mana was not recovered that day. He did not stop running, his breath wild and pattering.

He leaned over and caught his breath as he made it into the tunnel and away from the steam-filled chamber. Sections of the roof had started to collapse inward as the structural integrity of the space gave way. The creatures seemed to be thinking of their next move as they stared at one another and clicked their mandibles together. All of the sudden, they split. One skittered away from the prince and towards the way he entered the cave with the other bolting directly for him.

Castor took a few steps back and prepared to run, but his legs gave out on him. He gave it his all, but his muscles just couldn't keep going. He turned over and sat up, gripping wildly for his sword and trying to hold it out in front of his body as he prepared for the creature to collide with him. It was moving in quickly. Fifty feet away, then forty, then thirty. It closed in and he felt weak again. He tried to hold his sword up but his fingers wouldn't listen. The cindering of his flesh left him weakened and his hands were not responsive. He prepared for the worst.

A calm feeling flowed across his mind again. It felt just like when he was visiting Alexander in that tomb. It told him to try backing away. He listened and crawled upward through the tunnel. He could hear the thing closing in on his position. It skittered across the floor. Then a loud crack emanated through the cave and he felt the ground shift and everything felt alive. Then it went quiet. Castor turned over to see the cave entrance covered in fallen debris. The cave had fully collapsed. And with it, those hideous things were crushed.

Only a few feet away did the last rock fall from the collapse. If he did not listen to that little voice in his head, he would have been crushed like those things. He sat there for close to a half-hour and just stared at the pile of fallen stone. He felt blessed, and sad, and tired. His hands were moving again, although the ends constantly throbbed where the blackened char had built up. His leg was moving again, and he continued to wiggle his toes as he sat.

He was free of this place. He could feel a cold draft coming from up ahead. He stood and steadily walked upwards. He let the trickle of mana flow through his back from the moonstone crescent and give his body enough energy to escape this living hell. He felt calm, though. He knew he had survived the events of that day. Whether it be luck or fate, he had survived.

The cave felt colder as he walked. He supported some of his weight by gripping the edges of the walls when he could. At one point he had to wrap his hands in cloth because of how cold it had gotten. Light broke a few hundred feet up ahead. He saw the light of the sun. He knew he had made it. As much as he tried to cry, the tears wouldn't come. He was too dehydrated for that. Instead, he just kept walking.

[335]

His vision was fading as he made it outside into the open world again. His lips were cracked and his muscles ached. He was so hungry and felt cold. Snow slowly descended from the sky as he walked. He was not where they entered the caves. He could not tell where he was. He overlooked a valley like before, but he could see the ocean in the distance. The cold air bit at his ears and nose.

He sat on a large rock near the edge of the hill. He could see smoke in the valley below. He could tell they were dwellings, but he was not sure who or what lived there. It didn't matter though. He would freeze to death if something did not come and get him soon. He had to take the risk.

With the little mana he had saved up from the crystal in his rucksack, he chanted a small prayer once more to his patron god. He knew he had pushed his luck that day. He knew he was asking too much. He normally wouldn't call upon his god more than once a day. But this day was different. If he was supposed to have a destiny in saving these lands and his fate was tied to the deity he had dedicated his life to, then he needed to ask for his strength once more. His mind felt heavy and hazy, but he remembered his favorite lines from the letters he read of his god. It was a short verse, and not the most eloquent, but it summarized his feelings well.

Oh, Radiant One.
I adore the greatness of your spirit.
Inspire in me the ways of your glittering soul.

As he finished the last line, a large ball of flame burst from his mouth. While it was not very hot, the sphere of flame was substantial in size and brightness. The valley lit in those morning hours from the light of the orb. Castor fell over and laid on the rock. His eyes were too heavy to keep open. He laid there in the morning shade and the cold snow covered his clothing. He wondered what would happen to him. Was this the end? What of his fate? Wasn't he supposed to help the world? Maybe this was just enough to enact those plans. Maybe by caving in that cavern, he saved the world from whatever those things were. The thought of them made his stomach hurt, but he did not have the energy to react physically to nausea.

He continued to lay on that stone for a while. He hoped he would be able to wake up after this. Hopefully, he would just sleep for a bit and then recover enough to get home. He heard some noises around him, but he was not able to make out what they were. His conscience slipped as he felt something touch him. The last thing he remembered was the warmth of long fur against his face. After that, he slept.

CHAPTER 15

A Long Gravel Path

37th of Azurite, 453 of the Age of Discovery

astor sat atop the Thymian lighthouse. The white granite stone below reflected the light from the sea and lit parts of the town like a sparkling piece of sea glass. The bonfire behind him warmed his back as he peered over his city. He let his feet dangle over the edge of the stone precipice and his wrapped sandals bounced against the hewn stone block.

He had his right knee tucked to his chest. With his normal street clothes on, he could sit comfortably on the edge without his armor digging into his skin. His helmet sat against a stone pillar behind him. He had just gotten off his guard shift and took some time to enjoy the sunset before going home.

He felt comfortable up here. The salty sea breeze peppered his nostrils as he breathed in the warm summer air. The waves below were mild and temperate. They had just had a storm but the sea seemed calm. Was the water level a little lower than normal? Castor could see a few triremes rowing into Thyma's two bays, their oars extended as the trierarch shouted commands to properly dock their ships. He could just barely make out the sharp barks of the captains as they came into port.

In the distance, Castor saw a dark shadow. He felt like he had seen it before, but he could not remember where it was. Thunder crashed in the distance and he felt a cool breeze flow up the side of the tower. He felt the winds pick up as large dark clouds moved over the horizon. The light of the dusk sun dimmed as their rays were snuffed out by the impending storm.

Castor held onto the pillar behind him as the weather took a turn for the worst. He could see that shadow again just far enough away for him to not be able to see it directly. It danced just on the edge of the dark rain clouds. He could feel it taunting him.

The ground rumbled and Castor gripped the pillar tighter. A wave grew in the distance. It slowly grew as it got closer. He could see the water building up as it closed in on the port town. The tower shook. He lost his grip as the stone below gave out and the lighthouse fell.

Castor awoke to the rumbling of a wagon. His back hurt from the hardwood underneath him. They must have hit a rock recently, as the cart was shaking back and forth before balancing out. A cloth tarp sat over the cart and blocked his view of the front. He had vision out the back and the gravel path of a mountain road was all he could see.

Around the edge of the cart came the face of a Maudian. The maneless lion man was startled by Castor, who had sat up and was only a foot away from the edge. Castor tried to suppress his surprise, but the Maudian did not. He leaped backward and bared his fangs, mewling in his confusion. The lion man's deep mewls started Castor. He sounded like a confused child. It took a little bit to not laugh at the lion man's reaction, but he did not want to offend. He sat there and nodded once the Maudian had calmed.

Instead of responding, the Maudian spoke in Pârsi, the Maudian language, and alerted the others around the cart. From the left, a familiar face walked into view. It was Mithra.

"Welcome back to the realm of the living, little prince." the exiled one said in a calm and commanding voice, making sure the rest of the caravan had realized the status of their guest. He got close enough to pat Castor on the head and kept walking with the pace of the cart. He had his bronze scale mail vest on with a set of light purple robes underneath. He seemed very much alive, much to Castor's astonishment.

His emotions got the best of him and he embraced the exiled prince with a bear hug. He fluffed his mane and rubbed the underside of his chin. Mithra closed his eyes and let the boy indulge in his mindless pettings, as he knew the young man had been through a lot. It was no doubt that his fluffy white fur was what Castor felt on that cold. snowy hillside before he had passed out. The air was still chilly and Castor's hands were cold to the touch. Once satisfied, Castor retreated to a more formal arrangement, seated as he would be at a formal dinner. He wrapped himself in as many of the pelts and pillows as he could find.

"I thought you were dead," Castor said in a timid voice, choking back his emotions. He had been through a lot and he was happy to have some semblance of normalcy back in his life.

"Yes, it is good to see you too, my friend," Mithra said after Castor had calmed down and sat comfortably under the few tanned furs within the cart. "You do me a disservice if you think the son of the sun could be finished off by a mere fall. For Ignus' sake, I am a great Maudian. We are known for our physical prowess."

"How was I to know how far the cliff descended?" Castor snapped back. "That damn fog hid the landscape from us. And we did not have much time to ponder as we were continuously attacked by those little, horrid things."

"Yes, well we will not have to worry about their leader anymore. I took care of him a little later." Mithra pointed forward, which focused on the staff of Quartz nestled with leather bindings into the front side of the cart. It was in perfect condition as far as gnarled wood and hastily tied crystals were concerned.

"Good... good," Castor murmured, his mood changing to a distant and tired state. Mithra put his hand on the young man's shoulder to console him. Castor bundled tighter under the furs. Mithra continued to walk with the wagon as they came down out of the mountain. The other Maudian had returned to the front and out of sight, no doubt trying to give the two princes their privacy. After a few minutes, Mithra continued their conversation.

"We looked through your bag when you were out, trying to make sense of your situation." Mithra focused his gaze on the young prince. "I made sure I did so myself, to not tarnish your reputation with rumors if you were holding anything that would be suspect. I was glad I did."

Castor saw Kyros' rucksack in the cart a few feet away. It was properly tied up and looked to be in good condition. Castor kept his eyes averted.

"That was not the way I wanted to find him," Castor mumbled. "He deserved better."

"The remains are from Kyros?" Mithra asked in an apologetic tone. "I never found him when searching the mountains."

"It is." Castor confirmed. "He protected me from these... things. I do not know where they came from but they were... terrifying. I passed out at one point and found him like this after I woke up."

"The mercenary died doing what he enjoyed and protected his friend in his final moments. I see no reason to be sad."

Castor rolled his eyes. "We Anthorans do not see the afterlife like you great Maudians do. We prefer to keep our friends and family in this realm for as long as we can."

"So do we, little one. So do we." Mithra purred. He took a deep breath, then continued. "But you cannot change the past. He did not die in a pervasive or depressive way. Give his memories the honor they deserve."

Castor played with a few hairs on the fur pelt he had bundled around his hands. He did not respond. He figured an argument on the importance of life would be wasted labor. The great Maudians believed in an impressive afterlife for those that died in a predatory state. From what Mithra had seen of Kyros before their separation that day, he included the young man in this category. Anthorans did not have this belief. Castor knew he did not mean to offend, but his death was too recent to not be bothered by his lack of cultural understanding.

After a few minutes of walking, Mithra spoke again. "You prepared his remains very well. They are bleached white and ready for burial. You honor him well. Do not be ashamed."

Castor looked at Mithra, confused. "I found them like that. All I did was wrap them up. I found him only a few minutes before I passed out on that rock."

"I thought you said you found him right after you woke up after our separation." Mithra rebutted. He then started to purr like when he found something amusing. "So unless you slept for thirty-two days, there must have been some sort of confusion in your story."

Castor looked at Mithra with eyes wide in shock, then horror. *Thirty-two days?* He had just seen them maybe a day or two ago. Was he actually gone for thirty-two days?

"Mithra." Castor got to his knees and put his hands on the Maudian's shoulders. His arms bobbed with the cat man's body as he walked behind the cart. "How long have we been missing?"

Mithra put his left hand in between them and counted on his fingers with his right. "Since the day we left, I believe it has been thirty-seven days as of today. We only have a few days until the start of Moonstone."

Castor sat back, trying to wrap his mind around the situation. He was safe and did not feel in danger, but hot needles pricked on the back of his neck. It just didn't make sense.

"Are you alright, little one?" the Maudian asked with his head cocked to the side. Castor took a second to compose himself before responding.

"Mithra, you may not believe this, but to me, it has only been one... maybe two days at most," Castor said in a serious voice. "Since we lost track of you down that cliff, there was only around half a day before I separated from Kyros. We rested for a few hours and we were stuck underground, but I do not think it was more than that. I slept in that tomb for another half of a day. And once I regained consciousness and my wounds were healed, I think it was only a couple of hours after where I came to the surface."

Mithra stared at Castor, weighing the statements he said carefully. Castor waited for a little while before realizing the Maudian did not have a response for him at that time, so he continued.

"What about my family?" Castor asked. "Do they think me dead?"

[343]

"Very much so," Mithra confirmed. "I believe your funeral was a week ago. Your family told me that was the plan before I left. I have been in those mountains searching for you for the last ten days. I assumed I would find corpses. But instead, the corpses came to me."

Mithra pointed out and poked Castor's left bicep, which had a wrapping. His long nail shot pain up his arm and Castor winced.

"When I found you on that stone, like a sheep ready for sacrifice, I did not think you would make it. There was poison running through you. Do you remember getting hurt?"

"No," Castor said, "I am pretty sure I made it out of the cave unscathed."

He thought about his fight with those things but did not recall them getting close enough to hurt him. Although there was that one time the creature snuck up on him...

"It is possible," Castor interjected before Mithra responded, "but it would have been a small wound. If it did get me, it would have barely been a graze."

"Graze or not, you were unconscious for the last six days of our travels," Mithra said with a pause, letting the impact of the statement set in. "You have been tossing and turning the last few days, so I was not sure if you would make it home. But lo and behold, here you are. Once again among the living. Seems your patron has different plans for you."

That reminded Castor of the events that transpired that first day. He moved close to the edge of the cart.

"I will say, in confidence to you, that I was greeted by a messenger of the gods when I was in that dreadful state," Castor whispered, making sure to check around the corners of the cart for Mithra's compatriots.

"Well, that is surprising news indeed," Mithra responded with a faint nod. "Then it seems the sacrifices of our labors were not in vain."

"It was a strange meeting." Castor continued, "There was no way I was there for that many days. But I did feel odd when I was there so maybe some sort of magic was at play."

"The gods can have many effects on us mortals." Mithra pointed out.

"That is true. I just did not expect the day to turn out as it did." Castor got closer to Mithra and whispered. "I have become god-kissed."

The cat man guffawed so loudly that Castor could feel the vibration of his large larynx a few feet away. Mithra pushed Castor's hair off of his forehead and scanned his face up and down with his sharp stare. He found nothing and moved to review the boy's neck, but Castor stopped after a few seconds.

"No, it is not on my face." Castor corrected. "I know that is the typical place to have the mark show, but this time is different."

Castor unbundled himself from the fur pelts that kept his heat in. He could feel the bite of the cold winter weather on his arms and neck as he removed a few knots on his shoulder and let his chiton down to reveal his chest. The raised skin and discolored marking of the sun god were clearly defined on Castor's sternum. The eight prongs of the day star extended outward a few inches in each direction. It was not the symbol commonly associated with Ignus in Anthora, but it was found in ancient temples in the lands of Maudif.

Mithra paused as he saw the symbol and thought for a few seconds before he stopped walking. His face was twitching and he had bared his fangs openly towards the young man. To Castor's surprise, he did not seem happy. Instead, he roared out in anger. His voice echoed multiple times against the sides of the canyon around them. His stare was fierce and dangerous.

Castor pulled back and covered himself as he recoiled in fear. He had not seen Mithra lash out like this before. He did not know what to do. The only person he had talked to since he had awoken and probably the only ally he had in a ten-mile radius looked as though he would easily rip the boy's throat out in his animalistic rage.

A few of his companions came around from the front of the caravan and approached the exiled prince. They called out, "My lord, are you alright?"

Mithra snapped out of his fit of rage after a few seconds, seeing the commotion he had wrought. He collected himself and said, "Yes, I am fine, I stepped on a sharp rock."

The Maudian servants looked around at the group, trying to find what bothered their lord. Mithra dismissed them with a wave of his hand.

"Do not fret, my friends." He said to the two that were closest. "Instead, fetch me some wrappings so that I can pad my feet further. I do not feel like going through that twice in one trip."

"Of course, my liege." the right one said and went to the front of the caravan to fetch some cloth straps. The left one asked, "Would you like us to stop and give you time to recover?"

"No, it will be fine. I will sit on the cart edge. You may return to your positions."

They bowed and returned to the front. As they passed Castor, they nodded to the Anthoran boy. Mithra walked over to the edge of the cart and sat along the back rim. His weight made the wood floorboards sag. He wrapped his fake injury with long cloth straps and stared off into the distance. Castor stared at the cat man until he said something, as he felt uncomfortable making the first move.

In a hushed tone, Mithra said. "It may have been better that you did not wake from your long rest, little one. It seems you do not know the severity of what you bear upon your chest. There is no doubt that the aša..." Mithra moved his hands around as he thought of the proper translation, "The truths of our lives were leading towards this moment."

Castor swallowed deeply as the crest tried to cool his overly active mind. He was worried about what Mithra was speaking of. "You mean like the fates?" Castor asked.

Mithra thought for a second before responding. "Yes, you could say that. That is most likely the closest idea between our religions. Consider the fates to be personally interfering with our lives."

Castor thought for a bit in silence as Mithra finished wrapping his feet. He believed what Alexander had told him during his time in that realm. Was he lying? He was not honest about the amount of time that had passed while he was there. Was there more to what Alexander had initially let on?

"You do not bear the kiss of Ignus, little one." Ignus whispered, "The mark that you bear is older than what you would be referring to. Maybe not as common in your lands, but that symbol is no doubt of the old faith. Before the reformations, many centuries ago. I believe that to be the mark of Ez Nakhasht."

The way that Mithra pronounced the word felt very Maudian. It was guttural and left his tongue like a purr. He made sure to say it quietly, as he no doubt wanted to keep this conversion away from prying ears in the front of the caravan. Mithra always trusted his followers to the utmost, so seeing him be weary was more than enough to worry Castor.

"Our lands had many wars over the new and old faiths. Ultimately, the new teachings won. They are more in line with your faith, most likely done to quell the tensions after the old wars. The Maudi-Anthoran wars lasted over a century, and the schism followed soon after."

"But Mithra, that was over eight hundred years ago. Are you saying this mark is older than that? What we found was..." Castor trailed off. His brain felt overwhelmed. He knew those ruins were old, but to be that old, then they would be from an age long lost to history.

"Yes, heir prince of Thyma. What you hold upon your chest is the mark of an ancient god. A god spurned by many today and older than the city you will rule over. It may not matter to you much what you call your patron, as you already use his anthropomorphized image. But I would beware of allowing any word of it to get out, lest you gain the hatred of every other Maudian you meet."

Castor took his word heavily on his shoulders. To see Mithra speak as such meant his words had weight behind them. It explained his reaction and his subsequent commands to dismiss his followers before they spoke. While it may not matter much to himself and his people, it would be bad to have an entire continent against your rule.

"Why do you defend me then?" Castor asked. "I believe you, of course. You have not done me any wrongs in the past. But why hide it from your followers as such?"

"My following is weak, little prince. I have only this handful around now. I left my home with over a hundred people, and it has dwindled to less than a dozen. While I cannot act against you, as per our life debt, that doesn't mean my followers must abide by such. They are free people, not slaves. If they see me as a heretic of the old gods, they can easily renounce me and my claim."

Castor nodded. "I understand. Then I thank you for your understanding and your secrecy, exiled prince."

"Our lives were tied together when you saved me during the attack on Thyma many months ago," Mithra said in a confident tone. "Have no worries that I will uphold my life debt. I only hope that the gods see us in a favorable light over the coming years."

"If we make it that long," Castor muttered. Mithra smacked him on the back of the head and mewled. Castor smiled a faint smirk but hid his doubts internally.

Mithra patted Castor's head as the cart made its way through the canyon and into a grassy plain. Castor recognized the landscape around him. They were close to Thyma. The hills were more arid here on this side of the mountains, yet not desolate like the northern steppes of Anthora. He had traveled these hills many times when on scouting patrols during his younger years as a guardsman.

Mithra said, "I had sent one of my cats out earlier before you awoke. I wanted your family to know of your survival before you arrived so we would not surprise them. I pray they have had enough time to prepare for their revenant son's safe return."

Castor nodded. He was staring at the gravel path as it passed underneath. The last few days for him had been more eventful than he would ask for in a year. He was tired, even though he had just slept for the good part of a week. He was mentally drained. Even though a month had passed since he left, and for him only a few days, he felt like he had not seen his home in a decade. His arm still throbbed from where the poison had set in. He just wanted to rest and recover in his bed with homely food and a recognizable environment.

"Your pains will ease," Mithra said somberly. "Give them time, and they will ease."

"I have a funeral to plan when we get back," Castor said glumly. He had set his hand over the rucksack.

"I am aware. And you will. In due time." the great Maudian said.

Mithra arched his back and reached into the cart. Castor flinched. He felt bad for doing so near his friend, but his fit of rage earlier had him feeling unsure of his motives. He trusted the Maudian, but he still reacted instinctively.

Mithra pushed a linen-wrapped bundle into Castor's lap. Castor looked at him and he said, "I believe our fates are not as gloomy as you are currently thinking. Take a look at the one thing I found salvageable at our old campsite from that dreaded day a month ago."

Castor unwrapped the bundle to find his prayer shrine to Ignus in pristine condition underneath except for a few dirt smudges around the edges of the pocket shrine. He unfolded the wings of the wooden tablature to show the intricately carved panels. The wood was in good condition and had no water damage. The wood was not warped, scratched, or cracked. The scenes of the triumphs of Ignus were just like how they were before their trip. The young man reviewed the scenes in detail.

"It was the only thing I found of worth that was left," Mithra said as Castor stared at the wood panels. "Those little gray bastards stole everything else. They even took the remains of the auroch. I am glad I was able to kill their leader after I fell off that cliff, but it doesn't seem like their numbers dwindled in those mountains that day."

They sat in silence for a little while as the gravel path continued to grow longer into the distance.

The hills were not like Castor remembered. Castor knew a month had to have passed since he left. The once green hills were tan from the winter cold and the animals had moved onto greener pastures or warmer barns. The Ephysian deer that he would occasionally see on the hillsides were completely gone, moving onto the more temperate climates of central Anthora. He saw no shepherds with their flocks, no farmers with their plows, just empty fields. Winter had truly moved in.

CHAPTER 16

A Celebration Of Ash And Blood

40th of Moonstone, 453 of the Age of Discovery

he revenant prince leaned against a marble pillar in the city square as he sipped on his mulled wine. The powdered cinnamon and cloves gave the drink a warm and comforting feel. The day was not that cold, but it helped soothe his naturally heat-inclined body. He watched as citizens of Thyma slowly gathered into the town square for the festivities. A giant bonfire sat in the middle, easily ten feet in diameter, and smoldered near the edges as some city servants pulled the spent ashes from the ever-burning conflagration. The stalls of food and drinks had already started the laborious task of feeding a whole city. The smell of grilled fish and vegetables permeated the air and drew hungry customers in for a snack before the start of the festivities.

He could see his family dispersed into the crowd. While his parents were already at the temple preparing for the day's celebration, he could see his Acco and Aretha in the area. Acco was with a few of his forge mates who had finished their smelting quotas early to celebrate with the rest of the town. Aretha had a small crowd around her as she weaved and whittled her way into more political and economic contacts. He was glad to see them enjoying the winter festivities as they saw fit.

"You are not going to grab a snack? It will be a while before the sacrifices are cooked for tonight's celebration." a voice said from behind the pillar.

Castor turned to see Nikitas and his grandchildren walking toward the young prince. It was a nice turn of events. He had to speak to many dignitaries, nobles, and otherwise pompous people during the time he had been in town. His reemergence after a month of being missing was not something to be taken likely, and many came to show their regard to their revenant prince. He liked the ring of that title. He hoped Mithra would pick up on it. The day's events had already drained him of his mental energy. He hoped the mulled wine would heat his body and his soul, but it had not kicked in yet. A short break from politics to talk with an old friend was welcomed.

"Hello, little ones," Castor said as he bent down onto one knee to be at the right level to speak to the children. Teris and his older sister Clio stood with big smiles in front of their grandfather. Clio ate a light and fluffy honey pastry as Teris stepped forward.

"Hello there! Are you ready for the sacrifices tonight? I am!" Teris announced to Castor with a grin. The boy was very excited about the celebration, and Castor smiled at him.

"That is good to hear," Castor said. "I am excited about it too."

"Oh, and I'm glad you didn't die in those mountains." Teris said with a wider smile, "Welcome home!"

The comment caught him off guard. Castor had hidden from the town for the last month. The ruling family had not publicly disclosed Castor's missing status until after he had come home and brushed the event off as an extended scouting and survival training program. The death of Kyros was stated to be a camping accident when he lost his footing on a cliff during their adventures. Mithra was also asked to confirm these as facts when talking openly in town. The loss of the heir prince would destabilize the region and could spark a civil war, considering Castor was the only viable heir right now. Acco was adopted and Aretha was not a male heir. The number of people that could die from a civil war outweighed Castor's want of openness with the people. He had to bite his tongue and accept the outcome for the sake of Thyma.

That did not stop Castor from hating the way it was stated to the public. His friend deserved better. Kyros, an able-bodied and experienced mercenary, just fell off a cliff? Without anything to cause it? It seemed suspicious to him but after talking to many people today, it seemed to be a more common occurrence in Anthora. People go missing in the mountains. It seems to be commonplace.

Castor patted the boy on the head. "So am I." he spoke, "So am I. But today is not about me. Today is about our celebration of the new year! Make sure your grandpa gets you all the best food from the stalls and a good view of the rituals!"

"Mhm!" Clio interjected cheerfully. "We already told him that. He knows. We want to see the oracle as close as we can!"

"That is a great idea," Castor said as he ruffled the Teris's hair and stood up. "If you end up near the top of the hill, make sure to bundle yourselves up in your cloaks, alright? It will get windy and you do not want to catch a cold."

"Ok!" She said, "We will!"

Nikitas stepped forward and locked arms with Castor. "I am also glad you made it out of those mountains alive."

[353]

Castor nodded and looked away, trying not to remember some of the sights he saw that week. "I am as well. But I doubt its effects will go away any time soon. That was not a fun time."

"I understand that." Nikitas confirmed in a hushed tone. "And we will keep the details corrected for the time being. I am glad you were able to have a proper funeral for Kyros. You were able to bring his family the solace that not many mercenaries are privy to."

"Yes." Castor said shortly. "I am glad I was able to at least do that."

Nikitas slapped Castor on the upper arm and almost spilled his cup of wine. "Cheer up, at least for today. He wouldn't have wanted you sulking for this long."

Castor nodded and smiled. "You are probably right. Today is about the town. Not some failed adventure."

"Exactly so," Nikitas said. "Take your time coming to terms with it all. It is not every day you lose your best friend. But the dead care not for the living. Today is for the living. Enjoy yourself as much as you can."

The grizzled veteran pulled on the fabric on each of his grandchildren's shoulders. They went to his sides and each grabbed one of his hands, making sure to hold tightly so as to not get lost in the crowds.

"Come now, kids. Let our heir prince enjoy his day with friends and family." the grandfather said.

"You are a part of that list too, Nikitas." Castor shot back, making sure his mentor did not feel obligated to leave.

He knew he had a more off-putting demeanor as of late and he wanted to fix that. Moping about won't change the fact that his friend is dead or that the fates had their hands in the state of their nation. He had his time to mourn and mourn he did. He had to get back into his princely visage.

"I am well aware, my prince. Do not fret. I have not taken offense to your demeanor. I want to give you the ability to mingle with others closer to your age." He pointed to the back of the crowd where a familiar palanquin was surrounded by a group of young adults. It looked as though many young scholars and soldiers were trying to talk to the exiled prince as his companions kept the crowd at bay. The curtains were rolled down on the sides of the large platform, but the front was open. Within it lay a well-dressed Maudian staring intently at the young prince.

"Very well, I will do my best to spare our giant cat man in distress." Castor joked as he clasped arms with Nikitas once again.

"I am glad you made it back alive," Nikitas said again, this time in a much more serious tone.

"Thank you. I am as well." Castor nodded in agreement.

The children escorted their grandfather towards the temple hill as Castor walked towards the group of people surrounding Mithra's platform bed. They were not aggressive and did not try to overstep their bounds, but Mithra's companions were having a hard time keeping up with all the questions the people were asking. Cyrus stood on the ground in front of Mithra and answered any questions that the others did not have the ability to answer, whether it be a dialect issue or a lack of knowledge.

It was not every day a Maudian noble joined a public Anthoran celebration. The locals were both curious and excited. It felt like when he had first joined the city guard, where everyone and anyone would come to him for an idle chat to learn more about their upcoming leader. Anthorans were inquisitive people and always yearned for more information. Gaining knowledge from a Thrimic group of travelers could be a vault's worth of valuable information. As Castor had not spoken to Mithra much in the last week due to Kyros' funeral and the bereavement time afterward, he wanted to extend his gratification to his furry friend.

When Cyrus saw Castor, he nodded and extended his arms for the standard Maudian greeting. Before he could greet Castor with words, a few gasps from the crowd drew their attention. Mithra had risen from his bed of pillows and leaped forward towards Castor. He embraced the boy and nuzzled the prince on each side of the head with his bushy mane and the bristles tickled Castor's neck. He was happy to see his friend too and tried to reciprocate the non-verbal greeting as best he could.

"Men and women of Thyma, your prince has returned!" Mithra announced to the group around them. His voice was loud and clear. Castor knew he had experience as a leader in his homeland, but his distinct ability to speak to a crowd was showing off in this instance.

"What are you doing?" Castor asked in a hushed tone. "You know we do not talk about what happened that day."

"Relax, I am just raising the spirits and giving you a little renown in your city."

He turned back to the crowd and said, "You all are so curious of me and my people. And I appreciate your curiosity. Thrim and the greater Maudif have a rich history and there are many things to learn from my people! But what about your prince? Your revenant prince has returned from a long and arduous journey into the mountains to better himself for your sake. And I watched while my companions answered your questions and your prince stood alone in this courtyard for most of his time here. Maybe you were being courteous and giving him space, but he chose to be here. If I was disregarded in my homeland like that, it would have been an outrage. Join me in celebrating the return of the revenant prince!"

Castor expected the crowd to be stunned and confused. Mithra was not one to talk to the common citizen. Maybe something changed since they left on their journey because this was not the case. Instead of confusion, he was met with a large roar of cheering and clapping. The crowd had expanded from the group near the palanquin to most of those who had entered the town square at this point, numbering over a few hundred.

"Go ahead," Mithra whispered, "they are looking for a response from their prince."

Castor nodded and spoke to the crowd. "Our esteemed guest gives me, and indirectly you all, a great compliment. We may not be the largest city in Anthora, but our history is rich and our ports are full. Great gems flow from our mountains and metal tools are forged daily in our lands. It is through our hard work and our tenacious curiosity that we have become so successful over the last few decades. Thank you all for your love of our region and thank you for giving me a fantastic city to call my home."

The festivities felt truly welcoming after the small tirade of the friendly princes. Although Castor felt tired from his earlier conversations, his renewed energy allowed him to speak freely and openly with everyone that came to talk to him afterward. Mithra sat on the edge of his palanquin and the two of them spent close to an hour talking with the locals. Many wanted to know more about Maudif, while others asked about the prince's trip into the wilderness. The two of them answered to the best of their ability to keep to the set story his parents and the local council came up with to ensure a consistent and light-hearted feel. The only focus of discontent was on Kyros, who became the sacrificial lamb for their sake and was the only casualty of the "survival training gone too far". It was said that he had fallen when the side of a cliff path gave out under Castor after a long thunderstorm and he sacrificed himself to save the prince. This rendition was much better in Castor's eyes and he had to fight to alter the government's less heroic version when he returned home. As they talked, Castor felt relieved that Kyros would be remembered as his savior. It was the only thing to do.

Mithra seemed far more sociable compared to the first time he met the large cat man. His brash nature seemed to have dulled during his time in Thyma. Castor knew his port town had a more laid-back atmosphere, but he did not think it was only that. Mithra was safe here. After the failed assassination attempt those years ago, Thrim had a large opposition force to the current rule. To try and assassinate a political rival rather than fighting in open combat was a serious social blunder that the nameless king had committed. Mithra had mentioned the political strife in his homeland and informed Castor that another attempt on his life was very unlikely.

Castor and Mithra had also been training each other on their respective languages while Castor was hiding from society over the last month. Since he had taken time off from his guard captain duties due to his injuries, he had an ample amount of free time to spend on learning and recovering. Mithra had become more fluent in Anthoran and Castor had started to pick up basic phrases in Pârsi while they discussed their linguistic differences. His capabilities in Anthoran made him more confident in his casual conversations as well, as Castor noticed from his impromptu speech a bit ago.

After an hour or so of casual frivolities, events of the day unfolded as the temple's esteemed guest was heard to have arrived in town. The Oracle of the White Tower was seen entering the gates and the town square prepared for his arrival. The conversations gradually dulled to a weary silence as the information passed from one person to another. As the square had become all but silent, an entourage made their way through the packed streets.

A group of thirty people, clad in long white robes and cloaks, moved gracefully into the open area meant for the Oracle's company. They looked as though they glided across the stone tiles as their flowing clothing followed smoothly around them. Within the center of the group stood one person without a hood. Only adorned in a stark white robe, this tall, bald man stood out in the midst of the attention-grabbing procession. He was lighter skinned, an uncommon trait for the tan and swarthy Anthorans. Castor had heard that all the Oracles were of light skin, like that of Acco, but never knew why. They did not come from the colonies, as they rarely left their towers. This celebration and the summer solstice were the only times Castor knew them to leave the confines of their established estate in the mountains on a normal basis.

The procession came into the square and stood in the middle of the ever-growing crowd. The people that had come to see the day's events had spilled over into the surrounding streets, and their numbers grew to the thousands. The procession had a few of the tower priests playing handheld harps, which rang a soft and beautiful lullaby through the city's open alleys and streets. Incense filled the streets in a light haze which made the bright sunlight coming through the cloud cover as rays of light.

The smell of juniper and saffron filled Castor's nose as the scent made its way to where he was standing. The holiday incense was always his favorite. It was sweet and felt cleaner than normal incense. He knew it was very expensive too and saved his enjoyment of the mix to only holidays so as to not make the special scent less special. The music he heard was also gentle and mellow. He recalled that a few of the tunes they played were verses common in the temple of Keanas. While the solstice was given piety fairly between the gods of the Kalotrapia, the celebration leaned in favor of the ocean goddess. It was only fair to celebrate the city's matron deity when the entire city was together in commemoration.

The two people that stood out within the procession were the fully armored soldiers that flanked the Oracle. Castor could tell with just a glance that they were a part of the Carillon, the most well-respected military organization in the nation. Funded and trained within the capital, the soldiers of the Carillon were fully clad in bronze and armed with ornate weapons that were both deadly in physical battle and bejeweled for channeling combat. Their bronze bell panoply covered just about every inch of their bodies and the symbolic crests on their helmets were both elaborate and impressive. They marched in sync, their meticulous training allowing them to perfectly match the Oracle's gait. Their polished bronze armor stood out within the crowd of white gowns.

Castor could see the Oracle clearly now, and the man was stunning. His features were chiseled like a statue and his eyes were a stormy gray. His gaze was as intimidating as Mithra's. It seemed like his view was searing into its target. As if in sync with Castor's thoughts, the Oracle turned his head directly at the young prince as he processed through the square. They kept eye contact as he walked with his entourage of cloaked master channelers past the crowds and into their predesignated spot in the center where the day's ritual would start. His eyes were intense and Castor felt like he was in danger. A wave of calm passed over him as he gripped his holy symbol and it gave him mental fortitude. Content with the stare-off, the Oracle broke their eye contact and passed as though nothing had occurred.

From the eastern street that led from the docks, a group of animals was led by a few of the guild leaders. The local guild paid for and ensured the quality of the animals that were to be sacrificed on the solstice. Castor saw his sister amidst the merchant representatives. She walked with dignity among the other old merchants. He knew that if she was there, the quality of the animals would not be taken lightly.

Once in the center of the town, a few of the white-cloaked tower priests claimed clay bowls near the bonfire and had the city servants fill them with ashes. The light and fluffy residue from the burning inferno filled the air around them with soot and stained some of their outfits. A few surrounded the Oracle tightly and made sure no black marks made their way onto his vestments. Once the bowls were full, the ash bearers made their way to the edge of the procession and started to cast the ash onto the ground.

They covered the tile lightly near the southern edge of the town square and made a giant circle around the group. Before they finished the circle off, they left a thirty-foot gap in the ash markings and continued forward north towards the temple district. The path continued as the rest of the procession followed. Once the Oracle was on his way, the crowds of citizens moved into the circle and followed the procession through the town.

Castor asked Mithra if he would have his companions guard the palanquin, but he shook his head.

"Not needed," Mithra explained, "We had cleared out any valuables yesterday so that we all could take part in your celebration together. If a thief is so in need of my palanquins gossamer, then so be it."

With that, the two princes and the Maudian companions led the rear of the giant mob as they all walked towards the temple hill. The crowd walked half a mile to the base of the temple district. As though raised to the gods themselves, the temple district sat atop the tallest hill in the city. It was in the most northeastern section and overlooked the sea down below its steep cliffs. The procession made their way up the many stairs that climbed the edge of the plateau and came to surround the open paths of the temple hill.

Around the edge of the mount sat the individual temples of each of the gods. Pyrrus was the closest and most renowned god of the Anthorans. Keanas had her temple adorned with many tapestries and sat closest to the sea. Nerea was next in the circle and sat between her friend

Keanas and her husband Vrontir. Vrontir's temple sat at the back and was the tallest temple, designed to be as close to the skies as the temple priests could be. Beltunia's temple had large pelts of exotic animals covering the stone walls and antlers were hung between the well-crafted columns. Gargrin and Brömli came next, the Durulian godsmiths having many braziers lit in their honor. Calcothwyn and Arimilia were the Elvari deities accepted in Anthoran lands and had their temples made of wood and natural materials. They stuck out on the temple hill, but their following in Anthora were devout and kept the temples in pristine shape.

One small shrine sat away from the rest, behind the foreign gods, as though it was not planned for during the construction of the temple hill. The temple of Ignus was not built with the rest here, as the Maudi-Anthoran wars were being waged during the time of the founding of Thyma. Instead, a small temple was put up many centuries later to ease tensions with Maudif and appease the followers of Ignus within the city.

In the center of the temple hill sat the main temple that houses all religious ceremonies and rituals; the Kalotrapia. The Table of the Gods kept any individual bias out of the celebration and allowed for the appeasement of all the gods during the year's many celebrations. This temple was clearly the most cared for, with its many well-designed brass sculptures, braziers, and linen adornments. The front of the Kalotrapia had an outdoor altar area that could be overlooked by most of the temple hill. It was here where the procession was heading. Castor and Mithra were still at the very end of the procession and had not made their way onto the plateau yet. The main landing filled as the entire crowd moved into the temple grounds.

Castor overheard a few young adults in a group talking about who was going to catch the Oracle's fate today. When the sacrifices were completed, the Oracle would throw the auroch's heart into the crowd, and the person who caught it would have their fortunes for the year read. The randomness of the toss gave everyone a fair chance at being the one to get the blessing. The few people who were speaking were clearly dock workers, as their clothing was bleached and worn from many years of working near the salty spray.

"It is strange to me that your people are so close to the ritual," Mithra said as they walked up the street towards the temple hill. He eyed a lower-class citizen in tattered clothing.

"We all have a right to celebrate our gods here," Castor said. "Even those who are not always welcome in normal affairs."

"They could have prepared a little more for a sacrifice to your divine deities." Mithra retorted. "It would not be acceptable in Thrim to wear such tattered sacks. Our gods are worth more than that."

Castor raised an eyebrow and frowned at Mithra. "Do you think my gods are so petty as to judge the poor for being poor? Not all are privy to ornate vestments and pungent perfumes. If you look closely, you can see their hair is well washed from the ocean's salty waters. Their clothes may look stained, but I am sure they washed them before the ceremony started."

Mithra guffawed. "My gods are not petty. They hold their positions with great regard. It is our duty as mortals to give them the respect they deserve. If you are poor, you should acquire the proper attire or leave the ritual to those that do."

Castor nodded. "I understand where you are coming from. You have taught me a lot of Maudian culture over the last few months. But Anthora is different. We do not believe in the idea of deserving anything, but rather earning it. This region was built on heavy industry and hard labor. It was hit hard by war and weather for centuries. No one here was given their worth for what they deserved. They earn it."

"Then they should earn a little more." Mithra conceded to Castor's understanding of his own culture.

Castor smiled and patted Mithra on the shoulder. "It never hurts to show some kindness every once in a while."

As the crowd made their way around the raised stone platform and the animals were led up the temple stairs, the ritual had begun. The ashes were scattered across the platform floor and thrown into the open air above the people in the street below. Many people were covered in the black ash and prayed to their gods as they were coated in the soot. The "honored ash" was a great boon for anyone close enough to come in contact with it and would give good luck to all that it touched.

Below the main platform was another large bonfire that heated the area and cast ambient shadows across the many stone pillars and plinths of the temple hill. It was centered below the altar and added an immense amount of backlighting to the sacrificial area. It was very easy to see the platform from the streets below.

"Look at all those dirty people, Mithra." Castor jabbed at the Maudian prince, "They are far too dirty for this celebration, do not you think? You should tell them to wear clean clothes."

"Poking and bothering a giant beast is unwise, prince of Thyma." Mithra shot back. "Where is that kindness you mentioned earlier? Maybe you can offer them your clothes instead?"

"I did not earn the honored ash this year." Castor laughed. "Those people were probably here since dawn just waiting to be blessed by it. They earned that right. So I would not take it away from them."

"Suit yourself, little one." Mithra purred.

The ritual continued as the two princes joked from the rear of the crowd. The Oracle stood in front of the altar as the animals were led to their places beside him. He removed his garments and stood almost naked in front of the four or five thousand people who had shown up for the city's winter sacrifice, only wearing a loincloth in the cold winter air. If he was not cold already, the purification ritual would change that. He got down onto his knees and proselytized himself in front of the altar while two of the white-robed priests poured water upon his bare skin from a large ceramic krater. The ceramic jug was large enough to require two people for pouring and the excess water that ran off the oracle flushed the spread ashes down the stairs of the temple. Before the container was empty, the little remains were poured on the heads of the animals which were to be sacrificed to the gods. The auroch bellowed, the goat bleated, and the chicken clucked. Streams of black water trickle across the temple hill.

The two Bronze Bells stood motionless on each side of the sacrificial altar. The large granite slab was in clear view of the whole area to see from below. The Bells faced outwards towards the crowd, standing guard as the disciples prepared the altar for the Oracle's part of the ritual.

Once cleansed through the pouring of the water, the Oracle stood and came closer to the altar. His disciples helped him attach a long white skirt to his lower half but allowed his upper body to remain bare. His body steamed from the difference in air and water temperature as though a mystical force had taken a hold of his body. The animals were inspected by the temple priests and each was led to the altar for the sacrifice.

From the smallest to the largest, the animals were bled and their lives given to the gods. Blood pooled on the altar as the livestock were given a swift and peaceful death. They did not howl nor bark, as they had been fed many herbs for the week prior and were in a dreamlike state by this time. Aretha had explained the process to Castor in the past and he found the immense number of preparations the local government completed for the city's holidays to be fascinating. No detail was left out in the entire ritual process.

The blood that overflowed from the altar drained into the same channels that the ashen water had flowed down. Instead of spilling off the platform and down the stairs, the animals were placed near the base of the altar and the blood poured down notched grooves in the stone floor. They coalesced into a single spout that rained from the altar's area and into the street below. It fell directly onto the giant bonfire below the altar and allowed the sacrifice to reach the gods in a timely manner. The animals were butchered on the altar as the blood drained downward.

The naked Oracle was a sight to behold. He was fully bald and much lighter-skinned than the rest of the citizens. Without his clothes, he steamed in the winter air. The blood from the animals had caked against his hands and forearms and stained his feet where he stepped in the stone channels. As was Anthoran tradition, the Oracle read the entrails of the beasts and deciphered the god's will through their divination. As he whispered the results of the future year's fortune to the tower priest beside him, the fortunes were announced to the crowd.

"This year's climate will be wet and humid, prepare your crops early and harvest before they rot!" the priest announced as the Oracle went back to reading the entrails.

"The seas will be calm and storms will be few, travel as you can this year!" he announced after another set was divined.

As the announcements were made, the Oracle cut pieces of the flesh and fat. He would toss the special parts down over the altar and directly into the fire below. The entire temple hill smelled of cooked beef and baked herbs. Castor wished he had listened to Nikitas earlier. He was getting a little hungry after the smells permeated his nostrils. He sipped from his wide-brimmed kylix and finished off the rest of the warm wine.

The Oracle whispered to the priest and his eyes widened for a second before he regained his composure. Most of the crowd would not have noticed, but Castor did. He had trained enough in the courts and government meetings to realize when one is surprised. The priest whispered back and nodded after the Oracle's response.

"Steel your hearts this year." the priest said as monotone as he had the other statements, "Prepare for violence in the coming months. The severity of the situation is not yet decided but you should prepare for the worst."

Faint whispers and pallid murmurs made their way through the crowd. Usually some things would be negative during the readings, but nothing of this severity. What could this violence be? Would bandits grow in the region? Could it be an insurrection? Was he speaking of war?

Without missing a beat, the Oracle whispered again and the priest made an announcement, this time on a calmer note.

"Our mountains will be abundant and our veins rich in ore. Regardless of upcoming events, we will have the materials we need to prosper and grow."

The murmuring stopped. It was not like there was a way to change the fates. Thyma was a strong and well-defended city-state. If it was to fall into a war, then they would march forward with a smile on their faces. Usually, the Oracle's readings were much less severe than what they sounded like during the solstice celebration, so many put the last statement aside and focused on the celebration at hand. The readings continued for a short while as the different aspects of the city-state's culture and industries were discussed. While some other points were negative, the overall story of their fate was positive.

As the Oracle finished his divinations, he dismissed the priest and cleaned the altar. He tossed the entrails that were left over his shoulder and into the fire below, singeing upon contact with the smoldering embers. The meat was prepared into large sections, ready to be roasted over the fire below to feed the people. Castor saw as food carts wheeled their way up the temple hill and set up near the back of the crowd, hard-pressed into the hill's short walls. The carts with open flames for their cooking were protected from the chilly winter winds behind the stone face.

The meat that had now become the crowd's food was taken down to the fire below and some of the white-robed tower priests prepared the meat with herbs and spices. While it would not sate their hunger, every person in the crowd could eat from the celebratory meal as the auroch was large enough to give everyone a handful of clean, well-flavored protein. As the herbs and oils were slathered on the different cuts, the Oracle left one object on the altar: the auroch's heart. He prepared himself for the tossing by tying up his clothing around his legs and girding his loins. He grabbed the heart in both hands and, in one singular motion, crouched and jolted upward. He let the heart arc through the air across the holy mount and into the crowd.

Castor could see the flying organ was heading his way. He laughed to himself that the dockworkers from before had a good chance of catching the heart. He saw Mithra step forward. He couldn't remember a time when a non-Anthoran was given a prophecy. He saw the crowds follow the heart across the plaza and ever downwards. Mithra reached out. He would have been quite happy if he would have caught it.

It seemed the fates had a different plan. Mithra made contact with it, now around twelve feet off the ground. His claws were not able to gain purchase on it though, as it was still wet from the butchering. Instead, it bounced off the back of his paw and fell against Castor's face. It rolled down his chest and into his kylix, barely staying within the confines of the container.

The crowd was speechless. Those around him saw as the heart fell flawlessly into his hands. As though guided by the gods, his fate was sealed.

The crowd erupted in cheers and celebration as the people around him realized who the lucky fated one was this year. It was their very own heir prince.

Castor was lifted off the ground and a mob of civilians cradled him above their heads to the Kalotrapia's stairs. There, only the strongest around dared to help lift their prince up the climb and onto the Oracle's platform above.

As they reached the peak, Castor saw the enormous masses of people in the temple's courtyards. While it may be hard to see the entire scope of the event from down where he was before, it was very clear that the numbers stretched close to ten thousand people. The entire hill was covered, even some people standing on the individual temple's open walkways between the temple walls and the columns that skirted their frames. Children sat on their parent's shoulders to get a better view. There were more people that ended up joining the procession to the hill and the crowds extended part of the way down the steep ramp up the hill. A breeze hit Castor in the face as he stood at the top of the ritual platform. The crowd cheered and stared intently at the outcome.

Behind the platform and in an open tent that helped block the cold winter winds sat his parents. His father had a raised eyebrow and his mother smiled beamingly. His father nodded and Castor walked to the Oracle. The only two other people left on the platform were the Oracle and the elderly head priest.

The Oracle's disciple approached Castor and bowed slowly so as to not throw out his back. "Welcome my lord. In all the years I have supported the mighty Oracle, never have I had the pleasure of greeting the ruling family during the fate reading. This process may be different than what you are accustomed to, but I will do my best to serve you both during this ritual."

"Thank you." Castor said politely, putting his hand over his heart and warding it away. He wanted to give the temple headmaster an easy time with the process. He had a soft spot for the elderly of his city, even if they ran a temple complex.

The oracle stared at Castor and said nothing. He pulled an ornate knife from the bowl of ash and rinsed it in a bowl of clean water. He handed the blade to the head priest and nodded.

"My prince, at this time we will need to take a bit of your blood in order to complete the reading. I am well trained in making the blade hurt as little as possible, but it is up to you whether you or I draw the blood. Normally I would just do it myself, but I dare not strike a lord without consulting him first of the ritual's standards."

Castor nodded to him in acceptance and they walked to the front of the altar to allow the crowds to watch. There, the priest rubbed the blade across the muscular part of his left thumb and a steady stream of blood flowed from the wound. The priest was right, Castor barely felt the incision happen. The only time when it hurt now was when he moved his hand closer to the catching bowl. Once an acceptable amount of the viscous liquid was within the bowl, the priest applied pressure with a patch of clean linen and tied up the prince's hand.

As Castor and the head priest walked back to their original positions, the Oracle grabbed the cup and started to complete the reading. He took the blood and applied a liquid to it, used his fingers to rub a bit onto the altar, and even licked the blood off his fingers when he was done. Castor was always surprised that the Oracle never caught a disease over the hundred years he completed these readings. He guessed the immortal part of his name was there for a reason.

The Oracle turned his head after examining the blood and ointment mixture and glared at Castor. He had a scowl and bunched eyebrows. It was the most emotion he had seen from the immortal devotee of the gods during the entire celebration. He called the head priest over and used him as a mediator for their discussion.

"The oracle would like to know who you are." the head priest said rather dismissively. "If you could recite your full name and title, I believe he just wants your confirmation in the proceedings."

"My name is Castor Alexios Daimos, heir to the principality of Thyma and the revenant prince," Castor responded back.

"And you have not traveled to the capital or to other lands as of yet in your life?" the Oracle asked vicariously through the head priest.

"I have not. That will be this coming year. I have only heard great stories of its culture and architecture." Castor said politely.

"Have you ever visited the other Great Towers across Anthora?" He said, continuing his inquisition.

"I have not left the region of Thyma in my lifetime," Castor confirmed.

The Oracle whispered to the head priest and the exasperated sigh he released seemed to give off the type of conversation they were having.

"He is not lying, and I am not going to scare the people like that again." the head priest whispered in a heated tone. The two clergies may have thought Castor was out of hearing range, but his young ears picked up the priest's words quite easily. "You have to think about the stability of the region, Immortal One. I doubt your old stories just so happen to be tied to the ruling family of one of the smallest regions in our lands. As happy as I would be for it to be my prince, you have to think reasonably."

The head priest took in a deep breath and exhaled slowly. He composed himself before turning to Castor.

"Do not fret, my prince. We just needed to discuss how the reading would be announced to the people below. Since we do not rehearse the readings, we have to prepare the statements of your reading in real-time while we are up here. I think we covered everything we needed. I will go announce your results to the people. You can stay back here while I make the announcement."

The head priest walked in front of the altar and started to slowly announce the good fortune and specifics of the prince's fate this coming year. It sounded well-rehearsed and was eloquently said like the rest of the readings the head priest announced. He had clearly been doing this for quite a while.

Castor stood by the Oracle behind the altar as the announcements were made. While he was staring forward without any emotion on his face, Castor could feel the heavy stare of the Oracle's gray eyes on him. He turned to glance at the oracle and found he was correct. He quickly turned his view towards the crowd again.

The Oracle gave off a very different aura than Castor expected. He seemed like a reserved man full of energy rather than a decrepit artifact of a bygone age. Just from the conversation he heard earlier, he could tell the Oracle was opinionated and seemed to want to tell a much less positive story to the people. The crest on his chest cooled his mind as he felt the gaze continue on him. Was his fate really that bad? He knew from his dreams that Alexander told his fate as such. Was this a confirmation in the material world that his fate really was set by the gods?

Castor remembered his talk with Alexander in more detail when the holy symbol was activated. He could recall their conversation about fate quite clearly and the stipulations that came with it. Maybe he had made the mistake of leaving that day. Not knowing one's fate seemed like a cruel tantalization.

Castor's mind snapped to another idea as he scoured his mind from that day. There was a saying that Alexander made him remember. It was clearer in his mind now. He was not sure the Oracle was the right person to say it to, but he had no leads thus far.

"They are coming again and we must prepare," Castor said under his breath. He made sure it was loud enough for the Oracle to hear but not too loud as to alert the head priest.

Castor heard a deep inhale from his right, loud enough to startle him. When the head priest came to a pause between the lines of his speech, he turned to the Oracle to ensure everything was alright. The Oracle dismissed him with a wave of his hand.

Castor heard the oracle clear his throat and he turned to look at him. Instead of a half-cocked glare, he saw the oracle had turned around and was pointing at the ground in front of him. His long slender fingers were almost skeleton-like and his long nail pointed distinctly at the floor in front of him.

Castor, taking that as a sign to stand in that position, did so. He did not take his steel eyes off his target. The oracle leaned in and spoke in a toneless voice.

"You know things you say too freely to strangers. I would warn you to keep your phrases to yourself. Your enemies could be listening at any moment."

Castor nodded. "Thank you for your advice. I take it that you are not one of those enemies. Are you the keeper?"

The Oracle raised an eyebrow in confusion. "I know not what this keeper is. I do not commune with others as much now as I have in the past. But I believe my brother in Pynos has said that phrase before. He may have more information for you."

Castor nodded, suppressing his surprise at this revelation. The High Oracle of the capital city was more reclusive than the Oracle of the

White Tower. To gain his audience may be an issue, even if he was an heir prince in the nation.

The Oracle saw his distraught look and said, "I cannot get you access to my brother directly but you can try to convince their temple guards that you are fulfilling a contract for me. I doubt the temple guards would argue much to a prince with an Oracle's blessing, but my brother has been stubborn in the past. I know not the outcome of that interaction. I have not seen my brother in..." the oracle paused for a second before responding "seven hundred and fifty-six years."

That amount of time was inconceivable for Castor, as his entire city's history was less than a third of that span. Thyma was built because of the White Tower, not the other way around.

Castor nodded and said, "Thank you for your help. I will stay quiet on this subject until then."

The Oracle repositioned his long finger to point back at where Castor was standing before. "I would advise you to do so."

As he stepped back into formation, their conversation ended.

CHAPTER 17

The Founding Of A Feldspar Prince

6th of Quartz, 454 of the Age of Discovery

treams of cold wind passed through the cracks of the abandoned building. The quarried stones that made up the walls of the building were leftovers from the mining days of the small town. The once stucco walls were now worn from weathering over the decades once the mines ran dry. Only a few feet of the protective coating remained near the bottom of the walls and the naked stone was laid exposed to the elements.

The cracks on the wall allowed a bit of the snow to drift through, which made a small puddle under the openings where it coalesced. The hot interior air was easily able to keep the cold draft from reaching the Anthorans inside.

Castor and Acco stood near the old forge with the hot coals glowing softly. A crucible full of bronze scraps sat within the bed of glowing embers of the hearth. It was nestled in a bed of orange coals as the heat soaked into the container's ceramic walls. Acco stared into the bed of coals as Castor pulled on the bellow's piston handle to force fresh air into the ever-burning core of the old bronzesmith's workshop.

"Thank you again for working on this in secret," Castor said politely to his brother as a sweat pooled on his brow. The workshop had gotten warm enough for him to take off the thick furs he had brought with him into the mountains.

"Do not mention it." Acco huffed. "I thought you were dead all of a few months ago. We had the funeral rite and everything. When my once dead brother returns and asks me to work on a legendary weapon with him, do you think I would turn that down?"

"Good point." Castor laughed. The bellow rasped and creaked as the warped wood frames rubbed against the support structure.

Castor looked over to find Acco picking the crystal crescent off the small wood workbench in the corner of the room. He admired its glittering facades and inspected the ends. He used a stylus to outline certain parts of the long gem onto the wax sheet that covered half of the wood table below. Beside the table were sand molds he had prepared earlier in the day. When he was done imprinting the object, he made small changes to the sand in the cast molds below with a metal rod.

"So where again did you find this?" Acco prodded. He kept his attention on the drawing and fidgeted with small details as they talked.

"As I told you before, I couldn't tell you if I wanted to. We got lost and stumbled across it. And if I did know, I wouldn't tell you. I know you would go looking for more and I can assure you it is not worth the risk. The things we found there..." Castor trailed off. The crest cooled his thoughts as he remembered those horrible things.

"It's a pity," Acco said, unfazed by his brother's remorse. "This thing is unlike anything I have ever seen. I do not understand how it is so strong yet holds such a vastness of mana. I mean, the forgemasters have shown us some unique gems and adornments that took years to finalize in their workshops, but this is just...wow."

"It was strange, the way we found it," Castor said as he took a quick break to drink some water from his waterskin. "It was on a mound of stone. And it just protruded from the edge. We were so deep in the mountains that I was surprised there was light at all that deep. The moonlight that was on it made it twinkle as I have never seen before."

Acco held the crescent up and angled it so that the light of the forge would refract off the cleavage within the stone. As there was just a single sheet of refracting crystal under the surface, the entire piece shimmered as though it was a polished sword of bronze. The colors were far different, however. It gleamed brilliantly with streaks of blue, green, and purple. When the light hit it just right, a small glint of gold glittered on the edges.

"I honestly could not tell you what type of gem this is. It appears to have the properties of labradorite and moonstone, but it isn't either of them. I tried to ask around without raising any suspicion at the foundry, but no one seemed to have any idea what it could be."

"That is fine, I appreciate you checking." Castor sighed. "I had the same amount of luck in the library. I checked my collection of military documents in the barracks and the scrolls on gems and minerals in the main library chamber. Neither seemed to have any records of such specimens."

"Well, it is fine with me. I know I have to keep quiet about our work today, but it is still a great project to work on. I have seen the forgemaster's work on gemblades before. The process of connecting the handle and supports will be tedious, but I think I'm up to the task."

"Are you sure it is not too big to be made into a gemblade?" Castor asked honestly, "The records I did find of such weapons were only daggers and highly refined fittings on metal weapons. This is at least three times the size of the largest one I had seen in the records."

Acco waved his hand dismissively as he continued to draw angles and sketch the shapes for the bronze handle. He rubbed his thumb against his pointer finger to warm it up and pressed into the wax to remove some of the writing he had created. Once the new markings were to his liking, he nodded. Noticing the coals had dimmed, he pointed back at the bellows for Castor to continue the forging process.

A steady dripping of water fell from the ceiling. One tile was missing from the slate roof and allowed the melted snow to drip into the room. The wall near the back of the forge was damp from a leak as well, its lowest stones occasionally hissing from the water flashing off the hot surfaces.

"A day like this was perfect for our covert operation," Acco said proudly as he grabbed his long tongs off the anvil. As the liquid bronze pooled at the bottom of the crucible, Acco lifted it out and poured the molten metal into the sand mold. Steam erupted from the edges of the wood frame as the liquid metal permeated the open cavity and formed the hilt of Castor's future sword.

After a tedious minute of pouring and checking for leaks, Acco placed the crucible back into the bed of coals and tossed another handful of scrap bronze into the opening. He had many failed projects and trimmings from his summer forge job that could be smelted down for future smithing like this. He accrued a decent stockpile in the hidden compartment under a stone at the base of the forging structure.

"I am glad we found a place to work on this in secret. The locals seemed very fond of you." Castor said to Acco as he forced air into the fireplace. The glow built back up as it heated and the crucible was starting to regain its melting temperature.

"I helped them out around a half year ago." Acco recollected, "Fixed a few tools and helped restack a few homes. The forgemaster of this town used to use this building. I worked here for a week with him and learned a few tricks."

Acco rubbed some soot off his nose. "He died a few months ago. The locals let me continue to use his forge as gratitude. Too bad the old man didn't have an apprentice; this workshop is perfect to just tinker away on a project."

"In a way, you are his apprentice," Castor said. "You use his tools, work in his workshop, and help his people."

Acco scoffed. "In a way, sure. But I won't stay here. I like forging weapons and smelting metals, but you know I enjoy my stone working far more. I would much rather become a mosaicist. Besides, I already have one adopted father. I do not need to think about gaining the legacy of another."

Castor chuckled. "That's fair. You could do either, but your mosaics seem to have...more life to them. It is easy to see you enjoy them more."

Acco squinted and frowned at Castor, pointing his stylus at the prince. "Are you saying my metalworking is bland and lifeless? After I volunteered to make this weapon?"

His frown turned into a cocky grin and his eyes relaxed. Castor played along.

"Oh, never would I ever suggest such a thing. You are but the finest craftsman in the land! All the forgemasters of Thyma proper pale in comparison."

"Now that's the type of praise I want to hear! Boost my ego even higher!" Acco nodded with his hand on his hips.

The brothers enjoyed their getaway together. Since this three-day holiday allowed them to appreciate time away from their daily occupations and political sphere, they were able to catch up on each other's lives. Castor was missing for a month and was reclused for another. A little break to craft a legendary weapon was very welcome.

"Actually, let's cut the boasting for a minute." Acco frowned, his serious face showing as they made strides towards the weapon. "We have to discuss the design."

Castor reviewed the indentations and marked angles on the table. He could see the patterns Acco had formed and could tell the difference between stone and bronze. The framework for his weapon was laid out before him in a two-dimensional way.

"As we discussed, there is no way for me to make this weapon into your current style," Acco stated bluntly. "Only having one edge makes it all but impossible to make a xiphos. If I added a false edge of bronze, it would become too heavy to wield with your frame."

Acco looked Castor up and down. "I'll be honest, I think it is going to push the limits of your size as it is. This will be over five pounds. While that weight will give you more impact, you are going to have a hard time swinging this around without some channeling being involved."

Castor tapped the side of his head. "You do not have to worry about that. I have a good plan to overcome that hurdle."

Acco scoffed. "Oh ya? Are you planning to disappear for another few months to just lift boulders and get to my size?"

"No, no." Castor wagged his finger. "I would never want to be as big and brutish as you. I have a far more useful resource."

"Let's say I ignore that comment and I won't put a handful of frogs in your bed sheets this coming spring. Care to enlighten me about your plan?" Castor noticed his gaze was focused on the forge. He was checking on the color of the coals to ensure the bronze was still heating.

"I have a Kimpian mace bearer as my mentor. It may be a grueling plan but learning the Kimpian war dances would allow me to wield this sword with ease."

Acco purses his lips in grudging approval. "Not a bad plan at all. As long as you understand the training that will entail. I have a failed initiate I work with at the foundry. That guy puts my tenacity to shame. And Nikitas is a failed Koukouloföroi. That is going to be another step above. Aren't you worried your build may not be up to it?"

"I will take the time to do that," Castor said confidently. "I feel I need to wield this weapon. This is the only way I know that I can do so. It may be difficult but I will figure something out. I think it will be worth it."

"If you say so," Acco said, measuring a few angles on the sword's framework. "Going back to our previous conversation, I think an Anthoran design just won't fit the shape of this crystal."

He pointed between a rough outline at the top of the wax section and the main design. "See how the added metal here is almost twice that of the bottom design? I just do not see how we could create a good plan for this weapon by making it a kopis."

He pointed at the bottom design and the extended neck of the weapon's hilt. "I'm sure you have seen these Maudian designs before, but to explain in detail, these are a newer rendition of a Thrimic khopesh. I extended the hilt to give you more of a lever advantage and added this hook to the end so you can disarm your opponents."

Castor reviewed the plans with Acco on the wax. The design was similar to the ones Mithra's companions would wield when outside the city limits. While theirs were a bit shorter, they had the same extended hilt that flowed into its unique sickle shape. As the bronze weapons were designed with the hooked end already integrated, Castor's khopesh would need the hook added to the casting design.

The extra functionality would help Castor offset the disadvantages of this design too, as there were a few. Its single side and extra weight meant his current sword techniques were no longer applicable. Starting fresh at age nineteen would put him at a disadvantage in combat. The thicker designed small point at the end also meant his attack patterns would have to focus on slashing or hacking over piercing. It was doable with a shield, but his heavy aspis would limit his battle movement. He would have to consider that change as well.

The sword did still have a point, albeit less functional than on his xiphos. The way this crystal was faceted gave a sharp and narrow point on the far end. While it wasn't focused on stabbing, it gave Castor the versatility of piercing, slashing, and bludgeoning when the right call was to be made in battle. He liked that aspect of this weapon.

The largest advantage of a gemblade was its mana reserves. Unlike a typical bronze weapon which only allowed the mana to conduct through its length, this blade could store a vast amount of mana within the crystal and be of use to its wielder during their travels. This expanded mana pool would give Castor a great advantage over his friends and foes alike.

Castor nodded as Acco confirmed the details of the bronze connections between his hand and the crystal. The guard was thin and tapered but covered the backside of his hand in case a blade slid up the crystal's surface. The stem of the khopesh's central trunk was partially hollowed with circular indents that reduced the weight and kept the core strong.

"You really planned this out, didn't you?" Castor exclaimed as he realized the complex intricacies of this new design.

Acco chuckled, "Planned it out? Brother, I have spent half of my waking minutes over the last few weeks on this design. To create a gemblade at my age? This opportunity comes up once in a generation. I have not seen a crystal like this before. I want to make a weapon worthy of this gem's value."

Castor clasped his brother on the shoulder. "Thank you." he said appreciatively.

Acco rolled his eyes. "Here we go again, the caring prince with his heartfelt responses. I know you appreciate my workmanship. You wouldn't have asked me to create this blade if you did not. So do not worry about making me feel better. I feel better when I have a hammer or tongs in my hand."

Castor laughed and stepped back to the bellows, forcing more air into the system to ensure the crucible was getting enough heat. "Then let me ensure you get back to your hammering as soon as you can."

Acco once again measured the angles in the sand molds so that they were the same in every way as the wax design. He added a little bit of wet sand and poked holes in other sections.

Acco looked up from his squatted position on the floor. "You are good with the design then? There is nothing major you want to change? I can't edit the design once we pour the bronze into the mold."

"Yes." Castor confirmed, "I see nothing that needs fixing. I am happy with this gemblade's design."

"Fantastic!" Acco said as he grabbed the crystal crescent off the table and placed it into its indent in the sand. It fit perfectly between the opening for where the metal would be poured. "Then this is where the fun begins."

He stacked the sand molds on top of one another. The crescent was fit between them, and the open cavities enveloped the crystal from all sides. The voids would become the bronze that held the blade in place.

Before they could do so, Acco pierced the sand from the top to add openings for air to escape. He added three holes and expanded the middle one with a brimmed lip. He was very delicate with the sand for such a large man.

Castor held the wood frame as Acco prepared the surface for the pouring of the molten metal. He used a small ceramic jar with tiny holes in the top to drizzle water onto the surface. The dampness helped him mold the holes without them falling apart.

From across the room, Castor heard a loud crash as a damp stone from the wall collapsed onto the forge. The leak from the melted snow must have weakened the mortar and allowed the loosely packed cobblestone to cave inward. Most fell onto the floor below but a large, rounded river stone plopped into the bed of hot coals. The stone's surface sizzled.

"Castor, the stone---!" Acco tried to call out before a thundercrack shook the room they were working in. Sharp stone chunks shot across the room in every direction as the waterlogged river rock exploded from the high heat. The water in the stone vaporized and created a massive barrage of debris across the room. Tiles of slate shattered above them as the superheated pebbles blasted through them. The top of the crucible exploded next to the stone from the sheer force of the explosion.

Around the brothers, a wall of small pebbles was suspended in the air. Acco looked up as the noise dissipated to see no damage to his table, molds, or body. Castor held up his hand as he levitated the shrapnel.

"What just happened?" Castor exclaimed with wide eyes as he held the wall of pebbles in their place.

Acco rubbed his temples as he got off the muddy floor. "I believe a wet stone fell into the fire and exploded. They'll do that when they are waterlogged. I had it happen in a firepit once before."

Acco looked up, saw the suspended rocks, and nodded approvingly.

"Well, that's a neat trick." he said flatly, still stunned from the explosion.

"Looks like my fate is still sealed with bad luck." Castor sighed. "I am glad I got dad to teach me this trick."

Acco squinted at Castor. "He taught you that? Castor, you have only been back home for two months. I haven't seen someone below the age of forty use that type of barrier. You are trying to tell me you just learned how to do that?"

"Since my epiphany, I have been able to pick up different ways to channel quite easily," Castor informed Acco as they stood to assess the damage. "The back luck seems to be the tradeoff for that."

The forge was more beaten than before but still stood in one piece. Small nicks and pinholes pierced the stone surface. Ashes and coals glowed on the cobbled floor, sizzling where they came in contact with leaks in the roof. The crucible was only a mere three inches in height now, the entire top half was blown off and fragmented across the bed of the forge. The molten metal was still in its basin. It glowed faintly as the residual heat from the remaining coals kept it in its liquid state.

"You may have saved this project still," Acco said as he grabbed his tongs and skimmed the dross off the top of the molten pool. "I think we can still do this."

"Then let us try," Castor said. He rolled his eyes before saying, "What else could go wrong?"

Luckily for the god-kissed, his cynicism was not met with divine chastisement. Acco was able to grab the broken crucible bottom with his tongs without the fragile ceramic shattering under his grip. He carefully pulled the metal over to the mold and poured it into the opening in the top. The liquid bronze flowed through the gap and into the mold, the surface bubbling as the steam forced its way out of the sand. While it would be ideal to have the mold fully dry, the weather would not allow it. Instead, the small hiss of escaping gas squeezed out of the mold and into the room's damp air. The surface of the molten metal bubbled and glowing splotches of copper alloy spattered across the top of the sand cast.

Acco placed the crucible back into the forge to keep it away from any more harm. While it would most likely not be used again, he did not want another rock falling and sending molten metal slag across the workshop. After their explosive encounter a few minutes back, he did not want to take any more risks around his unlucky brother.

He went outside and grabbed the brass basin he used for the quenching process. Using a shovel, he quickly scooped enough snow into the container and compressed it. The room was warm enough to turn the snow into a liquid. Water slowly formed at the bottom of the basin as he packed more and more snow on the top. As Castor caught his breath from pumping the bellows for the last half of an hour, Acco shoveled a few coals from the forge around the outside of the container with his shovel to help the melting process. Castor sat and stared at the mold, excited with anticipation as he awaited his new weapon.

The bronze bucket was fully melted as Acco prepared the mold for its quenching. As the metal was expanded from being so hot, Acco knew the cold water would help contract the bronze around the blade and form a tight fit. It also allowed the metal to be slightly stronger without him work hardening the frame for a few hours, so he figured he would save himself some time and quench the blade for its strengthening. He had plenty of tasks left to do after the rough form was completed, so he would rather focus on the fine details than an afternoon of beating the metal with some hammers and earning a harsh ringing in their ears when they were done.

The sand was crispy on the top surface of the mold as Acco put his thick leather gloves back on to his hands. With his tongs in one hand, he tipped the wood frame on its side and spilled the sand and metal onto the floor. The formed brick, which was hard to the touch from compression, crumbled as the sand and clay toppled onto the cobbled floor. As it fell apart, Castor's khopesh appeared from the casting and sat softly on the pile.

Using his tongs, Acco lifted the unfinished khopesh into the trough and allowed it to cool quickly in the frigid water. It sizzled as the water enveloped its shape, vaporizing in small inclusions across the bronze surface. The noise was muzzled as it sank into the water's depths. Castor stood over the container as it bubbled away and released any sand and clay that stuck to its surfaces.

Castor reached in and pulled his new weapon from the murky water. It dripped cleanly back into the basin as the water fell from the sparkling dark surfaces. The bronze was mottled and rough but still stood out against the inky vibrance of the crystal crescent. He could see the way the bronze wrapped around the gem and kept the piece suspended in its metallic grasp. Like geometric vines from a vineyard, the metal coiled and intricately entwined the brilliant feldspar arc.

"That is one fantastic gemblade," Acco said with a confident nod. "It's not finished. That's for sure. But it is a beauty even now."

"It really is," Castor said, handing the blade off to his brother. Acco had the work table prepared for the detailing already, with hardened files and coarse rocks ready to smooth the surfaces. The metal was not too rough, as Acco made sure to keep the inside of the mold lined with fine clay to reduce pocketing on the outside of the cast. There were still the finishing touches to the metal that needed twisting and engraving. Acco sanded away as Castor swept the casting sands into a wood bin with a straw broom.

"You know, for how much you complain about your current situation, you do not know how nice it is to have your god visit you in a dream," Acco muttered under his breath as they worked.

Castor was surprised his brother would want a conversation about the gods. He was not one to pray often nor one to visit temples. He turned his head and continued to sweep as he responded.

"Is that something you would want?" Castor asked. "You aren't one to venerate your patron very often. I hear you curse the Kalotrapia more than you praise them."

"Well, sure." Acco shrugged as he nodded his head, "I'm not looking for a divine revelation. I do not need Brömli to come down and pat me on the back when I am working or Vrontir to join me in battle. But I know I wouldn't be cursing my luck if they did."

Oh. Castor thought to himself, *That is what this is about.*

"Acco, there are some things I cannot tell you about that trip," Castor said, nudging into the topic on eggshells to not say anything he was not supposed to.

"I am well aware," Acco said flatly. The pause afterward was palpable.

"Then I hope you understand that the trip was not all rainbows and roses," Castor said to break the silence.

"I am well aware," Acco said flatly again. "You disappeared for a month and your best friend was killed."

This time the silence was not broken by Castor, as he had no good response after Acco's brash comment on Kyros' death. Castor knew his brother was trying to force an instinctive response out of anger, but Castor had far too much political training to allow for such an outburst. Instead, they let the silence sit for a bit as Acco rasped against the metal and Castor brushed the sand. This time it was Acco who broke the silence.

"Listen, I get that there are parts you can't talk about and it was not a fun adventure for you in the slightest. I just wish I could know more about it. I mean, I understand that I am not an Anthoran citizen by birth, being born to the colonies. But I have lived with you all for fifteen of my nineteen years of life. Being left out has made conversations somewhat awkward around the house as of late."

"I understand that, but that's not my call." Castor said. He tried to understand Acco's side of things, but he did not have a good answer for him. "Dad and his council decided on the rules for what I can share and to whom. That information in itself was not something I was supposed to tell you. It is not to cut you out of things, but more to keep you less liable. You just have to trust me. I have no personal reason to keep you out of the loop."

"Just so you realize the awkwardness is there and that it is not my fault," Acco said gruffly. "I do not care if you have to boil it all down for me, so long as I'm not the one being blamed for the awkwardness."

"I appreciate it," Castor said. Trying to switch off of this topic, Castor brought up Acco's prior statement. "So would it make it all better if Brömli came and joined us?"

"Ha!" Acco blurted out. "You think I want that angry little man in the forge with me? No way. He would hog the workstations and tools for his projects and I wouldn't be able to get anything done."

[389]

Castor couldn't help himself from chuckling. It was such a profane way to talk about the gods that he couldn't even comprehend such a mindset. He knew Acco was eccentric when it came to his beliefs. He heard the colonies had a different way of speaking about the gods, especially those who came from the other races. He could only try to understand their ways of worship.

"Truth be told, I wouldn't mind having a conversation with Brömli on a day like this. I am sure his tutelage could be of great help with this gemblade." Castor stated honestly.

"You do not need him, you've got me!" Acco said confidently. "I may not be as talented, old, or as short of stature as the lord of the smiths, but he works through me when I get into my work. I have toiled enough hours over the coals to earn his grace."

Castor asked, "Who do you follow more, Brömli or Gargrin? You work with stone and tile so often with your mosaics that it feels like you could be split on your patronage."

"Before I answer that, can you hand me that pendant you wanted in the pommel of this weapon?" Acco replied. He put out his hand without looking back, tinkering feverishly at the fine edges of the sword's hilt.

"Oh, right." Castor sheepishly agreed. He pulled the onyx pendant from around his neck, unclasping the silver chain and balling the cord up in his other hand. He placed Kyros' family crest gently into Acco's palm with his thumb. Acco quickly pulled away and gilded the crest into the end of the khopesh.

Castor watched as Acco worked on the fine details of the blade. He placed the onyx gem in between the prongs of the hilt. It fit perfectly into the indentation that was cast for it on the bottom flat of the pommel. Castor could see the imprint on a small wax tablet that Acco had made a few days prior which held many calculations and measurements of the valued gem. Acco worked away, bending the prongs and filing the shoulders of the pommel. Once it was fully attached, he pounded the end of the sword onto the stone floor. When he looked and found no broken or shattered bits, he knew his work on the back half was complete.

"Very good, very good indeed!" Acco exclaimed proudly. "I think it is just about ready!'

He put a finger up, catching himself as he rubbed on a few uneven angles with a gritty rock.

"I can't get too ahead of myself. We still have to give it a name." Acco stated accordingly. "As per tradition, we must abide by the rules of the forge lords."

Castor remembered reading about that in his searches over the last week. He paused quizzically before he recited the line.

"Yes, I think it goes along the lines of 'All gemblades must be named by their patron with a title denoting its value and worth.' I believe it was in the Anthoran Manual of Gemblades and Focusing Pendants. Acastus lent me that scroll from his collection in the barracks."

"I do not think I ever met him." Acco pointed out as he stretched his arms behind his head. Castor knew they had been working for a few hours straight already, but his brother did not seem to falter. He really did enjoy his smithing endeavors.

"You are welcome to read it when we get back. I haven't returned it yet. I could introduce you two when I do return it. It would allow you to meet one another."

Acco glared at Castor. "You know my rule. I stay out of your political affairs, and you leave the smithing to me. I have no doubt you would use the opportunity to get me into the city guard."

"Not anymore," Castor answered with genuine honesty. "Everyone has their role in our realm. If yours is to work stone and metal, it is not up to me to try and change that."

Acco nodded approvingly. "Maybe some good did come from your trip in the mountains. I like this new way that you think!"

"I cannot stop him from trying to recruit you." Castor added, "but you won't have me pushing for it. I know that Acastus is a fan of intricate weapon smithing and a collector of fine blades. That could be where you lead the conversation."

"I may do so." Acco trailed off and pondered for a few seconds in silence before coming back to the situation at hand. "But that doesn't matter right now. We still have to breathe life into this gemblade. Do you have the name you want to give it?"

Castor had thought about that for quite some time over the last month. It was not an issue he cared about. The blade would serve its purpose regardless of the name he gave it. At least, that's what he thought before he read more about gemblades and their history. It seemed that when the secret was out and the world found out about his gemblade, its name would be one of the most important bits of information to the forgemasters, smiths, and nobles that yearned so desperately for information on it.

Castor thought about the trip he took and the hardships they went through to acquire the crystal crescent so deep in the core of the mountain. He remembered those horrible things, with their vile white skin and voracious mouths. He remembered the ancient ruins of a long-lost civilization and the marvels of architecture he saw in Petrus' depths. He recalled the goblins and the harpies and his two friends he thought lost. But one aspect of discovering the crystal stood out to him.

"Fengos," Castor said. Acco looked up and squinted at his brother. After realizing the wordsmithing his brother made about this blade, he smiled.

"I like it!" Acco fervently exclaimed. "Is that Fengos as in 'moonlight', or Fengos as in 'glimmering'? The accent matters in this case, does it not?"

He went over to the wax table and wrote out the word with his stylus. Each strike of the short wood rod pressed softly into the wax; φ ε γ γ ο ς was written onto the table in pristine handwriting.

Castor smirked. "You tell me, oh master smith. Which one fits this blade better? It was found within a column of moonlight deep into the ground, so it could be spelled as φεγγος. Yet it shimmers and glitters when any light touches it, so φέγγος could also work. Which spelling do you think it should be?"

Acco nodded and pressed an accent mark over the epsilon. It now read φ έ γ γ ο ς.

"You said yourself that this should be a secret," Acco stated. "To give information away freely of its origin through its name would oppose that idea. So I think you should call it for what it looks like and leave the hidden meaning to those who know."

Castor was shocked. His brother, the hard-headed colonist from the Hem Durulian colonies, was not one to mince words so easily. As a foundry worker and mosaicist, he was not known for his wordsmithing. Castor only asked his opinion out of politeness and an urge to coyly toy with him. But his answer struck true within Castor, and he had no option but to agree with his conclusion.

"That is perfect," Castor agreed, "then let us stick with that name. I agree with the name of Fengos, the glittering moonlight khopesh."

Acco nodded continuously as he prepared the blade for its naming. "I will need you to pour a steady stream of mana into it as I engrave the letters. I'm sure you can do that. Are you ready now?"

"Lead on." Castor nodded.

Castor put his right hand on the pommel of the sleek sickle sword and gently caressed the crest of onyx within the bronze clasps. He focused his mana and channeled a slow and steady stream of his energy into the blade. Acco stood to his right and chiseled out the grooves of the letters with a pointed ferric rod. The metal made Castor's mana feel jittery as he worked, but he was far more controlling of his channels now than a half year prior. A little bit of the mage-killing metal was not going to stop him from finishing this masterwork weapon.

A faint glow of gold emanated from the khopesh. Dust in the air lit like little yellow particles and floated in the stagnant air. Each strike of the hammer against the chisel caused small sparks to skitter across the bronze blade. The crystal crescent seemed unfazed by the entire ordeal, nestled tightly in the bronze branches of the sword's framework. The geometric patterns etched into the surfaces allowed his mana to flow easily down the flats and through the gem core. The loud ting of each strike resonated within the small workshop.

Acco wiped the sweat from his brow as he finished the engraving. The soft glow faded as Castor released his grasp of the weapon. The final touches of the process were at hand. Castor drew his xiphos from his belt and cut a small indent into the base of his thumb. A thin streak of crimson trickled down his hand as he held the wound over the engraving. Drop by drop, Castor dropped his lifeblood into the divots his brother had just carved. He filled the minor channels to their brims before wrapping his hand with a piece of cloth. Sheathing his old blade, he grabbed the hammer from the workbench and prepared the final strike.

Without another word, Castor said a small prayer to his patron and struck the blade. The mellow note reverberated across the room, vibrating his ears and causing dust to lift off the ground. The faint glow from before lit brightly across the blade before dying completely. Placing the hammer on the table, Castor lifted the sword into the air. The red carvings were now etched in a deep umber. His weapon was finished; the moonlight khopesh Fengos was completed.

"You did well!" Acco chortled as he went and poured the quenching basin out the door. "Your final act looked just like the way the forgemasters sealed their gemblades during the summer months."

Castor smiled. "Thank you. Your craftsmanship made the process effortless."

"Ha!" Acco bellowed. "Do not say your brother never did anything for you. Just remember this whole ordeal the next time you find a good deal at the market for gem tiles and other minerals I could use for my mosaics."

"I will not forget." Castor agreed. He looked the blade up and down, noticing the finest of details that were carved and molded into the weapon. "I will never forget."

He thought of all the pain and suffering Alexander had mentioned in the realm he had visited deep underground. There were many things he still did not understand from that journey and many more that he expected to come. It was a great relief to have a step forward to gaining the strength to overcome the obstacles the gods had put him up against.

"Very well." Acco grinned and started to tinker at the workbench again. He tossed a few chunks of charcoal into the forge from a bucket and pulled on the bellows. "We are not done yet. Still have a few details to hammer out."

"Alright," Castor said, giving the feldspar crystal crescent one last look before handing the weapon off.

"Let us finish this."

To be continued...

Made in the USA
Monee, IL
16 September 2022

13891753R00236